"Footprints lead off this way."

Merci came up beside him. She touched his arm for support. "Do you suppose the other two thieves were already at the camp?"

Nathan studied the two sets of prints partially drifted over from snow. "Maybe." They trudged forward in the darkness, heads down.

The wind had distorted the footprints, and Nathan took a guess at where they were leading. The temperature had to be hovering below zero. The wind picked up, making it even colder.

He felt a tug on his coat. "It's getting worse. I think I need to stay closer."

Nathan draped an arm over Merci's shoulders as both of them put their heads down and leaned into the wind.

He only hoped they had not made a mistake. They had taken a gamble that the weather would hold. Conditions were hazardous at best. A little more wind, a few degrees' drop in temperature and they would be fighting for their lives.

HIDDEN ON
THE MOUNTAIN

USA TODAY BESTSELLING AUTHOR

SHARON DUNN

&

TERRI REED

Previously published as *Zero Visibility* and
Secret Mountain Hideout

LOVE INSPIRED
INSPIRATIONAL ROMANCE

LOVE INSPIRED®
INSPIRATIONAL ROMANCE

Recycling programs for this product may not exist in your area.

ISBN-13: 978-1-335-46621-1

Hidden on the Mountain

Copyright © 2021 by Harlequin Books S.A.

Zero Visibility
First published in 2012. This edition published in 2021.
Copyright © 2012 by Sharon Dunn

Secret Mountain Hideout
First published in 2020. This edition published in 2021.
Copyright © 2020 by Terri Reed

This edition published by arrangement with Harlequin Books S.A.

For questions and comments about the quality of this book, please contact us at CustomerService@Harlequin.com.

Love Inspired
22 Adelaide St. West, 40th Floor
Toronto, Ontario M5H 4E3, Canada
www.Harlequin.com

Printed in U.S.A.

CONTENTS

Ever since she found the Nancy Drew books with the pink covers in her country school library, **Sharon Dunn** has loved mystery and suspense. Most of her books take place in Montana, where she lives with three nearly grown children and a hyper border collie. She lost her beloved husband of twenty-seven years to cancer in 2014. When she isn't writing, she loves to hike surrounded by God's beauty.

Books by Sharon Dunn

Love Inspired Suspense

Broken Trust
Zero Visibility
Montana Standoff
Top Secret Identity
Wilderness Target
Cold Case Justice
Mistaken Target
Fatal Vendetta
Big Sky Showdown
Hidden Away
In Too Deep
Wilderness Secrets
Mountain Captive
Undercover Threat
Alaskan Christmas Target

Visit the Author Profile page at Harlequin.com for more titles.

ZERO VISIBILITY

Sharon Dunn

And this I pray, that your love may abound yet more and more in knowledge and in all judgment; That ye may approve things that are excellent; that ye may be sincere and without offence till the day of Christ.
—*Philippians* 1:9–10

Faith is the substance of things hoped for, the evidence of things not seen.
—*Hebrews* 11:1

To my Lord and Savior who is patient with me
as I learn to "see" people for who they really are
and respond not to appearances, but what is
really in a person's heart just as God does for me.
I love you, Jesus.

ONE

Merci Carson sucked in a fear-filled breath as the car she was a passenger in swerved on the icy country road. The jumpy view through the windshield fed her panic. Her stomach clenched. She braced her hand on the dashboard.

The driver, Lorelei Frank, gripped the wheel and pumped the brakes. The car fishtailed. Lorelei over-corrected. Both girls screamed at the same time as the car veered off the road and wedged in the snow. Lorelei killed the engine, let out a heavy breath and pressed her head against the back of the seat. "That was really scary."

Merci sat stunned. She pried her fingers off the dashboard and waited for her heart rate to return to normal. "I wonder how badly we're stuck." She took in a deep breath and rolled down the window. Frozen air hit her face as she leaned out for a view of the front wheel. This high up in the mountains, there was snow almost year round. Still, it felt unusually cold for March. "It doesn't look that bad. Maybe we can back out."

Lorelei clicked the key in the ignition, but the engine didn't turn over. Her hand fluttered to her mouth. "Oh, no."

"Try one more time. Wasn't the engine still running when we got stuck?"

Lorelei nodded and reached for the key. She clicked it back and forth several times. Each time Merci felt as if a vise was being tightened around her heart. The bleak winter landscape only made her more anxious. If they couldn't get the car started, who would come to help them? The last car they had seen was right before they had turned off the highway to take Lorelei's shortcut.

"This is my fault." The deep crevice between Lorelei's eyebrows gave away the level of guilt she must be wrestling with. "I've only taken this road in the summer. It's almost spring, I didn't think the snow would be such a factor."

"It's okay." Merci hoped she had been able to hide the encroaching fear from her voice. Lorelei had been kind enough to offer her a ride to her aunt's house in Oregon for spring break after her own car had broken down finals week, two days before she needed to leave. After a stressful quarter, Merci had been desperate to see her Aunt Celeste. She patted Lorelei's hand. Playing the blame game wouldn't get the car on the road again. "You were only trying to get us there faster."

"Let's try one more time." Lorelei's hands were shaking as she reached to turn the key in the ignition.

Merci held her breath.

Please, God, let the car start.

Nothing. No engine noise. The car was dead.

Lorelei pulled the key out of the ignition and sat back in her seat, staring at the ceiling while she bit her lower lip. "We must have damaged something when we went off the road."

Merci pressed her palms together. They were stranded, but they were not without hope…not yet. They still had options.

Merci took her cell phone out of her pocket. She stared at the purple sequined cover. Who could they call? They were seven hours away from the college and six away from her aunt's house in Oregon.

Lorelei combed her fingers through her short blond hair. "I'm not sure where I put my phone."

If she called her aunt, she could look online for them and find out if there was a tow truck in this area that could come to get them. "I've got some charge left on mine." She flipped it open. The "no service" message flashed in front of her.

Lorelei sat up and looked at her.

Merci tried to ignore that sinking feeling in her gut. She closed the phone and responded in a monotone. "The mountains must be blocking the signal." Nobody was going to come for them.

Both women sat staring out their windows, not saying anything for a long moment.

Merci said a quick prayer and mustered up some optimism. She wasn't giving up that easily. "Let's see if we can dig the car out of the snow and then figure out why it won't start." She didn't know much about cars, other than how to put gas and oil in, but they were running out of options.

Lorelei's expression, that mixture of fear and despair that caused her forehead to wrinkle, didn't change, but she shrugged and said, "Okay. What else can we do, right?"

"Exactly." Merci pushed open her door. Strong wind assaulted her before she could get her hands into the sleeves of the lavender dress coat she grabbed off the seat. She let out a breath. The chill cut right through her even after she put the coat on. Rolling the window down had only given her a taste of how cold it was. They'd been insulated in the heated car.

The dark clouds in the sky indicated that a storm was on the way. Bad weather was not what they needed right now. They would have to work fast.

Moving both their suitcases out of the way, she checked the trunk for a shovel. Empty. Okay, so Lorelei didn't believe in bringing tools with her. Maybe it had been her responsibility to make sure they were better equipped for emergencies. Lorelei was at least four years younger than her. Because she had paid her own way through college by working a year and going to school a year, Merci was older than most college seniors. Her own car had everything she needed for any kind of emergency, but it wasn't running. She knew about being prepared in the harsh Northwest winters.

She closed the trunk and walked around to the front of the car where Lorelei kicked snow away from the driver's-side tire. Merci pulled her gloves from her pocket. The snow didn't look that deep, and only the front tires were stuck. The back tires were still on the road.

Lorelei leaned over to examine the car tire. "Sorry, I should have brought a shovel."

"You must have a bucket or some kind of container

in the car. If so, then we'll need something to create traction like sand or kitty litter." As cold as it was, they weren't going to last very long before they had to return to the car to warm up. Without the ability to run the heat, even that survival tactic wasn't going to do them much good for long.

"I don't think I have either of those, but I can look for something to shovel with." Lorelei returned to the car's backseat to search.

Merci crossed her arms over her chest. She stared at the winding path the car had taken though blowing snow had already drifted over some of their tracks. It was too far to walk back to the main road that way. Besides, didn't all survival shows say to stay with your vehicle? Anxiety knotted her stomach all over again. Had it come to this already, thinking about how they would stay alive? Just moments before, they had been singing along to one of Lorelei's CDs.

The graying sky indicated that more snow was on the way. This time of year, it got dark early. They had maybe a two-hour window before darkness and colder temperatures meant they would be huddled together and freezing in the car. They had to get out of here.

She leaned down and pushed away the snow with her gloved hand. Working at a frantic pace, it took only moments before she was out of breath. Fighting the wind drained her strength, and her face felt like it had been dipped in a block of ice.

Oh, God, we need help or a better idea about getting this car moving.

The car door slammed, and Lorelei let out a yelp that sounded almost joyful.

Merci pushed herself to her feet. Up the road in the direction they had come, headlights shone. Merci breathed a sigh of relief. Sometimes God took forever to answer prayer, and sometimes He answered on the spot.

The car pulled ahead of them and came to a stop.

A man in a leather jacket and thick sweater got out of the driver's side. "What seems to be the problem here, ladies?" The man's dark black hair was cut short and slicked back. The huskiness in his voice gave away a smoking habit.

Lorelei rocked from heel to toe. "Boy, are we glad to see you. We got ourselves stuck and now the car won't start."

A second shorter, broader man dressed in a puffy orange down coat got out of the passenger side. He looked to be in his early twenties and had long wavy hair. The stringiness of his hair indicated that a shower was a couple of days behind him. Duct tape covered two holes on his oil-stained coat.

The taller man walked toward them, addressing Lorelei. "Why don't you ladies warm up in our car? I've left it idling. We'll see what we can do."

"Oh, thank you," Lorelei gushed.

Treading through the snow, Merci followed Lorelei. It seemed a little odd that the guy had pulled out in front of them instead of stopping behind, and the men had a greasy unwashed quality that was off-putting. But what did she care? She needed to get beyond her own prejudices. God had sent help; that was what mattered. Besides, these men were their only hope of getting back on the road. She slipped into the backseat while Lorelei occupied the front passenger seat. The car was toasty warm.

Lorelei took her gloves off and laced her fingers together. "This was a stroke of luck."

To Merci it was an answer to prayer, but she didn't know Lorelei well enough to know if she would understand. They had only had a few classes together and lived in the same dorm.

From the backseat, Merci turned around to see what was going on. One of the men had popped the hood, which blocked most of her view. She couldn't see where the tall man in the leather jacket was. From this angle, it was hard to tell, but it looked as if the trunk was open, too. He'd figure out soon enough that there wasn't a shovel in there. Guilt washed through her. It wasn't right for her to just sit here. She needed to get out and help.

Lorelei had put her earbuds in and closed her eyes. No need to disturb her.

Merci pushed open the door and stepped outside. As she walked to the back of the car, she heard the car door open. Lorelei must be following her.

Merci saw that the man in the orange coat had unzipped her suitcase and was rifling through it. Lorelei let out a loud gasp behind her.

"Stop stealing our stuff," Merci screamed at the men.

Did they intend to rob them and leave them here to die? What kind of people would do something like that?

The man reached into his coat and pulled out a gun. "Just back off."

Merci froze in her tracks, focusing on the barrel of the gun. Intense fear made it impossible for her to scream.

The other man pushed open the door of the backseat, stepped out and absorbed the situation. "No way man, it wasn't supposed to go down like this," said the tall man in the leather jacket.

"Yes, put the gun away." Merci's voice trembled uncontrollably. She felt as if someone was shaking her spine from the inside.

"We'll give you whatever you want," said Lorelei. "Just don't hurt us."

The short man placed his finger inside the trigger guard.

In the pensive silence, snow fell softly on Merci's head in sharp contrast to the tornado of fear raging inside her. Would her next breath be her last?

With his snowmobile idling and partially hidden from view by trees, Nathan McCormick flipped up the visor on his helmet and watched the two parked cars. A man in a leather jacket had lifted the hood and then got into the car. A man in an orange coat had popped the trunk and was looking for something. It was unusual to see anyone on this road next to the mountain acreage he and his brother Daniel had inherited. There was no reason for traffic anymore. His dad had closed down the small ski hill three seasons ago to take care of his ailing mother, and the kids' camp only ran in the summer. Then a year ago, his mother had died and his father only six months after that. He'd come back to the family cabin one last time to say goodbye and pack up before putting the place on the market.

He wondered why the cars had stopped. It looked like engine trouble. One of the cars was positioned as if it might be stuck. Maybe he should go down and see if they needed an extra hand. He watched a moment longer. A woman in a purple coat got out of the car in front followed by another woman.

He angled the snowmobile downhill and revved the engine preparing to go down to help. The man standing by the trunk pulled out a gun and pointed it at the woman in the purple coat. Nathan's heartbeat kicked up a notch. He'd stumbled onto a robbery.

Without hesitation, Nathan flipped down the visor on his helmet and zoomed down the mountain. Those women weren't going to be harmed, not on his watch. Adrenaline shot through him like quicksilver as he increased his speed.

As he drew closer, Nathan saw the second man in a leather jacket get out of the car and a moment later pull a gun, as well. The two women huddled together, stepping back away from the men. The thieves looked up and saw him coming. One fired a shot. He swerved the snowmobile away from the line of fire. The women collapsed in the snow in an effort to protect themselves from flying bullets.

Nathan headed toward the man in the orange coat as though he was going to plow him over. At the last second, he stood up and angled the snowmobile sideways, spraying snow on the man and hitting him with the runners. The man in the orange coat reeled backward. The gun flew out of his hand and fell into the snow. Nathan was between the two women and the stunned would-be robber, who was digging through the snow for his gun. The other man had retreated behind the second car. He was probably waiting to see if Nathan was armed.

Nathan flipped up his visor and yelled to the women, "Get on, get on right now."

The first woman, the one wearing mostly purple, scrambled to her feet. She grabbed the wrist of the blonde woman, who glanced side to side but didn't move. The woman in purple pulled her friend toward the snowmobile. She got on the snowmobile, and her friend got on behind her.

The second gunman came out from behind the car just as they sped up the hill. Nathan could hear the gunfire behind him. Leaning down, he steered toward the protection of some trees, while driving the snowmobile around the edge of the forest. The snow fell in big wet clumps, and the wind picked up.

The first woman had wrapped her arms around him and was holding on for dear life. He only hoped the other woman was secure on the seat, as well. The gunmen couldn't go very fast pursuing them on foot. The route he took on the snowmobile to the family cabin was over the mountain, not on the road, so they wouldn't be able to follow along in the car. Chances were the men would take whatever was of value in the women's car and head straight out to the highway.

They traveled in ever increasing cold, wind and snow for about twenty minutes. He felt a gentle pounding on his shoulder and brought the snowmobile to a stop, but let it idle.

He flipped up his visor. "Yes."

"Where are you taking us?" Fear saturated the woman's voice.

She was probably wondering if she had just gotten out of one dangerous situation only to land in another.

"Sorry, I was kind of focused on getting you away from the gunfire. We'll go to my cabin. It'll be safe there. We'll call the police. I have a truck. I can take you into town to the police station to file a report. Maybe they can catch these guys before they get too far."

Her response came after a long pause. "Okay."

She didn't sound totally convinced, but what choice did she have? Going back to the cars was unwise, and they couldn't stay on the side of the mountain with the wind and snow blowing at them.

"It's going to be okay," he said, hoping to lessen her anxiety.

By the time they reached the cabin a few minutes later, the storm had become full blown. Tiny sword-like snowflakes came at him sideways. Air seemed to freeze in his lungs.

He brought the snowmobile to a stop, took off his helmet and leaned very close to the woman in purple to shout into her ear. "You and your friend go on inside. The door is unlocked. I've got to put the snowmobile away." He pointed toward the cabin twenty feet away and almost not visible through the blowing snow. "Get warmed up."

After watching them safely enter, he put the snow-mobile in the three-sided shed then stumbled toward the house, reaching out for the rough pine stairs.

He pushed open the door. The two women huddled by the dying fire, bent over and shivering. Both were wearing dressy winter coats, fine for a church service, but nothing that would keep them warm in this kind of weather. They needed to thaw out from the ride on the snowmobile before they headed down the mountain to the police station.

Nathan stoked the fire and threw on another log. From the guest room, he retrieved blankets for them. He placed the blanket over the shoulders of the woman who wore purple.

She pulled her long strawberry-blond hair free of the blanket and whispered, "Thank you."

The other woman stared at the floor as though she weren't seeing it. He had worked ten years as a paramedic straight out of high school. His job had taught him a few things about people's responses to violent crime or any kind of trauma. The blonde would come out of the shock in time. He just needed to keep talking to them, pulling them away from the memory of the violence and back into this safe part of the world.

"How about I get you guys some hot tea? I'm Nathan, by the way."

"Tea sounds nice." The strawberry blonde lifted her head and looked at him. "I'm Merci and this is Lorelei. We're students at Montana State in Bozeman." He liked the trust he saw in Merci's eyes. At least she had come around.

"Well, Merci, it's going to be okay. Soon as you are warmed up, we'll call the police, go into town and get this taken care of," he said.

Nathan went into the kitchen and prepared two cups of tea. They really needed to get moving, but neither of the women was in the state of mind emotionally or physically for a ride down the mountain. It wouldn't hurt to give them a few minutes to recover.

The blonde didn't take the cup when he offered it,

so he placed it on the table beside her before returning to the kitchen to clean up. A moment later, when he peeked out, he watched Merci gently place the steaming mug in her friend's hand and encourage her to sip.

He stared at the storm through the window as he made his way back through the living room. With the amount of snow falling and the intense wind, visibility had been reduced.

"I suppose we should make that call to the police," Nathan suggested. "The sooner we get this done, the faster the police will be looking for the guys that robbed you."

Merci set her empty cup down. The color had come back into her face, and her eyes looked brighter. She was kind of pretty. Lorelei had at least raised her head and taken a few sips of tea. The almost invisible freckles on Merci's cheekbones and her white eyelashes gave her a soft, translucent quality, like a water color painting.

Lorelei shuddered and wrapped her arms around herself. "I don't want to talk about what happened. I don't want to go to the police."

"She needs a few more minutes." Merci rose to her feet and walked over to Nathan. The fear had returned to her eyes. "Could you make the call? You saw what the men looked like and what they were driving. I don't think either of us is ready to talk about this just yet."

"Sure, I can do that." His heart filled with compassion. Because he was an EMT, he was used to handling traumatic situations. But this might have been the first time these women had even seen a gun. He tempered his voice, hoping not to stir up the fear again. "When we get to the station, they will want more details. Can you tell me what you were doing down there? Did you know those guys?"

Merci explained about the shortcut and getting stuck and how the men had shown up.

Nathan kept his thought to himself, but it sounded as if the women had been targeted. The only thing more vulnerable than two college-age women traveling together was one traveling alone. The men had probably been following them and waiting for an opportune time to rob them.

He kicked himself for not having gotten there five minutes earlier. Then this whole thing could have been prevented. He would have helped them with their car and gotten them on their way.

Nathan picked up the phone and dialed into the sheriff's office. He recognized Deputy Miller's voice.

"Hey, Travis, I'm up at the cabin and I've got two young women here who were robbed up on Jefferson Creek Road." He briefly described the men and the car they were driving. "They should be able to give more details by the time I bring them in. They're still a little shell-shocked."

"I haven't noticed a car in town matching that description. Doesn't sound like they're from around here." Travis Miller's slow drawl came across the line. "So you're up there playing hostess with the mostest to college co-eds. Tough duty, huh?"

Nathan rolled his eyes at the friendly jab. Clampett, Idaho, was not a big town. Driving an ambulance in a town of twenty thousand meant that he was cozy enough with all of the first responders to joke around.

"That's right, I'm the Martha Stewart of the mountain. I'll bring them in shortly."

"Better hurry, that snow is coming down fast. Getting the road up to your place plowed isn't county priority since there is no traffic up there anymore." Travis said goodbye and hung up.

Nathan returned to the living room. Merci had risen from her chair and was looking at family photographs on the mantel. She picked up one of the framed pictures. "Is this your mom and dad?"

A sharp pain sliced through him. He hadn't been up to this cabin since his dad's funeral. He had a place in town. When his mom and dad were alive, the cabin had been used for family gatherings and vacations. He had come up here to clear away all those photos, to pack them in a box where they wouldn't evoke sorrow every time he looked at them. "Yes, they passed away a little bit ago."

"Oh, I'm so sorry." Her voice filled with compassion as she placed the photo back on the mantel with care. "You look really happy in these pictures."

"I suppose we were." He laid the photo facedown, not wanting to think about what his life used to be. "I don't live up here, and all this stuff is just gathering dust. It needs to be packed up so the place can be sold."

"I think pictures are a beautiful treasure." She picked up a second photo. "Is this you with a friend?"

Nathan felt himself retreating emotionally as he took the frame from her hand. The image was of him and his older brother, Daniel, when they were maybe twelve and fourteen, practicing archery at the camp. Their hair shimmered in the summer sun, and both were smiling.

His relationship with Daniel had been strained for the past ten years and had only gotten worse when their mother and father died.

He really didn't want to talk about his brother…not to a stranger. Not to anyone. "He's my brother." Merci had probably thought she could make up for having reminded him of his parents' death by talking about his "friend." Instead, she had opened an even deeper wound. "We need to get going. If we wait too long, even my four-wheel drive isn't going to get us off this mountain."

TWO

Merci slipped into the truck next to Nathan, and Lorelei climbed in beside her. It had taken some coaxing to even get Lorelei to agree to go. She wasn't handling this well at all.

The sound of the engine turning over made Merci breathe a little easier. At least the truck was running. Snow fell in clumps. The wipers worked furiously to keep it off the windshield. At best, they could see maybe five feet in front of them.

Nathan pressed a button, and a blast of heat hit her. "Warm enough for you?"

Nathan had found them both extra clothes to put on underneath their dress coats. "Yes, that's good." She stole a glance at the man who had saved their lives. His brown eyes held kindness. "Thank you…for all you've done for us."

"No problem." He leaned forward to see better through the window, focusing on his driving. His answer was so abrupt. Maybe he was still upset over her asking questions about his family. He probably thought she was nosy. She hadn't meant to step on toes or reopen old wounds. It was just that in the pictures of his family, everyone looked so happy. She only understood the concept of happy families from television shows.

She'd been an only child. Her father, an international businessman, traveled all the time. Having to raise a child alone had made her mother depressed and resentful. Merci had always felt as if she was in the way of their happiness, not a part of it. Though her mother would never say it, she seemed happier when Merci was old enough to stay with relatives, and she could travel with her husband. Her aunt Celeste, her father's sister, had been the stabilizing force in her life. When her parents left for Hong Kong or London, she had stayed with Auntie in the little town of Grotto Falls, Oregon, that never changed. Even though she would be twenty-six in a month, she found herself running to the stability and the love that her aunt provided.

"I'm just grateful you came along when you did, that's all." Merci folded her hands in her lap.

"Once I saw what was going on, I couldn't very well have left you there." Nathan gazed at her for a moment, offering her a lopsided smile that sent a charge of warmth through her. "Besides, I'm an EMT. I can't help myself. I had to rescue you."

She was glad he was able to look past whatever pain she had caused by talking about his family. In addition to showing bravery in facing the armed robbers, he seemed like a truly kind and decent person.

The truck slid, and Nathan gripped the wheel tighter. Lorelei let out a tiny scream, and Merci patted her leg.

"This is scary." Lorelei's voice was barely above a whisper. "We should have stayed at the cabin."

"Don't worry. We'll make it. I can handle this snow just fine," Nathan said.

Up ahead, the mountain road intersected with a flatter road. That must be the country two-lane they'd taken when they turned off the highway.

Nathan slowed the truck down. "There's something on the road down there."

Merci couldn't make out anything but windblown snow.

Nathan braked. The truck slid before coming to stop. Now she could discern the dark lump at the intersection of the two roads.

"Sit tight." He pushed open the door. "Let me go check it out. I'll leave the engine running so the cab will stay warm."

He stepped away from the truck. Within a few feet, the blowing snow consumed him. It cleared momentarily, and she saw his bright-colored ski jacket as he made his way toward the dark mass.

Nathan's boots sank down into the deep snow. He pulled his leg out and tried to find the center of the road where the snow would be more hard packed. He'd been on the mountain in winter before, but this was the worst he'd ever seen it. At least a foot of snow had fallen in a short amount of time.

He wasn't worried. He'd get the two women down this mountain. He had confidence in his skill as a driver, and his truck was designed for these kinds of conditions. If the women could file a report, it would make capture that much more likely. Taking action would also help them get past the trauma. Lorelei seemed to be shutting down by degrees. The compassion her friend Merci showed her touched him. Merci seemed like a strong, capable young woman.

The wind cleared and a dark colored car partially covered in snow came into view. It looked as though the car had slid off the road. As he drew closer, he saw that it was the car that belonged to the thieves. He slowed his pace.

The car was facing east, which meant the thieves were headed back to Clampett when they got stuck. The impending storm must have made them decide to go back the way they had come, rather than face the unknown of how long the country road stretched on before it met up with the highway going west. From the way the car was wedged, lack of familiarity with the road and reduced visibility had caused them to veer over into a ditch and get stuck. The car blocked enough of the intersection between mountain road and country road to make it hard for him to get his truck around without ending up stuck, too.

He approached the car with caution. When he peered through the windows, he saw that it was empty. Where had the men gone? The wind had blown quite a bit, but he could make out the soft impression of foot tracks leading back up the mountain road.

Nathan exhaled, creating a cloud. His eyes followed the direction the men had walked. The two thugs might have seen the tall light by the cabin or maybe it had cleared enough for them to see smoke rising out of the chimney. In any case, they probably thought they could find shelter up the road, not realizing the cabin belonged to the man who had just seen them trying to rob the women. Though it looked as if they had veered into the forest, the thieves were headed up the mountain where he had left the women alone in the truck.

Adrenaline kicked in and every muscle in Nathan's body tensed. He ran back toward the truck.

Lorelei tapped her feet on the floorboards of the truck. "I don't see what good going to the police will do. Those guys are probably long gone."

Merci cleared her throat. Part of her just wanted to get on a bus to her aunt's house where it was safe and forget all this had happened. "I know it's hard to think about, but what if those guys try to rob someone else? We need to tell the police what we know. We have to make every effort to make sure they're caught."

Lorelei crossed her arms over her chest and bent her head. "I guess I just don't like police very much."

Merci sighed and listened to the rhythmic movement of the windshield wipers. She took in her surroundings, what she could see of them. This road looked as if it had been cut out of the side of the mountain. Out of Lorelei's window was a steep bank where the road dropped off. On the driver's side was a slight upslope that jutted against an evergreen forest. The mountain road was a single lane at best.

Merci stared out the windshield. Even before Nathan emerged from behind the veil of snow, running and shouting something they couldn't hear, she knew they were in trouble.

Lorelei raised her head like a deer alerted to a distant noise as she gazed out the driver's-side window. Merci turned her head, zooming in on the movement in the trees. She saw flashes of color, branches breaking and then the man in the orange coat was on the road pointing the gun through the driver's-side window. Merci reached over and locked the door.

Time seemed to be moving in slow motion as her heart pounded in her chest. All of her attention focused on the barrel of the gun. The man in the orange coat stepped closer. He had a scar that ran from his lip to his ear. Murder filled his eyes as he lifted the gun.

Lorelei shouted, "No," and pulled Merci's head down to the truck seat, a quick reaction that saved both their lives.

Glass shattered, sprinkling everywhere. Cold wind blew into the cab.

"Give me the truck." The man shouted through the broken window.

Nathan came up behind Orange Coat, grabbing him around the neck and wrestling him to the ground. The second man, the one in the leather jacket, emerged from the trees.

Nathan rattled the handle and then reached through the broken window to unlock the door.

The second thief was free of the trees and close enough to take aim.

Nathan jumped behind the wheel, clicked into reverse and hit the accelerator. His arm covered the women and pushed them lower as another bullet hit the truck, creating a metallic echo.

Nathan continued to back the truck up, swerving and looking behind him. Another shot was fired. This one fell short.

The truck labored to get up the road backward. When

she peered above the dashboard, the two men were on the road coming after them, and a third man emerged from the trees. Lorelei gasped. She saw the third man, too.

The blowing snow enveloped the three figures on the road.

Going back to the cabin didn't seem like such a good idea. The men would know where they were. "Isn't there some way we can get into town?" Merci found the courage to sit up a little straighter.

"Their car is blocking the intersection. If I try to go around it, I'll get stuck." Nathan craned his neck, focusing on the narrow road behind him.

The cab of the truck grew colder as the wind blew through the shattered window. The passenger-side window also had a spider-web break where the first bullet had exited.

The back tire slipped off the edge of the road. The truck leaned at a precarious angle. Nathan gunned the engine and then let up several times trying to rock the car out of the rut.

"I can't get any traction." His voice filled with tension.

"We can push it out," Merci suggested.

Nathan tapped his thumb on the steering wheel. "I don't know if that is a good idea in this cold weather."

The truck slid again. Lorelei let out a moan and dug her fingers into Merci's forearm.

"This thing is sliding off the bank." Nathan commanded, "Get out now on my side."

Nathan pushed on the door, crawled through and then reached first for Merci, lifting her easily onto the road. He held his hands out for Lorelei to grab on to. Wind drove the snow into their skin like thousands of icy needles. At least, the trunk of her body stayed warm. She was grateful for the extra clothes Nathan had given them.

"Stay linked together," Nathan shouted above the wind. "We're not that far from the cabin." He hooked his arm through Merci's and Merci grabbed onto Lorelei. Heads bent and leaning into the wind, they trudged up the hill.

Merci's heart still hadn't slowed from their close encounter with the gunmen. Though her muscles grew tired after only a few minutes, Nathan's strength pulled her forward. She couldn't see anything in front of her. She had to trust that Nathan knew his way back to the cabin. She leaned against him, sliding her feet one after the other.

She tightened her grip around Lorelei when she felt her weakening, slipping away. It was useless to shout words of encouragement. She bent over at the waist ignoring how cold her face and hands had become.

After a while Nathan slipped free of her. She had a fearful moment of wondering what had happened and then his gloved hand found hers. He placed it on something solid…the railing that led up to the cabin.

They were here.

They had made it.

She collapsed on the stairs. A moment later, strong arms lifted her, and she rested against a warm chest. She clung to the flannel shirt that smelled of wood smoke and musk. He laid her on the couch. She opened her eyes.

She didn't have to fight the strong wind anymore. No

more icy chill embedded under her skin. Warm tears formed.

He placed a blanket over her and pulled it up to her chin. "You're just exhausted and cold. No frostbite or anything." His hand covered hers. The heat of his touch seeped through to her core.

Merci shook her head. "This has all been a bit much." Her arms and legs felt like cooked noodles.

Lorelei had resumed her position, sitting bent over by the fire. How had she had the presence of mind to pull Merci out of the trajectory of that bullet? She owed Lorelei her life for her quick thinking.

"What are we going to do now?" Merci's question held unspoken fears. If the men couldn't get out, they'd be seeking shelter, too. The cabin would be the first place they'd look, and now there were three of them. She could only guess at where the third man had been during the robbery. Waiting down the road to be picked up or hiding in the trees? There must not have been a second car or they would have used it to escape. "I don't know if we should stay here."

Nathan shook his head. "Even if we didn't have to deal with this storm, the snow will be too deep by morning to get anywhere on the snowmobile. The truck is probably not viable. We can't get out, anyway, with the thieves' car blocking the road."

Merci sat up. "Is there another road out?"

"Not from the cabin," Nathan said. "There's a kids' camp not far from here and a ski hill farther up the mountain. They both have roads that come out on the other side of the mountain."

Lorelei looked at him. "All that is on this mountain?"

He nodded. "It doesn't help us any, though. I don't think there are any vehicles left at either place."

Merci absorbed what he was saying. "There's nobody at the camp or the ski hill or a house that is close by? Nobody who might be able to help us?"

"There are no other cabins on this section of the mountain. We hired a security guy to do periodic patrols, but he doesn't live there," he said. "It would be suicide to try and go anywhere in this storm on foot."

"So we stay here…and wait?" Fear coiled inside Merci.

"You might as well try to get some sleep. You two can have the guest bedroom." He pointed across the living room. "I'll call the police station again and let them know what is going on."

Lorelei shook her head in disbelief and wrung her hands. "I can't believe this is happening this way."

Lorelei was even more shaken than she was. Merci lifted her legs off the couch and placed her feet on the carpet so she faced Lorelei. "It'll be all right. We'll get this all straightened out in the morning. We can get the car towed and fixed and be on our way. In no time, it's all going to feel like a bad dream…." Her voice faltered. Though she had always been an optimist to a fault, even she was having a hard time believing her own words.

"Once the roads are clear, I can even take you back down to the car. We might be able to get it started." Nathan offered.

All their attempts at trying to put a positive spin on what had happened did very little to change the look of anxiety on Lorelei's face.

"I'll grab you guys some extra blankets." Nathan rose to his feet and disappeared around a corner.

Lorelei got up and trudged toward the door where Nathan had pointed. She stopped for a moment to look out the window. She was probably thinking about the thieves, too. Chances were the thieves would come looking for shelter. They weren't safe here. Lorelei shut the door quietly.

Nathan returned, holding a pile of blankets. "It can get kind of chilly in the rooms."

Merci took the blankets, grateful for the care Nathan had shown. Maybe that was the one good thing about all of this. She had met someone who cared about the welfare of strangers. "You are truly a good Samaritan. I'm so sorry that helping us has led to even more trouble."

"It's not your doing." He offered her a faint smile. He walked to the front door and slid the bolt in place. He made his way across the living room, checking window latches. "If you don't mind, I might sleep out here on the couch just to keep an eye on things." He clicked the deadbolt on the back door into place.

The sound of the bolts sliding was like a hammer blow to her heart. Nathan hadn't said anything about owning a gun. Though she was grateful for Nathan's vigilance and his effort at remaining calm, if the thieves decided to break in, she knew they were no match against three armed men.

THREE

For the fifth time in the night, Nathan woke up in darkness. He lay with his eyes open, absorbing the sounds around him. Wind rattled the windows. The big living room clock ticked. He got to his feet yet again and made his rounds through the house to make sure everything was secure.

He stopped before checking the front door and stared out the big living room window. Snow whirled and danced in the beam created by the porch light. The storm looked as if it had let up a little. At least two feet of snow, maybe more, had fallen.

He glanced back at the door to the guest bedroom. He hadn't heard any noise from them. He was glad the two women had been able to sleep. When he had tried to call the police station a second time, the phone was dead. The weight of the snow on the phone lines had probably destroyed the connection. The house ran on a generator, so that had not been affected. He hadn't brought a cell phone or a laptop, intending for the weekend to be a time of prayer and saying goodbye to the cabin that held so many fond memories.

His hand touched the windowsill as he peered out into the darkness. Maybe they had gotten lucky and the thieves had opted to seek shelter in their car instead of hiking up the mountain to the cabin.

In the morning, he would find out if either of the women had a cell phone, but for now he didn't want them to worry. It would be easier to face tomorrow's challenges after a full night's sleep.

He stared out the window. Something moved just beyond the circle of illumination created by the porch light. He watched. There it was again. He saw a flash of yellow, the same color as Lorelei's coat. Then he noticed that the bolt on the door was slid back. She hadn't been in a clear mental state since the robbery. Maybe she had really lost it and was wandering in the cold. He needed to get out there ASAP.

He slipped into his boots and put his coat on. He'd yell for her. If she didn't respond right away, he'd have to go back inside and get more winter gear on. He stepped out on the porch, but couldn't see anything.

His breath formed clouds when he called her name. He studied the forms and shadows through the falling snow, trying to pick out movement.

The blow to his head came without warning. He tumbled off the side of the porch into the snow as blackness descended.

Merci stirred beneath the covers of the twin bed. The bedspread was baseball-themed, something a young boy might like. Nathan and the brother he didn't want to talk about must have shared this room when they were kids. Funny that he called it the guest room instead of referring to it as his old room.

Merci reached over and clicked on the light by her bed. Lorelei's bed was empty.

Concerned about her friend, Merci sat up and pulled back the covers. She plodded across the room and into the living room. Nathan's door was shut. He must have found the couch uncomfortable and gone to his room. Lorelei wasn't in the living room or in the kitchen. When she checked the bathroom, it was empty, as well.

Lorelei had been traumatized by the attack, even more so than Merci. Maybe she wasn't thinking rationally. Merci took a deep breath to try to minimize the rising panic as she walked toward the living room window.

The wind wasn't blowing quite so hard, but the snow fell in heavy clumps. She pressed a little closer to the window. Though she was covered in shadow, Lorelei was outside. What was she doing?

Merci flung open the door, and the cold wind hit her. She yelled Lorelei's name. Lorelei turned slightly, but didn't look at Merci. Maybe she couldn't hear through the howling wind.

Merci ran back to the room, slipped into a sweater and jeans, grabbed her coat and put her boots on. She opened the door and stepped out on the porch. Silence greeted her. Where had Lorelei gone?

Her heart drummed in her ears as she scanned the empty landscape. One set of footprints looked newer than the others, where less snow had drifted over.

She stepped off the porch. "Lorelei." She sank down

into the deep snow as she followed footprints away from the cabin.

A mechanical noise, the sound of an engine starting up, broke the silence. Headlights sliced through the darkness and then the snowmobile emerged from a three-sided shed. The tall man in the leather coat who had tried to rob them earlier was driving. Lorelei stepped out behind him. When the thief saw Merci, he grabbed Lorelei and pulled her toward the snowmobile.

Merci raced toward them. The man pulled a gun out of a coat pocket and pointed it at Lorelei. He said something to her, and she got on the snowmobile.

He pointed the gun at Merci and then at Lorelei. "Back off or she dies."

"You better do what he says." Lorelei's voice cracked.

"No, Lorelei, I won't let them take you." She grabbed Lorelei's sleeve.

The man reached up and hit Merci hard against the jaw with the butt of the gun. She fell backward. Pain, intense and hot, spread across her face. Her eyes watered. When she looked toward the house, Nathan was standing up at the far side of the stairs.

The man revved the motor, preparing to take off. Merci turned to face the thug as Nathan's footsteps pounded behind her.

Nathan, dressed in his boots and an open coat, jumped in front of Merci. "Get off my snowmobile." He hit the man across the face with a right hook.

Lorelei screamed and scooted back on the seat.

The man leaned sideways, recovering just in time to lift the gun as Nathan grabbed him and yanked him off the snowmobile. The gun flew out of the thief's hand.

Merci crab-walked backward in the snow. The two men struggled, rolling around on the ground. The thief freed himself of Nathan's grasp, scrambling for his gun where it had fallen in the snow.

Out of breath, Nathan lunged toward the man.

The man hit him with the butt of the gun just as he rose to his feet. Nathan reeled backward and fell in the snow, not moving.

The man crawled back on the snowmobile. Lorelei sat stunned. Her eyes glazed as though she didn't really comprehend all that was happening. The man revved the snowmobile and lurched forward. Merci waited for the backward glance from Lorelei, but it never happened. She tried to get to her feet to chase them, but sank down in the snow. The snowmobile disappeared into the trees, and the engine noise faded.

Out of breath and shaking, Merci crawled over to where Nathan lay. Blood dripped from his cheek.

She shook him. "Please, please be okay."

His eyelids fluttered. Brown eyes looked at her. "Hey," his voice was weak, but his eyes brightened when he saw her.

She breathed a sigh of relief, then noticed he had thrown his coat over his pajama bottoms. "You're shivering. Take my hand. Let's get you inside." The struggle had chilled her, but he was probably nearing hypothermia. She was dressed for the cold and hadn't had to roll in the snow with the thief.

He sat up swaying and blinking rapidly. "What about the snowmobile and Lorelei?"

"It's too late. We can't catch them." She slipped in

under his arm and helped him to his feet. "Let's get you warmed up."

"I'm an EMT. I know what to do. I just need to…" His voice trailed off.

She helped him up the stairs and through the door, easing him down into the chair by the fire.

"The coat needs to come off, it's wet." She peeled it off his shoulders and put it aside. She drew the same blanket he had offered her earlier over his muscular shoulders. His lips were drained of color, and he was still shivering. She touched his cheeks with her palms, forcing eye contact. "Better?"

He drew the blanket closer as he crossed his arms over his bare chest. "Getting there. I…he knocked me off the porch…hit my head." He touched the back of his head and winced.

She hadn't even seen Nathan as she had raced down the stairs in search of Lorelei. "How long were you there?" She covered his freezing hands.

"I was only out for a few minutes. I came to, and I saw you struggling."

She pulled his boots off. The inside lining of his boot was wet from where the snow had seeped in. His bare feet weren't blue, but they looked cold. She cupped her hand over one. "Can you feel that?"

He nodded. "Exposure wasn't long enough for frostbite, just kind of cold."

She grabbed a throw from the couch and secured it around his feet. "Now it's my turn to make you tea." She rose to her feet and went into the kitchen. She allowed herself only a momentary glance out the window. Lorelei was out there somewhere with those animals.

They were going to have to find her before anything bad happened. If it hadn't already.

Heat slowly returned to Nathan's body as he listened to Merci work in the kitchen. A tingling sensation came into his feet and hands. He wasn't accustomed to being the one needing first aid. She had handled herself like a pro.

In the kitchen, the kettle whistled. Merci hummed while she made the tea. He caught an undercurrent of tension in her singing. Her feet padded softly on the wood floor. She brought the steaming mug on a tray and set it on the table beside him.

She picked up a wet washcloth and pointed to his cheek. "You have blood on your face that needs to be cleaned." She leaned toward him and touched the warm cloth to his face.

He drew back, surprised by the pain. "It must be pretty bad, huh?" He was going to have a knob on the back of his head where he had been hit, too.

She dabbed at the cut. Her face was close enough to his that her cool breath fluttered across his lips. "It's a pretty big gash."

"I have a butterfly bandage I can use to get it to close up," he said.

"Let me get it. Where is it?"

He really wasn't used to being the patient. "There is a first-aid kit in my bathroom, but I can get it." He rose to get up.

She placed a gentle but firm hand on his shoulder. "Sit."

Something in her tone told him argument would be

futile. He listened to her open and close several drawers and then she returned, placed the first-aid kit on
the table by his chair and tore the bandage out of the
wrapping.

"Hold still." She leaned close, her touch as delicate
as feathers brushing over his skin.

Her proximity sent a surge of heat up his face. Surprised by the sudden smolder of attraction, he turned
slightly away.

"Hold still." She grabbed his chin and readjusted
his head.

She was all business. Obviously, the feelings were
not mutual. "Really, I could do this myself if I looked
in a mirror." She ignored him and finished the job.

"There, that should do it." She sat back on the has-
sock between the two chairs. Her hand brushed over
his cheek as she scrutinized her work. "You shouldn't
have any scarring."

He touched the bandage and then looked at her. He
studied her full lips, delicate—almost invisible—eyebrows and her freckles. Her green eyes widened. For a
moment, time stood still and he forgot what they had
just been through and what they faced. She was a lovely
young woman.

She cast her gaze downward at the bloody cloth
where she had placed it on the tray. Her expression
grew serious and her soft full lips drew into a tight line.

She didn't have to say anything for him to know
what she was thinking about. It had been on his mind,
too. Lorelei was out there with armed men who had no
qualms about using violence.

"What's going to happen to her?" Merci couldn't hide her anguish.

"I don't know. He must have come back for the snow-mobile, thinking that would get him and the others off the mountain. They might get a little ways, but even that won't be good in the deeper snow."

"But why would they take Lorelei?"

He shook his head. "Maybe he thought it would be easier to get away if he had a hostage."

Merci nodded. "He did say if I came close, he would hurt Lorelei."

"The others must have been waiting for him in the trees. You can't fit four people on that snowmobile. He might let her go once he thinks he's gotten far enough away."

Her eyes widened with fear. "That would mean she would be wandering out there in the cold." She brought her fingers up to her mouth and shook her head. "Or he might just kill her when she is not useful to him anymore."

Judging from what he had seen so far, that was a possibility. He kept the thought to himself. Merci was worried enough.

"She went outside in the middle of the night like she was not in her right mind. I remember reading stories in history class about pioneer women who just walked out in the cold and died because the struggle for survival just got to be too much for them."

Still feeling a little wobbly, Nathan rose to his feet. "She was kind of falling apart."

Merci shuddered, then lifted her chin. A look of resolve came over her face. "We have to rescue her."

He didn't disagree, but they were no match for armed men. If they were to get any distance at all, they needed a break in the storm. "We don't have any way to defend ourselves."

"She saved my life when they attacked us in your truck." Her eyes pleaded. "We have to do something. Maybe they'll just let her go in the woods."

That would be the best case scenario. "We might be able to bring her back to the cabin, but not if the thieves are close by."

Her jerky movement as she ran her fingers through her hair revealed how anxious she was. "Maybe the police will try harder to get up here now that they know what we are dealing with."

He hated hitting her with more bad news, but he needed to tell her the truth. "The phone line is not working. I wasn't able to make that second call." He braced for her reaction.

Merci sucked in a sharp breath before responding. "We have no way to contact anyone?"

"Do you have a cell phone?"

She shoved her hands in the pocket of her purple coat. "I thought I put it back in my pocket when we were at the car, but maybe I didn't...or it might have fallen out of my pocket outside." She rose to her feet and looked up at him. "What are we going to do to help her?"

His mind reeled, searching for possible solutions. "If they came back for the snowmobile thinking it would help them escape, they'll get bogged down in the snow eventually."

Merci's eyes brightened. "So they would be on foot.

That means we might be able to catch them and get Lorelei back."

Nathan nodded. "If we get a break in the storm, we can follow the tracks. I have snowshoes and warm weather gear."

She moved away from him and collapsed on the couch. "It's not a smart plan, is it?"

"It's the only viable plan we have." He paced. "We'll only go out a short distance. When the snowmobile becomes unviable, they might head back toward the cabin. We'll have the element of surprise on our side."

She laced her fingers together and bent her head. She stared at the floor for a long time as though she were mulling over what they were about to do. "We can't leave her out there. And we can't just wait here and hope they come back and that she is with them. You saw what those men were capable of."

"There is a lot of 'ifs' to this plan." He shook his head. "Taking her just doesn't make a lot of sense even if she was some sort of insurance policy to get away. Maybe this isn't a simple robbery. Is your friend rich?"

Merci shrugged. "I really don't know her that well."

"But you took a ride with her." He hadn't intended to sound accusatory.

"I was desperate. I had a terrible finals week. Someone stole textbooks out of my dorm room. I failed chemistry. My dad sent me a letter saying he and mom weren't going to be in the States for the spring break. He thought it would soften the blow if he sent a care package, too. The final insult was that my car broke down two days before I was supposed to leave. All I could think about was how being with Aunt Celeste would make the world seem right again. I was checking the *Share a Ride* bulletin board when Lorelei came up to me and said she was driving to western Oregon and could drop me off."

College students caught rides with fellow students all the time. Still, it seemed a little impulsive on Merci's part. "So how well did you know her?"

"We weren't best friends or anything." Merci gathered her long hair in her hand and twisted it while she talked. "We're in the same dorm, and we had a marketing class together last year. We worked on a project together. She's a serious student."

Nathan walked to the window and stared out at the deep snow. The wind wasn't as bad as it had been earlier and the snowfall was lighter.

Merci came up behind him. "We have to do this, Nathan. She saved my life. There is no one else to help her. I'm afraid for her."

He hated putting Merci in harm's way. But going alone would be foolhardy, too. His resolve solidified. They had to at least try. "I have an extra pair of snowshoes. I don't have another coat, so you will have to wear the one you have. Let's see if we can find all the winter gear we can."

In twenty minutes, Nathan gathered together everything he thought they might need and filled their backpacks with food and water. When he looked out the window, the storm seemed to be breaking up. There was less snow and wind.

Merci followed Nathan out onto the porch. Darkness still covered the sky, but the wind had stopped blowing. He took a moment to show her how to strap the snowshoes on. "Step lightly. Don't waste energy pulling yourself out of the snow."

She nodded, her face filled with trust. "Is that it?"

He picked up a silk balaclava that had been his brother's. "Wear this under your hat. It'll keep your face warm." He slipped it over her head.

"And it makes me look like a ninja."

He smiled, grateful for the moment of humorous relief.

"Stay close. The wind isn't bad now, but it's important that we always be able to see each other. I'll slow down if I need to. Are you sure about this?"

The trusting green eyes gazed up at him. "I couldn't live with myself if something bad happened to her, knowing that I didn't at least try to help her."

"Me, either," He said before taking in a prayer-filled breath. "Let's do this."

Nathan clicked on his flashlight and took the lead. Merci followed in his tracks. Snow swirled out of the sky. When he looked over his shoulder, she was keeping up, but the distance between them had increased.

The snowmobile tracks were easy enough to follow, making clear grooves as the snow got deeper and deeper. They were only about half a mile from the cabin when they found the abandoned snowmobile stuck in the snow.

Nathan lifted his head and shone the light. "Footprints lead off this way."

Merci came up beside him, breathing heavily. "Do you suppose the other two thieves were waiting for them somewhere?"

"Maybe." He studied the two sets of prints partially

drifted over from snow. "I can tell you one thing. He's not taking her back to the cabin."

Merci came up beside him and shone her flashlight. "There's not any blood. No sign of struggle. She must still be okay. Where are they going?"

"These footprints point toward the camp." He took off his gloves and tightened the drawstring around his hood. The temperature had to be below zero, but at least the wind wasn't blowing too bad.

"How would they even know about the camp?"

Nathan shrugged. "Maybe they saw the signs when they drove in and remembered it."

"How far is it to the camp?" She clamped her gloved hand on his forearm.

He turned and shone his light on the cluster of trees and the trail behind him. "It's only a little farther to go to the camp than it is to go back to the cabin." He remembered something that lifted his spirits. "My father used to keep a rifle in the camp office to use in case of bear attacks. Only the stuff that varmints will damage gets taken out of the camp in the off-season. I think the rifle is left there."

"If we had a gun, it would be easier to get Lorelei back." Hope tinged Merci's voice.

The decision was not a hard one to make. He knew the layout of the camp like the back of his hand, had keys to all the buildings and a rifle meant they could defend themselves if they had to. The odds had shifted a little. "Let's keep going."

They trudged forward in the dark. The flashlight beam illuminated a small path in front of them. Merci fell a few paces behind him. After about thirty minutes, the wind picked up again. The break in the storm had been short-lived as the snowfall became heavier again.

He felt a tug on his coat. "It's getting worse. I think I need to stay closer."

Nathan draped an arm over Merci's shoulder as both of them put their heads down and leaned into the wind. He only hoped they had not made a mistake. They had taken a gamble that the weather would hold. Conditions were hazardous at best. A little more wind, a few degrees' drop in temperature and they would be fighting for their lives.

FOUR

Merci held on tight to Nathan's gloved hand and trudged forward in the dark. She was grateful they had put on enough cold weather gear to ensure that they weren't chilled to the bone. Having to lean into the wind and fight the elements with every step meant fatigue was setting in, though. How much farther to the camp?

She bent forward to shield herself from the wind, which meant her flashlight only illuminated the three or four feet of ground in front of her. The tiredness in her leg muscles made her think that they had been walking for hours. In reality, it had probably only been minutes.

She put her foot down slightly sideways. The snowshoe came off. Her leg sunk down to the knee in a drift of deep snow, and snow suctioned around her calf. A cry of surprise escaped her throat, and she let go of Nathan's hand. She tensed the muscles in her upper leg to pull herself free, but her foot didn't budge. Nathan grabbed her at the elbow before she toppled face-first in the snow.

"You all right?" Clouds formed when he exhaled.

Even through the layers of clothing, she could feel the strength of his grip as he held her.

"I think my foot is stuck." Snow seeped in through the top of her boot. The biting chill on her calf was instantaneous as it melted down her leg.

"I'll pull you out." He bent forward and wrapped his arm around her waist, while she gained leverage by bracing her hand on his shoulder. "On my count, try to lift your leg. One. Two. Three."

She leaned, dug her fingers into his shoulder and put all her weight on the free leg while she pulled the other. "Got it." Though the thick socks slowed the encroaching cold, the snow had melted down her boot to her foot. "How much farther do we have to go?"

Nathan turned a half circle. "Not far now. And look." Moonlight revealed a plume of smoke rising up into the sky.

She tilted her head. With the wind blowing like it was, she wouldn't have noticed it if Nathan hadn't pointed it out.

"The camp is just beyond these trees," Nathan said. "And it looks like our friends have built a fire in one of the buildings. They must have found a way to break a lock."

The muscles at the back of her neck squeezed into a tight knot as the reality of what they were facing hit her. "So they are there for sure."

"It could be someone who got stranded up here, but I doubt it." He patted her shoulder and put his face close to hers. "The camp isn't far. It won't be long now." His voice held a solemn quality.

Were they walking to their deaths even if they did

find the rifle? Would they even be able to help Lorelei? They trudged onward. Her leg grew colder.

They stepped out into an open area away from the forest. Without the shelter of the trees, the accumulated snow had grown deeper. Walking became harder even with the snowshoes. They sank down repeatedly.

They made their way up a steep hill. Her leg muscles burned from the exertion.

"Stay here for a moment." Nathan walked back toward the trees that lined one side of the road. He disappeared into the forest and returned a moment later holding a large stick. He handed it to her. "Use that. It'll help you walk faster. We're really close, but the last bit is kind of hard going."

"I'm not sure if I needed to hear that." She'd tried to sound lighthearted, but the only thing weighing heavier on her than the walk was what they faced at the end of their journey.

"Just focus on how close we are. Look up ahead," Nathan said.

She followed the direction of his point. A flagpole without a flag was visible in the moonlight despite the blowing snow.

Their snowshoes slapped on top of the snow with each tedious step. She stopped for a moment to catch her breath. She aimed her flashlight up the trail as snow danced and swirled in the beam of illumination. Her spirits lifted. "I see the sign for the camp."

"Yup, that's it." Nathan's voice still had lots of pep to it. The hike hadn't worn him out.

As they neared, she raised her light again. Now she could make out the yellow letters against the brown background of the sign. "Why is the camp called *Daniel's Hope?*"

"It's named after my brother. He survived cancer when he was a kid. My parents developed the land shortly after he went into remission. They wanted to memorialize all the blessings that had taken place while he was getting better."

So the camp was named after the brother he didn't want to talk about. "That's a really neat story."

"It was a long time ago." His voice held a note of sadness.

She saw the two sets of footprints in the snow. They followed the tracks past the sign and down a hill. The two sets of tracks were joined by another set of prints.

When they entered the camp, the buildings were but shadows in the darkness. The smell of chimney smoke grew stronger.

"Hard to say where they are, but I'm thinking they are in one of the dorms," Nathan said. "Those would be the easiest to break in to. Each one has a fireplace."

Merci leaned on the walking stick Nathan had given her. "I need to rest and get this wet sock off my foot."

"The cafeteria is a bit of a hike across the camp, that's where the office and the rifle will be. You have to cook your food away from where people sleep, to prevent bear attacks. The main meeting hall is close. We can go there," Nathan said.

He pulled on the sleeve of her wool coat and led her through the camp. She had the impression that they were on a trail, though she could not be sure in the dark. From what she could discern, the camp was built in a bowl and surrounded by trees that must have served as a barrier to keep too much snow from drifting through.

She could make out the dark silhouette of a building. As they drew closer, the distinctive lines of a cabin came into view. "How are we going to get in?"

"I have keys, remember?" he said.

He let go of her hand and pulled his backpack off. "Can you hold the light for me?"

Merci angled the light at the door where a chain and padlock was drawn across. Hardly high tech. She heard keys jingling. Nathan brought his hand into the beam of light as he sorted through the keys and then unlocked the door.

The door swung open, revealing a large room shrouded in darkness. They slipped inside. The flashlight allowed her to only see portions of the room, benches and tables, a stage with a podium and a microphone laid on its side.

"We can't build a fire. That would alert them to our being here, and we should probably keep the flashlight use to a minimum." Nathan must have picked up on her anxiety because he added, "We have a lot to our advantage. We have the element of surprise on our side, and I know this camp like the back of my hand."

"Getting the rifle will help, too." Merci struggled to sound calm. Everything Nathan pointed out did nothing to alleviate the tightness in her stomach. Maybe they would get lucky and find Lorelei tied up in a room alone.

Nathan had slipped off the snowshoes. His boots pounded on the wood floor as he walked around. "It seems like we kept some basics supplies in the storage room in here. Why don't you sit down and rest? I'll see if I can find a replacement sock for you."

Merci swung the light around until a bench came into view. She plunked down, turned off the flashlight and pulled off her snowshoes, boot and wet sock. She hung the sock over the back of a chair. The cabin wasn't much warmer than outside. She crossed her arms over her body and sat in the dark.

She could hear Nathan's footsteps. A door screeched open. Judging from the distant sound of the footsteps, this place was pretty big. Their voices had seemed to almost echo when they had stepped inside.

The noise of him moving around stopped. She sat in the darkness enveloped by the silence. What had become of Nathan?

Moonlight provided only a little illumination. She could see the outline of the door where Nathan had gone. With one boot on and one boot off, she listed slightly to one side. Her steps had a clomp, pad, clomp rhythm to them. She twisted the knob, and the door eased open with a screech. "Hello, Nathan," she whispered.

No answer.

A thudding above her caused her to jump. Her heart revved up to rapid-fire speed. Scraping and squeaking sounds filled the room. A door above her opened up.

She heard Nathan's voice before she could discern his face above her. "Looks like they have been storing a bunch of stuff in the loft."

"You nearly gave me a heart attack." Her heart was still racing.

"I didn't find any dry socks for you." He tossed a

bundle to the floor. "But I found something that might work. If you can reach up and pull the string, the ladder will unfold, and I can come down."

She couldn't see anything as small as a rope so she retrieved her flashlight and shone it for only a moment to see where the rope was and pulled the ladder down.

Nathan descended. "That plastic bag I tossed down contains a wool blanket. It's a little moth bally, but we can tear it into strips and wrap it around your foot to make a sock."

"Guess mine is not going to dry out in time," she said. "Do you think we should try to get that rifle tonight and find Lorelei?"

"We have less of a chance of being seen in the dark." Nathan unzipped the plastic bag and pulled a pocket knife out of his coat pocket. "If we surprise them while they are sleeping, we have a better chance of success."

Merci sat down on the floor and scooted in beside him. He ripped the blanket down the middle and handed her half. "Put that around you to keep warm. Sorry we can't have a fire."

She wrapped the blanket over her shoulders. "I'll be okay. Once we get moving. I won't notice the cold so much."

He split his piece of the blanket in half again. "There should be a pocket knife in your backpack. This will go faster if we both work. Six or so strips about an inch wide."

"Maybe I could just survive without a sock, and we could get moving," she said.

Nathan shook his head. "Not a good idea. The inside of your boot is probably wet, too. This wool will pull the moisture away from your foot. When you put the boot on next time, put your pant leg on the outside of it."

Of course that made sense. She'd been so anxious about Lorelei when she had suited up at the cabin that she hadn't been thinking about pant legs and snow. Merci held the blanket scrap up to the window, cut a notch in the end and tore a strip off. "Did you come up to this camp quite a bit when you were a kid?"

"Every summer. My parents ran it themselves for years. They had the ski hill in winter and the camp in summer. When my brother and I got older, we kind of lost interest." His voice faded.

She watched Nathan work with his head bent. Even with the shadows the darkness created, she could see an expression of intense concentration. Her curiosity about Nathan had been piqued from the moment he risked his own life to save her and Lorelei. She wanted to get to know him better. There seemed to be some landmines where his family was concerned, so she needed to tread lightly. "So going to summer camp was fun for you?"

"Yes." His voice warmed. "How about you? Did you ever go to a summer camp?"

"No, my parents were into resorts. I've never even built a campfire."

"Really?"

"Yup, but I don't even go to resorts anymore. My father has the mindset that if he is paying the bills, he gets to tell you how to live your life. I've been on my own since I was eighteen. Paid for college by working one year and attending the next, buying secondhand and living on a shoestring."

"You sound like a pretty determined lady."

"I guess. It's also made me the world's oldest undergrad. I'll be twenty-six by the time I finish my business degree." She gazed at the stage and the chairs, trying to imagine it filled with laughing children. "What was it like, being at camp?"

"Best part of the summer in a lot of ways." He rose to his feet and walked over to the stage area. "We'd have worship service here and a talent contest. Mom spent the whole winter talking local merchants into all kinds of cool giveaways for the kids." His voice had become animated.

She pulled another strip of fabric from the blanket. "Sounds like it was a good part of your life."

"Yeah, I've got a lot of good memories connected to this place." She could hear his footsteps as he paced across the wooden floorboards. "Maybe some sad memories, too." His pacing stopped. "It's just not the same with mom and dad gone."

In the darkness and even without being able to see his face clearly, the depth of his pain vibrated through his voice. The sorrow in his life ran deep. Merci rose to her feet, wishing she could offer him some sort of comfort. His tall frame was silhouetted in shadow against the tiny bit of moonlight that shone through the window. She stepped close to him and slipped her hand in his.

He squeezed her hand but then pulled free and walked away. "Yup, I'm kind of sorry to see the place go, but I need to sell all of the mountain acreage. The ski hill, the camp. Everything." His voice was stronger now, more in control. He'd buried the raw emotions somewhere deep.

Why would he sell something he so obviously loved? "Is the camp in financial trouble?"

He shook his head. "My parents were smart about how they set it up. The ski resort did okay when it was operational, and the camp was a nonprofit. With the right management and staff, both of them stay in the black."

"So why are you selling it?"

Nathan paced some more before settling down and cutting another strip of fabric. "You ask a lot of questions."

She felt for the blanket, draping it over her shoulders. "That's how you find out things."

"My brother and I would have to run everything together. We don't always see eye to eye." He spoke in a clipped tone.

The strain in his voice indicated that he didn't want to talk about his brother. She'd treaded into dangerous waters.

After a moment he spoke. "Are you getting your energy back?"

The effect of only a few hours of sleep and all the trauma of the past ten hours had left her battle-weary, but they had come all this way and Lorelei needed help. She summoned what little strength she had. "I think I've caught my breath."

"Good, let's get this homemade sock around your foot." Nathan picked up one of the strips.

"Can I help?" Merci scooted against the wall.

"It's kind of a one-person job." Nathan gently lifted her foot, cupping her heel in his hand. "Your foot is like a block of ice." The warmth of his touch permeated her skin as he wound the fabric around her toes.

"Snow usually is cold," Merci joked.

His finger grazed her ankle when he braided the fabric up her leg. "My super special weave should make a good sock." He bent his head sideways and offered her a crooked smile.

Merci's heart warmed toward this man who was so willing to sacrifice everything for someone he barely knew. Even in the most dangerous of circumstances, they had found a light moment. "I'm sure your super special weave will work just fine."

Nathan was surprised how little Merci had complained about her wet foot. She must have been freezing. His finger glided over her smooth cold skin until he completed a sock that went up to her calf. "All done." He looked a little closer to assess his handiwork but was unable to see much in the moonlight. "Is it comfortable?"

Merci flexed her foot. "It's not too tight or anything. I'll get my boot on."

Nathan glanced up at the windows thinking he'd seen movement. But it was only the shadow of the trees close to the building.

Merci slipped into her boot. "So now we go to the cafeteria to get your father's rifle."

He wrestled with their plan and wondered if there was a better way to do it. They had to get to his father's office and find that rifle. Without that, they were no match for the thieves at all. Even once they got Lorelei free, they would have to contend with returning to the cabin or somewhere else until law enforcement could arrive. Had they been foolhardy in choosing to come up here?

He shook off the uncertainty as quickly as it had come into his head. Merci had been right. They didn't have a choice in waiting for the authorities where a human life was concerned. He stood up. "We can't waste any more time."

Merci rose to her feet. "Lead the way."

He'd never met someone as trusting as Merci. He had come up with a plan that maybe had a fifty percent chance of working, but she had backed him and endured the physical struggle of getting here. He admired her positive outlook and tenacity. She'd done all of it without complaint or questioning.

He patted her back. There was a lot to admire about Merci Carson. If they made it through the next twenty-four hours, it might be nice to take her out to coffee where they could get to know each other under less traumatic circumstances.

A rattling sound caused both of them to jump and turn.

"What's that noise?" Merci's voice filled with panic.

Nathan's muscles tensed as adrenaline surged through his body. "It's the door handle. Someone's trying to break in."

FIVE

As a precaution, Nathan had bolted the door when they came inside. He hoped the thieves wouldn't be able to break the lock.

Merci wrapped her arm through Nathan's. "How did they find us?"

"I don't know. Maybe they saw our tracks or the lights as we were coming in," he said.

"Is there a back way out?" she said in a frantic whisper.

Nathan shook his head. The rattling grew more intense and persistent. One of the men said something in a harsh tone. An object thudded against the door.

Nathan took a step back and stood between Merci and the intruders. The thieves were going to break the door down.

He grabbed her hand. "Get your stuff. Come with me." After gathering up backpacks and kicking the snowshoes under a table, he pulled her toward the ladder of the loft.

Merci scampered up the ladder. Nathan put his foot on the first rung.

The banging noises increased. He climbed the ladder and swung into the loft. "Help me pull it up." He leaned down through the loft opening.

The banging continued. An ax sliced through the door. The hole grew bigger with each blow.

Merci crawled to the other side of the loft and reached down. The ladder pulled up in three sections that folded on top of each other.

They folded the final section. The man in the orange coat came into the building, holding an ax. The loft door eased shut as they heard more footsteps. Though she couldn't discern the words of the conversation, it was obvious the men were irritated.

In the darkness, Merci pressed against Nathan's shoulder. Her breathing was a little more labored than his. His heart jackhammered in his chest.

The voices below them were muffled but angry. The stomping of feet overwhelmed the words.

Nathan leaned close to Merci and whispered in her ear. "We need to get to where we can hear them. They might say something about Lorelei. Follow me." He found her smooth delicate hand in the darkness and cupped his own over it.

"But it's so dark," she whispered close enough for him to feel the warmth of her breath on his skin.

"I could go through this place with my eyes closed." Which was pretty much what they would be doing. Without the generator hooked up, there were no lights in this building. He never would have foreseen that playing hide-and-seek in the dark in this building as a kid would benefit him as an adult.

"Okay, lead the way," whispered Merci.

He slipped out of his boots. "Take your boots off, so they won't hear us. We'll come back for them."

He grabbed her hand again and reached out for the rough wood texture of the wall. He led her through a narrow hallway to an opening. When he was the designated techie for the performances, he'd crawled along the catwalk and backstage area a thousand times. They came out to the stage manager's booth above the performing area.

The men's voices became clearer and more distinct.

If they leaned forward, they'd have an aerial view of the stage, but they also risked detection if they leaned too far out.

"There is no food in here," one of the thieves grumbled.

Nathan breathed a sigh of relief. They hadn't given themselves away with the minimal flashlight use or tracks. Hunger had driven the men from wherever they were holed up. Hopefully, their footprints would be blown over enough to avoid detection by the thieves once daylight came.

"There has got to be something to eat around here," said the second man. "What do you think, boss?"

There was a brief pause and then the sound of footsteps moving up stairs. One of them was on the stage. Nathan lifted his chin in an effort to get a look at what was going on. He could just see the blond head of the third thief, the one who hadn't been at the initial robbery, as he stepped center stage. He was younger than the other two men and more clean-cut.

His voice had a commanding, smooth quality. "I am sure there is some food around here somewhere."

"Look, Hawthorne, I don't work well on an empty stomach." The man in the orange coat approached the stage and plunked down on the stairs.

Nathan strained to see more without being noticed. It looked as if the men had fashioned torches out of logs and rags. Two torches had been stuck in plant holders. They may have had a lighter with them and must have located some kind of fuel to put on the rags.

"We need to get off this mountain." The voice came from a part of the room Nathan couldn't see. "This is way more than we signed up for."

"Use your brain." The third thief, the one they called Hawthorne, raised a calming hand. "We are not dressed well enough to go any distance. We nearly froze to death getting here. The weather will probably break up by morning. We'll find a way out."

"What are we going to do without any food?" said Orange Coat.

"I bet there is plenty to eat back at that cabin." Nathan couldn't see who was speaking but he assumed the voice belonged to the man in the leather jacket, the one that had come for Lorelei.

"I say we go back there and help ourselves." The other thief's voice took on a menacing quality. "I know what to do with that redhead and her friend on the snowmobile."

"Do you really want to walk back to that cabin?" Hawthorne's voice was insistent and demanding. "We don't have a snowmobile anymore. The less contact we have with those people, the better."

The other two men responded with silence.

"There's got to be a cafeteria around here. They

had to feed those rug rats something. Most of the food would have been hauled out, but maybe they've got some canned goods or something." Hawthorne stepped off the stage. "Let's get moving."

Nathan stretched his neck to try to get a view of what was going on.

Hawthorne had picked up one of the torn pieces of the wool blanket they'd left behind. He paced the room still holding the fabric scrap. The blanket didn't give them away. It could have been left there from a previous summer. "Let's take this. It'll come in handy to keep us warm."

Nathan's heartbeat drummed in his ears as his breath hitched. Merci's wet sock was still flung over the back of a chair. If anyone touched it, they would know someone had been in the building recently.

Merci let out an almost indiscernible gasp. Her hand clasped around Nathan's forearm. She must have noticed the sock, too. What he could see of the floor below was limited. As the men moved around the room, they went in and out of view.

Leather Jacket said, "Yeah, I don't know why we didn't just barge into that cozy cabin."

"Going to the cabin means I risk being seen. I don't want to be connected to this. That's why I hired you two." Hawthorne's voice was condescending.

"Besides," Hawthorne continued, "this was supposed to be done with no bloodshed until your friend here thought it was a good idea to pull a gun on the redhead and messed up my plan. So you being trapped here and hungry is your own doing."

"She caught me off guard." The second thief spat out

his words. "She was supposed to stay in the car getting warmed up where she couldn't see anything."

"Nevertheless, it's not my fault that you're stuck on this mountain." Hawthorne stepped into view. He was only a few feet from the chair that had Merci's sock slung over it.

He shook his blond head. "Bickering won't help us. Let's go find some grub."

The wavering light of the homemade torches moved across the floor as the thieves made their way to the door they had torn to pieces.

The voices faded. From the kneeling position in the stage manager's booth, neither Merci nor Nathan moved for a long tense moment.

Finally, Merci said in a voice that was barely above a whisper. "Lorelei wasn't with them."

"That doesn't mean anything. They might have her tied up somewhere. Let's not give up hope. It won't take them long to figure out where the cafeteria is. We need to get there before they do and find that rifle."

Though her stomach felt as if it had been turned inside out, Merci nodded in agreement. "I'll go get our boots."

"Let's leave the snowshoes here. Snow is not as deep in the camp, and footprints would be less noticeable," Nathan said.

It took only minutes for her to find the boots and for them to be ready to head out the door. Once outside, Merci listened to the rhythmic crunch of her feet in the snow as she walked beside Nathan in near total darkness. The decision had been made not to use flashlights. Since they had no idea where the thieves were in the camp, bobbing lights against the blackness of night would give them away.

Nathan moved at a steady pace. He knew the camp so well the darkness wasn't a huge hindrance. The sound of their footsteps seemed to harmonize.

"There is a tree coming up here on the right. You might want to step behind me," Nathan instructed. "Just walk where I walk."

She slowed and slipped in behind him. Without a word, he turned and found her hand in the darkness.

"How much farther?"

"Maybe another ten minutes." He stopped for a moment.

She pressed against his shoulder, grateful for the sense of safety she felt when she was close to him. She scanned the area around them looking for the telltale torches that would reveal that the thieves were on the move, but could see nothing. "It's that far away?"

"It just takes longer in the snow and the dark. We'll come to an open area and then it's just a little ways after that. It's at the top of the hill away from the rest of the camp." Her eyes had adjusted enough to the darkness that she could see his breath when he spoke.

The wind had almost died down completely, and the night had a crisp, cold feel to it.

Nathan said, "Let's keep moving."

Every choice they made seemed to be wrought with uncertainty. Would they find the rifle? Would it be enough to protect them against three men with handguns? What if they couldn't find Lorelei and free her? What if something had already happened to her?

A sense of foreboding and anxiety snaked through her as they stepped free of the trees and buildings.

They came to a sloping meadow filled with snow. The trees that surrounded the rest of the camp had blocked out much of the moonlight. But out here in the open the new fallen snow took on an almost crystalline quality. Flakes glistened like tiny diamonds. A calm came over her as she stared out at the pristine snow. God was in this with them. If they lived or died, they had done the right thing by coming for Lorelei.

"It's just up this hill," Nathan said. "Walk around the edge of the meadow where our footprints are less likely to be spotted."

"It's really beautiful out here, isn't it?" she said.

"I've always loved it. Too bad you aren't getting to see it under different circumstances."

They trekked down into the meadow and up the hill. A large building came into view. Nathan led her to the front door and filed through his keys. She stared down the hill at the way they had come. Underneath the moonlight, the snow took on a blue hue.

Nathan let out a groan.

"Is something wrong?"

"I'm concerned they may have changed some of the locks and not given me an updated key. I have a vague memory of the camp director saying something to me about it." He shook the doorknob. "With Mom and Dad dying last year, I really wasn't in any kind of shape to deal with those mundane details."

"Is there another way in?" Merci bounced up and down to stave off the cold.

"There is no alarm system. We can break a window. You're small enough to crawl through. Once you get in, I think the back door will open from the inside. Follow me."

She glanced back toward the camp. Her breath caught. Halfway through the camp, two torches bounced against the blackness of the night. "They're coming this way."

He pulled on the sleeve of her coat. "It looks like they are searching the other buildings for food. They've got a couple more buildings before they come up this way. We'd better hurry." He led her around to the side of the building where she could no longer gauge the progress of the thieves as they moved toward the cafeteria.

Nathan stopped and tilted his head. "The window is higher than I remember. I'm going to have to boost you up." He skirted around, turning on the flashlight and kicking away snow.

"Are you looking for a rock?"

"Anything that we could use to break the window. Then you can just reach in and unlatch it," Nathan said.

Her boot touched something hard. She reached down and felt through the snow, pulling up a metal cow bell. "Will this work?"

He shone his light on it and took it from her hand. "One of the instruments we used for music class. Someone must not have been too happy with the sound quality and thrown it out. It'll work for us." He drew his arm back as though he were about to throw a baseball pitch and tossed the bell.

The bell hit its mark. In the frozen air, the glass had a tinny quality as it shattered.

"You should be able to reach it if you stand on my

shoulders." He put his flashlight in his teeth and held out a cupped hand for her to put her boot into. "I'll boost you up."

Her heart raced a mile a minute. "I was never a cheerleader, and gymnastics was not my strong suit."

"I have every confidence in you," he said.

She placed her boot in his hand. He groaned.

She froze. "Am I hurting you?"

"Don't worry about it." His voice sounded strained.

Merci gripped his opposite shoulder and pulled herself up. She managed to position each of her knees on his shoulders. "I don't know if I can stand up. Move closer. Let me see if I can reach it this way."

Nathan wobbled a bit as he stepped forward.

By straightening her spine and stretching her arm, she was able to reach through the broken window pane.

"The latch should be right below the hole," Nathan said.

She felt around until her fingers found hard metal. She clicked the latch and pushed open the window. She hooked both hands on the bottom of the window frame. "Okay, push me through."

"Once you get in, check the back door. If memory serves, it opens from the inside even when it's locked on the outside." He gave her a final push through and then shouted. "I'll be waiting there."

Merci cascaded down to the linoleum floor. Table and chairs lined the walls of the big open eating area. She rose to her feet. When she glanced out the window that faced back toward the camp, she saw the torches as they headed toward the final building before the meadow. Her muscles tensed. They didn't have much time. Maybe six or seven minutes. She raced down a hallway with closed doors toward what she assumed was the back door Nathan had referenced and pushed it open with force.

A blast of cold air hit her, and she struggled to catch her breath. Panic tickled her nerve endings as she stared out into the blackness. "Nathan?"

She took in a deep breath.

He came around the corner. "They're on their way up."

"I know. I saw."

He directed her toward one of the doors in the hall and pulled out his key ring again to unlock the office. The eating area took up about half the building. The kitchen and pantry must be opposite the offices.

Nathan pushed open the door. He dashed over to a closet behind a desk and pulled out a rifle.

Through the open office door, they could hear the rattling of the doorknob in the cafeteria.

"Do you think they will crawl through the window like we did?"

"They would have to find it first." Nathan yanked open drawers in the desk. "I don't think they have that kind of finesse. They'll probably just break through the door with an ax like they did with the main building."

Nathan's mouth dropped open as he checked another drawer. He shook his head.

"What's wrong?"

"We've got a rifle, but no bullets," he said.

Merci's gaze darted around the room. "Maybe they are somewhere else?" No matter what, she wasn't going to give in to defeat. Those bullets had to be somewhere.

She walked over to a file cabinet and opened the box that was on top of it. Receipts.

Nathan shook his head. "They were always kept in his desk. I'm sure Dad taught the new camp director to do the same. The camp crew must have taken them when they closed for the season."

The crack of the wooden door being sliced by an ax became loud and insistent again.

"We have to get out of here." Nathan ushered Merci toward the office door.

The front door of the cafeteria banged open. The stomping of feet intensified. Though she could not discern all the words, the thieves' conversation was mostly about food.

Nathan led Merci down the hall to back door. "They will go to the kitchen first. That buys us a few minutes." He walked on his toes and opened the door only wide enough for them to slip through. "But we should hurry all the same."

The cold night air assaulted them as they raced out into the darkness.

SIX

As she ran, Merci glanced out at the meadow that was now marred with footprints. "They know we're here now, don't they?" She looked over her shoulder at the back door.

Nathan nodded, but didn't slow his pace. "Hard to say. They might have noticed the footprints, but our footprints are on the edge of the meadow, not in the middle like theirs."

"Only two of them came up this way. That means one of them stayed down there...probably with Lorelei." Merci still hadn't given up hope that Lorelei was okay. All of this risk couldn't be for nothing. But what were they going to do without a rifle?

They dove into the shadows the surrounding trees provided.

The priority for the two thieves was food, so even if they had suspicions, they might not come looking for them right away.

Nathan pulled her deeper into the forest. "I know where we can hide until we figure out what we're going to do."

He increased their pace enough that she was breathing heavily. He came to a cluster of cottonwoods. "There's a platform up there." He pointed at one of the larger trees.

Merci tilted her head but couldn't see anything but dark branches and sky. "I'll have to take your word for it."

"It was built to be camouflaged," Nathan said. "It was for the paint ball wars they have at the camp."

She moved a little closer to the tree, hoping to see spikes or wooden footholds in the tree. The trunk was bare. "How do we get up there?"

"We climb up on the tree next to it with the lower branches and then we leap," Nathan said.

Her breath hitched, and her hands grew clammy. "And then we leap?" She'd never been one to back away from adventure, but her adrenaline and desire for excitement had worn a little thin over the past few hours.

"They'll never find us up there, and in less than an hour when we have some daylight, it will provide us with a view of the whole camp."

Merci sucked in a prayer filled breath. "I guess that is what we have to do, then."

"I'll go first. Watch which branches I go on." Nathan walked toward the tree.

Merci stood beneath the tree as Nathan skillfully climbed from one branch to the next. Once he was on top of the shorter tree, he scooted to the middle of the branch that he had straddled. "You can see the platform from here."

He repositioned himself so his feet were on the branch. He eased up to a standing position, balancing on the branch that couldn't have been more than ten inches around. The branch wavered from his weight. He stretched his hands out and jumped.

Merci held her breath. She closed her eyes and braced for the sound of a body falling and branches breaking. A simultaneous thud and a grunt filled the air. When she opened her eyes, she couldn't see Nathan, but she could hear him.

"Now it's your turn," he said.

She pulled off her gloves and put them in her backpack. Fear overwhelmed her. "I've never been very good at falling." She stepped away from the tree. "Maybe there is some other way."

"Merci, the men have left the cafeteria. I can see their torches. You have to come up. We'll be safe up here even if they search the whole camp."

She had no choice. This had to be done. She stepped toward the tree. On wobbly legs, she placed her boot on the branch that Nathan had used. The initial climb was easy enough. Each time she pulled herself up a section of the tree, the next branch she should reach for was obvious. She swung onto the last thick branch near the top of the tree. When she looked up, Nathan waited for her at the edge of the platform.

"I'll turn on the flashlight for just a second when you are ready to leap."

"Okay." Her trembling voice gave away her fear. She swung her leg over the branch to a sitting position. Her pulse drummed in her ears as she gripped the rough cold branch and placed a boot flat on it. She lined up her other foot. The branch was thick enough to provide a secure platform for her boot.

Her throat constricted, and her leg muscles felt as if they'd hardened into granite. This was the moment of truth. She was going to have to let go of the branch.

"Ready?" Nathan whispered. He lifted the flashlight, but didn't turn it on.

"Wait just a second until I'm standing." She released the death grip she had on the branch and eased into a standing position. The branch bounced. She held out her arms to find her balance. She tilted her head. "Now."

He flashed the light on and off long enough for her to see the edge of the platform. She bent her knees and jumped. Time stood still as she held her hands out. One of her hands found the rough edge of the platform but the other slipped. Her heart seized. She was going to fall.

Nathan's strong arms grabbed her hand. She lost her grip on the platform. She dangled by the hand that Nathan held. Her body swung like a pendulum.

His grip on her hand tightened. "Give me your other hand."

She angled back toward the platform and reached her free hand up. He grabbed her hand and pulled her up, gathering her in his arms.

She shuddered, fighting back tears. Once again, she had nearly died, and Nathan had saved her.

His face was very close to hers. He brushed a hand over her hair. "Not so bad, huh?"

She couldn't form words, only nod in agreement. He tightened his arms around her and drew her even closer. "Hey, you were pretty scared there."

She sniffled, but still couldn't think of what to say.

She was trembling. Only the strength of his embrace calmed her.

His face was very close to hers. His beating heart pushed back against her palm where she rested it on his chest. She tilted her head. The rough stubble of his face brushed over her cheek. His lips found hers. At first he grazed over her mouth with his own and then pressed harder. She responded to the kiss, scooting closer to him. A calm like warm honey spread through her.

His lips lingered on hers. He pulled away and kissed her cheek. He opened his eyes, and even in the darkness, the power of his gaze melted her to the core.

"Better?"

She nodded, still not able to come up with the words, but not because she was still afraid. Nathan's kiss had stolen her ability to use language. She had become a speechless puddle of mush.

"Me, too." He rested his hand under her jaw. "I'm better now." His fingers traveled down her neck where her pulse throbbed. He studied her for a long moment. "I hope I wasn't out of line. I'm not sure why I did that."

She shook her head. The kiss had been wonderful.

He backed away. His voice lost that smoldering quality. "Maybe it's just all this life-threatening stuff we are facing."

Her heart crumbled into a tiny ball. Now he was regretting the kiss. "That must be it," she said flatly.

He pulled away as an uncomfortable silence descended. They looked at each other then looked away.

After a long moment, he reached over and touched her ear. "Those are nice earrings."

The inflection in his voice suggested that he didn't

want any awkwardness between them. He was trying to keep the conversation going. "Thanks. I got them at a garage sale right before break." His touch sent a zing of warmth down her neck. "I get most my things secondhand, part of how I managed to pay for college on my own."

Noises in the distance caused both of them to sit up. She turned back toward the meadow, but couldn't see anything. Then voices, growing louder and closer, separated out from the other forest noise.

Merci took in a ragged breath as fear returned. "I don't see them."

"I do." Nathan placed a gentle hand on her shoulder. "Get low, they're coming this way."

Nathan placed a protective arm over Merci's back as he lay flat against the hard wood of the lookout. The delight and excitement that had flooded through him from kissing Merci was replaced by a need to keep his senses tuned to his surroundings. He didn't regret the kiss, but he feared he had been too forward with her. He'd felt the need to apologize, but it had come out wrong.

He turned his attention back toward the approaching voices. The men had made their way back through the meadow and appeared to be carrying some items, judging from the way they were bent forward. They must have found food of some sort.

The torches bobbed across the blue-white landscape of snow. The men headed in the direction of the trees. The manner in which the thieves were stopping and shining the torches revealed that they were searching for footprints. So they had become suspicious.

The thieves stepped into the trees, and their voices grew louder and more distinct.

"Do you think it's that guy and that chick from the cabin?" That voice belonged to the larger man in the orange coat.

"Nobody else could have made it up here," said the taller, thinner man in the leather jacket.

"Maybe this place has a caretaker or something."

"I doubt it," said Leather Jacket. "Whoever it is, Hawthorne is not going to be happy."

The thieves were within twenty feet of the lookout. Close enough for Nathan to hear their footfall on the snow.

Nathan tensed.

Nobody ever thinks to look up.

Merci had turned her face toward him. Even in the near darkness, he knew she was afraid.

You're safe, Merci. You're safe with me.

The men stomped around a while longer. It sounded as though they were right at the base of the tree.

"I've had enough of this. Let's go eat," Orange Coat said.

"Yeah, I'm starving," said Leather Jacket. The thieves' footsteps crunched in the snow.

Nathan and Merci waited in silence, not daring to move, their cheeks resting against the rough wood of the platform. Nathan longed to tell her it was going to be okay. He longed to calm her with a kiss again. But they could only wait and be quiet and still. As they faced each other, he looked into her eyes, hoping to communicate all that he was feeling.

The footsteps faded and the voices grew farther

away. Gradually the sounds of the forest, branches creaking in the breeze, became distinct again.

"I think we are in the clear." Nathan lifted his arm off Merci's back.

Merci let out an audible breath as she sat up. "They know we are here now. They'll be looking for us." She wrapped her arms over her body.

Having to stay out in the elements without moving had probably chilled her. "Are you cold?" He lifted his arm, indicating that he would hold her.

She nodded and slipped underneath his arm as he wrapped it around her. "Thanks. That's better."

Just like it had been better a few minutes before when he had decided to kiss her. He'd never been so impulsive in his life. Now he knew why he had kissed her. They were in a life-and-death situation. There wasn't time for formalities and first dates. If they didn't get out of this alive, he wanted her to know he liked her.

Merci turned her face toward him. "What do we do now?"

"They probably won't start looking for us until full daylight. They're eating right now. We'll be able to see where in the camp they are at first light." He checked his watch. "Sunrise will be in about forty minutes."

"But we don't have any way to defend ourselves," Merci said.

The frustration over not finding bullets had been delayed by having to run out of the cafeteria so quickly. The full force of that reality hit him like a blow to the chest. "Why don't we eat and drink something from our packs, and I'll figure it out."

Merci pulled a protein bar and a water bottle from

her pack. Together they watched the slow warm glow of morning spread across the camp, rimming the trees in gold and warming the hue of the snow.

Nathan chewed his protein bar as he watched the camp and cycled through an inventory of solutions for getting Lorelei back. It was possible that the rescue would be a simple thing of finding her alone and breaking her free. On the other hand, she might already be dead. He wrestled with a possible solution when an idea popped into his head. "Crossbows."

Merci furled her forehead. "Crossbows?"

"In the activities shed. They are stored there. I'm pretty sure they are not hauled away in the off-season. I know it is hardly a fair match, but it is better than nothing. I used to be pretty good with a crossbow."

"It's worth a try. We've come this far." Her expression grew serious. "Do you think Lorelei is still alive?"

"We have to find out. If we can't find her, I say we head back to the cabin. If this weather holds, the plows will be up here in less than twenty-four hours."

"That long?"

"The deputy might push to get up here faster since he was expecting us in town. It's not something we should count on, though." The realization of how alone they were in this fight sank in.

Merci sat for a long moment with her head tilted toward the sky. He wondered if she was praying. Then she stared out at the camp and light slowly spread across it. "Look over there."

She pointed toward a long skinny building that was used as a girls' dorm on the other side of the camp. Smoke rose out of the chimney.

"That must be where they are?" He took in a calming breath. If things didn't go as he planned, it could cost them their lives. "Over there is the activities storage shed." He pointed to a small cabin.

"It's not that far from here. We should go before we have full daylight." Merci spoke in a monotone, probably an effort to push down any fear she might be wrestling with.

Climbing down proved easier than getting up. Merci followed behind him as he walked through the snow toward the small cabin. The thieves had not broken down the door of the activities cabin. They must have thought it was too small to be where the food was.

Nathan pulled out his key ring and released the padlock. The place smelled musty. As he shone the flashlight around the windowless room, it looked as if the storage procedures hadn't changed since he was a kid.

Various plastic boxes were labeled *Balls, Paintball* and *Frisbees*. The archery gear took up several boxes. He pulled one off a shelf.

Merci leaned over to peer in the box. "Maybe a bow and arrow would be better."

"The crossbows are more powerful. Once the string is cocked not as much arm strength is needed." He pulled one of the arrows out and turned it around in his hand.

He located two crossbows and two sets of arrows. For safety, these arrows were not as sharp as those used for hunting, but they would pierce a target just fine, so they might do some damage at close range. "You ever use one of these before?"

She shook her head. He took a moment to show her

how to cock the string and place the arrow in. He held the bow up to eye level. "Once the arrow is in place, you just look down your sight and pull the trigger."

Even as he instructed her, he prayed it wouldn't come to having to use these things to defend themselves. They stepped out of the cabin with the crossbows in their hands and the quivers slung over their shoulders.

They moved cautiously, slipping behind buildings and trees for cover. The smell of smoke became evident as they approached three identical buildings. All the buildings were long with small windows lining the long side.

The sky had begun to lighten up. They hid behind a large evergreen. Nathan could make out the smoke rising from one chimney. He tapped Merci's shoulder and pointed. She nodded in understanding. He signaled that she should stay behind while he moved in to see what he could.

Again, she nodded in agreement and settled down at the base of the tree. Crouching, he ran toward the next bit of cover, a woodpile that hadn't been stacked yet. When he looked back, Merci was leaning out, watching him.

He gripped his crossbow in his gloved hand and darted for the final bit of cover, the dorm closest to them. The thieves were in the middle dorm. He was about to edge around the corner to the short side of the dorm when he heard a door burst open. Leather Coat came into view with the gun in his hand.

Heart pounding, Nathan glanced back to the tree where Merci was. She had slipped into hiding. The thief stepped off the concrete slab by the door and walked a wide circle, stopping every few seconds to survey the area around him.

The man walked out quite a ways from the occupied dorm in a straight line. Then he turned and moved toward the first dorm. Nathan slipped to the other side of the building and sunk low to the ground. He could hear the approaching footsteps. When the man coughed, it sounded as if he was right in front of Nathan.

Nathan pressed harder against the building, not even daring to breathe. He adjusted his grip on the crossbow and slid the arrow into place. The time it took to hear the retreating footsteps seemed like an eternity.

Nathan waited for a long moment after the area had gone quiet before he dared to move. He angled around to look at the closed door of the second dorm. The man in the leather jacket had limited his patrol to a big arc around the front of the building.

The dorm was one long structure without any interior walls and only rows of beds with a bathroom at one end and a fireplace at the other. He would be able to see if Lorelei was inside by peering through one of the windows.

The problem was he didn't know where they were in the dorm. He ran toward the back of the building and hunkered down against the wall of the other dorm. He lifted his chin. He ran the risk of being seen here, if someone looked out the window, but it allowed him to look for movement in several windows.

He sat with the sound of his own breathing surrounding him like a drumbeat. It looked as though the thieves had managed to come up with some form of light. The middle part of the dorm was illuminated. Only the main building and the cafeteria were wired for electricity. They must have found a Coleman or another flashlight.

Crouching, he moved toward the window where the light was the strongest. He raised himself up slowly. If he moved into a standing position, he would have a clear view of what was going on in there, but he would also be spotted the second someone looked toward the window. Not a good idea. Most people could sense when they were being stared at.

He bent his knees and peered through the window with his eyes barely above the bottom sill. A bed was pushed up against the window blocking his view. He ran bent over to the next window. Most of his view was of the man in the orange coat with his back to the window.

The man moved slightly. Nathan angled his head to take in more of the room.

The third thief, the leader they called Hawthorne, was perched on the top bunk opposite the window. Leather Jacket lay on a lower bunk with his face to the wall. He couldn't see Lorelei anywhere. He moved down to the next window. Open, industrial-size cans of food were on one of the nightstands.

Hawthorne and Orange Coat were having some sort of loud discussion that sounded as though it verged on being an argument. Obviously, things had not gone as planned. They had intended to take whatever treasure two college girls might have and head for the highway. Now they were stranded and half starved. The quick gestures and set jaws of both men indicated that the conversation seemed even more tense than the earlier one they had overheard in the main building.

Hawthorne jumped down from the bunk. His swagger and expansive gestures suggested confidence and control. Growing frustrated, Nathan moved to the next window. Where was Lorelei? He refused to believe that she was dead. Maybe they had her tied up in one of the other buildings.

No, that didn't make sense. They would have put a guard on her. The view through the third window was covered in shadows as it fell outside the circle of illumination created by the lanterns.

Still no Lorelei. His spirits sank. Had they missed the signs of an assault or worse on the way up here? Maybe the darkness had hidden the blood trail in the snow. What if all of this had been for nothing? What if they were too late?

As he struggled with his doubt, a chill crept into his muscles from standing still. He moved back to the window where he had the clearest view. The discussion between Hawthorne and Orange Coat had lost much of its energy. The larger man slumped down in a lower bunk and Hawthorne paced and ran his fingers through his blond hair.

To get warmed up and to see if he could locate Lorelei, Nathan circled the building, peering in each window, hoping to see Lorelei tied up in some dark corner. Within a few minutes, he had rounded the building to the other long end. Much of the interior was still so dark it was hard to discern anything.

Another possibility nudged at the corners of his consciousness. What if the thieves had marched Lorelei into the woods and shot her once she was no longer of use to them? He shut down that idea almost as quickly as it had popped into his head. He couldn't give up hope…not yet.

He moved back to a window that provided better light to watch the interaction. Orange Coat lifted one of the industrial-size cans and looked inside it. Leather Jacket was no longer on the bed, and Nathan couldn't see where he had gone. Hawthorne continued to pace. There was really nothing going on here. He should probably just go back to Merci, and they could wait and watch for Lorelei to make an appearance.

Hawthorne took a cell phone out of his pocket, held it to his ear and pulled it away to look at the keyboard. He grimaced and held the cell phone at arm's length. People's actions in a crisis were sometimes illogical.

Unless Hawthorne knew a snowplow operator who owed him a big favor, nobody was going to come up here and whisk them back into town. Maybe Hawthorne had thought they could hike out, and he wanted to call someone to give them a ride once they got to the highway. Also, not a very viable plan.

Nathan had seen it in his work as an EMT a hundred times, the illogical coping mechanisms of people in crisis. People in burning office buildings returned to their desk to turn off their computers out of habit before seeking safety. Hawthorne and his gang probably didn't have lots of winter survival skills. If they were smart, they would stay at the camp where they at least had shelter and warmth.

Lorelei stepped into view. Nathan's head jerked back. She'd come out of nowhere. She walked toward Hawthorne. She hadn't been tied up. Nothing in her expression suggested a state of terror though there was a hesitation in her step as she approached Hawthorne. She waited for him to look up. Something in his expression must have communicated that it was okay to approach him.

She handed Hawthorne a purple phone that sparkled when it caught the light. Then he saw something that caused his old suspicions to rise to the surface again. The gesture lasted only a nano second, but Lorelei reached up and brushed Hawthorne's upper arm before she walked away. Nathan's mind reeled. The gesture appeared to be one of affection.

With the phone in his hand, Hawthorne turned toward the window. Nathan ducked down. A metal clicking sound caused him to look up. Nathan froze. He was looking directly into the barrel of the handgun held by the man in the leather jacket. The man smiled at him. "Find what you were looking for?" He pulled a knife out of his pocket. "A gun is too quick for you. Let's make this slow and painful, shall we?"

SEVEN

Merci shifted side to side in an effort to keep warm. She'd grown cold sitting on the ground behind the tree that hid her from view and had decided standing up and moving was a better option. Twice she'd peeked out from behind the tree. The first time she'd seen Nathan as he had headed behind the first dorm building. The second time she hadn't seen any sign of life anywhere.

She guessed that maybe twenty minutes had passed. She twirled the crossbow in her hand. She'd practiced cocking the bow and putting the arrow in place so many times she could probably do it in the dark. Nathan had been gone a long time. She peeked out from behind the tree again.

The emerging light allowed her to see the dorms and the rest of the camp. She saw the back side of the sign at the entrance of the camp where they had come in. After she checked her watch, a rising sense of panic made the hairs on the back of her head stand up. Too much time had passed without any signs of disruption or Nathan's return. Where was he? Did he need her help?

She couldn't just sit here while something bad happened to him. She moved in a little closer, using the pile of unstacked firewood for cover. When she looked out over the logs, the man in the leather jacket was headed back toward the dorm. He must have slipped out when she wasn't looking.

He walked deliberately toward the door then stopped abruptly and angled his head. Instead of going inside, Leather Jacket disappeared around the side of the dorm out of Merci's view. Merci clamored to her feet as adrenaline surged through her. The last time she'd spotted Nathan he was headed toward that side of the building. Unless Nathan had moved, the thief was going right toward Nathan.

Merci pushed past her fear as she raced through the snow. Ducking down into a crouch, she closed in on the lighted windows of the middle dorm. The thieves must be in there. She slammed herself against the wall. Her heart pounded out a furious beat. She closed her eyes. She prayed that Nathan had moved somewhere out of view and wasn't in danger.

She ran around to the narrow end of the middle dorm where there was less light spilling out. Her feet sunk into the snow. She pulled the arrow from her quiver and placed it in the crossbow just like Nathan had shown her. She swung around the corner.

It took her only a second to absorb what she saw. Leather Jacket twirled a knife that caught glints of sunlight. Nathan curled forward in a defensive posture, clutching his shoulder. Leather Jacket bent his knee and kicked Nathan across the jaw with his cowboy boot. Nathan fell backward in the snow.

Her finger trembled when she placed it in the trigger of the crossbow. Her whole hand was shaking. Before the thief had time to register that she had come around the corner, she lifted the crossbow, looked down the sight and pulled the trigger. The yelp of pain that sounded more like a dog than a man shattered the early morning air.

Noise came from inside the dorm. Doors slamming. People shouting. Feet stomping.

Nathan was next to her pulling her up. She must have crumpled to the ground after she shot the arrow. Leather Jacket's cry of pain acted like a direct blow to her eardrum. The thief bent over, clutching his leg. Drops of blood stained the white snow. She had done that. She had hurt another human being.

Nathan pulled her to her feet and dragged her away. When she looked over her shoulder, the other two men had come outside. She locked gazes for a moment with Hawthorne. His eyes grew wide, and his face registered rage.

They ran faster than she had ever run in her life. Dried tree branches grazed her cheeks. Nathan guided her still deeper into the forest. She stumbled, but he caught her and lifted her up.

"Come on Merci, you've got to keep going."

Her legs wobbled. She couldn't find the strength to stand.

"You're going into shock. Focus on moving forward. Can you do that for me?"

She couldn't let go of the images in her head. She had shot a man and made him bleed. "I don't know."

"They're after us, Merci. We have to keep moving." Then she noticed that he gripped his shoulder.

"Are you hurt?"

"It's nothing. Let's go."

She saw the blood on his hand and the sliced fabric of the coat. What had that animal done to him?

He grabbed her hand as they ran through the thick evergreens. She couldn't manage a deep breath. Her legs still felt like burning pillars. They had run for at least ten minutes. She couldn't hear any noise behind her.

Nathan planted his feet and bent over. He slumped to his knees and coughed. The snow below him grew red with blood.

She fell on the ground beside him. "What happened? What did he do to you?"

Nathan groaned, straightened his back and squared his shoulders. "He kicked me in the stomach. That's all. I'll be all right."

Then she noticed the blood on his face. "It looks like he did more than that." Her fingers trailed down to his chest. She unzipped his coat to get a better look at the bloodstain on his shirt. "Is that a knife wound?"

"The guy is one of those sickos who enjoys inflicting pain on people." Nathan gritted his teeth. The tightness of his jaw revealed how much pain he was in.

She peeled back his shirt and took in a sharp breath. "The cut is really deep and still bleeding."

Nathan rose to his feet. Though he tried to hide it, she caught the wince of pain. "It was a blessing in a way. If he had just shot me on the spot, there wouldn't have been enough time for you to get there."

"We need to treat that wound," she said.

Nathan shook his head. "We can't stop. Did you see Hawthorne's eyes? He's really angry."

She opened her mouth to protest. The raging voices of the thieves assaulted her eardrums. Nathan was right. They had to keep moving.

They ran for a full twenty minutes, until both of them were out of breath.

Merci bent over and clamped her hands on her knees. "I don't hear them anymore."

Nathan leaned his forearm against a tree. He stuck his hand inside his coat. "Maybe we lost them." He sucked in a breath between each word.

If her lungs hurt from running so hard, he must be in horrible pain.

She dug through her backpack and pulled out a glove liner, which she handed to him. "To stop the bleeding."

He nodded and placed the cloth inside his coat.

A twinge of empathy pain caused her to shudder. "Nathan, we have to slow down long enough to get that wound to stop bleeding. You're a paramedic. You wouldn't let someone walk away with an untreated cut like that."

Though he squared his jaw, she saw the flash of pain in his eyes. "I suppose we can double back to the cafeteria. If there are any medical supplies, they would be in there."

Merci nodded in agreement. "It'll throw them off, anyway. They think we are running deeper into the woods."

She turned, trying to orient herself.

"This way through the trees." He gritted his teeth as he spoke. He was in way more pain than he was letting on.

That he had managed to scoop her up and get them

out of danger was a testament to his strength and courage. They moved at a slower pace. Within twenty minutes, the far side of the cafeteria came into view. They had done a wide arc around the camp and come out on the side where they had previously broken the window.

"We can just use the door the thieves broke through."

The door had been almost completely broken apart with the ax. She pushed it open. By the time they got inside, Nathan was leaning against her for support.

"Guess I lost more blood than I realized." His voice had a faraway quality.

She led him back into the office and helped him down onto a wooden bench. His eyelids slipped over his eyes. "Nathan, you can't pass out. You have to tell me what to do."

She unzipped his ski jacket and unbuttoned the shirt. The cotton fabric stuck to his chest where the blood had soaked through. She swallowed the cry of anguish as she peeled back the blood-soaked fabric of the glove liner. Now she had a clear view of the cut. It looked as if the knife had been driven straight into his pectoral muscle.

He closed his eyes, and his head bobbed forward. She patted his cheeks. "Stay with me. Tell me what to do."

By sheer force of will, he raised his head and opened his eyes. "Compress to stop the bleeding."

Her stomach clenched. "It looks like you need stitches." She had no medical training beyond a first-aid class, but the gash was pretty deep.

He bent his head, placing his fingers close to the still bleeding wound. "No," he said, gulping in air. "It's better to leave it open so the pus can drain." He touched the wound, shuddered and closed his eyes.

She gathered his cheeks into her hands. "That's a really big open cut. You've got to tell me what to do." If her voice didn't give away her fear, her trembling hands did.

He looked at her with wide vulnerable eyes and wrapped his hand around hers. "Stop the bleeding first, then draw the edges of the cut together, place a sterile airtight dressing on it."

Merci searched frantically. Where in this place was she going to find anything resembling a sterile cloth? She opened and closed drawers. "I don't suppose there is a first-aid kit in here somewhere. That would be way too easy."

She found a box of outdated ibuprofen in a desk drawer. Nathan slumped over on the bench, still clutching his pectoral muscle. She pulled her water bottle out of her pack and approached Nathan, kneeling beside him. "Here, take these." She gave him three pills. He opened his mouth. She held the water bottle to his lips. He gulped the water. She placed the bottle of pills in his coat pocket. "In case you need more later."

"Check the kitchen," he said between breaths.

She shook her head, not comprehending what he was saying and wondering if he had started to become incoherent.

"Maybe there is a clean cloth in there, tin foil and some kind of tape." His words sounded weak as he rested the back of his head against the wall.

What on earth did he want her to do with tin foil?

"I'll explain." He took in a gulp of air. "Just find them."

Merci raced to the kitchen, taking a moment to look out the big window for any sign of the thieves. The landscape was empty. Maybe the men would give up.

Once in the kitchen, she opened and closed cupboard doors. She found a dishrag, but it was too dirty. She opened the drawer underneath the stove and found a small piece of tinfoil left on the end of the roll. She was on her way to the bathroom to search when Nathan called out to her.

When she returned to the office, Nathan lifted his head. His gaze was unfocused, and his face had a chalky pallor. "Look where that rifle was. Dad had cleaning cloths," he said.

Again she wondered if he was losing coherence. A cloth that had been used to clean a gun would hardly be sterile. She opened the drawer in the gun rack and found an unopened package of white cotton cloths. You don't get any cleaner than that.

He pulled his bloody hand away from the wound so she could place the cloth on it.

She remembered seeing some packing tape in a desk drawer. "Now what?" Her voice trembled. The cloth was already saturated with blood.

"Tear off a piece of that cloth for the bandage. The tin foil will keep it airtight." He sucked in a breath. "But first you have to draw the sides of the cut together, so it heals right."

She took in a breath that felt as if it had glass shards in it. His face had completely drained of color, and he slumped to one side. She peeled the blood-stained shirt off his skin. He pulled back the bloody compress and winced.

His hand rested over the top of hers. "A gash this deep could get infected." His Adam's apple moved up and down. He squeezed her fingers. "We want it to drain but don't want it exposed. Draw the edges of the cut together and hold them together with tape."

She nodded. "Won't that hurt you?"

"Let's just do it."

She stared into his glazed eyes. He'd lost so much blood. Was he going to die? And what for? They still didn't have Lorelei. What had even become of Lorelei? There hadn't been time to ask Nathan if he had seen her.

All the uncertainties were like waves of panic washing over her. She gripped the arm of the bench and took in a deep breath. So much she didn't have control over. She needed to focus on helping Nathan.

Nathan lifted his head and offered her a forced smile that didn't hide his anguish. "Are you ready?"

She nodded.

"I'll force the two pieces of skin together, and then you place the tape over them. Tear off narrow pieces first so it goes faster," he said.

Merci's throat went dry, and her stomach somersaulted, but she managed a nod.

He must have seen the fear in her eyes. He reached up and touched her cheek. "You'll do fine."

She bit her lower lip. "I know." She tore off three strips of tape.

"Let's do this." He gritted his teeth and drew the skin together. His back arched. He tilted his chin toward the ceiling and inhaled through gritted teeth.

Merci picked up the first piece of tape. For Nathan, she needed to do this. For Nathan, she needed to get past her fear.

"Quick is best," he said. His breathing had become labored.

She grabbed another piece of tape. Nathan's hands trembled. His face turned red, and his mouth drew into a flat line. She had to separate herself from his pain or she would fall apart.

She placed the white cloth over the wound and then the tin foil. Finally she taped over the whole dressing.

He let out a whoosh of air and slumped forward when she finished. He rested his glistening forehead against hers and cupped her neck in his hand breathing heavily. "You did it."

The victory was short-lived. From the front of the cafeteria, the sound of the battered door opening and someone stepping inside floated down the hallway to the office.

EIGHT

"Nathan, we have to go, they're coming."

Merci sounded as if she was talking to him from the next room, even though he could open his eyes and see her lovely face. He had enough coherence left to know that the loss of blood had made him lightheaded.

She placed his coat over his shoulders. When she helped him to his feet, the room spun. "You should go without me. I'll slow you down."

She slipped in under his good shoulder. "No, I'm not leaving without you. Come on, we can make it to the back door."

Though he still felt dizzy, Nathan willed himself to move forward. They pushed through the back door and into the forest. The cold air hit him almost immediately. His shirt was unbuttoned. He had only one arm in his jacket.

Glancing over her shoulder, Merci headed toward the cover of the trees.

"Can you see them?"

"Maybe they came back looking for more food." She

stuttered in her steps. "Oh, no, I left the backpacks there."

"All our food." Nathan heard the words, but it didn't feel as if he had spoken them. It took a moment for it to sink in how dire their circumstances were without food.

"Once they find those backpacks, they'll know we were there." Merci's voice filled with anguish.

Nathan fought to get a deep breath as he continued to lean on Merci. The chill had sunk clean through his skin. "Merci, you've got to stop."

She looked up at him, concern etched across her features. "Oh, Nathan, you're in really rough shape."

Merci helped him pull his coat on and then zipped it up.

Nathan summoned what little strength he had left. "I don't hear anything. Maybe they are not after us. Are you sure you heard them coming through the door?"

Her expression changed as though doubt had crept in. "I'm kind of jumpy. Maybe I was hearing things."

Nathan slid down to the ground. "Let me just rest for a minute. We'll go back for the backpacks."

"And then what, Nathan?"

He stared at her for a moment weighing options. He still hadn't told her about Lorelei. "If we go back to the cabin, they might come there looking for food." He took in a breath. Icy slicing pain riveted through his chest. He wasn't so sure he could make it back to the cabin at this point. He needed rest more than anything.

"If we can get the backpacks, we can survive a day, maybe two, even if we can't make it to the cabin. Help will come by then." Her pretty features grew tight. "But what are we going to do about Lorelei? Do you think she is still alive?"

Nathan cleared his throat. "I saw her."

Merci sat down beside him and grabbed his arm. "Where is she? Is she tied up? Is someone watching her?"

Nathan wrestled with how much he should tell her. Perhaps his suspicions were unfounded. "She wasn't tied up. She was walking around."

Merci let go of his arm. Her gaze probed and she spoke slowly. "So we could get her out pretty easy?"

"There was just something weird about what I saw. She seemed hesitant around that Hawthorne guy, but…" He shook his head. "Something in her body language suggested affection for him."

Her voice leveled out. "What are you saying?"

His physical weakness made it hard for him to form the question. "Do you think there is any possibility that she is somehow connected to these people?"

Merci shook her head. "No, that can't be. She's been on campus for at least two years. She saved my life in that truck." Merci rose to her feet and turned her back to him. "There must be some goodness in her. Maybe you weren't seeing things for what they were."

"That is possible." He had expected resistance from her. The look on her face told him that the news had crushed her. If Lorelei was involved, it meant that all this sacrifice and risk had been for nothing. They would have been better off waiting at the cabin and preparing for an assault from the thieves. "I don't know if trying to free her is worth our efforts."

Merci lifted her head and then stood up.

"Where are you going?"

"Give me a minute. Get your strength back." She sounded upset.

They shouldn't be separated. "Wait, I'll go with you." Nathan tried to push himself to his feet. He felt instantly lightheaded, and the pain was excruciating. Black dots filled the corners of his vision. A moment later he could see nothing. The last thing he remembered was the sensation of the cold snow on his cheek.

Merci moved through the trees away from Nathan. She needed a moment to calm down. His suspicions of Lorelei had opened old wounds. When he spoke, it was as if she was hearing her father talk to her in his judgmental way. She could picture him looking over the top of his half glasses. "Merci, your Pollyanna attitude, always thinking everyone is nice, is why you will never succeed in business. You are too trusting."

But Nathan wasn't her father. Over and over, she had seen how kind he was. He could have blamed her for the loss of the backpacks and he hadn't. He'd saved her life more than once. She needed to get back to him.

Ahead of her, a branch broke and she saw a flash of color. Her heart pounded. The thieves were moving through the forest. She stood paralyzed by uncertainty. She had only stepped thirty feet away from Nathan, but evergreens blocked her view of him. He was in no condition to run. She had to lead the thieves away from where Nathan rested. She dashed into the thick of the trees, breaking branches to alert them to her whereabouts.

She leaped over a fallen log. She could hear them behind her, growing closer. As she ran, she put together a plan. She'd lead them far enough away to keep Nathan safe and then find a hiding place or maybe double back to get him.

She glanced over her shoulder, but couldn't see anything. As she turned her head, she slammed into a solid mass. A hand went over her mouth. Leather Jacket's sour breath enveloped her. "Don't you dare scream for help or I'll shoot you." He pushed a gun against her lower back. "Now tell me where your friend is. He must be close by."

The thieves must have split up in their search for her. She had to keep Nathan safe. "He didn't make it. He was bleeding really bad."

The man let out a satisfied chuckle. "That cut I gave him must have done the trick." He leaned closer over her shoulder so his cheek nearly touched hers. The odor of dirt and cigarettes repulsed her. Her back stiffened. "He doesn't matter to us, anyway, but you do."

He grabbed her hair and pulled it so her head tilted toward the sky.

She drew her hand up toward her hair as her eyes rimmed with tears. Her whole body felt as if it was being shaken from the inside. What did he mean to do to her? "Please…please you're hurting me."

"Am I now?"

He pushed her forward. When she turned to sneak a glance at him, she saw the bloody strip of wool tied around his leg where she had hit him with the arrow from the crossbow. He walked with a limp.

"What are you staring at?" Leather Jacket barked at her, then yelled over his shoulder. "Check around for him just in case she's lying."

The other thief must be close by.

Please, dear God, keep Nathan safe.

A blindfold went over her eyes and a moment later, her hands were bound behind her. Her feet sank into the deep snow. As she was led through the camp, she lost all sense of where she was.

When Nathan awoke with his cheek resting against the snow, he was chilled to the bone, but the pain seemed to be subsiding. He willed himself to sit up. How much time had gone by? The sun had moved to the midpoint in the sky.

He waited a moment to ensure he was not going to pass out again from getting up too quickly. He pulled off his glove and gripped the tree trunk for support. The pain radiating through his shoulder threatened to send him toppling again. He gritted his teeth and straightened his back. If he didn't lift the arm that was connected to the injured pectoral muscle, he'd be okay. The trauma to his body had taken its toll. Under normal circumstances, a doctor would have loaded him up with antibiotics and advised him to stay in bed for a day. But these were not normal circumstances.

Where had Merci gone? He had upset her. Maybe that was why she had stomped off. He stumbled through the forest reaching out for tree trunks for support.

He almost cried out for her, but decided against it. When he came to the edge of the forest, he stopped. He had a view of the meadow. By now there were so many sets of footprints through the snow he couldn't determine how many comings and goings there had been.

His eyes wandered up to the cafeteria. His heart

thudded in his chest as he studied the bleak empty land-scape. Something had happened to her. He could feel it.

Leaning to one side from the pain, he made his way up to the back door of the cafeteria. The door was ajar. Each deep breath he took sent another jab of pain through him. He slipped into the hallway and pressed against the wall, listening for any sound. If someone was in here, they were being very quiet.

He eased down the hallway toward the office. His footsteps sounded as if they were being broadcast through a loud speaker. Once inside the office, it only took a moment to see that the backpacks were gone. The blood all over the bench where Merci had dressed his wound was evidence of the severity of his injury.

Maybe Merci had decided to go and get the back-packs on her own. He slumped against a wall. Somehow that theory just didn't seem to hold water. Their paths would have crossed if she had headed back to where he was resting after getting the backpacks.

Nathan pushed himself off the wall and rooted through the office to gather together whatever might be useful. He found several boxes of matches. He took two more of the out-of-date ibuprofen and put the rest back. He still had his pocket knife.

He left by way of the busted front door and set out toward the camp to find Merci. He had no food, his in-juries had weakened him and his only weapon was a pocket knife. It didn't matter. She had saved his life, and he intended to return the favor. More than that, he was coming to realize that he cared deeply about her. If the thieves had taken her, he was going to get her back no matter what.

NINE

Merci had no idea where she was. The fabric the thieves had tied over her eyes made it impossible for her to see. Even when she tilted her head to try and look underneath the blindfold, she couldn't make out shapes or even detect slivers of light. The room she was in must be dark and windowless. Her hands were tied behind her. It had taken only moments for the chill from kneeling on a concrete floor to penetrate the layers of clothing.

Her knees ached from putting pressure on them. She moved so she was in a sitting position with her legs out in front of her. In the quiet, her mind wandered. Nathan had been in rough shape when she left him. Would he have been able to slip away before the other thief found him?

The silence in the room was oppressive like a weight on her chest. She couldn't hear anything that indicated where she was. The air smelled musty.

After maybe ten minutes, she worked up the courage to scoot across the floor. Her foot touched something metal. She repositioned herself so her back was to the object, and she could touch it with her bound hands. She pressed her palm against cold metal. It could be a washing machine or maybe a hot water heater.

Above her, a door swung open and banged against the wall. She heard grunting and footsteps moving around her and then the door slammed shut.

"Is someone else in here?" a familiar voice said from across the room.

Her heart fluttered. The voice was faint. It seemed to be coming from across the room. "Lorelei, is that you?"

"Merci. Oh, Merci. You have no idea how glad I am to hear your voice."

Merci turned her head toward Lorelei's voice. "What is going on? Are you tied up, too?"

"Yes," Lorelei said.

Hope spread through her. Nathan had been wrong. Lorelei was a captive, not a conspirator in this whole terrible event. "Nathan said he saw you in the dorm walking around. What happened? Why did they tie you up?"

There was a moment's hesitation before Lorelei answered. "Could you keep talking, and I'll move toward you?"

"Okay, what should I talk about?"

"Just sing that song we were singing in the car." Lorelei's voice sounded closer already.

"You mean the one right before the car broke down?" Merci's voice trembled with emotion. Lorelei was as much of a victim as she was.

"Yeah, do you remember it?" Lorelei sang the first few lines of the song.

Merci joined it. Now the lyrics sounded so childish.

Had it been less than twenty-four hours ago that they had been singing and laughing in the car? The naive exhilaration of being on a road trip and the hope and excitement about visiting her Aunt Celeste now seemed a million miles away. The words of the song rang hollowly in the air.

She could hear Lorelei scooting toward her. And then their shoulders touched. She breathed a sigh of relief.

"What happened? Why did they tie you up?"

"I think they are leaving us. I think they are going back to the cabin." A silence fell between them before Lorelei piped up. "You said Nathan saw us when we were in the dorm?"

"That is what he said. Why did they take you on the snowmobile in first place?" Merci readjusted herself on the hard concrete floor. Though Lorelei's shoulder was no longer touching hers, she could feel the other woman's body heat close by. "What's going on here?"

"This whole thing has been kind of crazy." Lorelei's boot scraped the floor as she adjusted her position. "What do you suppose they were looking for back there at the car?"

Merci straightened her spine, struggling to find a comfortable way to sit. Lorelei's question seemed odd. Wasn't it obvious what they were looking for? "Probably iPods and laptops. Something they could sell for quick cash. Or maybe they thought we had some cash on us. They probably targeted us when we stopped for gas, followed us and waited for their chance. Why does it matter, anyway?"

"I don't know. I'm just trying to make sense of all this." Strain entered Lorelei's voice.

There was no need to visit the past. It was obviously upsetting. "Why don't we try to see if we can cut each other free? Maybe if we feel around, we can find something sharp. Could you see anything when they brought you in?"

Lorelei took a long time to answer. "They put a blindfold on me before they brought me here. I know I was led down some steps."

"Feel around. There might be something useful in this place." With the small range of motion she could manage, Merci scooted on her behind and patted the floor. She could hear Lorelei moving, as well. "I'm thinking maybe we are underground. It might be a laundry room or cellar or something." After a few minutes of not finding or feeling anything but hard cold concrete, she stopped. The room had fallen silent again. "Lorelei? Are you okay?"

Something thudded against the outside wall of the building. Merci took in a sharp breath. The door crashed open again. Footsteps, intense and fast, came toward her.

"Merci, I'm here."

Nathan's smooth tenor voice comforted her in ways she couldn't have thought possible. He cut the rope that bound her hands.

She reached up for the blindfold. "We have to untie Lorelei, too."

"Lorelei? What are you talking about?"

When she took her blindfold off, the only thing she saw in the room was a dryer that wasn't hooked up and some other broken appliances. "But she was just here. I was talking to her."

"Merci, please, we have to go." He pulled her up the stairs.

Merci's mind reeled as she struggled to understand what had just happened. The building was larger than she had expected. "Is there a back door?"

"Yes, there is. We need to go." Nathan's voice held a tone of desperation that told her now was not the time to be asking questions.

They burst out into the sunlight. Merci shielded her eyes. When she saw the man in the orange coat lying on the ground starting to stir, she understood why Nathan was in such a hurry. He must have been standing guard, and Nathan had knocked him out. He'd regain consciousness in a few seconds.

"Come on, we got to go. She may be running to tell the others right now," Nathan said.

He was talking about Lorelei? Her mind stalled out. This didn't make any sense.

He tugged on her shoulder. "Merci, come on, we have to get out of here fast."

She had to let go of her confusion for now. Nathan took off running. She followed.

When Merci looked over her shoulder, she saw the man in the orange coat rising to his feet. A moment later, the man in the leather jacket came around the side of the cabin. Nathan headed back toward the trees. His hand frequently went up to his pectoral muscle where the knife wound was. He bent forward as he ran. Though he didn't say anything, Merci knew he must still be hurting.

Nathan zigzagged around the pine trees moving in an

erratic pattern that would be hard to follow. She stayed close to him, pushing branches out of the way.

They ran for some time until both of them were breathless. Nathan stopped for a moment, leaning against a tree and gulping in air. When she had caught her breath, she said, "Maybe we lost them."

"I don't know," said Nathan. She could almost feel his pain with each ragged breath he took in. "I don't know why they are chasing us. They've already taken our food."

Shockwaves spread through her. "They found the backpacks?"

He nodded.

"We have to get back to the cabin before nightfall," she said. She still didn't understand why Lorelei had pretended to be tied up and blindfolded, but it no longer made sense to try to help her.

He raised his eyebrows in agreement. He turned a half circle as though he were trying to assess where they were. Finally, he pointed. "I think this will get us back on the trail without having to go near the camp again."

They had run only a short distance when the shouts of the thieves permeated the forest. The noise was coming from two different parts of the forest. The men must have split up. In the mix of voices, Merci detected one that was distinctively female. The voices grew louder, closer.

Nathan turned on his heel and led her in a different direction.

And though she couldn't totally sort through what had happened, it looked as if Lorelei was somehow connected to these men. She'd lied about being tied up and blindfolded and must have left the second Nathan burst through the door or even minutes before. The reason for the ruse was unclear.

They pushed through the trees without stopping to rest. Every time a human noise met their ears, Nathan led her in a different direction. They seemed to be working gradually uphill.

Any doubt about the tenacity of the pursuers was washed away by the shouts of the men that echoed through the forest. At one point, it was as if the two pairs of thieves had flanked them. The sounds of grunts, expletives and breaking branches seemed to come from both sides.

She picked up the pace, finding the strength to fill her lungs and keep going. How long before the thieves gave up? Even over the noise of their breathing and footsteps crunching through the snow, she sensed that the thieves were closing in.

Branches broke behind her. A single gunshot boomed within yards of her head. Though fear rushed through her like a river, she had the presence of mind not to cry out. Her knees buckled. Nathan gathered her in his arms. He wrapped his arm around her waist and supported her as they catapulted through the trees and bushes.

The cluster of trees thinned, and there were only junipers growing low to the ground and other brush. The deeper snow slowed their pace.

Another gunshot zoomed over the top of them. The breaking of the branches, the shouting, the footsteps, it all threatened to overtake them like a tsunami wave.

Nathan directed her uphill. "This way. Stay low. They can see the bright colors of our coats."

They made their way through brush. Each time they stopped to listen, thinking they had shaken their pursuers, they saw a flash of color in the trees or heard noise that indicated they weren't in the clear yet.

Nathan stopped for a moment, scanning the landscape. "We can't keep this up." He grabbed her hand. He pulled her toward a rock formation and then stepped into an opening in the rocks. Nathan really knew his way around this forest. She never would have seen the cave entrance on her own, and the thieves wouldn't see it, either.

He pulled her deeper into the cave where it was black. The temperature dropped at least ten degrees inside the cave. The opening was narrow enough that as they faced each other, their toes touched. Her inhale and exhale seemed to be turned up to high volume.

The voices and shouts of the thieves augmented and echoed inside the cave. It was hard to gauge how close they were. Hopefully, they were hidden well enough.

Dark small spaces had always made Merci anxious. Her gloved hand pressed along the cold cave wall. It felt as if her rib cage was being squeezed in a vise. She closed her eyes, trying to shut out all the pictures her imagination created of what might be in the cave. Bats and bears liked caves. She took in several shallow, stabbing breaths.

Nathan's hand found hers in the darkness. He had slipped out of his glove and tugged hers off, as well. His calloused hand covered hers. The warmth of his touch sank through her, soothed her. She dared not speak in case the men were close. The cave functioned almost as a loudspeaker with sound bouncing around it.

"They got to be around here somewhere." A voice boomed outside, not far from the cave opening.

Merci shuddered.

Nathan squeezed her hand. He leaned close, his cheek touching hers and whispered, "They can't see us."

The voices of two men pressed on her ear.

Hawthorne said something she couldn't make out. The footsteps were so close it sounded as if they were stepping into the mouth of the cave. Nathan held tight to her hand. Then she saw a flash of color at the cave opening. She dare not take a breath or move.

Hawthorne spoke up. This time she could hear him. "Lori and Ryan haven't seen anything, either. We need to find these guys before they can get off the mountain." His voice was filled with venom.

"What dummies." Orange Coat's laughter held an undercurrent of menace. "They should have just stayed at that cabin."

Hawthorne's voice grew louder and more intense. "Yeah, they've seen me now. My name can't be connected to any of this. After we get what we want from the girl, they both have to die."

TEN

Though she remained very still and quiet, Nathan sensed the waves of fear that must be radiating through Merci. Her delicate hand trembled in his.

Hawthorne did not want to risk being identified. That explained why he hadn't been a part of the initial robbery. He must have gotten out of the car before the other two got to where Lorelei and Merci were. They knew Hawthorne's name. They knew his face. For that, he wanted to kill both of them. Apparently, his vow of nonviolence ended when he was at risk of going to jail.

Nathan waited several tense minutes until he was sure the men had headed away from the cave, then he gathered Merci into his arms.

She let out an anguished cry. "I heard…what he said."

He held her for a long moment until her shaking subsided. Then he pulled back and placed his hands on her face. "Listen to me, we are going to get off this mountain alive. Don't doubt it for a minute."

"How are we going to do that?"

"I don't know yet." He eased past her and stepped through the narrow cave opening crouching behind a bush. He stared up at the late-afternoon sky as one idea after another tumbled through his mind. He couldn't see or hear any sign of the men.

Merci came out and crouched behind him. She tilted her head toward the sky. "Is there time to get back to the cabin before dark?"

The thieves would be expecting that. They could be walking into a trap. "At this point, it's not that much farther to get to the ski lodge."

"How is that going to help us?"

The resort hadn't been operational for three years. There probably wasn't any food to speak of. They hired a security guy to check on the place once a week, but he doubted he would be up there. "I just think we'd be safer going to a place they're not familiar with. We can wait it out until the plows can get up the road." His keys were in the backpack the thieves had taken. They would have to break in.

She cupped a hand on his shoulder. "Okay, that's what we will do, then. You are the one who knows this mountain."

He turned and kissed her forehead. She was so willing to trust him. "It's just this way." Sunset was early this time of year. Even if they walked at a steady pace, part of their journey would be made in darkness.

As they trudged forward, Nathan stayed tuned into his surroundings. Maybe the thieves had given up and started to look for them elsewhere. Then he remembered the venom contained in Hawthorne's vow. It would be foolhardy to drop his guard altogether.

They hadn't eaten since early morning, and now it was getting close to dinner time. Hunger had started to gnaw at his belly. Merci walked beside him with her head down as the snow started to fall again. Though she hadn't complained, she must be getting hungry, too.

As they walked, he picked up a tin can. "Let me know if you get thirsty. I have some matches. We can melt some snow." At least he could give her that.

She nodded, but her body language indicated that her mind was elsewhere.

He had a pretty good guess about what was occupying her mind. "So what happened back there?"

She stopped and met his gaze. "You mean with Lorelei?" She looked off in the distance. "Hawthorne called her Lori. They must be involved. I guess you were right about her being a part of this. She pretended to be tied up and blindfolded in that cellar."

"Yeah, that seemed really odd to me. Why would she do something like that?"

"Hawthorne said something about getting something from me before…before he killed me. Some of her questions were odd. Maybe Lorelei was trying to get some kind of information out of me. That's why they put her in that room with me." Merci looked at the trees up ahead and took a step forward. "The whole thing was staged." An undercurrent of anger colored her voice.

They walked on in silence for a few minutes as the snowfall increased. At least they weren't fighting the wind. Nathan didn't want to push her. She seemed pretty raw emotionally. If she wanted to say more, she would.

Once Lorelei saw that Hawthorne was with them, she must have contacted them on that purple phone she had. She must have told them about the snowmobile and the camp. What they thought was a kidnapping was just Lorelei being picked up.

After about five minutes of walking, Merci piped up. "I just can't believe I trusted her. I really am naive." Her voice faltered.

"There is nothing wrong with thinking the best of people," Nathan said.

Merci's foot slipped on the snow, and Nathan caught her by the elbow. Her eyes were filled with tears.

Compassion flooded through him. "Hey, we don't have to talk about this."

"No, it's not that. It's just that my father was right. I'm too trusting of people. I just really wanted to believe that Lorelei was who she said she was. Maybe it was just reflexes that made her save my life in that truck."

"Don't be so hard on yourself."

She crossed her arms over her chest. "My father says I'll never make a good businessperson because I don't see past people's veneer."

"I wish I could trust more easily," Nathan said. His thoughts turned to his brother. Daniel's past history of gambling meant he was a bad financial risk as a business partner. It just seemed easier to sell the mountain property than to go through the heartache and humiliation of losing it to pay off debt if his brother returned to his old habits. Still, there was a part of him that wanted to believe that his brother had changed after his last time in rehab.

Merci stared at the ground as she walked. "Taking people at face value just means I get burned a lot."

"I guess," Nathan said, his voice becoming distant.

His issue with Daniel wouldn't matter at all if they didn't get off this mountain alive.

The sky over them darkened to a deeper gray. Nathan watched the path in front of them. A dark lump lay in clearing up ahead. He put his hand up to stop her.

"What is it?" she whispered.

Now he could discern what the lump was. "Fresh kill. Stay here." He moved in quickly. The fawn was still warm. Maybe their voices had frightened the predator away. In any case, he'd be back quick enough. He pulled his pocketknife out and cut from the back flank where the muscle was exposed. He packed snow around the meat and placed it in the kangaroo pocket of his ski jacket.

Merci had stepped closer. She let out a sad cry when she saw the dead fawn. He paced toward her and grabbed her hand. "Come on, we got to go."

"Why?"

"Because whatever killed this has got to be close by, and they aren't going to be very happy that we stole some of their dinner."

He broke out into a trot and she followed. "I thought the bears were asleep this time of year."

"The wolves and the bobcats aren't," he said picking up the pace.

By now they were moving at a run, slowed down only by the drifts of deep snow. He pushed hard for at least an hour. When they stopped, the sky was black.

"We can build a fire here, cook this meat and melt some snow to drink. Look around for some dry wood." A tall order considering the amount of snow that had fallen. "Sometimes branches that are covered by other deadfall aren't too bad."

She hesitated, moving only a few feet away from him. "Do you think whatever killed that fawn is still out there?"

Nathan looked around as he cleared a dry spot under a tree for the fire. "We would have heard or seen the wolves by now." She was afraid, but he couldn't lie to her about the level of danger. "Bobcats are quieter. Sometimes they stalk their prey for miles."

"Have we become the prey?" Her voice faltered when she asked the question.

"Tell you what, why don't we just look for that wood together." They foraged for about twenty minutes. Dead branches on standing trees proved to be the best source of fuel. Nathan gathered twigs for kindling.

As he struck a match, he said, "We've got to keep it small and let it burn out quickly so they don't find us."

Nathan filled the tin can with snow and positioned it close to the flames. As the fire began to die, he placed the meat on a makeshift grill he'd fashioned from willow sticks.

They passed the can of melted water back and forth. Nathan jabbed at the meat with a sharpened willow stick. He cut it in half. "It's kind of black, but it will fill the hole in your belly."

"Bon appétit." Her cheerfulness sounded forced. After she had taken several bites, she said, "This tastes better than a lot of restaurant food I've had."

"That's just because you're starving," he said.

"This is pretty gourmet," she joked. "Maybe you should think about getting your own cooking show."

"Or at least write a cookbook." He played along, grateful for any humorous relief they could find. Merci's ability to find something positive or funny in the worst situation never ceased to amaze him.

She laughed. A branch broke somewhere in the forest. Her head shot up as she swallowed her laughter.

Nathan spoke in a low, solemn voice. "Maybe we should think about covering this fire up and getting out of here." It didn't matter if it was the bobcat or the thieves. They needed to move pronto.

As they piled snow on the fledging fire, he listened to the forest for more signs that they weren't alone, but didn't hear anything. By the time they got moving, the sky was pitch black with only a few twinkling stars. The flashlight had been in the backpacks. Any torch they could have fastened from the fire wouldn't have lasted long without fuel to keep it burning.

Darkness slowed their pace.

Merci came up beside him. "How much farther do we have to go?"

He didn't see any familiar landmarks in the darkness. "Let's just keep going." He hadn't lost confidence that they would get to the ski hill. They were headed in the right direction. Their escape from the thieves had been a little erratic, and they'd gotten off course. He just couldn't be sure how far away they were.

Night chill set in as the temperature dropped. The knife wound started to hurt again, sending radiating pain down his arm.

Merci stopped and leaned against a tree. She looked up at the sky. "I wonder what time it is?"

"Seven…or eight o'clock." The temperature had dropped, too. Spending the night out here was out of the question. If they stopped to sleep, they would freeze.

"Hey, what's that?" She pointed up at the sky back toward where they had come from.

He tilted his head, studying each twinkling star and then noticed that one of the stars was moving. He stared in stunned amazement. "It's a helicopter."

Merci clapped her hands together. "That's good news. That's means they are looking for us."

His deputy friend, Travis Miller, must have become concerned when he didn't show up at the station. Maybe his brother, Daniel, had even said something. Nathan shook his head. "The problem is they are looking over by the cabin. I don't know if they will extend the search to this side of the mountain."

Merci felt hope slip away like air out of a deflating balloon. Nathan hadn't said anything, but something in the way he talked indicated that they were off track in getting to the ski hill. And now the searchers weren't even looking in the right place.

"I'm surprised they are out looking this late at night. They probably had a lot to deal with closer to town because of the storm," said Nathan.

The tone in Nathan's voice sounded pessimistic. Had he given up hope?

"There must be some way we can signal them." She couldn't hide her desperation. They had to try something. This might be their only chance for rescue.

"A big X made out of logs in an open area is the standard distress signal, but they would only see that in daylight."

"And we will be at the ski hill by then, right?"

Nathan didn't answer. He turned and trudged forward

through the snow. Merci scrambled to find some morsel of optimism. The night chill had grown worse, and she could feel the cold getting under her skin. The moonlight only allowed her to see a few feet in front of her.

After a while Nathan craned his neck and then said, "I don't know how soon they'll decide to look for us on this side of the mountain. Days, maybe."

Merci scrambled to keep up with Nathan as he increased his pace. When she looked behind her, she could no longer see the flashing lights of the helicopter. Had it landed or headed back to town? "If they do come this way, we can build a fire. They can see that at night."

"A town the size of Clampett has limited resources, and they are probably overextended already with all the problems the storm caused." Nathan's voice filled with despair.

"You must know someone in town. They would report you missing…they would put pressure on the authorities. I know my aunt Celeste is probably frantic by now. She's probably called everyone but the president."

"My brother…maybe," Nathan said.

"Your brother lives in Clampett. That's something."

He stopped. "Merci, you have to stop. You're grasping at straws. No one is coming for us. We have to get ourselves out of here and…" He placed his hands on his hips and turned from side to side. "And right now, I don't know if I can do that."

"I'm not grasping at straws, Nathan. I know a little bit about survival. I know the thing that will kill us faster than not having food or shelter is losing hope. We can't give up, Nathan."

Nathan took a step back. He hesitated in answering

as though he were stunned by the forcefulness of her speech. "I guess I owe you an apology. I let doubt creep in. That'll kill us faster than a bobcat or a snowstorm."

Aware that she had taken Nathan aback, she softened her tone. "I'm not Pollyanna. I know we'll die out here if we don't find some shelter soon. It looks bleak right now, but that is what faith is about. Like it says in Hebrews, faith is holding on to hope even if everything around you says otherwise."

She couldn't read Nathan's expression in the darkness. He spoke in a quiet voice. "I guess you're right." He turned and studied the landscape. "I guess we better keep walking toward what we can't see."

As they walked, her mind went through a catalogue of possibilities for how they could get back on track. "I don't suppose there would be any lights on at the resort?"

He replied. "I don't think so."

The sound of their feet pressing into the snow was the only thing she could hear for what seemed like an hour. The wind picked up, and the chill intensified. Her eyes watered. Unable to see much else, she focused on watching Nathan's back as he walked several feet in front of her. The darkness held a foreboding she didn't want to think about.

Nathan stopped abruptly. "The chairlift, we should be able to see the chairlift in the moonlight."

His voice broke the rhythm of their footfall in such a dramatic way that it startled her. "What?"

He spoke over his shoulder. "It's not a big resort. There is one chair lift and two ski runs. But if we can get to a clear open spot, we might be able to see the chairlift 'cause it's up high."

So that was what he had been doing this whole time, trying to come up with a way to find the resort.

"Glad to see you haven't lost hope." Her voice held a note of teasing.

"Guess I needed to hear about how important hope is," he said.

As the trees thinned, she studied the night sky hoping to see some signs of the wires and chairs. No clouds covered the twinkling stars or the half moon.

Merci shivered, and she could feel herself nodding off as they walked. She swayed to one side. It had been almost a full day since she had slept back at the cabin.

"Whoa, you okay?" Nathan grabbed her coat at the elbow.

Her limbs felt as if they were made of lead. "I'm getting really tired. Can't we just stop for a moment?"

"It's better if we keep moving."

"I know, but if I could just rest for twenty minutes." She was having a hard time keeping her eyes open.

Nathan nodded. "I'll stay awake. If both of us fall asleep, we could freeze to death." He led her to a large tree.

She sat down and scooted close to his uninjured side. "Now after all that fuss, I hope I can fall asleep." He wrapped his arms around her, and she rested against his flannel shirt where he had unzipped his coat. She fell asleep to the sound of his heart beating in her ear....

She awoke when Nathan shook her. "Merci, wake up." His voice sounded frantic.

She was still foggy headed. "What is it?"

"It's the helicopter. I saw the lights. It's coming back this way."

ELEVEN

Nathan burst to his feet and raced uphill. He could hear Merci's footsteps as she followed behind him. It had just been a momentary flash. Two distinctive blinking lights against the night sky and then they were gone.

They ran nearly to the top of hill. His legs ached from the effort of treading through deep snow. They both stopped, doubled over from the exertion.

"Where...was... it?" Merci scanned the sky.

Nathan pointed. "He might have dipped back behind that peak over there."

"It doesn't matter. The point is they are here on this side of the mountain. They are looking for us."

"There has to be a way for us to get the pilot's attention." He tugged on her sleeve then they made their way up the rest of the hill.

"I see it." Merci jumped up and down, her voice filled with excitement. "Over there, he's coming back this way."

Nathan waited for his breathing to even out. "Quick, find wood for a fire. They might still see us."

Merci disappeared into the darkness of the forest.

Nathan kneeled down and frantically cleared away

snow in an effort to create a dry spot. Merci returned a moment later with an armful of dried branches of various sizes.

"We need something for kindling," Nathan said.

"I can go find some little twigs," Merci said.

Nathan looked up. The flashing lights were distant but appeared to be moving toward them. They had to make this work. "No time, we've got to get this started right away and build it as fast as we can. Find what you can close by, anything that might burn."

He slit open his coat and pulled out a handful of down. He gathered some of the thinner twigs Merci had brought. His hand was shaking as he struck the match. He leaned in and blew gently on the embers. A golden edge rimmed some of the kindling. He held his breath. The ember burned out, and the down feathers curled in on themselves.

Again, he glanced up to get a bearing on where the helicopter was. It was still moving this way. He stuffed more kindling into the triangular structure he had made with the wood and pulled another match out of the box.

Merci came and sat down beside him. "We need something that catches fire fast."

Nathan nodded. "Yeah, paper or something."

Merci searched her pockets and retrieved several receipts. She bunched them up into a ball. "This will work."

The clacking of the helicopter engine and the whir of the blades broke through the darkness.

Nathan struck the match and an orange flame sparked to life. "It has to work."

His bare hands were cold and stiff from exposure. He struggled to hold the match steady.

"Give me a box of matches, too, it'll go faster." She held out her hand.

He caught that look in her eyes, that desperation. He felt it, too. Everything depended on getting this fire going.

He handed her one of the boxes of matches.

She struck the match and pushed it toward the kindling. The small flames burned the paper and ate up the twigs around it. Careful not to quench the fledgling flames, they added more twigs and then the bigger pieces of wood.

The noise of the helicopter had grown louder and the lights brighter. Merci placed a larger log on the crackling fire.

The mechanical hum of the helicopter seemed to engulf the forest as it drew near. Merci jumped up and waved her arms. "We're here. We're here."

The helicopter spun around and wobbled, but drew nearer. Nathan waved his arms and yelled, as well, when the helicopter got lower to the ground. Hope burst through him like a flower opening to the sun. They'd been spotted.

The helicopter listed to one side. Was the pilot having trouble or was something wrong mechanically? The helicopter created its own whirlpool of wind as it drew closer and lower to the ground.

Merci wrapped her arm through Nathan's. "We're going home."

The helicopter hovered above them at a diagonal. A moment before he heard the gunfire, Nathan recognized one of the thieves as he leaned out of the open doors of the chopper.

Merci released an odd gulping sound that told him she had registered the threat, as well.

"Run." He draped a protective arm over Merci as they dove for the trees.

The pistol shot went wild, but was followed by three more as the chopper stalked them. They were a hundred yards from the trees. Three more shots were fired. Two of them stirred up snow around their feet. The noise of the helicopter engine surrounded them.

The forest loomed thirty yards in front of them. When he looked behind him, the helicopter was slanted even more to one side and losing altitude. They reached the edge of the forest as the helicopter soft-crashed into the snow. At least the thieves wouldn't be chasing them with the chopper anymore.

Again they ran through forest, slamming against the branches and debris when it was too dark to see. Nathan led Merci through the darkness until they had gone a long time without hearing any signs that their pursuers were close.

Their pace slowed as they struggled to catch their breath. His hands had grown cold. In their haste to escape, they'd left their gloves back by the fire.

"What was that about?"

"They must have hijacked the search helicopter. Either they tossed the pilot out and were manning it themselves or the pilot was injured and couldn't keep it in the air." Whether he was killed right away or later, chances were the pilot wouldn't make it. Hawthorne had said he didn't want anyone to connect him to all of this. Everything he had done revealed he was serious about that threat.

"There might be a radio in the helicopter." Merci shoved her bare hands in her pockets.

"I thought of that. It's just too dangerous to go back now. They might be waiting for us to do that. And what if they disabled the radio?"

"You mean because they want to make sure we don't get off this mountain." Merci's voice wavered.

He wanted to reassure her, but they needed to be cautious. "Maybe in the morning we can circle back around and see if the radio works."

She slammed her back against a tree and let out a huff of air. "You mean if we make it until morning."

"That's not what I meant." He could hear the frustration in her voice as he walked toward her. "What did you say about hope?"

"All of this has been too much," she sputtered. "I didn't think I would ever say this, but I don't see how we are going to get out of here alive. Now we don't even have gloves."

He could hear her soft crying in the darkness. He gathered her into his arms, but no words of assurance came to him. He had none to give. All he could do was hold her.

God, I need Your help. I am at the absolute end of the line here.

He brushed his face over her soft hair and waited until her crying had subsided. She had depended on him and trusted him, and he had let her down. She pulled away.

Without a word, he turned and pushed through the forest and she followed. He kept his freezing hands in his pockets.

Fatigue set in within minutes. He nodded off as they trudged forward. He had no idea where they were going. Nothing looked familiar in the darkness, and everything was covered in snow.

He struggled to keep his eyes open as the voice of condemnation grew louder inside his head. They should have tried to get back to the cabin. He'd been foolish to think he could get them to the resort. His memory of the landscape was imperfect. Nothing looked right in the dark.

If only they had stayed at the cabin in the first place. If only they had gotten on to Lorelei sooner. His foot caught on a log, and his top half lurched forward. His hands went out as a protective measure.

"Are you okay?" Merci was beside him touching his elbow and helping him to his feet. The sweetness of her voice renewed his strength.

He'd caught his fall, but his hands were cold from being buried in snow. "I must have nodded off."

"We are both tired. Here, put your hands back in your pockets." He obliged, and she hooked her arm through his before putting her bare hands into her pockets. "We've got to try to keep each other awake."

"That is a good idea," he said. "What should we do?"

"I suppose singing is out of the question," Merci said.

"We probably shouldn't make more noise than we need to." It was just a matter of time before the thieves found them again.

"Do you suppose they are going to hole up in that downed helicopter or come after us?"

"Let's just stay alert." How much longer could they last? They were both beyond exhausted. Daylight was a good six hours away. "Just say something to me every few minutes, so neither one of us falls asleep."

They came to a field of snow touched only by rabbit tracks. Moonlight washed the snow in a blue hue. Their boots sunk into the snow in a rhythmic pattern. Twice, Merci faltered in her step, and he knew she was falling asleep. They weren't going to make it until daylight. Maybe they could find some kind of shelter, build a fire and take turns sleeping.

The wind picked up. Nathan walked with his head down. They had gotten so far off track trying to escape their pursuers it didn't make sense to try and find a familiar landmark. Only the distant outline of the mountains told him approximately where they were. His heart felt heavy as anxious thoughts tumbled through his head. He had to find a way to keep both of them alive.

Merci planted her feet and pulled free of Nathan. "Lights," she whispered.

He looked in the direction she had indicated, but saw only shadows. Nathan wondered if she had gotten loopy from lack of sleep. "Where? I don't see anything."

She pulled her hand out of her pockets and traced the outline of the ridge. "On the other side of there. Don't you see how it kind of glows up there, just real faint. I'm telling you, there is something just behind that mountain peak."

It could be a light glowing behind the mountain, or it could be wishful thinking brought on by a lack of sleep. "Maybe," he said.

"I say we move toward that mountain top, toward that light." She turned to face him, her voice thick with emotion. "What other option do we have?"

Nathan took in a breath that chilled his lungs. The wind cut through him, and his fingers were numb even though he had tried to keep them in his pockets. Both of them had grown weak and exhausted. Did they have the stamina to make it up that section of the mountain? And what if there was nothing but another mountain on the other side. Fifty yards down the hill was a stand of trees that would provide some shelter.

Merci leaned against him. "It's not that far a climb."

He didn't say anything—only wrapped his arm through hers and stepped forward. She was right. They needed more shelter than those trees could provide. Very little snow stayed on the rocky mountaintop. The incline became steep enough that they had to separate and pull their hands out of their pockets.

His fingers had grown tingling and numb by the time they made it to the top. They gazed down into the valley below and at the source of the light. Orange yellow light glowed in the window of a small cabin. Two dark cabins stood on either side of the occupied cabin.

"What is this place?" Her voice filled with amazement.

"This is the backside of the ski resort. We must have gone almost completely around it."

"Why would someone be in the cabin?" Fear entered her voice.

"It doesn't necessarily mean the thieves beat us here. Maybe that security guy did get stranded. Or Dad used to rent the cabins out to people who wanted some mountain solitude even after he closed the ski hill down. Maybe it's one of those people."

"So did you rent the cabin out?"

"No, but my brother might have," Nathan said.

She turned toward him. "You don't know if he did. Don't you run this place together?"

The question made him uncomfortable. "We both own it…we don't run it together. That's why we're selling it. Anyway, my brother and I don't communicate that well. He might have rented it out and not told me."

"I say we go down there and knock on the door." Merci took a step down the hill.

Nathan caught her arm. "Let's go down but watch the place for a while."

"Nathan, I can't feel my fingers anymore," she pleaded.

"I know…me, either. I'm just saying we need to be cautious."

"Okay," she said reluctantly.

They walked down the mountain toward the cabin. The snow had drifted up to their calves in some places.

Merci was shivering by the time they came within a hundred yards of the cabin. Neither one of them was in any condition to run anymore if it turned out the thieves had beaten them here.

"I really need to be inside." Her voice vibrated when she spoke. "Maybe we should go into one of the dark cabins."

Nathan watched the windows of the lighted cabin, hoping someone would walk by. "I know. We just got to wait a minute here. I'll move forward and have a look in the windows."

When he got within twenty yards, the door burst open and a small dog bounded down the stairs. The door closed before Nathan could get a look at who had opened it. The terrier jumped up and down and yipped at Nathan's feet.

"It's not them." Merci rushed toward the cabin. "They don't have a dog."

The door swung open again and an older man with snowy white hair stepped out. "What is all that racket, Leo?"

His eyes rested on Merci and Nathan. He took a step back as the dog's barking became more insistent. "Who are you?"

"Please sir, we are so cold." Merci stepped forward.

"Where did you come from?"

Nathan wrapped his arms around Merci. "I'm the owner of this resort."

The man leaned closer, probably trying to get a better look at them. "We rented this cabin from a Daniel McCormick."

"That's my brother. I'm Nathan McCormick."

The man stepped to the edge of the porch to study them. "What are you doing all the way up here?"

The man was obviously struggling to make sense of how two strangers would appear out of nowhere in such harsh conditions. "It's a long story that I would be glad to share with you," Nathan said.

Merci stepped closer to the porch. "I know this seems crazy, but we are hungry and tired and cold."

The man shook his head as though he were not totally convinced. He stared at them for a long moment. "Well, I suppose you should come on in if you are cold." He turned back around, leaving the door open as he disappeared inside. The terrier followed after him. Nathan grabbed Merci's hand and pulled her up the stairs.

Inside, an older woman sat reading a book beside a crackling fire. A look of concern spread across her face when she saw Merci and Nathan. She rose to her feet. "Oh, my, what has happened to you two?"

The old man wandered toward the kitchen. "This is my wife Elle, and I'm Henry."

Elle walked over to Merci. "You poor dear. Come sit by the heat and get warmed up."

Nathan looked down at his hands. The fingertips had gone numb and turned white, signs of frostbite. Merci plunged down to the floor and held her hands toward the fire. Nathan sat down beside her.

Elle hustled toward the kitchen. "I've got hot water on the stove."

"Get them some food, too, will you, Elle?" Henry took a chair close to them. "My wife and I made plans to come up here months ago. We go somewhere every year for some solitude and prayer time. This storm was so unexpected. Weather forecast didn't predict it this close to spring. We came up here in the four-wheel drive, but there is no way we can get out until the road is cleared. The car is buried under three feet of snow. That's how we got stranded up here. Now why don't you tell me your story?"

Nathan offered Henry the shortest version he could to explain how they had arrived at his doorstop. While he told his story, Elle brought them both hot chocolate and chicken noodle soup.

Henry shook his head. "And you don't know where these thieves are now."

"I'm sure they will be looking for a warm place, too," Nathan said. "I won't lie to you sir—these men are extremely dangerous."

"We'll deal with what is happening, not what might

happen. We got a week's worth of food for two, we can make it work for four."

"Thank you." Merci's eyes rimmed with tears. The expression of relief on her face did Nathan's heart good.

Elle gathered up the empty bowls and cups. "One of you can have the couch, and I will put some blankets down on the floor by the window for the other one."

A few minutes later, after bringing out the blankets, Elle and Henry disappeared into the only bedroom.

"You can have the couch." Nathan grabbed a pillow and blanket from the pile Elle had brought out.

"I don't know what would have happened to us if we hadn't found Elle and Henry here." Merci settled down on the couch.

Nathan nodded as a sense of gratitude for God's protection spread through him. He was warm and his stomach was full. "The electricity for the cabin runs on a generator, but they had to have supplied their own gasoline to get it going. They must have brought all the food, blankets and supplies with them. It's a good thing they were here."

Maybe they would have survived the night if they had broken into a cabin, but the frostbite might have cost them fingers, and there would have been no food and no warmth and no kindness.

Merci spread the blanket out on the couch and fluffed the pillow. "Do you think we will be able to get out in the morning?"

Nathan shoved his hands in his pockets and stared out the window at the quiet night as he stood by the window. "Hard to say. I'm sure there will be concern when that helicopter pilot doesn't come back."

He clicked off the two living room lamps. If the thieves did make it this far, they wouldn't see any light coming from the cabin.

After a long silence, Merci said, "Nathan, maybe you and your brother should work a little more on communicating better. It's kind of sad that you didn't even know he had rented this place to these people."

"I suppose so." His answer was calm, but her comment had stirred him up inside. It was hard to talk to Daniel about anything without unresolved pain rising to the surface. Things with his brother had not been good since Daniel's teen years, when he had started gambling. The torment had come in watching how Daniel's addiction hurt Mom and Dad. All the happy childhood memories were overshadowed by Daniel's later cruelties. "It's hard sometimes talking to family members."

He wondered if she would understand if he explained the whole story. He had to sell the acreage. He couldn't see himself working with his brother. Daniel said the gambling was a thing of the past, but how could he be sure? He'd watched his parents live through the cycle of Daniel vowing to quit and starting up again too many times to count. If he told Merci all of that, would she understand?

Nathan looked out the window one more time before settling down to sleep. He felt as if he could finally take a deep breath. They were warm and fed, but he knew they might not be safe yet. He picked up the remaining blankets and laid them down close to the door. If anyone tried to get in, he would hear them.

TWELVE

Merci awoke in the night to a faint scratching sound. She lay with her eyes open in the dark, trying to decipher what the sound was. Finally she sat up. She could make out the outline of the rocking chair that was opposite the sofa. Across the room, Nathan stirred in his sleep.

The scratching noises continued. When she heard an abbreviated yipping sound, she knew the dog must be trying to get out of Elle and Henry's bedroom. His scratching grew a bit more insistent. Henry and Elle must be deep sleepers, but why was the terrier so upset?

She wondered if she dared try to make it to the kitchen to get a drink of water in the dark. The longer she thought about it, the more parched her throat felt. She planted her feet on the rough wood floor and moved toward the kitchen. She stepped back when she bumped against a box and then felt for the wall that led her into the kitchen. She clicked on the light above the stove, found a cup and turned on the faucet. She took a sip of the cool liquid.

When she turned to face the window, her breath

caught, and her grip on the glass tightened. In the distance, lights flashed and bobbed across her field of vision. She hurried back to the living room, slamming into a chair on the way.

She ducked down to a kneeling position out of sight of the window. "Nathan, wake up. I saw a light outside."

Nathan went from sleeping to awake without so much as a groan or an incoherent comment. He sat up, threw off his covers and pushed himself to his feet. "Where did you see it?"

They were both crouching beneath the window. "Over by that large building, closer to the rest of the ski hill."

Nathan raised up to his knees so he could look out. He snapped his head around. "The light in the kitchen. They might see it."

Merci raced across the living room and turned the light off. The door of the bedroom opened, and the scratching of the terrier's feet on the floor filled the room. The little dog bounded around the room barking.

A moment later, Henry came out of the bedroom. "What's going on?"

"Henry don't turn on any lights." Nathan's voice was forceful.

"Are they out there? These men who were chasing you?" Henry whispered.

Nathan and Merci crawled on their knees toward Henry while Leo paced and barked in front of the door.

Nathan spoke in a rapid-fire delivery as he put his boots and coat on. "Chances are, they won't know we are in this cabin unless they saw the kitchen light on. I am sure they will search this whole place. It is only a matter of time before they find us. All of us have to get out of here."

Her spirits sank. There was no safe place for them, and now they had endangered Henry and Elle who had been so kind. She grabbed Henry's hand. "We have to find a way off this mountain."

"There are three feet of snow on our car. Even if we got it dug out, you couldn't get it to move." Henry slumped down in a chair.

Merci scrambled for a solution. There had to be a way to escape. "What about skis? Would there have been skis left behind?"

"Maybe in the rental area." Nathan had gathered up Merci's coat and handed it to her. "Dad always planned on reopening down the line. Something might have gotten left behind."

Merci turned toward the older man. "Henry, can you and your wife ski?"

The rocking chair creaked when Henry rose to his feet. "Elle and I are too old for spy games. We'll take our chances and stay here."

"But—"

Henry raised his hand to stop Merci's protests. "It's the two of you they are after. We can lay low until the plows make it up here."

Merci squeezed Henry's hand. Either way, the danger was substantial for Elle and Henry. If they stayed, they ran the risk of being discovered. Even if they got away clean, the physical stamina required to ski out might be too much for the older couple.

"Please stay in here and keep the lights out," she said.

Nathan stepped toward them. "These guys are hungry and cold. If they wander over this way and figure out you're in here, I don't think that any of them has enough of a conscience to not harm you."

Merci felt a quickening in her heart. Maybe Lorelei had a conscience. Could she have that hope?

While Nathan and Merci got their things together, Henry returned to the bedroom. Merci could hear him talking to Elle through the open door. Merci glanced out the window. The lights bobbed up and down close to the large buildings and then disappeared. The thieves must have located a flashlight instead of the makeshift torches they had used at the camp. No doubt they had helped themselves to the supplies in the downed helicopter.

Elle came down the hallway in her nightgown. She padded over to the kitchen and opened cupboards. She handed Merci several packets. "Here, take this food. It's a meal in a single package. We have some backpacks you can have."

Merci gave Elle a quick hug. Henry handed Nathan two pairs of gloves. "We have extra."

Leo had settled down on the rug but stood up when Nathan and Merci moved toward the door. Henry gathered the terrier into his arms. The dog wiggled in protest, but Henry held onto him.

Merci gave a backward glance as they headed out the door into the night. "Stay safe. Lock the doors. Don't stand in front of the window once there is daylight."

"We'll be all right," Elle assured.

Merci couldn't let go of the anxiety that made her stomach tight. If only there was a way she and Nathan could let them know where the thieves were and if they were still a threat, but once they left the cabin, they would have no means of communicating with these kind people.

After closing the door, they slipped down the stairs and out into the darkness. The guest cabins were about a hundred yards from the main buildings of the ski hill. Nathan stopped for a moment, his gaze darting from one building to the next. "I just thought of something. The trail groomer was kept here because it's too hard to move out. The garages are over there." He pointed at a large building set off from the others. "If there was even a little gas left in it, we might be able to make it some of the way down the mountain."

Hope stirred inside her. "Let's go see."

Without any trees to serve as a barrier, the snow in the valley where the cabins were was deep. The snow covered her legs up to her knees as she put one foot in front of the other. The air was crisp and bitterly cold. She was out of breath as they neared the equipment garage.

"The front of the building is this way." Nathan led her around a large metal structure. Now she could see the chairlift and the log buildings that must house the ski rental and lodge.

The equipment garage had two huge doors. Nathan moved toward the smaller one. "I don't know if this is locked or not." His hand reached for the knob.

A screeching noise caused him to take a step back. One of the garage doors eased upward, creating a cacophony of metal scraping against metal. The rattling door sent shockwaves of fear through Merci. Nathan grabbed Merci and pulled her around the corner. Bright headlights cut through the darkness. The thieves had beaten them to the trail groomer!

He pulled her toward one of the large log cabins. A shot went off behind them. They dove to the ground and crawled through the snow toward a small wooden shed with a window. Nathan pushed her into the tiny building.

Merci pressed her back against the wall while her heart pounded against her rib cage. "Where did the shot come from?"

"Too high up to be from the garage area," Nathan said. "One of them must be posted somewhere. Maybe on the chairlift."

She gasped in air. "He must have seen where we went."

"You do have a good view of everything from there, but it's still pretty dark. I say we make a run for it," Nathan said.

Refusing to give in to the impending terror, Merci nodded.

They pushed back through the door and hurried around to the side that was opposite the chairlift. They scrambled up the stairs to the porch of the huge log building. Nathan tried the door, but it was locked.

"Around the side, there is a window I should be able to get open," Nathan said.

Merci's heart raced as they ran around to the side of the lodge. Their feet pounded on the porch planks, an auditory beacon to their location. Merci hoped it was just her fear that made the footsteps sound so loud.

Nathan grabbed a log from the dwindled pile on the porch and kneeled down beside a window that must lead into the lower floor of the lodge. He shattered the window with a single blow and reached in, twisted the latch and pushed it open.

"You first." He glanced side to side as Merci crawled forward and slid through the window face-first, careful to avoid the broken glass. Her hand landed on carpet. She pulled her legs free of the windowsill and rose to her feet. Nathan slipped in headfirst and pulled himself to his feet in one swift movement.

He cupped his hand over her elbow. "This way, hurry. If there are any skis, they'd be in the equipment rental room."

He led her upstairs past a room with a large fireplace and tables that must have functioned as a cafeteria.

"This way," he said.

He pulled her into a carpeted room with lockers and benches. Nathan ran toward a door at the back of the room.

When she followed him into the room and looked around, she felt as if she had stepped into Christmas morning. All three walls were lined with every size and brand of skis. The boxes below the racks held ski boots. "It doesn't look like they got rid of any of the rentals."

"Not a huge danger of theft. Dad probably thought it was just easier to leave stuff here. I really think he thought he'd only close down for a season." Nathan reached for a pair of skis and handed them over to her. "These should work for you. What shoe size are you?"

"Eight," she said.

He dropped to his knees and pulled out a pair of boots. "You have skied before?"

"My father used to take my mom and me to Switzerland every winter."

A thumping sound from the basement below indicated that one of the thieves had come in the same way they had.

While Nathan got his own skis, she found a bench and sat down. As she slipped off her boots and put them in the backpack Elle had given her, a sense of urgency overtook her. It was only a matter of time before the thief who had shot at them figured out where they had gone. The head start they had on him because he had to jump down from the chairlift had bought them precious minutes, but would it be enough?

Nathan came and sat down beside her, yanking off his boots and buckling into the bulky ski boot.

Footsteps pounded on the floor above them. Merci lifted her eyes. "He went the wrong way. What's up there, anyway?"

"Administrative offices and storage. He'll be back down this way." He rose to his feet. "You ready? Let's go."

As they rushed through the eating area of the lodge, Nathan glanced out the back window toward the rental cabins. He stopped and let go of her hand. "Oh, no, I think we have a problem."

THIRTEEN

Tension snaked around Nathan's torso. He rushed toward the window to make sure he was seeing correctly. Just enough moonlight spread across the open field to reveal Henry and Elle's terrier scampering through the snow. He must have bolted away when Henry let him out to go to the bathroom. Given the level of danger, it seemed odd that Henry would take the dog out. The dog was a dark lump moving across the white snow.

Merci came up behind him and placed a hand on his shoulder. "The thieves will know that somebody is here if they see that dog."

Nathan ran toward the stairs and shouted over his shoulder. "We have to get to him before he's spotted."

His ski boots clunked down the stairs. He prayed that the noise was not loud enough to alert the thief who was stalking through the building looking for them. He pushed open the back door. Merci followed him.

He scanned the area in front of them, hoping that Henry hadn't been foolish enough to come after the dog and make himself known. The cabin Henry and Elle occupied was still dark. As the dog made a beeline for them, he saw that he dragged his leash behind him. Henry had taken precautions in not letting the dog run wild, but he must have broken free of the older man's grasp.

They leaned their skis against the building and raced toward the animal. The clunkiness of the ski boots hindered their process, but Leo ran toward them, bounding up and down through the snow like a dolphin on the waves, oblivious to the level of danger he was putting his master in.

His heart racing, Nathan glanced back at the window of the lodge, half expecting to see one of the thieves leveling his gun at him. The windows were black. When he looked toward the garage, the large door was still open but no headlights shone there anymore.

Leo came within twenty feet of them and sat back on his haunches. Nathan eased toward the dog praying that he wouldn't start barking. That would alert the thief for sure.

"Come on now, Leo, you know us," Merci coaxed. She eased toward him saying his name over and over.

The little dog hopped from side to side. While the terrier's attention was on Merci, Nathan took a wide circle around the dog and then moved in. Nathan slipped off one of his gloves. He dove for the leash just as the dog darted away from Merci. His hand wrapped around the canvas strap. Leo protested by running three feet one way and then three feet the other.

"Got you, you little rascal."

"I'll get the skis and meet you partway while you take the dog back to Henry." Merci's gaze darted around the dark landscape from the window of the lodge to the open area by the ski lift. She was thinking the same thing—that someone might be watching them.

"I need to throw them off from the cabin." He gathered the dog into his arms. Elle and Henry didn't deserve to have their lives in danger for having been kind to them. If they were being watched, weaving through the buildings rather than going across the open field to the cabin would not give away their location. The back door of the cabin was not visible from the lodge or the equipment garage.

The dog wiggled in his arms as he slipped behind the first cabin. Nathan couldn't see Merci, and that concerned him. He walked faster.

Noises from the other side of the cabin alerted him. Footsteps. He pressed against the cabin. The dog yipped and squirmed. Nathan clamped a hand around the dog's snout. Had the thieves already found Elle and Henry and that was why Leo was running loose?

His heartbeat drummed in his ears as he pulled the squirming animal closer to his chest. The crunch of footsteps in the snow was distinctive in the nighttime quiet. His thoughts turned to Merci and her safety. Had it been a mistake to split up? The decision saved precious minutes, but at what cost?

He couldn't discern where the footsteps were coming from.

Even with his jaw clamped shut, Leo emitted a low guttural growl. Nathan pressed even harder against the wall of the cabin, willing himself to be invisible. The footsteps grew louder…and then stopped.

The sound of his own inhaling and exhaling seemed

to surround him as he held as still as a statue. Seconds ticked by.

He heard a single footstep. He sucked in a breath and counted to five.

Henry was suddenly in front of him. A wide grin spread across his face, but he spoke in a whisper, "I saw you out in the field."

Nathan let out the breath he'd been holding. He handed the squirming dog over to Henry.

Henry leaned close to Nathan and whispered. "Leo was barking and making so much noise inside the cabin, the only way to quiet him was to take him out and let him do his business. I would've just come out in the open, but one of them is creeping around these cabins. It looked as if he had an orange coat on. He's after you. I don't think he saw Leo or me."

Tension knotted at the back of Nathan's neck. None of this was good. "Be careful getting back to the cabin. Do you want me to go with you?"

"You need to get out of here. We'll be all right. We'll keep the doors locked and do our best to keep Leo quiet."

"If they try to break into the cabin, get out the back way as fast as you can and find a good hiding place." Nathan wasn't sure if even that would work. Henry and Elle were no match for the thieves physically.

Henry held tight to the squirming terrier. "We can do that."

"Leave most of the food behind, maybe that will be enough for them to leave you alone." The chances that the older couple would be able to slip out of the cabin unseen were slim at best.

"Take care. And don't worry about us. We'll be home soon enough." Henry turned and slipped around the corner of the cabin.

Nathan prayed for the older man's safety as he raced back toward Merci. He remained on the perimeter of the area using the buildings for cover when he could. When he stepped out from behind the last cabin, Merci made her way toward him. She'd already snapped into her own skis. She handed him his poles and tossed his skis on the ground.

"Are they okay?"

"For now," he said.

"Maybe the thieves will leave Elle and Henry alone. It's us Hawthorne is after, so we can lead them away from the cabin."

Hawthorne's threat to kill them both before they got off the mountain still weighed heavily on his mind. "Let's get moving. We should have some daylight in just a little bit here."

The few hours sleep they had gotten in Henry's cabin had made a big difference. They skied toward the front part of the resort. The skis made a light swishing noise as they pushed out into the open. The chairlift came into view. Nathan was grateful that the skis stayed on the surface of the hard pack snow. They'd encounter deep powder soon enough. At least it looked as if the other side of the mountain had gotten most of the snow.

"There are only two runs on this hill." He pointed down the mountain. "This one is the longer run. We might be able to ski a little beyond the runs, as well. From there, we should be able to get to the road."

Merci craned her neck. "What's that noise?"

Before Nathan could even register what Merci as talking about, a guttural clanging filled the air right before they saw the headlights of the trail groomer come into view. The yellow lights glowed like monster eyes. Two figures sat in the cab. The machine lurched forward as the metal tracks bit through the snow. They were directly in the path of the groomer.

"We can stay ahead of it." Nathan dug his poles in and pushed off. "Let's go."

Merci's skis sliced through the snow behind him. The snow grew deeper and fluffier, creating a white powder cloud around them as they zigzagged down the mountain. The air smelled of diesel fuel. The mechanical groan of the groomer making its way down the mountain pressed on his ears. They could outmaneuver the big machine, but he wasn't so sure they could outrun it, not in these kinds of conditions.

They came to a smooth part of the run that was exposed so most of the new fallen snow had blown off. Nathan gasped in air as he tucked in and leaned forward. When he glanced over his shoulder, Merci was doing the same.

The groomer was about thirty yards behind them. Merci's ski hit a snag or rock. He heard her scream right before she somersaulted. Both skis broke free of the boots. The groomer loomed toward them. Merci sat up looking a bit dazed.

He worked his way uphill toward her. "You okay?"

She nodded as she pushed herself to her feet. Nathan skied uphill, stepping sideways to retrieve the lost ski. Merci grabbed the other one. The groomer was ten yards from him and was showing no sign of turning to avoid him. Skiing wasn't going to work. Nathan dropped the ski, turned and pushed down the mountain.

"Toward the trees. The groomer can't go there." He clicked out of his own skis. They pushed toward the forest with the clanging engine noise of the groomer consuming all other sound.

Moving in the ski boots was slow going. The plow on the front of the groomer lifted in the air, screeching like a dying bird. They were a good twenty yards from the trees. The plow slammed down only a few feet from them, stirring up a dust cloud of snow. Merci screamed.

Nathan grabbed Merci's hand and pulled her toward the safety of the trees. The groomer surged toward them. The trees were within five yards. The roar of the motor and metal tracks chopping through the snow engulfed them. With adrenaline surging through every cell in his body, Nathan summoned up a final burst of strength and pushed hard toward the edge of the forest.

Once they were beneath the shelter of the trees, it grew even darker. They could hear the groomer being powered down as they moved through the thick forest. Both of them were out of breath. The rougher terrain and the bulky ski boots didn't allow them to run. They could only take big steps. The physical exertion caused the cut in his pectoral muscle to flare with pain.

"We have to get out of these boots." Merci gasped for air.

He couldn't hear the groomer anymore. The people in the cab would come looking for them. He wondered what had happened to the other two thieves. The cab only held two people. Were the two who got left behind already attacking Elle and Henry? Would they search all the cabins looking for food or give up after the first one didn't yield results?

"We need to find a hiding place." He didn't know this forest like he did the area around the youth camp. "Come on."

They moved deeper into the forest, stopping to listen for any signs of their pursuers but hearing nothing. The snow wasn't as deep, but fallen logs hindered their progress. Early-morning sun peaked through the trees, and still they heard no signs of their pursuers.

Merci stopped when she came to a large fallen log. "My feet are killing me. Let's stop and switch into our regular boots." She plunked down on the log and pulled her boots out of the backpack Elle had given her. "I don't think they are going to chase us into here."

"They didn't come right after us." Given Hawthorne's resolve to see both of them dead, though, it didn't make sense that they would just give up. While Merci clicked out of her ski boots, Nathan patrolled a circle around her looking for any sign of their pursuers.

"Boy, my feet are freezing." She pulled one of her boots out of the backpack.

Nathan studied the pathway through the forest where they had just come from. No sign of movement, no noise, nothing.

He quickly stepped into his boots while Merci continued to lace hers up.

Merci's scream caused him to stand up and spin around. The man in the orange coat stood holding a gun. Merci scooted back on the log. One of her feet was still exposed.

The man in the orange coat offered them a toothy

grin. "When the helicopter flew over this area, we saw how small this forest was. It was nothing to circle around and find you in here." He raised the gun so it pointed at Nathan's chest. "Surprise."

Nathan held up his hands as he edged toward Merci. Terror was etched across her face. Why hadn't he been paying more attention? "Now hold on. I think we can talk about this. Is killing us really the best idea?"

"It's what the boss wants," Orange Coat said.

"Do you just do your boss's bidding no matter what? You pull the trigger, you'll be the one going to jail." Nathan's voice was steady.

The gun wavered a little in the thief's hand. The hardness of his expression changed, indicating that doubt had crept in.

"So you go to jail for something your boss set up." Nathan edged a little closer to Merci. "That doesn't seem very fair to me."

The thief lifted his chin and pressed his lips together. "Boss says the way he's got it planned, they will never find your body." A sense of self-satisfaction permeated his voice.

Merci's sharp intake of breath was audible. Her head jerked back. Nathan put a reassuring hand on her shoulder.

Though he looked the thief in the eye, his peripheral attention was on the gun. He didn't want to die today, and he sure didn't want Merci to die. All he needed was a moment of distraction. Nathan shifted his gaze and made his eyes go wide as though he was seeing something in the trees. The thief's hand holding the gun slackened, and his eyes moved sideways.

Nathan jumped on him, driving the hand holding the gun upward and pinching the nerves in his wrist so the thief let go of the gun. The man managed to get a solid punch to Nathan's stomach before they both tumbled to the ground. He fought past the pain and caught a glimpse of Merci scrambling to get her boot on as he rolled. Pain from his knife wound electrified his nerve endings. Once he was on top of the thief, he landed a hard blow to the man's neck. Not enough to knock him out, but enough to leave him gasping. He punched him a second time in the stomach. The man drew up into a fetal position.

Nathan glanced around the area. Where was the gun?

"I can't find it," Merci said.

The thief continued to clutch his stomach and struggle for breath.

"No time. Let's move." The others were no doubt closing in on them from other parts of the forest.

They ran. He had no idea where they were, only that moving downward would eventually connect them to the country two-lane. If they could follow that out, they could get to the highway…if the thieves didn't get them first.

When they came out of the forest back toward the ski run, the groomer was still making its way down. They slipped back into the trees and ran until they came to a river partially frozen over. Only the water in the middle of the river flowed, pushing ice chunks downriver.

"Now what?" said Merci, staring at the freezing water.

FOURTEEN

Merci's heart pounded erratically as she glanced over her shoulder at the trees they had just emerged from. The thieves would catch up soon enough.

Nathan gripped her gloved hand. "We've got to jump across. The groomer won't be able to follow us across the river. Then they'll be on foot, too."

"The ice looks really thin." The river was at least fifteen feet across, too wide to make in a single leap. A hard fall on the ice would break it for sure. Merci was still struggling for a deep breath from their run.

"The trick is to choose where the ice is thickest. I'll go out first. Walk where I walk." Nathan placed a tentative foot on a frozen edge of the river. It held him without cracking. She sucked in a shaky breath as he stretched his leg out and took another step.

One more step and he was able to leap across the narrow opening where the water still flowed freely. She cringed, fearing the ice would crack from his hard landing.

His feet touched the other side of the bank, and he turned to face her. "Did you see where I went?"

She nodded.

Nathan broke eye contact with her and glanced over her shoulder.

"Are they coming?"

He turned his head slightly as he searched the tree line. "I don't see them."

Merci took a breath and stepped free of the bank. The ice held. She lifted her foot and stepped forward. As she put her foot down, it slid on the ice, straining her leg muscles. The ice beneath her cracked. She screamed. Her foot went into the cold river water.

Nathan grabbed her and pulled her to solid ground, holding her in his arms.

Already the icy chill from exposure had seeped through her skin. "My foot is soaking wet."

"Can you run?" His attention was on the hill behind them.

When she turned, she saw the groomer lumbering over a bump that must have hid it from view.

"Do I have a choice?" Her leg already felt like a block of ice. This was way worse than having snow in her boot. Though the long underwear and thick jeans provided some protection to her leg, her boot had soaked clean through and saturated the sock.

Nathan led them downhill away from the river toward an aspen grove that provided a little cover. They ran for what seemed like miles. The sun peaked up over the mountain when they finally stopped by a rock formation. The river had to have stopped the groomer, and the thieves would not know exactly what direction they had gone once they crossed the river. They had a moment to catch their breath.

Merci pulled the prepackaged meal Elle had given her out of her backpack, and Nathan did the same. She chewed the meal, which was labeled lasagna but tasted more like cardboard with marinara sauce on it. It would be nice to wash the food down with something. She hadn't thought to ask Elle for water. "I'm really thirsty." She leaned down to scoop up a handful of snow.

Nathan grabbed her hand and brushed the snow off her glove. "Don't eat frozen snow. It'll kill you. Your core body temp will go down."

Her leg that had been exposed to the cold river water had gone numb, and her jeans were frozen. When she stepped on it, there was no sensation. She was pretty sure her core body temperature had already been affected. "I need a drink of water." She wrapped her arms around her torso and shivered. Her throat felt unbearably dry. "Do you still have the matches?" When she swallowed she couldn't produce any moisture in her mouth.

"They're in my pocket, but I lost the tin can somewhere. If we can find any kind of container, I'll melt some snow for you."

She appreciated the compassion she heard in his voice and the way he reached up to brush his hand over her cheek.

"Hang in there," he added. "We should keep moving. The more distance we can put between them and us, the better." He trudged forward.

She followed behind. Her mind was still on the water. If she could only have a drink. "How much farther to the road?" She stared at Nathan's back. He didn't turn around or answer her. "You don't know where we are, do you?"

He kept walking. A sense of hopelessness crowded into her thoughts. She had no feeling in her leg from the calf down. She was unbearably thirsty. They were lost, and it was only matter of time before the thieves caught up with them.

Merci crumpled down into the snow.

Nathan stopped and rushed toward her.

"I can't keep going." Tears formed.

"Sure you can." He pulled his gloves off and touched her cheek. "Come on, I'll help you up."

"You don't even know how far it is to the road." More than anything, she just wanted to lie down and sleep.

"Everything is covered in snow, and the way we left the ski hill was rather haphazard. Something will look familiar sooner or later." Nathan's voice was soft and undemanding. He kneeled beside her. "Who was it that told me we couldn't lose hope?"

The look of assurance in Nathan's expression renewed her strength. She managed a smile. "Talk about my words coming back to bite me, huh?"

"Come on, I'll help you walk," he said.

She wrapped her arm around his shoulder and leaned against him. "Am I going to lose my leg? There's no feeling left in it."

"I don't know. We need to get to a place where I can have a look at it." An undercurrent of worry colored his voice. Was there something he wasn't telling her? He of all people must understand about the effects of exposure to freezing water.

As they came out into an open area, the wind picked

up, forcing them to bend and stare at the ground as they walked. Merci pushed her knit hat farther down on her head so it covered more of her ears and neck. She'd lost the hat liner Nathan had given her somewhere along the way. When she tilted her head toward the sky, the charcoal clouds toppled what little optimism she had left. Not another storm.

Their feet sunk into the deep snow.

"We need to get near some trees for shelter." Nathan had to raise his voice to be heard above the wind.

Merci lifted her head to look around. A flash of orange in a sea of white caught her eye. It took her a moment to process the incongruity of what was seeing. "That's my sweater."

"What?"

"My sweater from my suitcase." She ran toward the orange object. The deep snow slowed her down. She stopped and stared down at the sweater with the large buttons half buried in the snow.

Nathan came up beside her. "For a moment, I thought you were so far gone you were hallucinating."

With a little effort she yanked the sweater out of the snow. "It must mean we're close to Lorelei's car." She glanced side to side but only an endless field of snow surrounded her.

"It could have gotten blown around during the storm." Nathan turned in a half circle.

"It couldn't blow too far, especially uphill. This is the first sign that we are close."

Nathan pressed his lips together and continued to study the landscape. "I say we keep heading downhill. Maybe cut toward those trees."

Merci agreed. They walked together, arms wrapped around each other. Nathan hadn't complained about the deep knife wound, but every once in a while she saw him wince with pain. They were both in rough shape.

Though it was no longer wearable, she held on to the sweater. Glancing down at it in her hand helped her to remain positive. They had to be close. They just had to be.

They edged closer to the trees, which blocked out most of the wind.

Nathan stopped and pointed at a purple-and-orange scarf hanging off a tree branch in front of them. "Look there."

"That's mine." Merci raced down the hill yelling over her shoulder. "Hurry, Nathan. We're close. I just know we are."

She ran so fast she tumbled and rolled in the snow. The fall did nothing to deflate her spirits. The road and the car were close. She could feel it. Merci pushed herself to her feet, scanning the field of snow for any dark object. She found a blouse half buried in the snow.

Nathan came up to her. "I know where we are at now." He turned and pointed behind them. "That ridge-line is where I was riding the snowmobile the day I saw you and Lorelei."

"That feels like a million years ago." She was a different person from the naive college student who had left Montana State almost three days ago.

"Feels like that, doesn't it?" His voice grew serious. Nathan looked up the mountain. "My guess is that we need to move west."

They trudged forward with renewed energy, encountering a few more objects that had been in her suitcase. The car, nearly covered in snow, came into view when they rounded a curve in the road.

Merci burst forth, but Nathan grabbed her arm. "Wait just a minute. We got ambushed with that helicopter; let's make sure they haven't beaten us here."

Nathan put his arm out to bar Merci from taking another step. He needed to make sure it was safe. "I'll go first. You wait here behind these trees. Wait until I give you the all-clear."

Nathan stepped out into the open and approached the car. He didn't see any signs of life. The footprints around the car looked old and drifted over. The trunk was wide open and shoes, books and smaller bags were strewn up the hill.

A foot of snow covered the car, and there was no sign of it having been brushed off anywhere. When he looked behind him, Merci peeked around the trees. He waved for her to come out. She ran toward him favoring her left leg, but slowed as she drew near. Her expression changed when her gaze darted around at the items that had been dragged out of the car and strung all over. Her features clouded and her shoulders drooped.

"Are you okay?"

Her gloved hand fluttered to her chest. "This is all my stuff. They went through everything I brought with me."

Nathan brushed away snow from the driver's-side door and clicked the door open. "Why don't we get in here, get warmed up, and I can have a look at your leg."

Merci ran to pick up a book and then a knitted scarf and a pair of jeans. Nathan brushed more snow off the car so they could see out the front windshield. When he looked up, Merci had gathered an armload of possessions. Her demeanor had changed. The way she bent her head and the redness in her face suggested that she was upset.

"Merci." He called over the hood of the car.

She stopped and dropped the items she had gathered onto the snowy ground. "These are my private things. They went through my whole suitcase, everything that matters to me."

He circled around the car and grabbed her hands. "We don't need to do all that. Let's get in the car. We need to get your leg thawed out."

She pulled free of his grasp and pointed to her suitcase. "They tore that to pieces. Why?"

"Merci, this is upsetting you. Once we're warmed up, we can hike out to the highway. Someone will pick us up." He brushed away the snow on the passenger side and ushered her in before getting in on the driver's side.

Once she was settled in the passenger seat, Merci pulled her boot off and untwisted the makeshift sock. "I think the wool helped a lot. The feeling is starting to come back into my toes."

Nathan looked down at her bare toes, which were so white it looked as if the blood had been drained out of them. "You've got some frostbite damage, but at least the toes aren't blue and frozen through. They'd amputate then."

She leaned back and stared at the ceiling. "That's one good thing, I guess."

He grabbed a sweater from the backseat. "Pull up

your pant leg a bit and wrap this around it. Do you have another pair of boots and socks around here?"

"I don't know." Her voice held a tone of sadness. "If the thieves didn't scatter them up the hill, there might be a pair back there."

After wrapping the sweater around Merci's leg, Nathan turned his attention to the car. The keys were still in the ignition. Driving out wasn't a possibility though with the roads still unplowed. Nathan tilted his head sideways to look at the wires underneath the dashboard. "I think I see how Lorelei made it look like the car wasn't running. It would be nothing to disconnect this ignition wire while you weren't looking."

"So their plan must have been to drive me to this isolated place, rob me and then…leave me here." Her voice held a distant quality as if she was trying to process what all of this meant.

Nathan looked into her sad green eyes. Sympathy flooded through him. She was dealing with so much all at once. He shook his head. "Remember, they said that things went wrong. The guy in the Orange Coat wasn't supposed to pull the gun. They were probably going to take what they wanted, and you and Lorelei would go down the road not even realizing you'd been robbed."

"And then I would never know Lorelei had set me up." Merci turned away and stared straight ahead through the small hole he had cleared in the windshield. After a long silence, she said, "They didn't touch Lorelei's stuff. I guess that seals the deal that she was in on this."

"Don't beat yourself up over this. She was a pretty good actress." He patted her shoulder.

She turned toward him and fell against his chest. "I can be so stupid sometimes. You know when those guys pulled up in their car, I had a bad feeling then, but I totally brushed it off thinking I was just being prejudiced because of the way they looked." The wavering in her voice told him that she was crying.

He drew her closer and held her while she cried. His lips brushed over the top of her head. As her sobbing subsided, he said, "It's so hard to know when to trust and when not to."

She pulled away from him and rummaged through the glove compartment for a travel-size bag of tissues. "Lorelei offering me a ride was a setup to get me out here." She combed her fingers through her long red hair. "They probably had something to do with my car breaking down, too. Now that I think about it, the timing was weird that she showed up right when I was checking out the *Share a Ride* board."

Nathan glanced in the backseat searching for a pair of boots. A laptop case rested beside an overnight bag. He reached over and grabbed the case. The weight of it told him that the computer was inside. "What kind of thieves leave a laptop behind?"

"I don't know." Merci's gaze was unfocused, and her voice still held a disconnected quality.

Something didn't fit with the whole robbery. Hawthorne had done a great deal of planning and utilized a lot of manpower for what would maybe be a thousand dollars worth of possessions, and then he didn't take the laptop. If the original plan had been for Lorelei to continue the ruse and take Merci to her aunt's, the thieves wouldn't have intended on taking anything that would be noticed as missing right away. Nathan nodded as a realization came to him. "I think they were looking for something in particular. Do you have any idea what that might be?"

She turned toward him, the glazed look in her eyes clearing up. "No. I can't think of what I brought with me that would be of enough value to go to all this trouble. But it does explain why they sent Lorelei into that room to pump me for information."

"Think about the week before you left. You said your car broke down. Did anything else weird happen?

"Someone slipped into my dorm room and stole some books." She leaned her head against the backrest and stared at the ceiling. "The break-in was a really freaky experience. I was sleeping, and I thought I heard someone in my room. But the next morning, I thought I had just dreamed it until I couldn't find my textbooks. I just figured it was someone selling them back to the bookstore for quick cash."

"Had Lorelei been friendly to you before?"

Merci sat up a little straighter in her chair. "She always seemed like a nice person. She sat beside me quite a bit last year when we had that marketing class together. We said hi when we saw each other, but we didn't do things together."

"Did you ever see Hawthorne with Lorelei?"

"No, I would have remembered that," she said.

"Tell me again everything that happened that week before you left or anything that was out of the ordinary even before that."

Merci bit her lower lip. "I failed chemistry, my car wouldn't start, I got a package from my dad and a letter saying they wouldn't be back in the States for the holidays, I called Aunt Celeste, I went to that all-dorm garage sale and bought too many things because I was so stressed out."

Nathan reached over and touched the earrings he had admired earlier. "Maybe these are worth more than you thought. What if Lorelei accidently put something in the garage sale she wasn't supposed to or her roommate did? Maybe it was something that belonged to Hawthorne, that she was supposed to keep safe."

The exuberance returned to Merci's demeanor. "Lorelei was there at the garage sale. I remember talking to her. She came up to me and started the conversation. Maybe it was something she saw me buy and realized the value of it."

"What exactly did you buy at that sale?"

"I went a little crazy and bought so many items. I don't know if I can remember all of it. These buttons on this coat for instance. They're antique buttons. I sewed them on right before I left. I can't imagine someone going to all this trouble though to get these button or the earrings," she said.

"What else did you buy?"

Merci let out her breath and stared at the ceiling of the car. "Some clothes. I really hadn't sorted through everything before I left. Maybe there was a box or some kind of container that had something of value in it."

"Maybe the thieves searched your dorm and didn't find it. They took the books for some quick cash. Because they couldn't find what they were looking for in the dorm, they must have thought you had it with you," Nathan added. "The thief was just going to look through your suitcase, grab what he wanted and they would have gone on their merry way."

"That makes sense. The guy in the leather jacket was in the backseat going through my stuff, too. Lorelei's job was probably to make sure I stayed in the car and didn't see what they were doing, but she got distracted by listening to music."

She looked down at the large crystal-like buttons. "Maybe they didn't notice I had already sown these on my coat."

"Maybe," Nathan said. "Can you think of what else it might have been?"

Merci shook her head. "Most of what I own is secondhand."

Nathan perked up. "Did you hear that?"

She listened, then shook her head.

He turned around to look out the back window, but couldn't see anything. "It sounds like an engine or something?"

Merci turned toward the side window and then twisted around to face Nathan. Her voice filled with fear. "Oh, no, they found a way to make it down here with the groomer."

Nathan's heart raced. "Let's get out of the car. They'll figure out we're in here. Stay low. I'm not sure what direction the sound is coming from."

FIFTEEN

Nathan crawled out of the driver's side and crouched down. Merci joined him a moment later. She'd placed an ankle boot from the backseat on her bare foot. He peered over the top of the car expecting to see the trail groomer headed down the mountain toward them.

Merci said, "See anything?"

A distant rumble penetrated through the wind, but he still couldn't see the source of the noise.

"There," Merci pointed up the road. A set of headlights cut through the blowing snow. She cringed and pressed closer to him.

Nathan stood up. Was he seeing right? The vehicle coming up the road wasn't a trail groomer. He swallowed as his heart skipped a beat. "Merci, I think that's the snow plow."

Merci rose up and stood beside him. She let out a joyful gasp. "Are you sure?"

They waited, paralyzed by anticipation, as the vehicle drew closer. Nathan planted his feet, but he was prepared to run and take Merci with him if he had to, if this turned out to be just another ambush. At this distance and with snow whirling around the vehicle, he couldn't distinguish anything but the plow and the headlights. Then the machine turned slightly to push the snow that had accumulated in the bucket off the side of the road.

Elation surged through him and he hugged Merci. "It's them. They've made it."

Merci bounced up and down and started waving.

Even as the driver put the huge machine in idle and jumped out of the cab, Nathan half expected to see one of the thieves. They had been pursued so relentlessly that he couldn't imagine being in a safe place where the thieves couldn't get at them.

He breathed a sigh of relief when the plow driver removed his hat revealing a head of salt-and-pepper hair. They ran out to meet him.

Nathan recognized the man. "Joe, you have no idea how glad we are to see you."

"Nathan, good to see you." Joe sauntered toward them. "Deputy Miller has been looking for you. Where is the other girl?"

Miller must have informed the whole town when he didn't show up at the police station.

"It's a long story," said Merci.

"I don't have room in the cab for you, but I can radio out, and we can get a vehicle to come from the direction I've already plowed."

Nathan didn't like the idea of having to wait around too long with the thieves' whereabouts still unknown. "How long is that going to take?"

"We've got a truck out on the highway that can be here in twenty minutes," Joe said.

Nathan glanced up the mountain. "Tell them we'll be waiting in the car."

Joe nodded and returned to his plow. Through the window of the cab, they saw him pick up the radio. A moment later, he gave them the thumbs up.

They stood to one side as the plow pushed snow off the road, swerving around Lorelei's car. They watched the plow until it disappeared around a corner. "We got a little bit of a wait. Why don't we try to stay warm?" Nathan brushed more snow off the back window so they would have a clear view of the rescue vehicle coming up the road without getting out of the car. The blowing snow had reduced visibility by quite a bit, but they should be able to spot the headlights with time enough to jump out of the car.

As he opened the driver's-side door, Nathan glanced one more time up the mountain. He could see even less than before.

"I wonder what happened to them." Merci climbed in the backseat to retrieve the other boot and a pair of socks.

Had the cold and hunger finally become too much for them. Had they returned to the ski hill and hurt Elle and Henry? Or had they simply lost their way down the mountain and come out at a different spot?

The minutes ticked by. He caught Merci glancing up the mountain and down the road almost as often as he did. He half expected to see the trail groomer charging toward them or hear gunshots shattering the windows.

Nathan struggled to come up with something to say to break the tension. "Maybe you should have those antique buttons appraised. They might be worth more than you think."

Merci fingered the buttons. "I guess. I just wish I knew what they were looking for." Merci shook her head as a tightness came into her features. This wasn't easy for her.

Nathan placed his hand over hers. "It still bothers you what Lorelei did?"

"I just hate being the chump all the time. And I hate that my father might be right. He says that I am too trusting to ever succeed as a businessperson. My father can be kind of ruthless in his business deals, but he's really successful. I didn't major in business to be like him. I chose that career path to be different from him. I think that managing or owning a business should be about people, not about making money at any cost."

"I don't think what happened with Lorelei is any indication of how you'll do as a manager," Nathan said. "Sometimes when you give people a chance even if you have doubts, they blossom."

"I suppose you're right." When she looked at him, the gratitude he saw in her eyes sent a charge of electrified warmth through him.

Merci turned and looked out the back window. "He's here."

They jumped out, bending forward to cut through the blowing snow. The driver left his headlights on, opened his door and walked toward them.

The big ear flaps of his furry hat covered most of his face. He leaned close and spoke to them in a loud voice. "Hop in and we'll get this thing turned around."

Once they settled inside the warm cab of the truck,

the driver removed his hat, revealing a mop of coppery hair. "I'm sure you folks are glad to be getting off this mountain."

"You have no idea," said Nathan. He glanced over at Merci whose green eyes communicated a sense of relief. "We should probably go to the police station and give a description of those men."

The sensation had come back into her frozen foot. At least that wasn't a worry anymore. "I'm dying for a hot meal and shower, but you're right, that should be our priority." She turned to face the driver. "As soon as we have cell service, can I borrow your phone? I need to call my aunt. I'm sure she's worried sick."

The driver nodded.

"Guess I can take a bus to Aunt Celeste's house after we're all done with the police." She bent her head and gazed at Nathan.

His heart fluttered when she looked at him that way. Then, an unexpected sadness descended on him as she offered him a smile. After they talked to the police, they would have no reason to stay together. They had been through so much in such a short time, he felt as if he knew her better than he'd known any woman. He admired her strength and her optimism. And the memory of his impulsive kiss still lingered, but would she ever want to see him again under less trying circumstances?

The ride down the mountain was a white-knuckle affair even with the roads plowed. The truck jostled from side to side and slid on the road. They passed by the thieves' car where it had blocked the mountain road. The snow plow had pushed it out of the way and buried it even deeper. No way could the thieves use it for their escape.

When they were at the base of the mountain, the driver checked his cell phone. "Still no good."

Merci folded her hands in her lap. "I can call from the police station."

"That sounds like a plan." Nathan shuddered and drew his hand up to his shoulder where he'd been cut.

"Actually, could you take us to the hospital first?" She patted Nathan's hand. "I think you should have that knife wound looked at."

"I'll be all right." Even as he spoke the pain had returned.

"I don't mind stopping there." The driver glanced over at Nathan. "I'd be glad to wait while you go in."

"Please, Nathan, at the very least, they can give you something for the pain."

He didn't like the idea of the thieves having an opportunity to get away. "I still think we should go to the police station first."

Merci rolled her eyes at Nathan's objections. Why was he being so stubborn? What a guy thing to do. "You can't talk to the police if you pass out from the pain," Merci insisted.

"I'm not going to pass out from the pain." He sucked in a ragged breath and turned his head, probably trying to hide how much he was hurting.

Guilt washed through her for having pushed so hard. She softened her tone and rested her hand on his arm. "I'm just really worried about that cut. I can tell it's hurting you again. Maybe the wound got reopened."

He pulled away his coat. His shirt was already so bloodstained it was hard to tell if it was bleeding again. "Okay, for you, I'll stop and have it looked at. But you've got to let them check out your foot and fingers, too."

"Okay, I will…for you." She was pretty sure her foot would be okay, but whatever got him to the hospital.

A spark passed between them when she met his gaze. They had traveled a thousand miles emotionally in less than three days, faced death over and over and gone from being strangers to being two people who could depend on each other. What would they be to each other now that they were in a safe place?

As they drew nearer to town, Nathan said to the driver, "You can just take us around to the emergency room. I know everyone there. They'll get us looked at quickly."

The driver dropped them off in front of the emergency room doors. "I'll just be waiting over there in the parking lot. Take as much time as you need."

Nathan grabbed Merci's hand as they walked toward the emergency room. Nurses, doctors and EMTs cheered and clapped when Nathan stepped through the door.

A slender blond man in a paramedic uniform rushed up to Nathan and slapped his back. "You made it out alive. My church group started praying for you the moment we figured out you were trapped on that mountain."

"Thanks, Eddy. You have no idea what that means to me." The tremble in his voice suggested that Nathan was genuinely moved by the gesture.

Eddy turned toward Merci. "Is this one of the ladies you rescued?"

The deputy Nathan had talked to must have informed the whole town about what had happened before the storm hit.

"Actually, we kind of rescued each other a couple of times." A warm glow came over Nathan when he looked at Merci. "This is Merci Carson. She's got some toes and fingers with frostbite, and I've got a bad cut that needs looking after."

Nathan was ushered into an exam room, and a nurse led Merci to the room beside his. Petite and with her brown hair pulled back in a ponytail, the nurse was about Nathan's age.

"So you've got some frostbite?"

"It doesn't feel numb anymore." Merci sat down in a chair and pulled off her boot. "My fingers were exposed, too."

The nurse cradled her toes in her hand. "Definitely did some damage there."

"Not too bad I hope," Merci said. "Nathan said it looked like just the surface skin got frostbitten."

"He's probably right. Doesn't look like deep tissue damage. The doctor will have to have a look. I don't think you will lose the toes or anything. I'm Beth by the way. I went to high school with Nathan." She scooted back in her chair and looked right at Merci. "We dated for a while."

"Oh." Merci wasn't sure how to respond to the information. Was Beth just being friendly or had her comment been to let Merci know Nathan was off-limits?

Beth smiled as she examined Merci's fingers. "We're

just friends now. I'm pretty serious with the guy that owns the hardware store downtown."

An unexpected sense of relief rushed through Merci. She must really care about Nathan if even the slight indication that he was dating someone else sent a twinge of panic through her.

"I just brought it up because I have known Nathan most of my life. He's had some relationships in the past, and I've never seen him look at a woman the way he looked at you when he came in here."

"I think I like him, too." Merci placed her hand on her heart. "I hope it's not just because we were in such a life-or-death situation."

Beth sat in the chair opposite Merci. "That's true. I've seen it before. Sometimes a relationship can't be sustained when life becomes ordinary again."

The suggestion was like a blow to Merci's stomach. What was she to Nathan now that their lives didn't depend on staying together? "That's something to consider." Doubts tumbled through her head even as the memory of his kiss made her feel warm all over again.

Beth rose to her feet. "The doctor will swing by in just a minute. I'm glad to have met you."

After the doctor gave her the same diagnosis Beth had, Merci slipped her boot back on and stepped into the reception area. Nathan's face brightened when he saw her.

Beth's words echoed in her head. She liked Nathan. But was it an attraction nurtured by extreme circumstances?

She walked toward him. "Did you get a clean bill of health?"

"I got some painkillers and pills to keep it from getting infected. The doctor was impressed with your dressing." Nathan offered her a crooked smile.

"Maybe I have a future as a nurse," Merci joked.

"I don't know if I could have made it off that mountain if I had had to deal with an open and bleeding wound alone." His expression grew serious. "You saved my life."

She searched his deep brown eyes. "I was only returning the favor." The look in his eyes was like a magnet. She stepped toward him and tilted her head.

Who are we to each other now that we are safe?

Though it was foremost in her mind, she couldn't bring herself to voice the question. As he leaned toward her, she stepped free of the force field of attraction.

He dropped his gaze to the floor. "Guess we better get to the police station."

They walked back to the truck where the driver was waiting. As they drove through town, she dreaded having to relive their encounters with the thieves, but it had to be done. The sooner these guys were in jail, the safer she would feel.

SIXTEEN

The driver dropped them off in front of the police station. The high walls of dirty snow that surrounded the lot revealed that almost as much snow had fallen in town as on the mountain.

Deputy Travis Miller came out to greet them as they were climbing out of the truck.

"Man, am I glad to see you." He offered Nathan a big bear hug.

"Right, who would you have to beat at racquetball if I wasn't around?" Nathan joked, but a sense of gratitude toward God for getting them out alive rushed through him as he hugged his friend. Everything seemed more precious to him. His throat tightened. He loved his life here. He loved the people. Though he still didn't know what he was going to do with the mountain acreage, facing death had clarified what really mattered to him.

Deputy Miller looked at Merci and then back at Nathan. "Where's the other girl you told me about when you phoned in?"

"Long story," said Merci.

"We now think she was involved, and the robbery wasn't random," said Nathan.

"Let's get some descriptions of these guys you had a close encounter with." The deputy led them into a small office that had three cubicles. Nathan recognized Officer Amy Fernandez sitting at her computer. She offered him a tiny wave.

"We've got a computer program that will help us put together a sketch." Travis offered Merci a chair by Officer Fernandez. "Amy, you want to help Merci get started on that? Nathan, we have to take your statements separately if you want to come this way."

Nathan nodded. As Travis led him into a separate room, he glanced over his shoulder. Merci looked so vulnerable as she sat down in the chair beside Officer Fernandez. It wasn't going to be easy for her to relive the past days. He would prefer that she not have to do it alone. He longed to sit beside her, to be a support to her.

She looked up at him with wide, fear-filled eyes as Travis ushered him into an interview room and closed the door.

Officer Fernandez tugged on her long dark pony tail and scooted her chair toward the computer. "All right, Miss Carson. This computer program isn't as good as a police artist, but it at least gives us some basic idea of what the perpetrators look like." She turned the monitor so Merci could see the oval head shape on the screen.

Merci took in a deep breath. "I know it's important to deal with all this, but can I call my aunt first? I was supposed to be at her house days ago. I'm sure she's worried sick."

Officer Fernandez's features softened, and her voice held a note of compassion. "Sure, I understand." She picked up the phone and handed it to Merci. "I'll give you some privacy." She squeezed Merci's shoulder as a sign of support, rose from her chair and disappeared into a back room.

Merci stared at the phone panel for a long moment before dialing in the number. The phone rang twice.

"Hello?"

Her aunt's bell-like voice sent a measure of joy and relief through her. Merci's eyes grew moist. "You have no idea how good it is to hear your voice."

"Oh, Baby Girl." Only Aunt Celeste called her that. "I saw the news of the storm on the television and knew you must have been delayed, but when I didn't hear from you, I got so worried. What on earth happened?"

"I'm okay now." She couldn't keep the tremble out of her voice. "I don't want to talk to you about what happened over the phone."

"Oh, my, this sounds serious. It might require a double dose of hot chocolate and peanut butter cookies." Even over the phone, her aunt's voice soothed her frayed nerves. "When can you get here, dear?"

The warmth in her aunt's voice made her tear up all over again. "I'll call you when I know the bus schedule." She pressed the phone harder against her ear. "I can't wait to see you."

"You know how I feel about you. When I couldn't reach you by phone, I prayed and I just felt a peace that you were going to be okay."

"Thanks, Aunt Celeste. Can you call Dad and Mom and let them know that I'm okay? I just can't right now."

"Sure honey. And you call me as soon as you know when you will be here. I can't wait to see you."

"I can't wait to get there." She put the phone back in the cradle and wiped her eyes.

Officer Hernandez emerged from the room a few minutes later. "Everything go okay?"

Merci nodded. "I suppose we should get started."

Hernandez walked back to the desk and resumed her place by the computer. "Travis said there were two men who tried to rob you?"

"Actually, there were three men...and a woman." A pang shot through Merci's stomach. "Her name was Lorelei Frank. She's a student at Montana State. I think that she befriended me so she could lure me out to a place where they could stage the robbery. She's probably the girlfriend of the one who planned this whole thing, the one they called Hawthorne." Merci took in a quick breath. Her racing heart and sweaty palms didn't make any sense to her. She was in a police station. She was safe. What did she have to be afraid of? "It's all kind of complicated and confusing."

Amy nodded. "I'm sure it will make sense to me by the time we are done talking. Why don't we start with the physical description? This guy they called Hawthorne, he's the one who you think was the leader. Why don't you tell me what he looks like?" Hernandez typed on the keyboard. "Take this one step at a time. Let's start with the shape of his face."

Hawthorne's threat to kill her and Nathan because they could link him to the crime remained prominent in her memory. Her thoughts stalled as old fears rose to the surface.

Hernandez leaned close. Her voice filled with concern. "I know this isn't easy."

Merci cleared her throat. "But it has to be done. I know that." She stared at the computer and tried to recall what Hawthorne had looked like.

"This face shape is just a default setting." Amy coaxed, her voice gentle and undemanding. "We can change it any way you like."

She'd seen him so briefly, yet his face was etched in her mind. "His jaw line was more square, I think. He had what some people would call a lantern jaw."

Officer Fernandez clicked through different choices on eyes, nose and lips until a complete face emerged. Merci felt a prickling at the back of her neck. Why couldn't she let go of this fear?

"Now tell me about his hair," Fernandez said.

"It was blond, almost white, short and curly."

Amy clicked on her keyboard. "Is that him? Is that what he looked like?"

With the final touch of the hair in place, Merci stared at the picture in front of her. She nodded as a realization matured inside her head. They'd been running so fast, just trying to stay alive. She hadn't really had a chance to think about who this man might be. "I think I have seen him somewhere before."

Officer Hernandez swiveled in her chair to face Merci, her eyes growing wide with anticipation. "You know him."

Merci shook her head. "Just seen him. He's not an acquaintance or someone I have frequent interaction with. I may have seen him once before." She probed her memory. "I think somewhere on campus." She shook her head. "I'm just not sure. I can't place him."

Amy studied the picture. "Hawthorne is a pretty common name. It could be a nickname, too."

"I hadn't thought of that." While Merci tried to remember where she had seen Hawthorne, Amy guided her through the description of the other two men and of Lorelei and then asked her for details about everything that had happened. Merci kept her emotions at bay until she talked about seeing the helicopter and then discovering that the thieves had hijacked it. "Do you know what happened to the helicopter pilot who was looking for us?"

Fernandez's gaze dropped to the floor. "We lost contact with him."

"That means he is most likely..." She couldn't bring herself to say the word.

"The last I heard, they hadn't been able to get far enough up the mountain to the site of the crash."

"There was an older man and woman staying at the ski hill, Elle and Henry. Have you heard anything from them?"

Amy shook her head. "The plows just haven't gotten up that far yet."

Amy must have seen the anxiety in her expression. She reached over and covered Merci's hand with her own. Her soft voice filled with compassion. "One thing to keep in mind. If we can't get up that mountain, then the thieves are going to have a heck of a time getting out. It was amazing that you and Nathan made it as far as you did."

"You think the chances of catching them are pretty good?" Merci asked.

Amy nodded and pointed at the computer screen where Hawthorne's face was still up. "Even if they get off the mountain, chances are they are going to come into town or at Derlin on the other side of the country road. We'll send these sketches out within an hour. All law enforcement in the area will be looking for them. They won't get far."

The news was reassuring. She wondered, though, if small-town law enforcement was ready to deal with the kind of cunning and tenacity she had witnessed with these thieves. "They've got no qualms about using extreme violence."

"You said this guy Hawthorne wanted to kill you because you could identify him. Maybe now that we have a description of him, he'll go into hiding," Amy suggested.

Merci pulled some lint off her sweater, a nervous habit. Officer Hernandez hadn't heard the venom in Hawthorne's voice when he made the threat. "I think he would want to make sure neither Nathan or I made it to testify against him and then he would go into hiding. He wouldn't do the killing himself. He would just hire someone."

The interview room door opened, and Nathan stepped out.

Deputy Miller said, "I think we are all done with Nathan's statement."

Hernandez swiveled in her chair. "Mr. McCormick, if you want to look at these computer sketches, we'll be finished. I have Ms. Carson's statement."

Nathan walked over to the computer, nodding in approval of each sketch and offering suggestions for minor changes.

The door of the police station opened, and a tall man with sandy-colored hair stepped in. Nathan lifted his head. His jaw went slack and his head jerked back. Merci couldn't quite read his expression, but she thought she saw pain behind his eyes. "Daniel."

The tall man removed his hat and shifted it from one hand to the other. "Hey Nathan, Travis called me. I heard your truck was out of commission. I thought you could use a ride home."

Nathan nodded. "Guess I don't have any choice." He turned to face Merci. "You can come with me if you want. We can feed you and you can get cleaned up before you head down the road."

His words stung in an unexpected way. Of course, the next step was for her to get on a bus, to finish the journey she had started. But that meant she would probably not see Nathan again. She was looking forward to her visit with Aunt Celeste. Being with her in that safe cozy house would go a long way in helping her get over the trauma of the past few days, but all of that meant parting ways with Nathan.

Daniel nodded. "We'll go to the Wilson Street house. Everything in your refrigerator is probably green by now. My car is just outside."

The tension between the two brothers was almost palpable as they walked outside and headed toward Daniel's older-model car.

Nathan opened the passenger-side door. "You can sit up front, Merci. I'll take the backseat."

Daniel's head jerked up from the driver's-side door, and he peered over the top of the car. He shot Nathan a pain-filled look, but said nothing. They drove across town. The clacking noise of the engine seemed to indicate that the car was headed toward some kind of breakdown.

Though the brothers had looked to be close in age in the photo she had seen at the cabin, time had not been kind to Daniel. Intense worry lines and a hardness in his eyes made him look ten years older than Nathan.

Daniel looked over at Merci. "Sorry for the noisy engine. It's all I can afford right now. It actually runs pretty good, just needs a tune-up."

Daniel parked in front of a redbrick house framed by two barren weeping willow trees. They got out of the car and made their way up the sidewalk.

Daniel stuck the key in the lock and then turned to face his brother. "I was worried about you." He patted Nathan's shoulder.

"I can take care of myself. You know that." The smile Nathan gave Daniel didn't quite reach his eyes. His words weren't hostile, but filled with an undercurrent of sadness.

They stepped into a cozy living room done in rich burgundy and shades of green and gold.

Daniel pointed toward a door. "I'll get started with dinner if you two want to get cleaned up."

Merci wandered into the living room. More family photos decorated the walls. Nothing about the room said bachelor pad. "Is this your mom and dad's house?"

Nathan nodded.

"But your brother called it the Wilson Street house."

"We started referring to it that way sometime after Dad's funeral. Guess it's just less painful than calling it Mom and Dad's place."

Merci studied the photos that chronicled a happy family. "Your brother lives here, but you don't?"

"I have my own place across town." Nathan turned slightly away from her so she saw him in profile. "Daniel has lived here since he got out of his inpatient addiction treatment program."

"So has he gotten some help for his problem?" Merci moved around the large living room so she could made eye contact with Nathan. Something in his posture and the tilt of his head suggested vulnerability. It hadn't been easy for him to share that bit of information. "Is that what the tension and lack of communication between the two of you is about?"

"I'm sorry you have to be in the middle of this. Daniel developed a gambling problem when he was a teenager."

"But he's better now?"

Nathan's forehead furled, and his voice filled with anguish. "I want to believe that. But I've lived through too many relapses." He turned toward the kitchen door and let out a heavy breath. "I think Mom and Dad dying was the deepest rock bottom he's ever experienced. Mom was sick for a long time with complications from diabetes. After she died, my father's heart just gave out. He does seem different this time, but I just have no way of knowing."

Merci chose her words carefully, aware of how hard it was for Nathan to talk about Daniel. "Is your brother the reason you are selling the resort and the camp?"

"We inherited equal shares. Maybe my dad thought we would work through unresolved issues by running the ski hill and the camp together. I know Dad wanted to keep the acreage in the family."

Merci sat down on the plush couch. "But gambling usually involves people going through a lot of money."

Nathan took a chair opposite her. "If I go on his track record, Daniel's just not a trustworthy business partner. If he relapses, he might steal from the business. I could wind up with unbelievable debt. Mom and Dad worked so hard to run a business with a solid reputation. All that could be destroyed." He rested his head in his hands. "I don't know what to do. I wish I could trust him."

She hated seeing him so tortured by such a hard decision. "There are no clear answers, are there? I think if I were in your place, I would pray for days and days."

"I have been." He laced his fingers together and rested his elbows on his knees. "I like my job as a paramedic. It would be easier to sell the place and use the money for retirement, maybe set up some kind of scholarship program for the camp. It's never been about the money. It would break my heart, though, to see the businesses my parents poured their lives into fall apart and have a bad reputation because of my brother's destructive choices."

Merci leaned forward and covered Nathan's hand with her own. "I'm probably the last person to dole out advice on when to trust people. But I can see how much you love the property…especially the camp."

Nathan's brow creased as he drew his mouth into a hard line. "Nobody likes to admit that they can't trust their brother. I want it to be like it was when we were kids."

The door that led to the kitchen swung open, and Daniel poked his head out. "I got about twenty minutes left on this stir-fry."

"Thanks, Daniel." Nathan rose to his feet and offered his brother a weak smile. He waited until the door closed again. Anguish hardened his features. He turned to face Merci when she stood up. "I know he is trying really hard. I want to think the best of him." He shook his head as his voice faltered. "But he's broken promises, he's been through treatment twice before, he stole from Mom and Dad, and from me, from his friends, all to feed his habit."

Merci thought her own heart would break over the hurt Nathan was going through. She rushed over and hugged him. "I understand why it would be hard to believe he has truly changed for good. I don't have any great wisdom on what you should do." She pulled away, placed her hand on his cheek and looked up into his eyes. "I just hate to see you so torn up like this."

He took her in his arms and held her for a long moment, nestling his face against her neck. She closed her eyes and prayed that in some small way, she could ease some of his pain. He turned his head and pressed his mouth over hers. She welcomed the kiss. He pulled her closer by resting his hand on the middle of her back.

A clattering of pots and pans in the kitchen caused them to pull away from each other.

Merci giggled. "I don't know why I did that. We're not fifteen. It's okay if your brother sees us kissing."

He let out a single laugh but his eyes held no joviality. She searched his deep brown eyes.

Was that a goodbye kiss?

He turned away as though he didn't want her to see the emotion that his expression would give away. "We should probably get cleaned up. There's a downstairs bathroom with fresh towels if you want to use that."

She pointed toward the computer she had noticed earlier. "Actually, I think I would like to check bus departure times first."

"Be my guest." He still hadn't looked directly at her. Did he fear he would fall apart if he made eye contact with her?

How was it possible that two people who had been through so much could just walk away from each other like this?

She sat down at the computer and pushed the power button. The phone in the entryway rang. Nathan excused himself and left to answer it.

She waited for the computer to fire up. The gentle tenor of Nathan's voice landed on her ears when he answered the phone. As she typed in the name of a bus line she knew had routes in the Northwest, she thought her heart would burst into a million pieces.

SEVENTEEN

Nathan picked up the phone and uttered a greeting. His mind was still on Merci and the lingering power of her kiss. He peered around the corner at her. Her long hair fell over her face as she leaned over the keyboard. *You can't tell someone you have only known less than three days that you love them. That would be crazy.* Yet when he pictured dropping her off at the bus station and never seeing her again, the image was like a knife through his heart.

"Nathan," said a man on the other end of the line.

Deputy Travis Miller's voice jerked him out of his musing about Merci. Nathan pressed the phone harder against his ear. "Did you locate the thieves?"

"No, but we got a hit on two of your thugs almost right away. Lots of small-time stuff, petty thievery and assault. Both of them are from a town not far from the college where Merci goes. Local law enforcement there recognized their pictures when we sent out the alert. Now we got names to go with the faces."

"That's a good start." A knot of tension formed in his lower back. Though he knew the authorities were stretched thin and doing everything they could, he had hoped for news of a capture.

Deputy Miller continued. "Your ringleader Hawthorne must have found them there. Both of them had a thousand dollars deposited in their accounts three days ago."

The thugs were probably feeling a bit underpaid, considering all that they had gone through. "Nothing on Hawthorne, though?"

"No, the guy certainly isn't known to law enforcement like the other two," Deputy Miller said. "Lorelei Frank is exactly who she said she was. She's registered as a senior at Montana State. She's lived there for four years. No priors on her."

Nathan pivoted so he could see Merci sitting in the computer chair. "So they are all still at large."

"Look, we are going to get these guys. I promise you. And I have a bit of good news you can pass onto your friend Merci."

"What's that?"

Travis said, "She was worried about that older couple that got stranded in one of your cabins."

"Elle and Henry are okay?" Nathan couldn't hide his elation.

"They were pretty delighted when the plows made it that far up. They are resting up at a bed-and-breakfast and have some good stories to tell."

"I'm glad to hear that." Nathan massaged his chest where it had grown tense. "So those guys are still out running around."

"Or they are dead. They didn't go back to the cabins and harm your friends. That means they are without shelter or food."

"Merci and I got out," Nathan said.

"There has been no report of stolen vehicles. So that means they are probably still on foot. We're going to get these guys. I promise you." The deputy spoke with intensity.

"I know you will, Travis." His friend had always had a strong sense of justice.

"I wish we could provide some protection for you two. All our resources are being consumed by the aftermath of the storm. Highway patrol pulled in this office for extra manpower in dealing with wrecked and stranded motorists. It's going to be a week before everything gets back to normal."

"I understand. Merci and I will be okay." Nathan said goodbye to his friend and hung up. He returned to the living room.

Merci's long strawberry-blond hair cascaded down her back. She lifted her fingers off the keyboard and turned to face him. "Who was that?"

"Travis. I mean Deputy Miller. Looks like the thieves are still at large." He ran his hand along the back of the couch as he watched the disappointment spread across her face.

He didn't like the idea of putting Merci on a bus by herself. Anything could happen in the six-hour bus ride. "I would feel better if you would let me drive you to your aunt's house."

Merci rose to her feet. "You would do that for me?"

"'Course I would." Her green eyes glowed with affection. He could drown in them. He was grateful for the excuse to be with her a little longer. If he told her how he felt about her, would she think he was out of line? A six-hour drive would give him time to decide.

The kitchen door swung open. A mouthwatering blend of stir-fry spices drifted into the living room when Daniel stuck his head out. "Chow time."

The tension between the two brothers seemed to lighten a little with the addition of good food. When Daniel shared funny stories of things they had done at camp, Nathan laughed and offered his own details to the stories, but she could still see the sadness behind his eyes.

As the final bites of dinner were being consumed, Nathan turned toward his brother. "I'm going to drive Merci to her aunt's house. Can you give us a ride across town, so we can get my car?"

Daniel sat his napkin on the table. "Sure, no problem."

Snow fell softly from the gray sky of early evening as they drove across town. Merci checked her watch. It would be close to ten o'clock by the time they got to her aunt's house, but she had already missed part of the vacation, and she didn't want to wait another day. Nathan's offer to drive her had lifted her spirits. She'd feel safer with him than on the bus. Maybe the ride together would only delay the inevitable, that they would be parting ways, but she intended to enjoy whatever time they had together.

Daniel brought the car to a stop and got out, along with Merci and Nathan.

"Are you driving back to Clampett tonight?" Daniel spoke to his brother.

Merci stepped forward. "My aunt has a little guest-house. I'm sure she wouldn't mind putting you up, then you could get a fresh start in the morning."

"We'll just play it by ear," Nathan said. "I think it is important that we get you out of town. Maybe by the time I get back, they will have these guys in custody."

"You mean because if they do get off that mountain, they will come looking for us here. That seems like a pretty good argument for you to stay at my aunt's house, too."

Nathan's eyes grew wide as though something had occurred to him that he hadn't thought about before. "Didn't Lorelei know where you were going?"

"She knew the town, but not the exact address. I was going to give her directions once we got there." A knot formed in her stomach. Would there ever come a time when she wasn't looking over her shoulder for the thieves? "We'll be okay, don't you think?"

"We'll certainly be safer there than if we stay around here," Nathan said.

Having Nathan close by made her feel safer, but she knew the cloud of fear would not lift until all four of the fugitives were in custody.

"Take care," said Daniel. He pivoted from side to side, a movement that communicated that he didn't quite know how to handle a goodbye with his brother.

"I will." Nathan held out his arms and took his brother into an awkward hug. Both of them were treading so lightly around each other. What would it take for them to find healing, for Nathan to feel he could trust his brother again?

Nathan led Merci up the walkway as Daniel drove

away. "I'll just grab a few things if you want to come in for a moment."

Once inside, everything about Nathan's house screamed bachelor, from the sports equipment in the foyer to the lack of artwork on the wall.

"Daniel was right about me not having anything edible in the refrigerator, but could you fill up some water bottles for us? They are in the cupboard under the sink. There might be a box of granola bars in there, too. My car is pretty well outfitted for winter travel otherwise." He disappeared down a hallway.

Merci searched the cupboards, found the water bottles and filled them up. When she turned to face the living room, Nathan had just emerged from a back room. He opened a drawer in a living room cabinet and pulled out a gun.

Merci drew in a breath.

Her gasp must have been audible because Nathan turned to face her. "It's just a precaution." He grabbed his cell phone off the top of the desk. "Just like this is a precaution."

Merci placed her hand into the empty pockets of her coat. "I still don't know what happened to my purple sparkly phone."

He turned his head sideways. "Your phone was purple?"

Merci placed the granola bars and water in a canvas bag she found. "Yeah, why?"

"Lorelei was trying to dial out on a purple phone when I saw them in the camp dorms."

The realization stirred up a mixture of anger and sadness. She tapped one of the water bottles on the counter and shook her head. "She must have taken it and been able to pick up enough reception to call the men to come and get her when they escaped on the snowmobile. She probably wanted to be with Hawthorne or felt she couldn't continue the ruse anymore since things had gone so wrong. She probably wasn't even going to go back to college."

Nathan walked across the room and stood on the opposite side of the counter from her. "It's hard to say what she was thinking."

"She must have met Hawthorne in Bozeman, and recently, or I would have remembered seeing them together." The knot in her stomach got even tighter. "When I saw that police sketch of him, it made me think I have seen him before somewhere, but only briefly."

"Maybe it will come back to you," Nathan commented as he moved toward the door.

They walked out to Nathan's car, got in and drove out of town as a light snow started to fall. "Most of the highway should be plowed by now. Should be a pretty easy drive, not much traffic."

The sky darkened as they drove for several hours. Nathan put on the windshield wipers to clear off the falling snow. He glanced in the rearview mirror.

She jerked in her seat. "Something wrong?"

Nathan tightened his grip on the steering wheel. "That car has been behind us for a long time. He could have passed us on that last straightaway."

Merci craned her neck at the two golden lights. "Maybe he is just being cautious because of the weather."

They drove a while longer. The snow had stopped

and the roads looked much clearer. When they came to another straightaway, Nathan slowed to way below the speed limit. The car remained behind them.

"There are cautious drivers in this world, you know." She sounded more as if she was trying to convince herself than him. The sight of the glowing lights in the rearview mirror sent a shiver up her spine.

Merci leaned forward and studied the button on Nathan's CD player. "Maybe we should just listen to some music, huh? Get our minds off everything."

Nathan pushed a button and the strains of violins from classical music filled the car.

"That surprises me," she said.

"What's that?"

"I had you pegged as a country music fan. You just seem like the type," she said.

"I like Handel and Mozart, very big in the country music scene," Nathan joked.

"I guess I shouldn't have assumed. There's probably a lot I am wrong about with you. Like your favorite color."

"What do you think my favorite color is?" Though their banter was light, Nathan continued to check the rearview mirror.

She thought for a moment. "Blue."

"Ding ding ding." Nathan made a noise that mimicked the bell ringing on a game show when a contestant gets the answer right. "What do you think my favorite kind of food is?"

"Pizza," Merci said.

She didn't have to glance through the rear window

to know they were still being followed. The stiffness of Nathan's neck and shoulders told her.

Nathan cleared his throat. "Roasted chicken with red baby potatoes and broccoli."

"Your mother must have loved you," Merci said. "Pizza is my favorite, actually."

Nathan drew his attention to the rearview mirror again. "They turned off at that exit."

"That's a relief," she said. "I think we are both just a little jumpy because of all that has happened." Merci laced her fingers together in her lap.

"We would be abnormal if we weren't a little skittish after all of that." A few minutes later, Nathan pointed to a sign that indicated a rest stop was up ahead. "We can stop if you want?"

"That would be great," she said.

When they pulled over into the rest stop parking lot, there was one other car and a semi truck parked way off in a corner. No interior lights glowed from inside the semi and no one wandered around it. The driver had probably stopped to get some sleep. Someone was sitting in the passenger seat of the car with his or her back to them.

"I'll make it quick," Merci said as she pushed open the car door.

Nathan got out, as well. "I'll just wait right here for you."

Their fear hadn't subsided; both of them were still on heightened alert, expecting the thieves to jump out at any moment.

Merci entered the bathroom. Her boots tapped across the linoleum. Tension threaded down her back. The bathroom felt chilled as though a breeze were blowing in from somewhere. She checked all the stalls, half expecting Lorelei to jump out at her with a knife.

Once she had washed her hands, Merci hurried back outside.

Nathan was standing by the car unharmed. "You okay?"

She put an open hand to her racing heart. "I just hope they catch these guys soon."

Nathan nodded. "I think we will both be less of a target when we get to your aunt's house. I think you are right about me staying there. I might hang out until we get word that all four of them are in custody. The police are watching all the roads. I'm sure they will have the thieves in custody within twenty-four hours."

Merci couldn't shake off the fear that made every muscle in her body tight. "I know it's not realistic, but it feels like we could go to the ends of the earth and they would still find us."

Nathan nodded. "I know the feeling."

Nathan got behind the wheel. They talked for a while longer until Merci could feel the heaviness of sleep invading her limbs. Turning sideways, she rested her head against the head rest and drifted off.

As he checked his rearview mirror for the fourth time, Nathan was grateful that Merci was resting. She would have picked up on his nervousness. The car that had been behind him since the rest stop was different than the one before. The headlights were higher up.

The road was so curvy there had been no opportunity to pass.

Of course, it was entirely possible that the car was just another person who had decided to travel on this road at night. That was the most logical explanation. The sense that he had to remain vigilant while the thieves were at large was driving his paranoia.

Rationalizing didn't make the knot of tension at the base of his neck any less tight. He glanced over at Merci. She was kind of cute when she slept.

He rounded a curve, aware that there might still be ice on the road. The road evened out into a straight-away, and he slowed down. They were within an hour of Grotto Falls and would be out of the mountains and into nicer weather shortly.

Merci awoke with a start. "I just thought of something."

Nathan thought better of alerting her to the car behind them. "What is that?"

Her voice filled with an icy fear. "If Lorelei has my phone, then she knows Aunt Celeste's address. It's in the phone. What if they are waiting for us to show up there?"

Nathan didn't have time to answer. The car behind him sped up and switched to the left lane.

He took in a breath, gripped the steering wheel and waited for the car to pass. Even through the closed window, he could hear the other car accelerate and come up beside him.

Why wasn't the other car passing and pulling in front of him? He slowed down even more. The other car slowed, as well. Adrenaline shot through his veins as he sped up, and the car kept pace with him. He glanced over long enough to see the thief's leering face in the passenger seat.

Merci tuned in to Nathan's fear. She sat up straighter. "What's going on?"

The other car turned its wheels, slamming into the front end of Nathan's car. Nathan swerved, struggling to keep the car on the road.

Merci dug her hands into the seat rest. "They found us," she said in a panicked whisper.

Nathan scanned the road up ahead for a turnoff or a possibility of escape. The thieves' car surged slightly ahead and rammed against them by the wheel well.

Their car jerked and wobbled. Nathan gripped the steering wheel struggling to straighten the tire and get back on the road. His car swerved, veering off the road.

Merci screamed. The car rolled down the hill. The seat belt dug into Nathan's chest when they were upside down. His body felt beaten and stretched in all directions at once. They were right side up and then upside down again. He hung in space for a moment. An object flew past his face. The crunching of metal surrounded him.

The car came to rest upside down. Nathan felt woozy and foggy brained. Merci hadn't made any more noise since he'd heard her scream.

His hand trembled as he felt around for his seat belt buckle. "Merci, are you okay?"

She didn't answer.

He tried to turn his head so he could see the passenger seat. The car was mangled in such a way that his view was limited. Had she been thrown clear of the car?

The interior of the car seemed to be spinning around

him, and he couldn't orient himself. His fingers fumbled along the seat belt until he found the clip and pushed down. The belt didn't release. Black dots formed at the corners of his vision as he summoned all the strength he had left and pushed harder on the seat belt clip. He fell down to the roof of the car and passed out. As consciousness faded, he heard a harsh and familiar voice.

"Deal with him in a minute. First we need to get her to talk before she says bye-bye to the world."

EIGHTEEN

Nathan struggled to maintain clarity as his hand fumbled around the glove compartment where he had put the gun. The door on the glove compartment was bent. He couldn't get it open. The voices of the thieves had come from outside the car. Merci must have been thrown clear in the crash. He broke the remainder of the glass out of the driver's-side window with his elbow and crawled through.

Freezing night air surrounded him. He stumbled down the hill. He had to find Merci, to save her. The ground leveled out, and he continued to run into the darkness until he heard voices.

He slowed his pace.

He heard the sound of skin slapping skin and Orange Coat saying, "Wake up. You need to answer a few questions."

His heart squeezed tight when he heard Merci let out a cry.

Nathan stepped softly, hoping not to make any noise. He walked toward where light streamed out. The two thugs came into view. One was kneeling over Merci, and the other stood with his back to Nathan holding a flashlight.

More slapping sounds. "Where are they? Where are the books?"

Merci let out a cry of confusion. "The books? What are you talking about? You mean the textbooks that were in my room?"

Nathan's hands curled into fists. He'd heard enough. They weren't going to hurt her anymore. Nathan scanned the ground around him and picked up a small log. His feet pounded the ground as he lifted his arm and thwacked the standing thief hard against the side of the head. Leather Jacket tumbled to the ground. Nathan pushed Orange Coat out of the way and turned to look at Merci. From where she lay on the ground on her back, she reached out her arms to him.

He grabbed her hand and pulled her to a sitting position. Orange Coat recovered and lunged toward him. Nathan angled out of the way while Merci scrambled to her feet. He grabbed her hand and started to run.

From the ground where he lay, Leather Coat grabbed his ankle as he ran by and pulled him down.

Nathan hit the hard ground. "Run, Merci."

She hesitated.

Nathan managed to land a hard hit to Leather Coat's stomach and break free of his grasp before Orange Coat pulled out a gun.

"I don't think anyone is going anywhere," said Orange Coat.

Merci moved toward Nathan, who stepped in front of her, shielding her.

Leather Jacket doubled over from the blow to his stomach.

"Now give me the girl. We are not through with her yet," Orange Coat snarled.

Nathan knew he was of no value to them. They'd shoot him and take Merci. His mind reeled as he stared at the barrel of the gun. What could he do? They had turned a half circle in their struggle, so Orange Coat's back was to the hill that led up to the highway.

Nathan looked over Orange Coat's shoulder where he saw shadows moving. The thieves' flashlights had been kicked off into the brush, and it was hard to discern anything.

Merci let out a fear-filled gasp as she pressed closer to him. Nathan scanned the area around him. Maybe the darkness could work to their advantage.

He talked to Orange Coat to distract him. "Now you don't want to shoot me. What if you accidentally hit the girl? And you said you still need her. All this trouble you have gone to. It can't be worth it."

"It's worth a couple of million, and we get a cut of it now for all our trouble?"

What could be worth a couple of million dollars? While Nathan talked, he took an almost indiscernible step back, communicating to Merci that they needed to dive into the dark underbrush.

Orange Coat lifted the gun. On cue, Merci fell to the ground and scrambled on all fours toward the darkness of the bushes. As he turned to run, Nathan spotted a flashlight, grabbed it and shone it directly in Orange Coat's eyes.

Orange Coat put up his hand. The distraction allowed

Nathan time to reach for the other man's gun. The gun flew out of Orange Coat's hand and off into the shadows. Nathan wrestled with the thief. An arm hooked around his neck. Leather Jacket must have recovered and now had him in a vise.

"Get off of him."

He could hear Merci shouting and see flashes of her face. Orange Coat landed a blow to his stomach. Nathan gasped for air as the hands around his neck tightened. In his peripheral vision, he saw Leather Jacket dragging Merci away.

He clawed at the hands around his neck. He kicked Orange Coat in the shin, which caused him to let go of Nathan's neck. Nathan gasped for air and saw spots in front of his face. He wrestled Orange Coat to the ground and pinned him only to have Leather Jacket return and jump on top of him.

What had happened to Merci?

He wrestled and fought with both men, getting in several good blows, but growing tired. How much longer could he keep this up? Nathan had knocked Orange Coat to the ground and hit Leather Jacket across the jaw when a voice boomed out of the darkness.

"Leave my brother alone."

Both thieves threw their arms up.

Daniel stood before him, holding the gun that had been tossed out into the darkness.

"You came." Gratitude washed through Nathan like a flood.

"Of course I came. I would move heaven and earth for you, little brother," said Daniel. "I don't ever want to hurt you again or see you hurt. You have to believe that."

"I'm starting to. Thank you." Nathan retrieved the flashlight and shone it in the brush looking for Merci. "How did you know?"

"Right after you left, the sheriff's department called. They had a stolen vehicle report that was delayed in getting in because the driver had to hike into town. They tried to call your cell first."

"Mountains must have blocked the reception," Nathan said.

"I knew where you were going. I got in my car and headed down the mountain."

Nathan's heart swelled with love for his brother. "You did that for me."

Daniel nodded.

"Help me." Merci's strained voice came from the brush.

"Go find her. I can handle these two." Daniel leveled the gun at the thugs. "Get on your knees, both of you."

The thieves complied.

Nathan swung the flashlight back and forth searching until he found Merci lying facedown with her hands tied behind her back. He untied her.

She fell into his arms but pulled away quickly. Her voice filled with panic. "We have to go to my aunt's house. I know what they are looking for."

"What are you talking about?"

"They wanted to know where the books were. The only books they could be talking about are the ones my father sent me in the care package to give to my aunt."

"Your father sent your aunt books worth millions of dollars?"

Daniel said, "Nathan, I think we need to get something to tie these guys up with. I can't hold this gun forever."

Merci picked up the rope she had been restrained with. "This is long enough. We can cut this in half."

While Daniel tied the thieves' hands behind their backs, Merci pulled Nathan out of earshot of the thieves and continued, "My father didn't know the books were worth that much...or maybe it's just one of the books. He probably bought them at some little street stall in Spain. They were books that were written in Spanish. My aunt used to be a missionary in South America. She likes to read Spanish books. When I got the care package, I put the books in the mail to Auntie. I didn't want them taking up space and adding weight to my suitcase."

"But for some reason Hawthorne knows how much the book or books are worth."

"I know now where I saw him. When I got that care package from my dad, I opened it up in the student union. Hawthorne walked by me. He stopped and asked me directions to some place on campus. It was such a quick conversation. I don't even remember where he wanted to go. I must have just taken out the books, and he saw them."

"So he recognized that at least one of the books was valuable. Why go to all this trouble? Why not just offer to buy the book from you for a couple hundred dollars?"

"Maybe he was afraid I would do research and find out the book was worth more. It doesn't matter." She walked to where Daniel still held a gun on the two thieves. She addressed Leather Jacket. "You were supposed to call Hawthorne if you were successful, right?"

Leather Jacket stared at the ground. His voice filled with defeat. "Yes, if he doesn't hear from us, he knows it didn't work."

"Nathan, we need to get to my aunt's house. I mailed the books to my aunt right after the package arrived. If Lorelei has my phone, she knows where my aunt lives. Even if they don't know that the books are there, they might be waiting there to ambush me once they figure out these guys' plan didn't work." Merci stepped toward thieves. "That was the plan, wasn't it?"

Both of them nodded.

"Please." Merci grabbed Nathan's coat, her voice filled with desperation. "Aunt Celeste is in danger."

NINETEEN

"Nathan, we're ten miles from town." Merci couldn't hide the sense of terror that had invaded every cell of her body. "We have to go and make sure Aunt Celeste is okay."

"Couldn't you wait five minutes?" said Daniel. "I called the police in Grotto Falls when I saw the wreck. They're on their way."

"We have to go now," Merci pleaded.

Nathan looked at his brother.

"I can watch these two until the police get here. You can take my car since yours is wrecked." Daniel tossed Nathan the keys.

Nathan patted his brother's shoulder. "Thanks...for saving my life."

"I'd do it again tomorrow if you asked me."

The walls seemed to have melted between the two brothers.

Merci and Nathan scrambled up the hill past the wrecked car to where Daniel's car was parked beside the thieves' car. Once Nathan had started the engine, he handed Merci his phone. "Phone the police in Grotto Falls. Maybe they can meet us at your aunt's house."

Merci nodded. Her stomach twisted into a tight knot as she dialed.

Please, God, don't let them hurt my aunt.

The lights of the city came into view, and the landscape changed from mountains to rolling hills. Merci phoned the local police, explained the situation and gave them her aunt's address. When she tried her aunt's number, there was no answer.

She pulled the phone away from her ear. "Sometimes she doesn't hear the phone if she is in the back part of the house."

As they came closer to the city limits, they passed a gas station and a hotel. Hardly any snow had fallen at this lower elevation. Merci directed Nathan through the streets until they arrived at a white house with a stone walkway and chain-link fence. The windows of the house were dark.

A sense of apprehension skittered over Merci's nerves. "Where are the police?"

"Maybe they're still on their way."

"They should have gotten here before us," she said in a trembling voice.

Nathan knocked on the door.

"She wouldn't have gone to sleep. She's expecting me, and she would have left the living room light on." Merci checked the door. It was locked.

"Let's look around." Nathan took Merci's hand and led her around the side of the house.

"I think we need to call the police again." Merci looked at the cell phone panel.

A hoarse whisper from behind her caused her to freeze. "The two of you better be really still." Hawthorne stepped forward and placed a gun on Nathan's temple. "Don't try anything heroic."

Hawthorne's voice would haunt her dreams. If she lived to dream again. A sense of terror spread through her. "Don't hurt him."

Hawthorne raised an eyebrow. "I won't if you tell me what I need to know. Now, why don't all of us go inside? The back door is unlocked. Merci, you go first and if you try anything, your boyfriend dies. Are we clear on that?"

Lorelei must have told Hawthorne her name. How else would he have learned it? As she eased open the back door, she prayed that her aunt was still alive. Hawthorne was the type to get someone else to do his dirty work. Was he capable of killing?

Merci stepped through the door first. She gave Nathan a backward glance.

"It's okay," Nathan reassured.

Hawthorne pressed the gun harder against Nathan's temple. "I meant what I said."

Merci shuddered. The fire in Hawthorne's eyes told her he had no problem with killing.

Merci stepped inside and reached for a light switch. Their footsteps seemed to echo in the hallway. Maybe Aunt Celeste had run out for a last-minute errand to the grocery store. Was it too much to hope that this animal hadn't had the chance to do harm to her aunt?

"To the kitchen," said Hawthorne.

She reached out and switched on the light in the kitchen. Merci gasped. Aunt Celeste was tied up in a kitchen chair. Tears streamed down the older woman's face. Merci fell to floor and hugged her aunt.

"I'm so sorry this had to happen." Merci stroked her aunt's hair and wiped the tears away.

Celeste nodded but was unable to respond because of the gag in her mouth.

Hawthorne shouted toward the dark living room where the curtains were drawn. "Lori, get me two more chairs and some rope."

Shadows covered Lorelei as she moved around the dining room and then came into the lighted kitchen carrying two chairs. Lorelei's face was drawn. She looked as if she hadn't slept in weeks. She kept her gaze on the floor.

Hawthorne took the gun away from Nathan's temple and ordered him to sit down in the chair. He looked at Merci. "You, too."

Nathan's gaze moved around the room as though he were trying to come up with a strategy for escape. Hawthorne kept the gun on Nathan while Lorelei tied his hands behind his back and to the chair.

"Put your hands behind your back," Lorelei whispered to Merci.

Lorelei tugged on Merci's hands as she wrapped the rope around them. Merci bent down and angled her head so she could talk to Lorelei. "Why, why did you do this?"

"Shut up." Hawthorne waved the gun at Merci.

Lorelei tugged harder on the restraints, causing the rope to dig into Merci's wrists. Merci winced.

Lorelei stood up. "All done."

"Good girl." Hawthorne leaned toward Lorelei and

kissed her. "It won't be long now, Babe. We'll be rolling in dough."

Hawthorne narrowed his eyes at Merci as he loomed over her. "Now all you have to do is tell me where you put that Spanish language book. We'll go get it, and you'll be free to go."

Merci knew he was lying. Once he had the book in his hand, she would be of no use to him. He'd probably kill Nathan and her aunt even sooner. "What book are you talking about?"

"It's a nineteenth-century book about fruit trees written in Spanish with illustrations. The *Un libro de arboles* disappeared sixty years ago. It was suspected that it was stolen. How it ended up in some European street market is anyone's guess. The bookseller obviously didn't know what he had."

He leaned over her. "So where is it?"

Merci shook her head. "I'm still not sure what you are talking about." She had to stall long enough for them to come up with a plan, or for the local police to show up. Certainly, her call wouldn't have been ignored… unless Hawthorne had found a way to throw the police off or to harm them.

Hawthorne leaned close enough for her to feel his hot breath on her cheek. "That day you were in the Student Union. I stopped to ask you where the cafeteria was. You had just opened a package with a European post mark."

"Oh, yes, now I remember, the one my father sent."

Aunt Celeste's eyes grew wide, and her gaze turned toward the dark living room. The books were there stacked on the table by the couch. All Hawthorne had to do was turn on the lights, glance in that direction and he would see them. And then they would all be dead.

Hawthorne held Merci in his stone-cold gaze. "Yes, where is it?" He cocked his head to one side. "Don't tell me you got smart and put it in a security deposit box."

"I…umm… Let me think. There was so much in that package. I'm trying to think what I did with all of it."

Hawthorne's features tightened, indicating impatience. "Tell me what you did with it."

Lights flashed across the curtains.

Lorelei ran to the window and pulled back the edge of a curtain. "It's a cop. He's driving by real slow. Jonathan, I think he's going to stop here."

Hawthorne's gaze darted around the room and then he untied Celeste. "Now you listen to me, old lady. You're going to tell this guy that everything is fine here and that your niece has already gone to sleep."

Lorelei came back into the kitchen, put a gag in Merci's mouth and turned off the lights. There was no chance of the policeman seeing them when he stood at the door. Maybe she could knock the chair over and make a loud noise.

Hawthorne pushed Celeste to her feet. "And if you try anything. I'll shoot you and then your precious niece."

There was a knock on the door. A dog barked somewhere in the neighborhood. Celeste trudged toward the door. Hawthorne turned on the lights and crouched by the door where Celeste could see him but the police officer wouldn't be able to. He kept the gun pointed at her.

With the lights on, the books were clearly visible.

Merci held her breath. All Hawthorne had to do was pivot ninety degrees, and he would see the books.

Her aunt opened the door. The older woman gripped the edge of the door with trembling hands, but her voice was steady. "Hello Officer, what brings you out so late?"

Merci could hear the policeman but not see him. "We got a call earlier that you might be in some danger."

"In danger?"

In the kitchen, Lorelei touched Merci's wrist and whispered in her ear. "I did it because he promised me the moon and said I'd be rich. I thought I loved him." The ropes around Merci's wrist loosened. "But it has gone too far."

The conversation continued at the door. "A Merci Carson called in a while ago concerned that you might have had a break-in."

Celeste hesitated for a moment before answering. "I don't know what Merci was so worried about. Everything is fine here. She arrived a little bit ago and went straight to bed. She must have forgotten to call you and say everything was just fine."

"Good to hear. Sorry I was so slow in getting over here. I was on my way out to an accident just outside of town when the call came in. We've only got two officers on duty tonight. Well, you have a good night, ma'am."

Celeste closed the door. Hawthorne jumped to his feet and shoved the gun in Celeste's back. Hawthorne's face grew red with anger. "Now, Merci, I suggest you tell me where that book is or I'll put a bullet in your aunt and then in your boyfriend."

Merci's thoughts moved at light speed. Hawthorne might keep her alive long enough to get the book, but as soon as she told him, even if it was a lie, he'd shoot the other two. She saw murder in his eyes. Her throat had gone dry. "Why do you want it so bad?"

"That book is unaccounted for because it disappeared for sixty years. I'm in the antiquities and rare books trade. I could say I found the book at a bookseller's stall just like your father did, no one will ask any questions, and I would be a couple million richer."

She flexed her hands while he talked. If she made a run for it, would he chase her or simply shoot Nathan and Celeste? Lorelei continued to stand back in the shadows by the hallway. Merci focused on the doorknob shining in the dark living room. It wasn't that far to the door. She could cry out for help. Maybe Hawthorne would run rather than risk exposure.

In an instant, she jumped out of the chair and bolted toward the living room. She took long strides. She heard a scream of indignation behind her. A gun was fired and then she felt fingers clawing her back.

She reached out for the doorknob, her hand inches from it. Just as she turned it, a heavy weight fell on her back, knocking her to the ground. Her stomach hit the floor with a hard thud. Hawthorne was on top of her. She screamed and struggled to get away. His hand went over her mouth.

And then, he stood up and backed away.

Merci turned over and struggled to her feet. Hawthorne had seen the stack of books and was walking toward it. He still held the gun. Her heart rate soared as her mind raced. Now there was no reason for any of them to be kept alive.

Nathan burst out of his chair and tackled Hawthorne

just as he picked up the book. Lorelei must have cut him free, too. The two men wrestled. The gun skittered across the floor, and Merci picked it up.

"Stop right there, Hawthorne." Both her voice and her hands were shaking.

While Hawthorne's attention was drawn to Merci, Nathan subdued Hawthorne and held his hands behind his back.

Outside, Merci saw flashing lights. The policeman had come back. He must have suspected something was up.

"Here, take the gun, Nathan," she said.

Merci ran to her aunt who was huddled in a corner. There was no sign of Lorelei.

"That girl left out the back door after she cut Nathan free," said Aunt Celeste.

Outside a car pulled up. Merci ran to the door and opened it. The police officer who had come by earlier came up the walkway. A moment later, a highway patrol car pulled to the curb, and Daniel got out along with the officer.

Once Hawthorne was in cuffs and secured in the police car, Nathan walked over to Merci where she stood on the sidewalk. "You were right about Lorelei. There was something redemptive in her."

"I imagine the police will catch her. She'll go to jail. I'm going to try to at least visit her. We can't give up on people." Merci turned toward him and looked into his brown eyes. Then she looked over at Daniel who was making a statement to the local police officer.

"I agree." He placed his hand in hers. "That was enough excitement for the day, huh?"

"Enough excitement for a lifetime."

Aunt Celeste came up beside them and wrapped an arm around Merci. "I think we could all use a quiet morning after all that drama. How about I make us all some breakfast?"

"I'll see if Daniel wants to stay," said Nathan.

As Nathan walked toward his brother and slung an arm around him, the genuine warmth she saw between them touched her deeply.

The four of them made their way back up the stairs. Nathan's hand slid easily into hers as they stepped inside.

TWENTY

Daniel and Aunt Celeste's laughter floated out from the kitchen as they prepared breakfast together. The aroma of bacon sizzling and cinnamon filled the living room where Merci and Nathan snuggled on the couch.

A faint smile crossed Merci's face. "Your brother really likes to cook."

"Yes, he does." Nathan settled into the plush couch and drew Merci closer. "In fact, that's what he is going to do up at the ski hill when we reopen, be the head cook in the cafeteria and at the camp. He doesn't want full responsibility. We'll have to work everything out on paper, but he said I could gradually give him financial control of his share of the property."

"I think the way he came to our aid at the car wreck reveals a lot about who your brother is," Merci said.

"I agree, but this is the way he wants to do it. He wants to prove to me that he is trustworthy." Nathan let out a heavy sigh. For the first time in three days, he felt as if he could let his guard down and truly relax. Hawthorne, whose real name was Jonathan Drake, was the son of an antiquities dealer who had been on campus to give a lecture the day that Merci had received her package from her father. Jonathan Drake was in custody, and the thugs were already in a jail cell.

As Merci turned to face Nathan, her wide green eyes held a question. The same question that had been on his mind since they had gotten off the mountain.

"So, after breakfast, when it's time for Daniel and me to go…?"

Her expression communicated confusion.

Nathan slapped his forehead. He was really messing this up. "I guess what I'm saying is I know three days in not enough time for people to fall in love."

She pulled away from him, scooted back on the couch and looked directly at him. "Fall in love?"

Fear crept into his heart. Was she about to tell him it couldn't work out between them, that the need to stay alive on the mountain was what had kept them together? He rubbed her cheek with the back of his hand. He wasn't going to let her go that easily. "But we've been through more trauma and trials than most people face in a lifetime."

"And we worked together and kept each other alive." She leaned toward him "Do you think we could handle just an ordinary boring life together?"

He searched her green eyes. She did understand. "I'd like to try." He took her hand in his.

"I won't graduate until May. We'll be in different towns."

"I like driving, and I have a feeling there will need to be a manager for that ski hill about the time that you graduate." Nathan gathered her into his arms.

"I think I would like boring and ordinary."

"Me, too." He pulled her close and kissed her, pressing harder and relishing the fruity scent of her hair and the softness of her skin as his whiskers brushed over her face.

From the kitchen, Daniel said, "Chow is on."

"Breakfast will have to wait just a minute." Nathan kissed the woman he wanted to spend the rest of his life with one more time.

* * * * *

Terri Reed's romance and romantic suspense novels have appeared on the *Publishers Weekly* top twenty-five and Nielsen BookScan top one hundred lists, and have been featured in *USA TODAY*, *Christian Fiction* magazine and *RT Book Reviews*. Her books have been finalists for the Romance Writers of America RITA® Award and the National Readers' Choice Award and finalists three times for the American Christian Fiction Writers Carol Award. Contact Terri at terrireed.com or PO Box 19555, Portland, OR 97224.

Books by Terri Reed

Love Inspired Suspense

True Blue K-9 Unit
Seeking the Truth

Classified K-9 Unit
Guardian
Classified K-9 Unit Christmas
"Yuletide Stalking"

Northern Border Patrol
Danger at the Border
Joint Investigation
Murder Under the Mistletoe
Ransom
Identity Unknown

Visit the Author Profile page
at Harlequin.com for more titles.

SECRET MOUNTAIN HIDEOUT

Terri Reed

Hear my voice, O God, in my prayer:
preserve my life from fear of the enemy.
Hide me from the secret counsel of the wicked;
from the insurrection of the workers of iniquity.
—*Psalm* 64:1–2

To the ones I love. May God shine His face
upon you always and give you peace.

ONE

It couldn't be.

Ice filled Ashley Willis's veins despite the spring sunshine streaming through the living room windows of the Bristle Township home in Colorado where she rented a bedroom.

Disbelief cemented her feet to the floor, her gaze riveted to the horrific images on the television screen.

Flames shot of out of the two-story building she'd hoped never to see again. Its once bright red awnings were now singed black and the magnificent stained-glass windows depicting the image of an angry bull were no more.

She knew that place intimately.

The same place that haunted her nightmares.

The newscaster's words assaulted her. She grabbed on to the back of the faded floral couch for support.

In a fiery inferno, the posh Burbank restaurant, The Matador, was consumed by a raging fire in the wee hours of the morning. Firefighters are working diligently to douse the flames. So far there have been no fatalities, however, there has been one critical injury.

Ashley's heart thumped painfully in her chest, reminding her to breathe. Concern for her friend, Gregor, the man who had safely spirited her away from the Los Angeles area one frightening night a year and a half ago when she'd witnessed her boss, Maksim Sokolov, kill a man, thrummed through her. She had to know what happened. She had to know if Gregor was the one injured.

She had to know if this had anything to do with her.

"Mrs. Marsh," Ashley called out. "Would you mind if I use your cell phone?"

Her landlady, a widow in her mideighties, appeared in the archway between the living room and kitchen. Her hot-pink tracksuit hung on her stooped shoulders but it was her bright smile that always tugged at Ashley's heart. The woman was a spitfire with her blue-gray hair and her kind green eyes behind thick spectacles.

"Of course, dear. It's in my purse." She pointed to the black satchel on the dining room table. "Though you know, as I keep saying, you should get your own cell phone. It's not safe for a young lady to be walking around without any means of calling for help."

They had been over this before. Ashley didn't want anything attached to her name.

Or rather, her assumed identity—Jane Thompson.

Putting the name she was using in some system where it could be flagged and she could be discovered in Bristle Township was a disaster she wanted to avoid at all costs.

So far, using the identification Gregor had given her had worked. She'd been too stunned at the time to question where he'd obtained the driver's license, social security card and credit card, all with the name Jane Thompson. She suspected she wouldn't have liked the answer had she asked. No one so far had questioned that she wasn't Jane Thompson. She didn't know what she'd do if the thin line keeping her safe disappeared and her true identity became known.

A shudder of dread, followed closely by a jab of guilt at deceiving the good people of Bristle Township, made her gut tighten. She prayed God would forgive her for doing what she had to in order to survive.

"I just need to make a quick phone call," Ashley assured her landlady as the urgent drive to know who was injured consumed her.

If she could have bought a burner phone in Bristle Township she would have, but that wasn't an option. First, none of the local stores carried one—she'd discreetly searched—and second, everyone would know about such a purchase the moment she made it.

Thankfully, Mrs. Marsh's data plan included free long distance, as well as Wi-Fi. Mrs. Marsh's children, who both lived in Texas, had sent her the phone so that they could communicate with her.

With phone in hand, Ashley quickly searched for the hospitals in and around the Burbank area. She called each listed and on the fourth try found the hospital where the critically injured victim of The Matador fire had been taken.

Her heart sank to have her fear confirmed that Gregor Kominski, the restaurant's manager, had been the one hurt. Anxiety made her limbs shake beneath the khaki pants and long sleeve T-shirt sporting the Java Bean logo on the front breast pocket and the back. She had been on her way out the door for work when she'd seen the news.

Had the fire been set intentionally? Had Gregor suffered because of her?

"Are you a relative of Mr. Kominski's?" the woman from the hospital on the other end of the line questioned.

Biting her lip, Ashley debated her answer. She didn't want to lie, but she doubted they would give her much information if she admitted she wasn't related to the man. Finally, she hedged, allowing the woman to make her own assumption. "I'm calling from out of town. What can you tell me? Is he going to be okay?"

"He remains in critical condition," the woman said. "Would you like to leave a name and a number for updates?"

Ashley quickly hung up. No, she didn't want to leave a name and number. She didn't want there to be any trace of her reaching out for information. The call had been a risk. One she hoped she wouldn't have to pay for with her life.

Gossip in Bristle Township traveled faster than the wind off the mountain. Ashley couldn't help but overhear several customers of the Java Bean coffee shop talking about a detective from California asking questions about a mysterious woman.

Heart beating in her throat, Ashley spilled milk all over the espresso machine. With shaky hands, she quickly wiped up the mess and finished making the specialty drink.

Just this morning she'd learned of the fire that had destroyed The Matador restaurant and sent her friend to the hospital. Now a police officer from the same state was in town. Coincidence? Or was she on the verge of being discovered?

Ethan Johnson, a local farmer, stared at her from beneath the brim of a well-worn baseball cap as she handed him the steaming cup of mocha cappuccino. "Do you have a sister?"

Her tongue stuck to the roof of her mouth as she mutely shook her head.

"Hmm. I guess we all have a doppelganger," he commented. His blue veined hands cupped the to-go container as if the warmth of the liquid inside was soothing to the arthritis evident in the swollen joints of his fingers.

Forcing herself to speak, she asked, "Why do you say that?"

"You vaguely resemble the woman in the photo the lawman was asking me about," he replied with a shrug. He lifted the cup and blew through the hole on the lid as he walked away.

Though she barely resembled her old self, terror of being exposed ripped through Ashley. She'd been careful to keep her appearance understated so she could blend in better. Though the dye job she'd done right before landing in Bristle Township hadn't turned out quite the way she'd expected. Much too flashy.

The carton of hair dye had claimed she'd end up with honey blond hair. She touched the short platinum blond strands curling around her face. Sudden sadness and anger at the circumstances that had forced her to change not only her hair color and style but also her whole life swamped her, weighing her down.

One simple distracted moment and her world had spun out of control.

Knowing things could be so much worse—she could be dead—she quickly removed her apron and hurried over to the owner of the Java Bean, Stephen Humphrey. He was a big teddy bear of a man with two teenage kids who helped out on the weekends.

"Hey, boss. I need to take a break, if that's okay. I forgot I promised Mrs. Marsh I would help her with something." Like protecting her from me.

Ashley's insides twisted with guilt. She hated having to keep her true identity a secret from these people who had shown her such kindness.

She knew Stephen had a soft spot for Mrs. Marsh. The whole town did. Mrs. Marsh and her late husband had been beloved grade school teachers. Everyone who had grown up in town had been in her or her late husband's classes. Ashley had heard so many wonderful stories of how Mr. and Mrs. Marsh had made a difference in people's lives.

Just as Mrs. Marsh was making a huge difference in Ashley's life. More guilt and regret heaped on her head, making her scalp tingle. She wanted to scrub the past year and a half away, go back in time and undo what was done. But she couldn't.

The only thing she could do was run to stay alive.

"Sure," Stephen replied. "Just be back for the afternoon rush."

She smiled tightly but refrained from promising. It was time for her to leave Bristle Township as soon as possible. The thought pinched, creating a pang of sorrow. She liked the town and her job. She'd started to make friends, letting people into her heart. Foolish on her part.

Over the last year she'd saved up so she could afford to move on. She'd only stopped in the small mountainside community and taken the job at the coffee shop because she'd run out of the money Gregor had given her. He'd told her never to contact him again and she hadn't wanted to put her mother in danger by contacting her.

Not that Irene Willis would have been in any position to help her only child, nor would she have made much effort if she could. Irene barely made a living waiting tables at a truck stop outside Barstow, California, and Ashley was positive her mom's life was less complicated without her daughter to set off her temper. One of the many reasons Ashley had left as quickly as she could when she turned eighteen.

Ashley's only option had been staying in one place long enough to earn more money to keep running for her life. She hadn't meant to stay so long. But life had become comfortable and she'd believed herself secure in this quaint mountain hamlet. Maybe if she'd stayed in Barstow or chosen a different path, she wouldn't be here now.

An illusion of safety had kept her here. Another mistake she couldn't afford. And now she was on the brink of being found out. She had no doubt that the detective was hunting for her. She couldn't let him succeed in tracking her down.

She hurried out the back entrance of the Java Bean, taking a deep breath of the pine-scented air. She crossed the town park, trying to keep a low profile. The park was filled with moms and their children too young for school. A few elderly couples strolled along the street. A horn honked, startling Ashley. She glanced around, fear slithering through her, making her muscles tense. Two cars vied for the same parking space in front of the bookstore on the main street. Breathing a little easier she hurried on, cutting through the library parking lot, and walked fast down the residential street leading to Mrs. Marsh's place.

The trees along the sidewalk were beginning to blossom. Soft pink petals floated to the ground on a slight breeze. Ashley barely noticed the beauty today, her mind tormented with anxiety.

Managing to reach the boarding house without being seen, she gathered her meager belongings, left an apologetic note and some cash for Mrs. Marsh. Then putting up the hood of her navy down jacket to cover her bright hair, she retraced the same path she'd taken earlier and made her way to the Bristle Hotel where the interstate bus picked up and dropped off passengers.

A teenager on a bike rode by, waving at her. She had no choice but to wave back to Brady Gallo. Maybe he wouldn't mention to his older sister that he'd seen Jane. It pained Ashley to leave Maya, Leslie and Kaitlyn—the three women who'd befriended her—without a goodbye, but it couldn't be helped.

At the Bristle Hotel, a beautiful old building that dated back to the township's conception, Ashley checked with the front desk clerk and learned a bus was due to arrive within minutes and was headed to Montana. She bought a ticket and then took a position behind a pillar on the wide porch to wait for the bus. There were a couple of other people waiting and she purposely ignored them. The last thing she needed was to engage in idle conversation.

She hoped and prayed she made it out of town before she was found or stopped.

The bus rolled in and she hurried to stow her bag in the undercarriage compartment, then moved to wait at the door behind a guy who needed a shower. The stench coming from his unwashed hair made her eyes water. He'd probably been hiking on the popular trails that began right on the edge of Bristle and threaded up into the mountains.

She hung back as long as she dared, allowing space between them. There were already several people on-board the bus. Seemed Montana was the destination of choice today.

The guy in front of her showed his ticket to the driver and boarded.

"Jane! Wait."

Hesitating, Ashley warily turned to find Deputy Chase Fredrick striding toward her, undeniably hand-some in his brown uniform. His sandy blond hair swept over his forehead in an appealing way and his intense blue eyes bored into her. He'd always been kind and charming when he'd come into the Java Bean for coffee.

In different circumstances, she might have been tempted to flirt with him, but there was no place in her life for a man. It was bad enough she'd made friends who were going to be hurt and disappointed by her de-parture. She regretted causing anyone pain and wouldn't make that mistake again.

What did the deputy want? Dread clawed through

her. Was her ruse up? Would she find herself in jail? Or worse—dead?

Desperate to get on the bus, Ashley thrust her ticket at the driver, but he didn't reach for it as he stared at her a moment and then turned his gaze to the deputy who'd come to a halt at her side and touched her elbow.

Panic revved Ashley's pulse. "What are you doing here?"

"I could ask you the same thing." His blue gaze searched her face. "Why are you leaving town?"

Stiffening her spine, she replied, "It's none of your business."

"It is my business if you're a criminal," he stated in a low voice.

She drew back. Fear fluttered in her chest. "I don't know what you're talking about."

Turning to the bus driver, Chase said, "She won't be taking this bus. Can you unload her bags?"

Giving Ashley a cautious glance, the driver's head bobbed. "Straight away, Officer."

"No! I have to go," she protested. "I need to get on this bus."

The driver hurried to the cargo hold and dragged her duffel out, setting it on the ground before resuming his position at the bus door.

Drawing her away from the curious gazes, Chase said, "Jane, be straight with me. There's a detective from Los Angeles here searching for a woman wanted in connection with a murder. And I'm pretty sure the woman in the photo he has is you."

Her stomach dropped. Fear squeezed her lungs, making breathing difficult.

"Did you kill a man?"

She swallowed back the bile rising to burn her throat. "Of course not. I could never—I wouldn't—"

She wasn't a murderer.

But she knew who was.

Gregor had warned her not to tell anyone, not even the police. They were not to be trusted, he'd said. "I've got to go. This is the only bus out today."

"You're not going anywhere—" Chase's voice was hard and his eyes glittered with warning "—until you tell me the truth."

"Last call," the bus driver called out, sliding a cautious glance their way.

Her gaze darted from the bus to Chase. "Please," she pleaded. "I need to leave. You don't understand. If he finds me, he'll kill me."

Confusion tampered down the hardness of Chase's features. "Jane, trust me. I can protect you. Just tell me what it is you're running from."

She shook her head and took a step back. "No. I was warned not to say anything. Not even to the police. I can't trust you. I can't trust anyone."

The driver stepped into the bus and closed the door. The bus's engine rumbled and a few seconds later a plume of exhaust filled the air as the bus drove away. Frustration pounded a rapid beat at her temple. Now she was trapped with no way out.

Chase snagged her hand and gently coaxed her fist open. "Jane, listen to me carefully." His voice softened to a smooth tone that seemed to coil inside of her. Her pulse leaped. His touch soothed.

"My job is to protect and serve the citizens of Bristle Township. You are one of its citizens." The intensity in his clear gaze mesmerized her. "I will protect you. If you committed a crime, it is better for you to face it than to run."

Though his hands were warm and reassuring, her heart turned cold. She jerked away from him. "No. I didn't commit a crime. I didn't see anything. I don't know anything."

He stepped closer, invading her space. "I understand you're afraid. Whatever it is, I will be with you the whole way. Please, trust me."

She angled her head to stare at him. "Why is my trust so important to you?"

As if her words were a splash of cold water, he abruptly stepped back. "It's my job to protect you."

She shook her head with a dash of cynicism. "I know you want to believe you can protect me, but the type of people I need protection from don't respect authority. They'd just as soon kill you as look at you."

Chase stood tall as if her words had been a personal assault. "Jane, tell me what you know."

She glanced around to make sure she wouldn't be overheard. She hated how exposed and vulnerable she felt out in the open. She gestured for him to follow her beneath the shade of a large Douglas fir. "If I tell you, will you help me get out of here?"

"If you tell me, I promise I will protect you."

More frustration bubbled inside her. What choice did she have? Her only option was to trust Chase and his promise of protection until she had an opportunity to run again. She had to stay vigilant if she wanted to stay alive.

Her heart raced. Her gaze darted from shadow to shadow, half expecting Maksim Sokolov to step out from behind a tree like a bogeyman from a horror movie. "A year and a half ago—" her voice dipped as the secret she'd held inside escaped like a bat out of a dark cave "—I witnessed a murder."

Jane's words echoed through Chase's brain. Sympathy squeezed his heart. Ever since the detective, who'd appeared this morning without warning at the sheriff station, had shown Chase the photo of a woman with long dark hair and bangs dressed in a black dress and pumps at the back door of a brick building, Chase's stomach had been tied in knots.

Though only the woman's profile had been visible, there had been something vaguely familiar about the curve of her cheek, the line of her jaw. And then it had come to him. The woman in the photo was Jane.

And she apparently was hiding in Bristle Township because she'd witnessed a murder. "Tell me what happened."

She shook her head. "If the killer finds out that I can identify him…" A visible shudder rippled through her. "He will kill me and anyone else in his path."

Her palpable fear sent all his protective instincts into high gear. She was in danger. Her life threatened by what she'd seen. Reining in the urge to comfort and assure her that she was safe, he let his training prompt him to ask, "Why is Detective Peters convinced you're involved?"

She turned to pluck the bark off the tree. Her shoulders slumped. "I don't know."

Was he being played? He sent up a quick prayer, asking for God's wisdom and guidance here. Keeping his voice from betraying the anxiety her words caused, he said, "We have to get you to the sheriff's station so you can give your statement. You need to be brave now."

Chase hoped she would come willingly. He didn't want to have to compel her by putting her in cuffs.

For a long moment, she simply stared at him. He could see her inner debate with herself playing out on her face. Trust him or not.

He couldn't help her with the decision.

Finally, she seemed to deflate. "I'm so tired of being scared. I want to be brave."

He covered her icy hand. "I'll help you."

Snagging her duffel with his free hand, he walked with her away from the hotel. They hadn't gone far when a black SUV pulled up alongside them and Detective William Peters hopped out. The tall, bulky man wore a wrinkled gray suit, white button-down shirt and red tie. His dark hair brushed the edges of his collar.

There was something about the man's gruff demeanor that had rankled Chase from the second they'd met. He chalked it up to city vs. small town. One of the many reasons Chase left the Chicago PD after only a year. He hadn't wanted to become jaded like so many of his fellow officers.

Chase believed in good over evil, that the right side of the law would win in the end. And justice wasn't prejudiced or affected by social status. Maybe that made him naive as some had said. He didn't care. He had faith that he was doing what God wanted for his life.

Detective Peters's dark eyes glittered with triumph.

"There you are." He opened the rear passenger door. "Get in. We have a plane to catch."

Jane clutched Chase's arm. She made no move to comply.

"Hold on a minute," Chase told the detective. "We need to do this the right way. We go to the sheriff's station so we can make a proper transfer to your custody."

Peters shook his head. "No way. She's coming with me now. I have a warrant that gives me the right to take her into custody on sight."

Chase didn't recall any mention of a warrant. "The sheriff will want to talk with her."

"There's no time for that." Peters stepped forward and grabbed Jane by the arm, yanking her from Chase's grasp. He pushed her inside the back passenger side of the SUV.

"You can't just take her away," Chase argued. "There's protocol to follow."

Peters got in Chase's face. "Back off. If you have an issue, then call the brass. I've got my orders."

"Chase?"

Jane's anxiety curled through Chase. "I'm going with you. I'll get my own plane ticket. Even if I have to fly on a different airline." He stepped forward to slide into the back seat with Jane when Peters slammed the door shut, blocking Chase from following her into the vehicle.

Peters shoved Chase back a step and glared. "This is my collar, not yours. I'm not letting some Podunk deputy interfere with my investigation."

Taken aback by the man's hostility, Chase put his hand on the butt of his weapon. Drawing on a fellow officer wasn't something he wanted to do, but if the man continued with his aggressive behavior, Chase would have little choice. "She's a witness, not a suspect."

"That's for others with a higher pay grade to decide. She's coming with me." Peters jumped into the vehicle.

Chase grabbed the back door handle but it was locked. He banged on the driver's side window. "You can't just take her like this."

The SUV's engine revved. Peters hit the gas and the SUV peeled away, forcing Chase to jump aside to avoid being hit.

This wasn't right. There was a proper way of doing things. Chase ran to the sheriff's station. At the front desk, he asked Carole if she could get the chief of the Los Angeles Police Department on the line for the sheriff. Then he moved into the inner sanctuary of the station. His voice shook with anger as he told the sheriff and the other deputies about Jane and what had just transpired.

"I've got the Burbank Police Department on the line," Carole called from her desk. "Should I send the call to your desk, Sheriff?"

"No, send it to Chase's," Sheriff Ryder replied.

Stunned, Chase stared. "Sir?"

"You're running point on this one," the sheriff replied.

Not about to question his boss, Chase sat at his desk and punched the blinking light. A second later a man's deep voice came on the line. "Chief Macintosh, how can I help you?"

Chase hurriedly explained the situation, giving his protest at the detective's manhandling of their citizen.

There was a long pause before Chief Macintosh replied, "You say this man had Detective William Peters's identification?"

A strange question. An unsettled apprehension curled through Chase. "He did."

"The man's an imposter," Macintosh said. "Detective William Peters is dead. Murdered during an undercover operation."

TWO

The air swooshed out of Chase's lungs. If he hadn't been sitting, he'd have fallen to the floor. His mind raced and his blood pounded. The man posing as Detective William Peters was a fake. The real detective was dead.

Jane was in danger.

Kidnapped. And Chase had let it happen.

Guilt reached up to throttle his windpipe. He'd made a horrible mistake by not stopping the fake detective. Now Jane would pay the price.

"Whoever this woman is, she could be a potential witness to the real Detective Peters's murder," Chief Macintosh continued.

Chase's stomach sank. "She claims she can ID a killer."

Excitement buzzed in the chief's voice. "Did she give a name?"

"No, sir." She'd been too afraid. He could only imagine how terrified she was now. She'd tried to warn him not to trust anyone. Chase had lost control of the situation. A rookie mistake. He wasn't a rookie anymore. Self-anger burned in his gut.

"You need to find this phony detective before he kills her," Chief Macintosh said, his tone grim.

"I will." Chase hung up with knots in his stomach.

The man said they had a plane to catch, which meant they were headed to Denver. He needed the state patrol's help. He jerked to his feet. "Carole, can you get the state patrol on the line?"

"Chase?" Deputy Kaitlyn Lanz rose from her desk. "What's wrong?"

"The real Peters is dead. The man posing as him most likely is an assassin sent to silence Jane. We have to find them."

Eyes wide with a mix of worry and surprise, Kaitlyn said, "Yes, of course."

Carole hurried from her desk. "Sheriff, the phones are blowing up again. A speeding black SUV nearly ran down Brady Gallo. Others are reporting the vehicle heading up Bishop Summit."

Chase was familiar with the forestry road on the backside of Eagle Crest Mountain, which led to the ski resort at the top. It was a dangerous, twisty climb with lots of cliffs on one side. The assassin wasn't taking Jane to Denver but to a remote area to kill her.

"Also, Lucca Chinn is here, wanting to know what's going on," Carole said.

Groaning aloud, Chase jerked his gaze to the sheriff. The last thing they needed was *The Bristle Township Gazette*'s publisher, reporter and custodian—the man was a one-person operation—sticking his nose into the situation. Even a small town had someone who insisted the public needed to be kept informed, and Lucca Chinn had appointed himself the resident news source.

"I'll take care of Chinn," the sheriff stated. "You go."

Galvanized into action, Chase ran out the door with deputies Daniel Rawlings and Kaitlyn Lanz on his heels.

"I'll be right behind you." Kaitlyn peeled away and ran toward her own vehicle.

Chase didn't stop to question why she needed to drive her own truck pulling a horse trailer as he slid into the driver's seat of one of the department-issued vehicles while Daniel hopped into the passenger seat. Chase lifted a prayer that he would get to Jane before it was too late.

Ashley stared out the window of the rear passenger seat of the big black SUV as the vehicle roared up the access road to the ski resort. Green trees and various other plants growing wild along the edges of the road were a blur. The SUV's tires squealed as the vehicle sped through a curve in the road.

"I don't understand," she said to the man in front. "I thought you said we were going to the airport. This isn't the way to Denver."

She could only see his profile at this angle. His nose had a lump on the top like he'd broken it and not had it set well. His dark hair was unruly. Everything about him was at odds with the button-down way Deputy Chase Fredrick presented himself. "Shut up," the detective growled.

Alarm raised the hairs on her arms. She didn't know what this man was up to but the dread squeezing her lungs urged her to escape. She tried the door handle, but the door wouldn't open. He'd activated the vehicle's child locks, keeping her trapped inside. She tried the window, but it too wouldn't open. Not that either option was an escape when the SUV was buzzing along like a rocket on the twisty road.

She kicked the front seat. "Hey! What are you doing? Where are you taking me?"

He ignored her.

Who was this man driving her up the mountain? Was he really a detective? Fear scraped along her nerves. Had her captor been sent by Maksim Sokolov?

The vehicle made a sharp turn into an overlook gravel turnout and came to an abrupt halt, throwing her forward. The seat belt snapped into a locked position, keeping her from flying into the back of the front seat. The strap cut into her chest. Once the pressure lessened, she rubbed at the place where the seat belt had no doubt left a mark.

The detective climbed out of the SUV and came around to her side of the vehicle. She quickly unbuckled and scooted across to the other side of the back seat as he yanked open the door. She attempted to climb into the front driver's seat but her attacker reached in and grabbed her by the ankles, dragging her toward him.

Frantic, she kicked, hoping to dislodge his grip, but his hands were like manacles, his fingers digging into her flesh and not letting go. He yanked her out of the SUV, her back bumping painfully on the edge of the door frame. She landed flat on the ground with a jarring jolt. Gravel and grit bit into her through her clothes.

Her assailant loosened his grip for a fraction of a second, which was enough time for her to break out of his grasp with a forceful jerk. She jumped to her feet and ran toward the road, hoping someone else would drive by. Feet pounded behind her. She pushed herself to move faster, but she'd never been a strong runner.

Her captor caught her, grabbing her by the waist and lifting her off her feet. She pummeled his arms and lashed out with her feet.

"You are so dead," he growled. "Even if I hadn't been sent here to kill you, I'd do it just because."

"Please, no. I haven't told anyone what I saw," she beseeched the man, hoping for mercy. "You can tell Mr. Sokolov I won't talk."

Ignoring her pleas, her kidnapper carried her away from the road, past the SUV and dragged her across the lookout barrier. There was an overhang not far below.

"Move it," he demanded, giving her a push, forcing her down the steep incline.

Her tennis shoes made the going rough, as the rubber slipped on the loose dirt and rocks. Using her arms, she tried to keep her balance, fearing that she'd take a header over the side of the cliff.

"But you're a law enforcement officer," she exclaimed, shocked by his words that he truly did intend to kill her. "You can't mean to really harm me. What about your oath to protect?"

He let out an evil laugh that sent chills down her spine. "The police think you're a killer. Besides, no one is going to care when you're dead."

His words sliced her open. "How much did Mr. Sokolov pay you?" she demanded, wishing she could offer him more, but she had no money. "How much is my life worth?"

"Enough to set me up for the rest of my life," he said. "No more talking. Time for you to die."

Terror consumed her. The man hauled her toward the ledge that dropped off to a steep cliff with a deep ravine far below. The nightmare she'd been trapped in was coming to a horrifying end.

At the edge of the outcropping, his rough hands reached for her. Acting instinctively, she dropped to the ground, wrapping her arms around his ankles. If she was going over the cliff, so was he.

Chase's hands gripped and re-gripped the steering wheel as he took the corners at a breakneck speed. Adrenaline pumped through his veins, giving him a lead foot.

"Whoa," Daniel said, bracing his hands on the dashboard as the vehicle careened around a curve on the forestry road on the backside of Eagle Crest Mountain. "It's not going to do Jane any good if we drive off the side of the mountain."

Heeding Daniel's words, Chase eased up a fraction. They had to find Jane. He'd already betrayed her trust by letting her go off with an assassin and failed his repeated vow to protect her. The heavy weight of responsibility descended on his shoulders. He couldn't let her die.

The black SUV came into view and Chase hit the brakes, skidding to a halt in front of the vehicle. There was no sign of Jane or the fake detective.

"Radio the sheriff our location." Chase jumped out of the car and ran to the SUV. A quick peek inside confirmed it was empty. He turned around, desperate to figure out where they'd gone. The ground was marred with footsteps and drag marks in the gravel.

His stomach clenched with dread as he followed the trail to the guardrail. Peering over the side of the cliff, horror filled his veins. On an outcropping stood Peters with Jane clutching his legs for dear life as he tried to pry her from him. His objective was clear. He was going to throw her over the cliff.

Chase vaulted over the guardrail and drew his weapon. He slipped and slid down the hill. "Stop! Put your hands in the air."

Peters twisted toward Chase with a 9mm Glock fitted with a noise suppressor aimed at him.

Chase dove to the side as bullets whizzed past him, so close the air heated. Staying in motion, he rolled to one knee, sighted down the barrel of his weapon and fired. The loud retort echoed over the mountain and battered against his eardrum.

The bullet hit its mark.

For a moment, the assassin's eyes went wide and his mouth dropped open as red bloomed across his white shirt. Then he stumbled back a step, taking Jane with him. The heel of his shoe dislodged a landslide of loose dirt falling to the bottom of the ravine.

Fear choked Chase. Jane was about to go over the cliff with her assailant. "Let go of him!"

Immediately, she responded to his command and released her hold on Peters's legs, scrambling backward seconds before the man took a nosedive down the side of the cliff, disappearing from sight.

Sending a quick praise to God for Jane's safety and asking forgiveness for taking a life, Chase hurried to

Jane's side and gathered her in his arms. She clung to him, her body shaking. Through the ringing in his ears, he heard her racking sobs. Her tears soaked the front of his uniform. Chase's heart beat in his throat. He thought he might be sick.

A landslide of rocks sounding from above jolted through him. He jerked his gaze up to the cliff as he tucked Jane behind him.

Daniel slid down the rocky hill much the way Chase had done. Chase let out a compressed breath of relief.

"Wow," Daniel said as he skidded to a halt. "Clean shot. I saw the whole thing. You good?"

His ears still ringing from discharging his weapon, Chase made out the gist of what Daniel said, though his voice sounded muffled. Chase nodded as he sucked in air, working to calm his racing pulse. Later, he'd deal with the aftermath of taking a life.

Daniel stepped past Chase and peered over the edge of the cliff. He whistled and turned to stare at Chase. "That's a long way down." He moved away from the ledge. "I better call the sheriff and tell him we need a recovery team. You okay to get her up the hill?"

"We'll manage." Chase helped Jane to her feet. He met her terrified gaze. "Take it slow and steady."

He wrapped an arm around her waist and they made the arduous climb up the incline. They ended up having to crawl on hands and knees to keep their center of gravity low, until they reached the guardrail. Chase lifted Jane over the metal rungs and set her on the gravel of the turnout. Then he climbed over, grateful for the stable ground.

Jane wrapped her arms around her middle; her lips

trembled and tears streaked down her face. "Are you okay?"

"I am." His hearing was returning and his heart rate had slowed. "You? Did he hurt you?"

"I'll have some bruises." She stared at him, her eyes wide. "You saved my life."

The wonder in her tone scored him to the quick. "If I had been better at my job, you wouldn't have been in the situation in the first place."

"This is not your fault." There was compassion in her tone. "He was a police officer, too."

Chase shook his head. "No. He was an imposter."

Her eyes widened in shock. She let out a shuddering breath. "If you hadn't come along…"

"But I did." And he was thankful for that small favor from God. He gestured toward his vehicle. "Let's get you inside my car where you can feel safe."

He hustled her to the back of the Sheriff's Department vehicle and opened the door for her. She hesitated, most likely remembering the last time somebody told her to get into an SUV.

"Trust me," he murmured.

She glanced over her shoulder at him, her pretty eyes intense. "I want to." There was doubt in her voice, but she climbed inside the vehicle without further comment.

Warmth expanded within his chest. At this point he'd take whatever confidence she'd give him, even though he didn't deserve it. The sound of sirens punctuated the air. "Stay put, okay? Let us sort this out."

She settled in the seat. "I'm not going anywhere."

He left the door open so she wouldn't feel trapped

and hurried to meet the sheriff, Deputy Alex Trevino, Kaitlyn and the EMT.

Taking a deep breath as the adrenaline letdown coursed through his body, Chase's legs wobbled. He tucked his thumbs into his utility belt so no one would see that his hands trembled, as well. He'd shot and killed a man.

Not something he'd ever hoped to actually do. Oh, he trained for it. They all did. Aimed for center mass as he'd been taught. Maybe if he'd shot Peters in the leg or the shoulder... He gave himself a sharp internal shake. He could've easily missed a smaller target or hit Jane. And Peters's next bullet could've torn through Chase's skull. No, he'd done the right thing.

The sheriff and Alex climbed out of the sheriff's vehicle and strode toward him. Kaitlyn joined them, having driven her own personal truck with the horse trailer behind it.

Putting his hand on Chase's shoulder, the sheriff said, "Daniel filled us in on what happened. Are you okay?"

Standing tall, Chase nodded. "Yes, sir. I will be. A little shaken."

Empathy shone in his boss's gaze. "That's to be expected. You did well."

The sheriff's praise slide inside of Chase, bolstering his confidence. "Thank you, sir."

"Alex will escort you and Miss Thompson back to the station." Sheriff Ryder turned to Kaitlyn. "You know what to do."

"Yes, sir." Kaitlyn's hazel eyes were kind as she

shifted her gaze to Chase. "I'm glad you and Jane are unharmed. Please tell her I'll check in with her later."

Mild surprise washed over Chase. He hadn't known that Kaitlyn and Jane were close. "I will. How did you know to bring your horse?"

She cocked an eyebrow. "Hey, when somebody heads up the mountain with a hostage in tow, you never know when a horse might come in handy. I figured if the kidnapper took Jane deep into the forest, it would be best to be prepared to follow."

As she strode away, Chase marveled again at being blessed to be a part of the Bristle Township Sheriff's Department. Each team member was smart, competent and trustworthy. He could not have asked for better people to work with. They were like family.

"I'll drive," Alex said. He hopped into the front seat of the SUV Chase had driven up the mountain.

Not wanting to alarm Jane, Chase slid into the back seat next to her and shut the door. Jane was watching Kaitlyn ride by on her horse, a big roan with a black mane and tail. The pair stopped for a moment. Kaitlyn appeared tiny on top of the huge beast. Her blond ponytail hung down the back of her brown uniform.

"What's she doing?" Jane asked, leaning forward to watch Kaitlyn through the SUV's front window.

"Plotting out her course down the side of the mountain," Alex supplied as he started the engine.

Kaitlyn steered the large animal to the left, skirting around the metal barricade and slowly began a crisscrossed descent down the side of the hill until she disappeared from sight.

"Okay." Jane turned her troubled gaze to Chase. "But *why* is she doing that?"

"She's going to locate the body. And help coordinate the recovery from down below," Chase answered without sugarcoating the work that would need to be done.

Surprise widened her eyes. "Is that safe for her to do?"

"Kait's an accomplished horsewoman and a member of the mounted patrol," Alex replied from the front seat. "Her family breeds and trains horses. Plus, she knows this mountain like the back of her hand. She grew up here, unlike me or Chase."

"The sheriff wouldn't have asked her to do this if he weren't confident in her abilities," Chase added. "All the members of the mounted patrol are highly trained. With terrain like we have here, there are places only accessible by horseback."

"Are you on the mounted patrol?" Jane asked.

Chase met Alex's gaze in the rearview mirror. "Not yet. Alex has been teaching me how to ride. One day I hope to be trained enough to join the patrol. But for now I'm content to be ground support to the others."

"Leslie offered to give me a riding lesson," Jane said.

"You should take her up on the offer," Chase said. "She's an auxiliary member of the mounted patrol."

"Auxiliary?"

"A fancy term for volunteer," he told her. Like many western state mounted patrols, the members were a mix of paid law enforcement and trained, unarmed civilians.

"Perhaps I'll take a riding lesson." Jane turned to stare out the window. "If I live long enough to."

He didn't like to hear the despair in her tone. "You're safe, Jane."

She shook her head. "No, I'm not." She faced him. There was determination in her expression. "That man was sent to kill me. There will be more. I have to leave Bristle Township. Disappear again."

"You can't," he told her. "You said you wanted to be brave and do the right thing."

"I don't want to die," she said.

How did he get her to trust that they could protect her?

He needed to know what they were dealing with and why so they could form a plan to keep her safe. "Tell me about the night you witnessed a murder."

Dread twisted low in Ashley's gut. She blew out a breath. Dredging up the nightmare wasn't something she wanted to do but there was no way around it. Chase had to know about the monster after her. And once he learned the truth, he'd want nothing more to do with her. He'd be happy to let her slither away into the shadows.

She flicked a glance at the intimidating man named Alex in the front seat, wishing she were alone with Chase. But then again, maybe it was better that they both hear this so she wouldn't have to repeat it. "I was waitressing at an upscale restaurant in Burbank, The Matador."

Chase's eyebrows drew together. "It recently burned down, right?"

Her chest tightened. She lifted the restricting seat belt strap away from her body to suck in air. "Yes. It was reported on the news. I'm sure the fire was set because of me."

"Why would you think that?" Alex asked from the driver's seat.

She let out a small dry laugh. "Because the only person injured was the man who helped me escape California."

Chase's intense gaze locked with hers. "Did your friend know you were here in Bristle?"

Shaking her head, she said, "No. I was so careful." Remorse swamped her. "Until this morning."

"What did you do this morning?" Chase asked.

"I called the hospital where my friend was taken." She wiped at fresh tears slipping down her cheeks. "I had to know if he was alive."

"Is he?" Chase's intense gaze locked with hers.

"For now," she said. "He's in critical condition."

Sympathy crossed Chase's face. "Were you able to talk to him?"

"No. And I didn't leave a name or number," she said. "I don't know how they found me. But they did."

"Probably tapped the hospital phone and traced the call," Alex supplied.

Her stomach knotted. She should have thought of that. Another move that put her life in jeopardy.

"Let's go to a year and a half ago," Chase urged. "What happened?"

With one hand, she pinched the bridge of her nose, forcing herself to go back to that horrible night. Her heart rate picked up as she spoke. "We were going through our closing duties like any other night. I went to take the trash out to the dumpster in the back."

She pressed her lips together for a moment as a flush of anger robbed her of speech. Finding her voice, she continued, "I forgot to put the doorstop in the door." She couldn't keep the self-recrimination from her voice. "If I had just remembered to prop the door open." She pounded her fist against her thigh. "I forgot and the door locked behind me."

His hand covered her fist. "Hey, don't be so hard on yourself. Everyone makes mistakes."

She glanced over at him and stifled a scoff. "A mistake that could get me killed."

"Not going to happen. Not on my watch."

She wanted to believe him, but there was no way he could make such a promise. Though the sentiment was heartwarming to hear and to know he meant it filled her with tenderness. But he didn't know her. And she feared if he ever really did, he'd think twice about his promises. "I'm always such a mess. I can never get anything right. I would have been fired from that job long ago if Gregor, the restaurant manager, hadn't taken a shine to me."

"A shine? Was this man taking advantage of you?"

His voice held a hard edge that startled her. His reaction gave her pause. But he was a cop. Of course his thoughts had gone to a dark place. She gave a quick shake of her head. "Oh, no. Gregor was more like a grandfather to all of us. I never knew my own grandparents. Gregor was kind and generous. He didn't deserve to be hurt."

Her words seemed to nullify the sharpness of moments before. "No, he didn't if he was willing to risk his own life to protect you." He considered her a moment. "You didn't have a spouse or boyfriend to keep you safe?"

She tucked in her chin. "Oh, none of those. I mean, I've dated, but most men either consider me more of the sister type or the best friend type."

He remained silent for a heartbeat, then said, "You took the trash out and then what happened?"

At his prompting, she refocused on telling her story. "There were people in the back alley." She bit the inside of her lip as the memory assaulted her. "Mr. Sokolov was arguing with a man."

"Who is Mr. Sokolov?"

"He owns the restaurant. I'd never seen the man he was arguing with. I tried to go back inside, but I was locked out, trapped." The helpless, vulnerable sensation she'd experienced that night was back tenfold. She smoothed her hands over her thighs, needing something to do with her hands other than wringing them like some victim.

But let's face it, she was a victim. A victim of being in the wrong place at the wrong time and seeing something that changed the course of her life.

"You must have been frightened." The fingers of his right hand laced through hers.

She held on tight, absorbing some of his strength. He was a steadfast man like a giant oak that wind could neither bend nor break. "I would have had to walk right in the middle of their argument to go around to the front of the building and be let back inside." She shuddered. "I shrank into the shadows of the garbage container, hoping they'd leave soon. But they lingered, continuing their arguing. Their voices were loud and angry."

"You heard what they were saying?"

There was no mistaking the anticipation in his tone. She hated to disappoint him.

"Some, not all. Mr. Sokolov was yelling at the man about betrayal and trusting him when he should've known better."

"This Sokolov character must have discovered the man was an undercover police officer," Chase said.

She gasped. "I didn't know. He wasn't in uniform." She tried to recall what the dead man wore. "He had on jeans, a T-shirt and baseball cap."

"His clothing would make sense if he was undercover," Chase said.

"Where was his backup?" Alex asked.

"That's a good question," Chase answered. "One we'll have to ask Chief Macintosh." Chase returned his attention to her. "Go on."

"Mr. Sokolov reached underneath his coat and pulled out a gun." The memory made her shrink a bit, her shoulders rounding and her chin dipping. She wanted to forget, to curl in a ball and pretend she hadn't seen any of it.

"You saw this?" Alex asked.

"Yes." She lifted her face and met Chase's gaze. "He shot that man. I had to bite my fist to keep from screaming."

Chase squeezed her hands.

Tears rolled down her cheeks. Anxiety fluttered in her chest. "The sight of that man crumbling to the ground and Mr. Sokolov stepping over the man he'd just killed like he was a piece of garbage will be forever etched in my brain."

Now she could add watching the phony detective going over the side of the cliff. Definitely, the stuff of nightmares.

"So you ran away?"

"Not at first. After Mr. Sokolov was gone, I ran to the man to offer help. But he had no pulse. And there was so much blood." She remembered gagging at the sight. "Then I heard a noise and ran back behind the garbage bin. Gregor found me there. He hustled me away from the restaurant."

"Did someone remove the body?" Alex asked.

She glanced toward Alex and met his gaze in the rearview mirror. "I don't know. I didn't hear anyone else and I didn't want to look again."

Chase's eyebrows dipped together. "How does Sokolov know you witnessed the crime?"

She'd wondered that, too. Had Gregor revealed her secret to Sokolov? No, wait. "Didn't you say Peters, or whoever he was, had a photo of me leaving the back door of The Matador?"

"He did," Chase answered. "But if you worked there, why wouldn't they have known your name?"

She shrugged, sadness filling her chest. "I can only guess Gregor took me out of the system and that the others…" She swallowed back the choking sensation in her throat. "They must have covered for me."

And risked their lives. For her. Why would anyone do that if that wasn't their job? She couldn't fathom it. But she couldn't deny the warmth layering upon her fear. The people she'd worked with had protected her. There was no way for her to ever repay them.

"How long before the police arrived?" Alex asked.

She bit her lip. "I didn't see any police."

"Surely someone would have reported hearing a gunshot," Chase stated.

She cocked her head, trying to recall more of that night. "It's strange. I don't remember hearing the gun go off."

"The weapon could have had a noise suppressor like the guy today," Chase told her. "But even those make a sound that would have likely echoed through the alley."

She didn't know what to say to that. She'd been frightened, her heart pounding so loud in her ears and her breathing labored from terror.

"What did you hear?" Chase pressed.

"I—I don't recall." She searched her mind, desperate to dredge up some answer, but there was nothing, just the looping images and the residual fear. "It was a year and a half ago. But I know what I saw."

"Are you sure it was Sokolov who fired the fatal shot?" Alex asked, as he parked the vehicle in front of the sheriff's station, a brick two-story structure that had been rebuilt after a fire last year.

Ashley couldn't see any signs of the damage done by the blaze. The image of The Matador flittered through her thoughts and grief over what was lost twisted in her chest. "Yes." There was no doubt in her mind about Mr. Sokolov's guilt.

Alex twisted in his seat to study her. "Did the other guy have a weapon?"

She shook her head, embarrassed for not knowing the answer. "Not that I noticed."

"Why didn't you go to the police?" Chase asked. "That would have been the best course of action."

Stung by his words and the fact that she hadn't done the *best course of action*, she tried to explain. "I wanted to. Once the shock of it all wore off, my first instinct was to run to the nearest police station." Her lips twisted. "But Gregor... He said I couldn't trust the police. Mr. Sokolov owned too many of them. Gregor said I couldn't trust anyone."

"But you trusted Gregor," Chase pointed out.

Ashley detected a hint of complaint in his voice. "I did. He was my friend and had helped me. But he couldn't protect me long-term. Mr. Sokolov was cruel. Gregor had a scar on his face given to him by Mr. Sokolov when he'd let one of the waiters leave early because his child was sick. Everyone was afraid of Mr. Sokolov."

"Why did any of you stay there?" Alex asked, his gaze genuinely puzzled.

She shrugged. "He paid well." She focused back at Chase, taking comfort in his attention. "And when Mr. Sokolov wasn't around, it was a great place to work."

Chase's gaze intensified. "Then why run?"

Her chin dropped a fraction. "Gregor said my only option to stay alive was to run, keep moving and never look back. Mr. Sokolov would kill me and everyone I loved."

A scowl dipped Chase's eyebrows together as if he didn't like what she'd said. Neither did she. Being on the run, looking over her shoulder, constantly afraid had wreaked havoc with her mind.

"How did you survive this last year and a half?" Chase asked.

"Gregor gave me some cash, and the identification of a woman my approximate age and height and put me on a bus for New Mexico." Those first few days were beyond stressful.

His gaze narrowed. He slid his hands from hers. "Wait, are you telling me you're not Jane Thompson?"

The moment she'd dreaded had arrived. It was said that the truth will set you free, but she had a sickening quiver in the pit of her stomach that, in this case, the truth would condemn her. Would he still want to help her, knowing she'd deceived him and everyone else?

THREE

Chase's breath stalled in his lungs. He sat back to stare at the woman sitting beside him, taking in the paleness of her complexion, her short curly hair and frightened eyes. She wasn't who she'd said she was. "What is your real name?"

Her lips twisted in a rueful grimace. She ducked her chin slightly. "Ashley Willis."

He rubbed the back of his neck as he absorbed this bit of information. She'd lied about her identity. Was she still lying? How did he even know if she was telling him her real name? Or if the story she'd just told him and Alex was true? Was she mixed up in something that had ended the life of a police officer? Or had she really witnessed his death, as she claimed? Chase didn't like all the questions and doubts. He wanted to believe she was now telling the truth. Should he give her the benefit of the doubt?

"Ashley." He said the name slowly, testing it. "It will take some getting used to."

"At first it was hard to remember to answer to Jane."

Exchanging a glance with Alex, Chase replied, "I would imagine. Living a lie would be difficult."

"It was necessary to stay alive." She met his gaze with a direct look. "I couldn't even go back to the apartment I shared with three other women." Sadness crept across her pretty, tear-stained face. "I can't imagine what they are thinking. Gregor assured me he'd take care of my things, so I hope he told them I'd landed an acting gig and was moving up in the world."

His stomach dropped. It was an actress's job to lie, in a way. No wonder she'd pulled off being Jane so long. "You're an actress?"

"Aspiring. I did a few commercials." Her mouth twisted. "Mostly I'm a waitress. Just like my mother."

"Where is she?" Alex asked.

She glanced at him. "Barstow, California."

Alex tilted his head. "Does she know where you are?"

Jane—uh, Ashley, shook her head. "I didn't want to put her in danger." She shrugged as a flash of hurt lit her eyes. "I doubt she'd care to know where I was, anyway."

Chase couldn't decide if she was courageous or foolish. Or playing him. "How did you end up here in Bristle Township?"

"I first landed in Albuquerque, then went on to Santa Fe. Every few weeks I kept moving. I intended to head to Canada. But by the time I arrived here, I was nearly out of cash. And I didn't know what else to do, so I rented a room and got a job."

"You did the smart thing by staying put." If the assassin had found her somewhere else, things might not have ended well for her. "Now, you have to do another smart and brave thing. You need to go back to Burbank and testify about what you saw."

She shook her head, terror darkening her eyes. "He'll kill me just like he did that man. You've already seen he's determined. Please, the best thing for me is to keep moving."

He couldn't let her disappear. There were too many unanswered questions. "I understand your fear. You were alone and on the run. But no longer. You have me and the Sheriff's Department watching your back."

His words didn't seem to reassure her. He dared to press, "You need to tell the authorities in Los Angeles what you told us."

A visible shudder rippled through her. "But what if the police there can't protect me?"

Knowing he was taking a chance that might backfire, he said, "I'll be there with you."

Her eyebrows rose. "You mean, you'd actually go with me to LA? Won't that interfere with your job here?"

"You let me worry about my job." He ignored Alex's snort from the front seat.

Chase had no doubt the sheriff would allow him to take his vacation days to accompany Ashley to Los Angeles. Whatever it took for her to feel secure in doing the right thing. His heart ached for her, for the hardship she'd endured and the horror she had witnessed. One thing he knew was that the trauma she'd gone through today was real. Someone wanted her dead. And guilt for letting the danger get so close to her ate at him. But it was time for her to come clean and help law enforcement put away a criminal. Getting her to agree to testify might take some work. Regardless, he would persevere.

She shook her head. "I can't ask that of you. I've deceived you. I don't deserve your sympathy or your protection." She lifted her chin high as if she were ready to take a punch to the jaw.

His stomach contracted. Had someone hit this woman in the past? Or was this all bravado? Did she think she deserved to take her lumps for hiding her identity? Did she really expect them to turn their backs on her? Empathy nipped at him. She had to be telling the truth. No one could fake that kind of fear. And the danger was real.

He gathered her hands once again in his. "You were doing what you had to to survive. No one can fault you for that."

She relaxed, blinking rapidly. "I should have gone to the police and taken my chances."

He agreed, but what was done was done. They had to move forward. "You were in shock. You witnessed something horrible. When people are in the middle of trauma, they don't make the best choices. And you were given advice that may, or may not, have saved your life."

She turned away from him. "That's true. Once I ran, I knew there was no going back."

"But there is," Chase insisted. "Once you testify to what you saw."

Alex popped open the driver's side door. "We should get her inside."

Chase helped Ashley from the vehicle and ushered her into the sheriff's station. "You'll stay here for the time being. Safer that way."

She nodded. "Good. I don't want to put Mrs. Marsh in danger. But I should tell my boss at the Java Bean."

"We'll call him later and explain." He directed her to the chair next to his desk. "From now on, I'm sticking to you like glue. We're in this together."

He was rewarded with tears and a wobbly smile. "Thank you," she whispered. "I've been alone so long."

"Not anymore." He grabbed the phone. "Right now, I'm going to call Chief Macintosh and find out exactly what is going on."

She put her hand on his arm. "Can you call the hospital and check on Gregor?" Her gaze beseeched him to comply. "He helped me when he didn't have to and he asked for nothing in return. It would make me feel better if I knew he was doing okay. That they haven't harmed him trying to get to me."

For some reason her devotion to this man irritated Chase. He marshaled the strange reaction. It was a small thing to do, considering all she'd been through. A favor he was willing to grant. His heart squeezed tight. "Of course."

She gave him the name of the hospital. A quick internet search gave him the hospital's main number. He identified himself and inquired about Gregor Kominski's condition.

What he heard sent his stomach plummeting. He thanked the woman and hung up. Turning to Ashley, he said, "I'm sorry to tell you this. Gregor Kominski succumbed to his injuries."

Gregor was dead.

Anguish tore through Ashley. She dropped her head into her hands as grief swelled, making her insides ache. Gregor had died because of her. Guilt like shards of glass embedded themselves into her heart. He died even though he hadn't known where she was and yet Mr. Sokolov found her through him, anyway.

Gregor's death had accomplished what Mr. Sokolov had intended. He'd found her. And he'd sent someone to kill her. A shudder of terror worked over her limbs. How many more killers would show up until she was dead?

Gentle hands landed on her shoulders. "Ashley, you are not responsible for what happened to your friend."

She lifted her gaze to meet Chase's. How did he know that she blamed herself? Was she that easy to read? Or was he that good at his job? She suspected it was the latter.

This man was so kind, so generous and honorable. She didn't deserve his help. And if anything happened to him... Her heart contracted painfully in her chest.

If anything happened to anyone in Bristle Township because of her, she would not be able to live with herself. Especially now that she had let down her guard enough to allow people in, even if only just a little. She'd made ties to this community that she'd never intended to form. That had to end here and now.

She gave Chase a tight smile. "I appreciate your trying to comfort me. But I know Mr. Sokolov is the guilty party. And he needs to pay."

For the first time since that night, the seeds of anger took root, making her limbs shake. She wanted desperately to be brave enough to bring Mr. Sokolov down.

She needed a moment to collect herself. "Is there a restroom I can use?"

"Down the corridor, door on your left," Chase instructed.

On wobbly legs, she made her way down the hall as the sheriff returned. Quickly, she ducked into the restroom, not ready to have a face-to-face with Chase's boss.

Once inside the small single-user space, she turned the lock and slumped against the door as the floodgates let loose and she sobbed into her hands. She was crying for herself and for her friend who had paid the ultimate price. It was all so unfair. But then she knew God never promised fair.

She wasn't naive. Even if Mr. Sokolov were behind bars, her life would be in danger.

Fair or not, she would have to leave Bristle Township. A deep cold numbness spread through her body.

She couldn't allow anyone here to get any more involved with her. She couldn't allow her heart to become more attached than it already was. There would come a point when she would find an opportunity to leave.

Until then, she would do what was necessary to keep everyone safe. And she would pray, with everything in her, that the handsome deputy would be able to protect her long enough to give her testimony. Then she would disappear again, despite how much her heart longed to stay in Bristle Township.

She left the restroom and headed back to Chase's desk, only he wasn't there. A flutter of anxiety hit her in the gut. Then she spied him in the sheriff's office talking with his boss. She put a hand to her stomach to quell the uneasy knot camping out there.

"Is it true?" Deputy Kaitlyn Lanz walked in. Her blond hair was mussed with little twigs sticking out from the long strands. Her uniform also showed signs of her trek into the forest and the distinct smell of horseflesh wafted in the air, teasing Ashley's nose. She sneezed.

"Alex told me your story," Kaitlyn said.

Ashley's heart thudded in her chest. Kaitlyn stared at her, waiting for an answer.

Swallowing back the bile rising to burn her throat, Ashley had no illusions that once she confirmed the truth, Kaitlyn wouldn't want to have anything more to do with her. She braced herself. "Yes, it's true. I'm not Jane Thompson. My name is Ashley Willis." The burn of tears pricked her eyes. "I'm so, so sorry."

Kaitlyn came to her and wrapped her in a hug.

Surprise rendered Ashley immobile, even as her nose twitched again with the urge to sneeze.

Drawing back to meet Ashley's gaze, Kaitlyn stated in her no-nonsense tone, "I would have done the same."

Kaitlyn's kindness made Ashley want to cry. "I hated not telling you."

"Don't apologize for doing what you had to. I'm just glad that we know and now we can help you." One corner of Kaitlyn's mouth tipped upward. "Ashley, huh?"

Ashley nodded.

"Okay, then," Kaitlyn said. "You're a survivor. A fighter. I can respect that."

As much as Ashley wanted to believe Kaitlyn's words, she knew they weren't true. If she'd had any backbone, she'd have gone to the authorities in the beginning and not lost a year and a half of her life to fear.

Chase stepped out of the sheriff's private office and joined them.

Putting her arm around Ashley, Kaitlyn addressed

Chase, "So what are we going to do to protect our friend?"

A small smile played at the corners of his mouth. "Bless you, Kait."

Kaitlyn's eyebrows rose. "What? You thought I'd turn my back on someone in trouble?"

Chase shook his head. "Actually, no." His gaze met Ashley's. "But I have a suspicion someone else might have had that thought."

Heat rose in Ashley's cheeks. She had expected the worst. Better to be pessimistic than to hope for the best and be disappointed.

Kaitlyn bumped her with her shoulder. "We good?"

Bemused, Ashley bumped her back. "Yes." For now. However, she really had to find a way to put some distance between them all so none of them were hurt. But for the life of her, she couldn't bring herself to pull away.

"She can stay with me," Kaitlyn announced.

"Actually, the Los Angeles district attorney, Evan Nyburg, is making arrangements for us to fly to California in the morning," Chase told them.

"You're going with her?" Kaitlyn asked.

Ashley held her breath. He'd promised to not abandon her, but she wasn't sure that was a promise he could keep.

"Yes," Chase confirmed.

"The sheriff is okay with that?" Ashley blurted out the question.

"Yes, he's on board for me to escort you to Los Angeles. The district attorney's office is arranging hotel rooms at the Denver airport for tonight and tickets on the first plane out in the morning."

"Good," Kaitlyn said.

"Kaitlyn," the sheriff called from the doorway of his office and waved her over.

"Excuse me, the boss calls." Kaitlyn left them to join the sheriff in his office.

Ashley put her hand on Chase's arm. "I don't know what to say. You shouldn't be taking time away from your work for me."

"Ashley, I'm doing my job. Keeping you safe is a priority." The phone on his desk rang. "I'm expecting a call."

While Chase took his call, Ashley marveled at the way these people were rallying around her. It didn't make any sense to her. In her limited experience, very few people would go out of their way to assist a stranger.

But they had signed up to do just that, she reasoned. And she shouldn't read anything more into their willingness to help her. She needed to keep an emotional barrier up and the best way for her to do that was to remember Chase and Kaitlyn were being paid to protect and serve.

Chase hung up the phone, his expression troubled. Dread filled Ashley. What now?

Chase stared at his desk phone for a moment, pondering the upsetting news he'd just learned. Ashley sat in the chair beside his desk, drawing his attention. He was glad to see she'd pulled herself together. He'd sensed she was on the verge of a breakdown when she'd hurried to the restroom. Empathy curled through Chase. Her guilt had been palpable when he'd told her of Gregor's demise. Chase hoped she really understood that the blame for her friend's death laid at the feet of the one who set the fire and the one who'd ordered the deed done.

"Is everything okay?" she asked.

He ran a hand over his stubbled jaw. "That was Detective Peters's boss. The real Detective Peters," he amended, because they didn't have a name yet for the man Chase shot. "Macintosh is sending over some photos and I want you to see if you can identify the man you saw killed."

Her chin dipped. "Do you think it might not have been Detective Peters?"

"Honestly, I don't know what to think. Did you know that Sokolov is believed to be the head of a drug cartel with ties to Eastern Europe?"

"No." Surprise colored her voice. "I never saw any drugs at the restaurant."

The ding of an incoming email drew his gaze to his computer screen. He opened the post from Chief Macintosh and clicked on the attachment. An image appeared with two rows of four mug shots, each one numbered. Chase didn't know which was the real detective.

He turned the monitor so Ashley could see the pictures. "Take your time," he told her.

She stared at the screen with uncertainty written across her face. "He was far away and it was dark."

"But not too dark for you to see Sokolov?"

"There was a street lamp. Mr. Sokolov was standing beneath it, but the other man was shadowed."

"Close your eyes and go back to that night if it helps."

She did as he suggested and after a moment she

opened her eyes. Taking control of the mouse, she blew up each photo and stared at it, before moving on to the next one. Finally on photo number seven, she sat back. "That was him. I'm sure of it."

"I'll let Macintosh know," he said. He sent off a quick email, telling the chief the witness had identified photo number seven.

A few seconds later, Macintosh replied. Chase read the email. "You've identified Detective Peters. The detective went rogue. They don't know why he was there in the alley that night. He told no one of his plans. Thus why there was no backup."

She winced. "Do you think he was dirty?"

Chase hoped not. "Hard to say at this point. It would really help if you could remember anything that the detective said."

"I've been trying," she said. "His voice was more of a murmur so I don't recall his exact words. But Mr. Sokolov didn't appear to be concerned with anybody hearing him."

Chase read the rest of the email. "Detective Peters's body was found dumped in the ocean and washed up on shore. If that hadn't happened, he would still be missing."

There was no mistaking the surprise in Ashley's red-rimmed eyes. "Someone moved him. And…" She grimaced.

She didn't need to state the rest. Yes, someone had tried to cover up the crime. "Are you sure, without a doubt, it was Maksim Sokolov who pulled the trigger?" Even though Alex had asked the question earlier, Chase needed to reaffirm her answer.

"Yes, I'm sure."

Chase was glad to hear her confidence.

She heaved a sigh. "Okay. Now you all know who was shot, when and where. Do I have to go back to LA?"

"Yes, you do. The district attorney wants to depose you himself and then at some point you'll have to appear before a grand jury, then in court."

She made a pained face. "He'll be there, in court, right?"

Chase wasn't going to sugarcoat the truth. "If we can make the charges stick and take him to trial. Then yes, Sokolov will be in the courtroom and he will be watching you. But you don't have to speak to him. All you'll need to do is testify that he was the one you saw pull the trigger."

"You'll be with me?"

He understood her concern. The case could take months if not years to go to trial. "I promise. No matter how long it takes."

"But what about your job?" The distress in her tone was touching.

"You let me worry about that. I'll work it out with the sheriff." Not wanting to examine why he'd make such a promise, he turned off his computer and gathered his personal belongings. "Come on. We'll head to my place. I need to pack a bag and change into clean clothes before we head to Denver."

"My duffel bag?"

"It's still in the SUV. We'll grab it on the way to my truck." He paused. "I'll need to text Lucinda to let her know we're on our way."

Ashley's eyebrows rose. "Who's Lucinda? Your wife?"

"No, the woman who raised me," he said. After sending the text, he put his hand to the small of Ashley's back and led her outside. "Lucinda Jones was my nanny as a child. When I moved here, I brought her with me. Her husband passed several years ago, and she didn't want to move to Florida where her adult son and his family reside."

"What about your parents?"

"They live in Chicago. Dad's a cardiologist and Mom's the hospital administrator." And not really a part of his life except for on holidays. They were too consumed by their professions.

After retrieving her bag, he helped her climb into his truck, a blue metallic 1987 Silverado pickup.

Once they were on the road, she smoothed a hand over the dashboard. "This is pretty cool."

He smiled. "Thanks."

"I think one of my mom's boyfriends had one of these back in the day."

He slanted her a quick glance. "Were there many boyfriends?"

Ashley sat back and gripped the edge of the bucket seat. "Yes. My mother is a difficult and complicated woman."

He understood difficult and complicated. Two words he could attribute to his own parents. "What about your father?"

"I was a baby when he left." She turned her head away. "Did you restore the truck yourself?"

Clearly, she didn't want to talk about her family.

There would be time to assuage his curiosity about Ashley. But for now the truck was a neutral topic.

"I did." He couldn't keep the pride out of his tone. "Rebuilding the truck was a labor of love and a challenge. It was one of my first purchases when I arrived in Bristle Township. I needed something to get me around, but I didn't want anything fancy. And because I was low on funds, I bought this beast from a local farmer who had it sitting in a barn. Over the next year or so, I refurbished her every night and weekend."

Ashley's laugh filled the cab as her gaze swung to him. "You call the truck a *her*?"

Enjoying the sound of her laugh, he said, "Yep. Blue Belle."

"Hello, Blue Belle."

Her smile tugged at him. Not for the first time, he battled the draw of attraction. She was so pretty. He recalled her words about men not thinking of her in terms of dating, only as the friend or the sister. He hated to think she didn't believe herself to be beautiful and attractive. But it wasn't his place to inform her that she was both. His job was to protect her.

He pulled into the driveway of his one-level mid-century modern home with a small yard and shut off the engine.

"Nice place," she commented.

"Thank you. It was a fixer-upper when I bought it. Someday I plan to get a dog but just haven't taken the time." He climbed out and came around to her side of the cab to open her door. She didn't move. "Ashley?"

"What if he sends more assassins after me? I

shouldn't be here. I shouldn't be putting you and Lucinda in danger."

"I can't leave you out here," he said. "We won't be long." He held out his hand. "Lucinda will have dinner ready. And we don't want to keep her waiting."

As they entered the house, Chase couldn't stop from glancing over his shoulder at the quiet residential street as Ashley's words rang through his head. There was validity to her fear.

What were the chances that a man like Sokolov would only send one assassin to Bristle Township?

FOUR

Ashley savored each bite of the home-cooked meal of spaghetti and meatballs as if it were her last. Which, she thought somewhat morbidly, it could be if more hit men came after her. All the more reason to eat every last bite.

After arriving at Chase's house and being introduced to the woman whom he shared the place with, Ashley had freshened up, putting on a clean light-weight pink sweater and cotton slacks, then helped get the meal on the table. "Thank you so much for this deliciousness," she said to the elderly woman sitting in a wheelchair at the end of the table.

"I'm so glad you enjoyed it." Lucinda Jones's dark eyes twinkled with pleasure. "Can't send you and Chase off on an empty stomach."

Ashley put her hand to her full tummy. "No chance of that."

"We won't be gone for too long," Chase assured the woman. He'd showered, shaved and changed out of his uniform into jeans that fit his lean form well. His sandy blond hair, still damp at the ends, curled at his nape.

The plaid shirt in hues of blue deepened the color of his blue eyes. "A day or two at the most."

Ashley wasn't sure he should be making such a promise on her behalf. Once she arrived back in Los Angeles, she might not be returning to Colorado. The district attorney may want her to stay put. Or at the very least, she would be heading off to another new place where she could disappear, until it was time to testify in open court.

She suppressed a shiver of dread. There was still much to do before that horrible day arrived. First, they needed to drive to Denver and fly to southern California where she would be deposed by the district attorney. So many things could go wrong between here and there. And Chase knew it, too. She'd seen the way he'd secured the house, making sure every window was shut, every door locked and the curtains pulled closed.

Chase's cell phone trilled from inside his front shirt pocket.

Lucinda arched an eyebrow.

He shrugged. "I'm expecting this. I have to take it." He rose from the table. "Excuse me." He walked away, his deep voice low as he answered the call.

Lucinda used the toggle on the console of her electric wheelchair to move closer to Ashley. She touched Ashley's arm. "Chase tells me you're in some trouble."

Startled, Ashley stared at the woman. "Yes. How much did he tell you?"

"No details, just enough for me to know to pray for you both."

For some reason the older woman's words caused Ashley's throat to close. She quickly drank from her water goblet, letting the cool liquid calm her throat and push back the rising tide of emotion. She couldn't remember ever having anyone pray specifically for her. When she was sure she had control over her vocals, she said, "I appreciate your prayers. I'm not sure I deserve them."

"Everyone deserves to be held in prayer," Lucinda responded with a pat on Ashley's arm.

Not wanting to debate the point, Ashley decided to give in to her curiosity and said, "You were Chase's nanny."

A smile crinkled the corners of Lucinda's eyes. "Yes. I started taking care of him not long after he was born. He was the crankiest, loudest baby ever."

Adjectives that Ashley wouldn't have attributed to the man she was getting to know. "But you have your own children?"

"I do. A son. He was ten when I went to work for the Fredrick family. After my husband passed, I no longer had a reason to stay in Chicago, but didn't want to go south to Florida where my son and his family now live. Too hot. I prefer to have seasons. Chase was a dear to invite me to come here."

A dear. What an apt phrase. "How long did you care for Chase?"

"Until high school," Lucinda answered. "Even then, he would show up on our doorstep more often than not."

"It beat eating alone," Chase interjected as he returned. "That was one of the district attorney's assistants. Everything's all arranged. She's texting me the flight information and the hotel confirmation."

No sooner had he said the words than a ding from his phone let them know the text had arrived.

Ashley was more interested in learning about Chase. "Your parents weren't home for dinner?" Not that her own mother had been home or made dinner often, but she'd imagined that Chase grew up with two attentive parents when they weren't working.

"Rarely." He picked up their empty plates and strode into the kitchen.

"If Chase were a different kind of man, he could've gotten himself into some serious trouble," Lucinda said as she backed her chair away from the table.

Chase stepped into the arched doorway between the dining room and kitchen, wiping his hands on a towel. "You taught me well, Lucinda. Hard work and service for others is what life is about. Not partying like most of my peers."

Lucinda beamed. "Yes and look at you now. You're a fine deputy." She turned to Ashley, pinning her with an intent stare. "A fine catch."

Ashley smothered a choked laugh. She had no words to respond with.

"Enough, Lucinda." Chase tossed the towel onto the counter and walked fully into the dining room. Amusement sparked in his eyes. "She's hoping I will find someone to settle down with. But I am settled. My life's just about perfect the way it is."

Something strange twisted in Ashley's gut.

Lucinda snorted. "You keep telling yourself that. I'd like some babies to cuddle." She winked at Ashley. "I like to tease him. But I can't wait for him to have more in his life than work."

"I'm sure he will." Except she wouldn't be here to see it.

Settle down. Babies. All normal, healthy things for anyone to want. A longing from some place deep inside of Ashley tugged for attention, but she staunchly ignored the pull. Her life would never be normal. Not that she even knew what that was. Her childhood had been chaotic and at times scary.

Besides, a family of her own wasn't something she could dream about, not when there was a man out there bent on killing her.

She would never be safe enough to have a life free from fear. The thought made her shoulders droop and fatigue set in.

Shaking his head with good-natured humor at Lucinda's not so subtle matchmaking, Chase kissed the older woman's cheek. "It's time that we head out." He straightened and held out his hand to Ashley. "We'll make it to the airport hotel just after dark."

Slipping her hand into his, Ashley cherished the comforting and warm contact as he helped her to her feet. The world spun and for a moment she clung to him.

His concerned gaze made her withdraw her hand and plant her feet as her equilibrium returned. "Head rush. Happens sometimes."

Accepting her explanation with a nod, he moved to grab their bags from the couch and walked outside.

Ashley bent to hug Lucinda. "Again, thank you. It was lovely to meet you."

"And you, dear," the older woman said. "I'll lift you both up in prayer. And you can be assured Chase will keep you safe."

But at what cost? Ashley stifled the question, not wanting to cause Lucinda any undue worry. Closing the door behind her, Ashley hurried to the truck. Chase stowed their bags behind the bucket seats. From a holster hidden beneath the right pant leg of his jeans, he removed a gun.

She noticed it wasn't the same sort of weapon he'd been carrying earlier. This one was smaller but she was sure just as lethal. He put the gun in the glove box.

"It's my personal weapon. I had to surrender my service sidearm at the station."

Her stomach clenched. He'd shot someone to protect her today. She hoped and prayed he wouldn't have to do that again.

"Are you close with your parents now that you're an adult?" she asked, hoping to learn more about this man she was trusting her life with.

He started up the engine and backed out of the driveway. Once on the road, he answered, "Not especially. Don't get me wrong. I love them. They're great people. They've accomplished so much. I just don't know them, and they don't really know me. Kind of hard to build a relationship when they were gone so much of the time."

"That must've been hard for you. But you had Lucinda." What she wouldn't have given to have someone like Lucinda in her life.

He darted a glance her way. "It was hard, I suppose. I didn't know any different. But you're right, I had Lucinda and her family. They became my family. And I much preferred their brownstone to the big house on the lake."

She couldn't imagine living a life with so many choices. "I grew up in a trailer park," she blurted out.

"No shame in that."

She smiled to herself. Old wounds ached but she'd

learned to hold her head high in spite of the circumstances of her past. "*You* can say that because you didn't live it. In school I was considered trailer trash. What was even more ironic was that our trailer actually sat next to the trash bins. Even the other kids in the trailer park called me trailer trash."

His jaw hardened. "Children can be mean."

"True."

"I was called less than complimentary names at my school."

"You were?" She would have thought he'd have been part of the popular kids. "I can't believe that."

His shoulders rose and fell. "Except for one stint on the football team my freshman year of high school, I kept to myself. I didn't want anyone to know who my parents were."

"Why not? They are successful and rich from the sound of it." She'd have told everyone and been giddy to have the life he'd led.

"Exactly. Once people knew, then they treated me differently. Or wanted something from me."

Her heart hurt to think that Chase had had so much yet had been unhappy. "Money doesn't buy happiness."

"Not for me. I would rather have had my parents' attention than a big house and fancy clothes."

"I can understand that."

"You had your mom. Was she a good mother?"

Ashley turned the question over in her mind. She had nothing to compare her childhood to other than what she'd seen on television or read in books. "I want to believe she tried but nurturing wasn't natural for her. Not like with your Lucinda."

Even in the short time Ashley had spent with Chase's former nanny, she'd been cared for and treated like she was special.

"My mother wasn't the most nurturing, either," Chase said. "She ran a large organization with a lot of balls in the air. She didn't know what to do with a child under foot."

"I doubt your mom was free with her fists or her criticism." As soon as the words were out, she wanted to retract them. She didn't want him to pity her.

"She hurt you?"

His quiet tone filled with indignation on her behalf was more compelling than knowing he was doing his job to protect her. She wanted to laugh off the volatile nature of her mother but she couldn't find it within herself to be less than honest with Chase. "Sometimes. She was a single parent raising a child she'd never wanted."

He made a noise she took as sympathy.

"Don't get me wrong, we would do some mother-daughter things, like give ourselves pedicures or have movie nights with popcorn and candy." The memories were faded and frayed at the edges, but not forgotten. Those were the times Ashley had treasured. "There were many nights when she didn't come home." A shiver raced over her skin. She'd hated being alone in the trailer.

Chase's hands gripped and re-gripped the steering wheel. "Wasn't there anyone to help you? A grandparent or neighbor?"

She smoothed her hands over her thighs. "Not really. As soon as I was old enough, I would bike to the library as much as possible. I found solace in the books. And had many wonderful adventures sitting in the alcove of the Barstow library."

"I'm glad you had someplace to retreat to when it was scary at home. Though it pains me to think of you mistreated by the one person who should have been sheltering you from the ugliness of the world."

She stared at him, mesmerized by his profile. He was handsome in so many ways. His kindheartedness was so sweet and appealing. She was thankful God had put Chase in her path.

After a long beat of silence, Chase said, "I spent a great deal of time at the library, too, when I wasn't with Lucinda's family."

Grateful to have the subject change from her childhood to his, she commented, "I noticed your bookshelves. Many classics, as well as popular fiction."

"A book doesn't judge or betray you," he stated.

"Or hurt you." She wondered if he was only referring to his childhood. Had he loved someone who then betrayed him? "Why haven't you settled down?"

He groaned. "Not you, too."

"I'm just curious. And surprised. You're a catch." The words slipped out and flooded her with embarrassment. "I mean, not for me. I'm not looking to catch you." She was digging herself a deeper hole.

His soft laugh filled the cab of the truck. "I'm not sure if I should be insulted or not."

"No! I didn't mean to be insulting." Remorse for her words made her pulse pound.

He slanted her a glance. "I'm teasing. In all seriousness, dating was painful as a teen. I was never sure if the girls were interested in me as a person or in my last name. And in college I was too focused on graduating quickly so I could join the Chicago Police Department. I never took the time for a relationship. And wasn't sure I could trust someone to love me for me. What about you?"

She related to not knowing if she could trust someone to love her unconditionally. "My focus was getting out of Barstow. As soon as I turned eighteen, I escaped to Los Angeles."

"Did you always want to be an actress?"

"What little girl doesn't when they're young?" She could remember wanting to be a part of a television family so badly she'd ached. "One of the girls in the house I ended up living in introduced me to her agent. For the next few years, I went on auditions. I landed a few bit parts here and there. Hard to learn the craft with no money for acting lessons. I wasn't a natural. The camera was intimidating, plus having all the people on set watching you, judging you." She made a face. "Only significant thing I did was a commercial for a national car company."

"I'll have to search for it on the internet. How did you end up at The Matador?"

"To pay the bills I started waiting tables. First at a fast food joint and then a pizza parlor. One of my housemates worked at The Matador and when a position opened up, she told me about it." For a time she'd thought she'd won the best prize ever. Then that horrible night happened, and her world spun out of control.

"Did you not want to go to college?"

She had, so badly. "Kind of hard to do without money."

"You could have applied for scholarships or financial aid."

She sighed. "I didn't know how to apply for them." And had no one to ask.

"It's not too late, you know. Nowadays you can take classes online and receive a degree."

There was no point in dreaming when her life would be about staying hidden from Maksim Sokolov. "What did you study in college?"

"Communications. It was a compromise with my parents. There was no way I wanted to be a doctor or administrator. I wanted to be a police officer. Lucinda's father was a retired Chicago detective. He would tell us stories of his time on the force. And I knew that that's what I wanted to do. I wanted to serve others, just not the way my parents did."

She appreciated Chase's honor and integrity. And his desire to do for others without any real compensation beyond his pay. He wasn't posturing for accolades. She liked that about him. Back in Los Angeles, the guys she'd met all wanted to be the center of attention. "At one time I thought I might want to be a librarian."

A smile spread across his face. "You could, you know. Mrs. Hawkins is always asking for volunteers at the library."

Turning her gaze to the window, she said, "Maybe someday." Only not in Bristle Township. The thought hurt.

The truck sped up, pushing her back against the seat. She glanced at Chase. He sat straighter; tension radiated off him and made the fine hairs on her arms jump with alarm. "What's wrong?"

"I think we are being followed," he said. "There's a

sedan that has been keeping the same distance behind us since we left town. Every time I slow down, they slow down. When I speed up, so do they."

She twisted in her seat to stare out the rear window at the dark car. "What should we do?"

Before he could answer, the sedan raced forward and kissed the bumper of the truck. The hit jerked Ashley forward. She let out a yelp of panic. Chase floored it, and the truck strained for more speed.

"Grab my phone from my front shirt pocket."

She reached for it, but the seat belt slammed her back against the seat. Quickly, she shrugged out from beneath the chest strap and managed to pluck the cell phone from his shirt pocket. "There's only one bar." Cell coverage in the mountains was spotty at best.

"We have to pray we can get through. Press one and enter."

Please let the call connect. She did as instructed. She could hear it ringing.

"Put it on speaker," he said.

She pressed the speaker button just as a woman's voice filled the cab, "Bristle County Sheriff's Department, Carole speaking."

"Chase here. Listen, we need help. Mile marker 15 headed. A dark sedan is trying to force us to crash."

"I'll tell the sheriff—"

The line went dead. Panic seized Ashley. Her breathing turned shallow. "They won't arrive in time."

"Brace yourself," Chase instructed tightly. "I have to get us off the road before they cause an accident."

Ashley grabbed the door handle with one hand and the dashboard with the other. At the last possible mo-

ment, Chase cranked the wheel, crossing the oncom-
ing traffic lane and taking a graveled road on squealing
tires. They shot down the road through the trees, gravel
flying in their wake.

Ashley kept an eye on the side-view mirror. For what
seemed like a long moment, she held her breath, praying the car would pass by and keep going.

The sedan made the turn. The truck bounced, and
she barely hung onto the phone. Ashley's breath hitched.
"Now what?"

Chase pressed hard on the gas. The truck shot forward.
The road began to climb. Behind them the car sped up.

"They're gaining on us!" Ashley's hands curled
into fists. It wasn't fair. She should never have allowed
Chase to talk her into this. If he had let her leave on
the bus this morning, he wouldn't be in danger now.

"Hang on!" He yanked on the wheel, taking a hard
right and going off road into the trees.

She clutched the phone, panic making her breathing
shallow and her head spin.

"Ashley!" Chase's voice whipped through the cab, co-
ercing her to focus. "I need you to be calm. And ready."

"Ready for what?" Her voice shook. She was on the
verge of hysteria.

"Behind your seat is a length of rope and a harness.
Grab them."

As they bumped along the rocky and rutted path just
barely wide enough for the truck, she forced herself to
reach behind her seat, tugging out the length of coiled
rope and a thick black harness. "I have them both. Why
do you have these in your truck?" Though she had no

idea how these would help them evade their pursuers. Rock climbing was not something she could do.

A spray of bullets hit the back of the truck, the cacophony of noise echoing through her head. Her heart rate jumped with terror. "They're shooting at us!"

A loud pop reverberated through the truck. The back end fishtailed. Chase slammed on the brakes and brought the truck to an abrupt halt. "The tire's blown." He yanked open the glove box and pulled out his gun. "Let's go!"

Frantic, she scrambled out of the truck. Chase took the rope from her and grabbed her hand, pulling her into the trees.

"This way." Chase led her deep into the thick forest.

"How can this be happening?" Ashley's legs burned with exertion as she pushed to keep up with Chase. The underbrush scraped at her clothes, snagging on her pant legs. They were running in the opposite direction of the mountain.

"Where are we going?" she asked, her breath coming in spurts.

"Hopefully toward the highway and backup."

Behind them, she could hear the thrashing of their pursuers as they followed them into the forest.

Please, Lord, let us get away. She dug deep for more speed while trying to maintain her balance over the rough terrain.

The setting sun dipped below the mountain peak, casting long shadows through the trees, making the already dim lighting harder to navigate the untraveled ground. Animals scurried beneath the brush. Startled birds squawked and took flight.

Chase skidded to a halt at the edge of a large meadow. Ashley tripped over her own feet as she tried to avoid ramming into him. He caught her by the elbow and drew her behind a tree trunk. The last of the sun's golden rays touched the green grass and revealed a grazing herd of Rocky Mountain elk. Ashley had never seen such large beasts in the wild. Several lifted their heads as if sensing the danger breathing down on them.

"If we go out there, we're sitting ducks," Chase said.

Anxiety squirmed in her chest. "We have to hide." There was nothing but tree trunks in every direction. The men's voices carried on the slight breeze. Fear trembled over her limbs and panic dried her mouth.

Chase's gaze went to the treetops. He stepped away from her with his head tilted upward.

"What are you doing?" Her terrified whisper sounded as loud as a shout in her ears.

He pointed his finger toward the sky. "We have to go up."

Up? No way. Her heart jumped into her throat.

He grabbed her hand again and tugged her forward. They stopped beneath a large ponderosa pine tree. "Here we go."

She followed his gaze to a dark shape about thirty feet from the ground. Dizziness forced her to grab the tree trunk. "I can't climb a tree. I've never climbed a tree in my life."

"There's always a first time for everything."

"You don't understand," she whispered. "I'm afraid of heights."

FIVE

"Are you more afraid of heights than bullets?" Chase didn't wait for Ashley to answer as he wrapped one end of the rope around his waist and secured it to his belt with a belaying device, the mechanical piece of climbing equipment used to control the rope. She was going up into the tree, even if he had to carry her on his back.

"Uh, both." Her voice quaked.

"Bullets will kill you." He held out the harness. "Put it on."

She hesitated.

"Quick," he bit out, needing her to move. Time was of the essence. They had to get up the tree and in place before their pursuers spotted them.

Her hand holding the harness trembled. "What if I fall?"

"You won't. I'll have you. I promise."

Obviously deciding she had no choice but to trust him in this, Ashley hurriedly stepped into the harness. She grabbed onto him for balance, her fingers digging into his biceps as she used him for support. She was clearly still terrified. Unfortunately, there was no time to reassure her more. Once the safety harness was on, he tightened it around her waist as much as possible.

"Now what?" She fairly squeaked the question.

He flung the other end of the rope up and over the lowest hanging branch of the tree and then threaded it through the second belay device attached to the harness. "You climb."

"Shouldn't we keep running?"

"It will be dark soon." He gave the rope a tug, locking it into place on the harness. "If we keep going, we'll risk a twisted ankle or worse."

"What about the flashlight on your phone?"

"Which would be a beacon for the bad guys, revealing our location." He drew her closer to the tree's trunk. Taking her hand, he guided her to the small horizontal slates nailed to the tree trunk. "Feel those. Just like a ladder."

"If you say so." Doubt laced each word.

"You're going to climb up this tree. And when you reach the tree stand—"

"The what?"

Biting back his impatience, he said, "It's a hunters' perch. When we hit the meadow, I figured there had to be one around. It's a perfect spot for elk hunting."

"Is that legal?"

"During elk season." He put his hands on her shoulders. In the waning light, he could barely make out her face but her bright eyes were large and scared. "You can do this. I'll help you."

She took an audible shuddering breath. "Okay." The word came out sounding more like a squawk. "Why don't you go first?"

There wasn't time to soothe her nerves. Didn't she understand? Getting her out of the line of fire was the priority. He could hide, fight or shoot his way out of the forest. But his job was to protect her. If he failed… A deep dread warned he didn't even want to contemplate the thought. He needed to stay focused and trust that God would protect them.

He spun her to face the tree. "Start climbing."

Ashley swallowed back the choking trepidation at climbing the tree in front of her. When she was a child, one of her mother's boyfriends had thrown her up in the air and then failed to catch her. She'd had an issue with heights ever since.

But her life depended on going up this tree. She tilted her head. She could just barely make out the bottom of a hunting platform attached to the tree trunk. It was a long way to the tree stand.

Noise of their assailants making their way through the forest reverberated through the trees and galvanized her into action. She groped the rough bark for the first rung nailed to the tree just above her head and did her best to pull herself up. Her arms shook. There was no way she had the strength to muscle her way up the side of the tree. But then the rope and harness secured around her waist lifted her off her feet. Stifling a yelp, she reached for the next rung.

"Brace your feet against the tree."

Chase's whispered instructions gave her the encouragement she needed to remain calm.

Slowly, she walked her feet up the side of the trunk as she used every muscle she had in her arms to pull herself toward the perch. But she was thankful for the leverage of the rope keeping her stable and adding some lift.

In the distance, another noise, out of place for the forest, filled the air. But Ashley ignored the sound to concentrate on climbing. A cold sweat broke out on her body. Her breathing came out in little puffs.

Finally, she managed to land one foot on the little ledge of wood. From there, it was easier to make the climb, grasping each rung with her hands and pushing with her feet until she was able to grasp the metal edge of the tree stand. Awkwardly, she maneuvered herself over until her feet found stability on a piece of protruding metal with crisscross beams.

There was barely enough light to make out a cushioned seat fastened to the tree and the footrest on which she now stood. She made the mistake of glancing down and nearly passed out. The ground was a long way away.

The rope around her waist went slack as Chase made the climb up. Within seconds, he was squeezing in beside her.

"Breathe," Chase whispered close to her ear.

Inhaling and exhaling, she lifted her gaze and searched for his blue-green eyes in the dim light. Staring at him gave her the courage not to disintegrate into a quivering mess.

Balancing himself precariously on the footrest, Chase whispered, "We need to be as quiet as possible. Be very still. Let's pray they aren't smart enough to look up."

A moment later, the two men hounding them burst from the woods and into the meadow five feet from where Ashley clung to Chase in the tree. The last of the sun's rays glinted off the guns held in their hands, sending a shiver of dread along her spine. Chase drew her just a little closer. The warmth of his reassurance flowed through her.

The two men conferred with each other, then split up, one heading away from Ashley and Chase, while the other one moved in their direction.

Ashley buried her face into Chase's chest and held her breath as the big goon walked right beneath them. *Lord, please don't let him look up.*

The sound she'd heard earlier grew louder, shuddering through the trees.

Chase's arms tightened a fraction more around her. "Yes," he breathed out in obvious relief, his voice barely audible in her ear over the roar. "So grateful for Ian Delaney."

Wind whipped by the helicopter's rotors threatened to fling them off their perch. The flying craft passed over the forest twice above their heads and then hovered in the middle of the meadow before slowly landing.

Their pursuers doubled back, running toward where they'd left their car.

The helicopter's door opened. Kaitlyn and Alex jumped out, dressed in full tactical gear with rifles raised. They hurried toward the trees.

"That's our ride," Chase said. "I don't want my co-workers to mistake you or me for the bad guys." He pressed the app button on his phone, dispelling the darkness around them.

"What are you doing?" Hadn't he said it was too dangerous to use the light function?

"Flashing out the Morse code for SOS."

She supposed it was normal for a law enforcement officer to know Morse code.

An answering flash of light came from Alex. Chase let out an audible breath before he said, "I'll go first. Hang tight."

Chase nimbly descended the tree trunk. Clearly, he was an expert climber. He gave the rope a shake, letting her know it was time for her to begin her climb down. She prayed going down would be easier and less scary than going up.

Keeping her gaze on the tree, she made the arduous descent and was grateful when her feet hit solid ground.

Unhooking the rope from Ashley, Chase gathered the thick length in one hand and grabbed her hand with the other. "Come on."

They ran toward the helicopter as the wind stirred through her short hair and caused the tall grass to slap against her shins. Every step that brought her closer to the flying craft sent more anxiety twisting through her.

Kaitlyn waved for them to hurry while Alex flanked them, watching their backs. Chase helped Ashley inside the open bay of the large dark blue helicopter. It took all her courage to settle herself inside the space, knowing it would leave the ground. And go up and up. Her stomach hurt and nausea rose to burn her throat.

A small overhead light illuminated the interior of the helicopter. She scooted onto one of the beige bucket seats facing forward, her limbs shaking. Ashley recognized the very good-looking Delaney brothers in the pilot and copilot seats. She'd seen them a handful of times in town.

Chase climbed in next and took the seat opposite her. Dropping the rope onto the floor, he leaned forward and threaded his fingers through hers. His mouth moved, but she couldn't hear him over the rumble of the rotors.

Kaitlyn jumped in, taking the seat next to Ashley, while Alex sat beside Chase and shut the door.

Ashley shuddered with dread. Panic roared in her ears as the bird took off, lifting effortlessly into the air. She scrunched her eyes closed, afraid to see how far above the ground they had flown. Her lungs constricted. She would start hyperventilating at any moment. Chase squeezed her hands until she peeked at him.

With his free hand, he used his index and middle fingers, pointing them at her, then at his eyes, his meaning clear. Keep her gaze on him, not on the fact that they were flying high in the sky.

Swallowing the anxiety clawing up her throat, she nodded. It was no hardship to stare into his blue eyes. Though as the helicopter banked and then slowly descended onto the roof of the sheriff's station, which now sported a heliport thanks to the Delaney family, her stomach lurched and she clenched her jaw so tight she was surprised a tooth hadn't cracked.

When she stepped out of the helicopter, she'd never been so glad to have her feet on solid concrete. Her nerves were shredded. Fatigue and adrenaline letdown made the act of putting one foot in front of the other seem as if she were wading through thick sand.

She could hardly believe the day she'd had. Assassins and heights.

All she wanted now was to find a nice hot bath and

bury her head between the covers of a warm bed. To-morrow had to be better.

She sent up a prayer of praise. The day could have ended so badly. With Chase hurt or dead. It wasn't fair for her to put him and the whole community of Bristle Township in danger.

She was safe for the moment, but this whole disaster proved the point that she needed to leave town sooner rather than later. Before someone did get hurt.

She settled in a chair beside Chase's desk. A few seconds later, the sheriff and Daniel returned from the mountain with the two assailants in handcuffs. Her attackers glared at her as they were led to a jail cell. She didn't recognize either one. And hoped never to see them again.

"What's their story?" Chase asked Daniel, when the deputy returned to the main area of the station. "Did they say anything useful? Did Maksim Sokolov send them?"

Daniel shook his head. "Only word they've uttered since we grabbed them was *lawyer.*"

Chase let out a soft growl of frustration. "What about the guy from this morning? Did we get any information off him?"

Ashley shuddered at the memory of the man who'd dragged her to the edge of the cliff. The man Chase had shot and killed.

"We got an ID on him," Alex said. "Randy Brennan. Has a rap sheet that goes back decades. Mostly breaking and entering in his youth, but then he graduated to armed robbery and assault."

"Known associates?" Chase asked.

"Once we get IDs on these two, we'll see if there's a connection," Daniel said.

"This Randy guy said he was being paid well," Ashley told them.

"No doubt," Chase said. "Money may not buy happiness but it definitely will motivate some people to commit crimes."

She nodded, thinking about their conversation earlier. "What happens now?"

"We need to find you a safe place to lay low." There was fire in Chase's eyes. "The Los Angeles district attorney has a leak in his department. And I'm not entrusting you to their care again."

"How do you know the leak wasn't from your department?" she asked.

Gregor had told her not to trust the police. Yet she had. And twice now she'd been attacked. Was one of the deputies in collusion with Maksim Sokolov?

The hurt on Chase's face dug at her. "I get why you're asking. I haven't done a good job of protecting you. But I trust everyone in this department with my life."

"But you did protect me. You saved my life, twice." Which made the idea of his working with Sokolov ridiculous.

But what of the others?

She didn't know these people, really. She wanted to believe in them, to trust them. Even call them friends. But she wasn't sure she could trust her own judgment. All the more reason she should go back into hiding.

"I'd like to talk to the district attorney," she said.

Chase rubbed a hand over the back of his neck.

"That's reasonable. Let's get to it, then." He picked up the phone.

Within moments, he had the Los Angeles district attorney on the line. Chase updated him on the situation. "You need to check your house," Chase said. "You have a mole working for Sokolov."

Ashley could hear the district attorney's deep, angry voice shouting into the receiver. "No way. This is *not* on us. It's on you. You said you could keep her safe."

Guilt flashed in Chase's eyes. Ashley wanted to reach out to reassure him that he'd done nothing wrong, instead she curled her fingers around each other and waited.

"Nobody here even knew what time or what road we were taking out of town except me," Chase countered hotly. "And I certainly didn't alert anybody in Los Angeles."

There was a long silence, then the district attorney said something in a much calmer, lower tone that prevented Ashley from making out his words.

"A video deposition is the best solution," Chase said into the phone. He listened, his lips pressing together. "Really. You're going to quibble over the cost?" He rolled his eyes. "We'll set it up here in the sheriff's station. Tomorrow morning." Chase glanced at her. "He'd like to talk to you."

Ashley's hand trembled when she took the receiver from Chase. "Hello?"

A deep masculine voice came on the line. "Miss Willis, I understand that you are ready to testify that you saw Maksim Sokolov shoot and kill Detective William Peters."

"Yes, sir, I am." Even though she was quaking in her tennis shoes, she was going to do the right thing this time. She turned her back to Chase. "Sir, it would be better for me if I disappear after my deposition tomorrow."

Chase's gaze burned a hole into the back of her head. But she knew she was right. Even if he was too stubborn to see it.

"No can do. You're in police custody now. Let me talk to the deputy again."

"But, sir—" she said.

"No. Now hand the phone over to Deputy Fredrick."

Frustration beat a steady rhythm behind her eyes as she held the phone out to Chase.

Giving her a censuring scowl, he took the phone. "Mr. Nyburg." Chase listened for a moment, then said, "Yes, I understand."

After Chase hung up, he was still for a moment before meeting her gaze. She couldn't read his expression. Was he angry with her? Disappointed? And why did it matter to her?

She had no answer to that question.

Kaitlyn walked in with Maya Gallo and Leslie Quinn following in her wake.

"Ladies," Chase greeted them.

Ashley held her breath, expecting the women to be upset with her for not telling them who she really was from the beginning.

"Jane! Uh, I mean, Ashley, are you okay?" Grasping Ashley's hand, Maya's brown eyes searched Ashley's face. She was dressed in jeans and a lightweight red sweater. Her dark hair was held back in a clip at the nape of her neck.

"Kaitlyn told us what happened to you today," Leslie added. Tall and slender, dressed in a navy pantsuit with a white crisp blouse, Leslie exuded an intimidating air of sophistication. Clearly, she'd come from the dress shop she managed for her mother.

"I'm fine," Ashley told them, though she couldn't hold back the threat of tears. Why weren't they angry with her?

"I found them outside," Kaitlyn said. "They weren't going to go away until they talked to you."

"Thank you. All of you." Though Ashley wasn't sure what she was really thanking them for. Not ripping her head off with accusations and recriminations? For caring about her when she didn't warrant their concern? "I don't know what to say, except I'm sorry."

Leslie waved a manicured hand. "Please, no apology necessary. And there's no better place for you to be than here." She turned to Chase. "Right?"

He held up his hands with the palms facing out as if surrendering. "I keep trying to tell her that. She wants to leave. To disappear."

All three women turned their gazes to her. Ashley squirmed beneath their incredulous stares.

"No way," Kaitlyn broke the silence. "That would be a huge mistake."

"The sheriff and deputies here are the best." One corner of Maya's mouth lifted. "Of course, I'm biased."

Considering the harrowing experience Maya and her brother, Brady, had had on the mountain when treasure hunters kidnapped them in their quest to find the prize,

Ashley didn't doubt that Maya was grateful to the sheriff and the deputies for rescuing them. Plus, Maya and Alex had fallen in love and were to be married this coming summer. A happy ending for them.

Ashley didn't hold out any hope for a happy ending of her own.

"But truly," Maya continued. "Kaitlyn, Alex, Chase, Daniel and the sheriff would never let anything happen to you or to any of us in Bristle County."

"That's good to hear you say," Alex interjected as he walked into the room and came over to his fiancée, putting an arm around her waist and pulling her close.

Maya glanced up at him. "You saved me and Brady and this whole town from those nasty treasure hunters."

Alex grinned at her. "I didn't do it all by myself."

"That's right. We're a team." Daniel, who'd been sitting quietly at his desk while this drama unfolded, rose and joined them.

"I trust these officers with my life," Leslie stated. "And so should you."

"We appreciate your vote of confidence." Daniel addressed Leslie, his eyes sparking with amusement.

Leslie slanted a glance at him. "Don't let it go to your head." Turning her attention back to Ashley, Leslie said, "I know you've been staying with Mrs. Marsh, but it wouldn't be wise for you to go back there. You can stay with me. If fact, I think it would be best for Mrs. Marsh to take a vacation to visit her family in Texas."

"I'll see that she does," Daniel said.

Leslie considered him a moment. "Thank you."

"I'm here to serve," Daniel said.

Leslie's eyebrows drew together. "Right. Okay, then."

She shifted her focus to Ashley. "You good with staying at my place?"

Taken aback by Leslie's kind offer, Ashley tucked in her chin. "You would do that for me?"

"Of course."

Her gaze swept over the group. She didn't want to be a burden to them. Or put any of them out. Accepting help didn't come easy. It made her feel vulnerable. "None of you really know me. I've done nothing to deserve your help. In fact, by staying, I'm putting you all in danger."

"That's what people do in a small town," Leslie said. "We watch out for each other."

"You're our friend," Maya said.

Kaitlyn pinned her with a pointed stare. "And we can take the danger."

Ashley turned to Chase. He regarded her with a curious expression on his face that she couldn't interpret.

"You should...could stay at my house," he said.

"No," Ashley protested. "I won't put Lucinda in jeopardy."

"Which is why my place is perfect," Leslie said. "I live alone, I have a gun and I'm trained in self-defense."

Running his hands through his sandy blond hair, Chase said, "I'll stand guard outside."

Kaitlyn stepped forward. "Not necessary. I'll stay with Leslie and Ashley."

"Me, too." Maya grinned. "I'll send Brady to Alex's." She rubbed her hands together. "It will be a ladies' party."

Alex groaned. "Maya."

She broke away from her fiancé, linking her arm through Ashley's. "It will be fine."

"No way. You and Brady will stay at the ranch with my dad," Alex insisted.

Maya opened her mouth, most likely to protest, but Kaitlyn intervened. "It's better this way. Safer."

"Fine." Maya obviously couldn't argue with logic.

"We'll take turns standing guard," Daniel said.

Ashley shook her head, not liking that everyone was going to so much trouble on her behalf. "You guys…"

"No more arguing," Kaitlyn said in a decisive tone.

"Then let's go," Leslie said, heading for the door.

The sheriff stepped out of his office. "Hold up. I need Ashley and Chase to give their statements before they leave."

"You all go on," Chase said. "I'll bring Ashley over when we're done."

"Sounds like a good plan," Daniel said. "I'll take first watch after seeing to Mrs. Marsh."

"No, I will," Alex said.

The sheriff held up a hand. "You two work it out." He turned to Ashley and Chase. "Shall we?"

Bemused by the way these people were willing to circle around her to provide a protective bubble, Ashley blinked back tears of gratitude.

She wasn't sure why God had seen fit to grace her with such a gift. She prayed, as she followed the sheriff and Chase into the sheriff's office, that none of them would regret their decision to help her.

SIX

"How will you get your truck back?" Ashley asked from the passenger seat of the sheriff's personal vehicle as Chase drove them through Bristle Township. Overhead, the sky was filled with stars and the temperature had dropped.

Noticing Ashley shiver, Chase cranked up the heat. "Tomorrow I'll buy a new tire and have Mack, the local auto mechanic and tow truck operator, bring it back to town."

Chase hoped a new tire was all that would be required. He hadn't taken the time to assess the damage before he and Ashley had fled into the woods.

"I'm really sorry about all of this," she said softly.

He turned off the main road onto the Quinns' gravel driveway. He slowed the sedan and reached to take Ashley's hand. "It's going to all work out."

She gave him a sad smile before turning her gaze to the side window. She didn't believe him. Was it that hard for her to trust? Not that he'd given her much reason to place her faith in him. But he was determined to do everything in his power to keep her safe.

Withdrawing her hand from his, she made a sweeping gesture to the ranch laid out before them. "This is really nice."

An L-shaped main house sat off to the right side of the long gravel road with a large patch of green grass in the front yard. A corral and pasture were to the left of the driveway, along with a barn and smaller house. "Is it all Leslie's?"

"The spread belongs to her parents, but they are off traveling the world," Chase told her. "Her dad had a medical scare a while ago. Leslie returned home from Europe to help her mom and stayed after he recovered. She lives in the guesthouse now."

He pulled the vehicle to a halt next to Kaitlyn's truck in front of the guesthouse, which was more of a one-story cottage.

Ashley popped open the passenger door, grabbing her duffel bag from between her feet. "Thank you, Chase. For everything."

She hopped out before he could respond.

He climbed out and hurried to catch up to her. Placing his hand at the small of her back, he walked her to the door, like they were returning from a date or something. A strange sort of uncertainty and anticipation that he couldn't explain ignited his blood.

When they stopped outside the cottage's closed door, she gazed up at him, her pretty eyes filled with gentle concern. "Please, go home and get some rest. We both need to recover from the day."

Tenderness filled his chest. Here she was lecturing him, when he should have been lecturing her about resting and taking care of herself. She was the civilian, not the one trained to handle stressful situations. But he had to admit, he liked her worrying about him, liked the warm and fuzzy feeling of knowing she cared about his well-being. An unexpected yearning to have her affection and attention gripped him.

"I'm not going anywhere." He skimmed his knuckle down her petal soft cheek. "You shouldn't have had to go through all of this. I'm sorry for what happened."

She put her hand on his chest, creating a warm spot over his heart. "You're taking on unnecessary guilt. Don't do that. You protected me and saved my life. End of story."

He covered her hand, marveling at how she was so generous and compassionate with everyone but herself. "I don't think it will be the end of the story. This Maksim Sokolov is awfully determined."

She glanced away, slipping her hand from beneath his and leaving an ache in its place. "I wish I'd never brought this to your door."

Wishing she wouldn't blame herself, he hooked a finger under her chin and drew her gaze back to him. "Now, *you* don't do that. The thought of you facing this danger alone…" A shudder of dread tripped down his spine. "I want to help you. To protect you."

To kiss you.

The errant thought nearly buckled his knees. His heart pounded in his ears. The vulnerability in her eyes tugged at him.

She seemed to lean toward him as if silently willing him to reassure her. Giving him permission to kiss her?

It would be so easy to close the gap and press his lips to hers. The longing pulsing through his veins was stronger than anything he'd experienced before for any other woman. He was captivated by Ashley in ways that both terrified and thrilled him. Her innate kindness, compassion and bravery were alluring.

But giving in to his yearning and taking advantage of her vulnerable state of mind wouldn't be honorable. He prided himself on always doing the right thing. Now was not the time to make an exception.

Clearing his throat, he took a half step back, putting some much-needed distance between them while he regained his composure. "Daniel and Alex will take turns guarding the ranch's entrance while Kaitlyn and I are here with you and Leslie."

She cocked her head for a moment and a slow smile touched on her pretty lips. "You really are a good guy."

Had his expression given him away? Had she known he'd fought the urge to kiss her? Had she wanted him to? He'd have to be more careful.

He turned to the door and knocked lightly. The door opened immediately to reveal Leslie and Kaitlyn crowding the entryway. Clearly, they'd been hovering, waiting for Ashley.

"Come in," Leslie said to Ashley.

Ashley put her hand on his arm, keeping him from leaving. "We'll be okay. You really don't have to stay."

"It isn't a matter of having to," he replied. He focused on Kaitlyn. "I'm going to walk the perimeter."

He moved back, allowing Ashley to enter the house. He needed a moment alone with God to figure out what he was going to do about his growing attachment and affections for the woman he needed to protect.

* * *

Ashley shut the front door with a soft click. The two women stared at her with similar expressions of mirth and anticipation on their faces.

A flush heated Ashley's cheeks. For some reason embarrassment squirmed through her. "What?"

Leslie grinned. She'd changed from her pantsuit into black yoga pants and a deep purple T-shirt, and had pulled her honey blond hair out of its bun to hang loose around her shoulders. "For a minute there, we were hoping…expecting…"

Kaitlyn shook her head, setting her dark blond curls shimmering around her face. She wasn't dressed nearly as casually as the other woman. Kaitlyn wore well-worn jeans and a light green Henley-style, long sleeve shirt with the sleeves pushed to the elbows. Her badge and holster were at her waist. "Chase blew it. We thought for sure he was going to kiss you."

So had Ashley. But then he'd stepped away, dashing her hope. He was a man of integrity. And evidently kissing his star witness wasn't in his wheelhouse. She should have been grateful he'd called a halt when she wouldn't have had the strength. She wanted to kiss him. Wanted to believe she was worthy of his attention, despite knowing it was better this way. It would make leaving easier not to have any sort of romantic attachment to Chase.

But how had the ladies known he had almost kissed her? "Were you two spying on us?"

Leslie's grin widened.

Kaitlyn shrugged, totally unrepentant. "The window is cracked open. We could hear and see everything."

Ashley rolled her eyes. "Okay, you guys, stop. Nothing is happening between Chase and me."

Only problem was she kind of wanted something to happen between them. She wished he had kissed her. A missed opportunity that might not occur again. She sighed inwardly. She knew there could never be anything between her and the handsome deputy. Not only were they from totally different worlds, but he'd made it clear he was happy with the way his life was now.

Besides, regardless of what the Los Angeles district attorney said about her staying put, at some point she was leaving this town, whether on her own or with an escort to LA. It would be better for everyone if she didn't get too emotionally involved. She was relying on him to keep her safe. But she couldn't give him her heart.

Leslie tucked her arm through Ashley's and drew her to the couch in the living room where she sat beside her. "I want to know all about you."

Kaitlyn moved to the window and looked out before securing the latch and making sure the curtains were completely closed. Was she expecting something to happen tonight? Chase was out there. Would he be safe?

As her heart rate ticked up, Ashley asked the female deputy, "Alex will be close by, right?"

"I think Daniel is taking first watch," Leslie stated.

"That's right," Kaitlyn confirmed. "And you'll have me and Chase here in case anyone gets by Daniel."

Sinking deeper into the cushions, Ashley asked, "Where will Daniel station himself?"

"At the entrance to the driveway." Kaitlyn perched

herself on the arm of the couch. "You don't have to worry. You're safe."

Taking a deep breath, Ashley tried to calm her racing heart. She had to trust these people, but she wanted to think about something other than the danger she was in. Curious about the people she'd surrounded herself with, Ashley met Leslie's gaze. "So…you and Daniel? You two have history, I take it."

Leslie curled her lip. "Yes, there is history. We practically grew up together. His family's ranch borders ours. And with our last names of Q and R, we were always table mates in school."

"And you dated," Kaitlyn interjected.

Leslie rolled her eyes. "You can't call attending one homecoming event dating. And we only went because our parents insisted, but he was a jerk then and he's a jerk now."

Ashley frowned. "Daniel doesn't come across as a jerk." But she couldn't speak to what he'd been like in high school.

Leslie waved Ashley off. "Enough about me. I want your story. Where did you grow up? How did you end up in Bristle Township and why is somebody trying to kill you? Who—"

Ashley held up a hand and turned to Kaitlyn for help.

"She can't really talk about the case," Kaitlyn said by means of rescue.

"It's not like I'll tell anybody," Leslie said. "You don't trust me?"

"Of course I trust you," Kaitlyn said. "It's just somehow the bad guys seem to know our every move. So if you don't know anything, then you can't slip up. And you can't tell anybody that she's staying here."

Leslie frowned. "Of course not. Although Maya also knows she's here, but I trust her not to say anything, either."

A soft knock on the front door had Ashley's nerves jumping. Kaitlyn strode to the door, her hand on her weapon. She peeked through the peephole, then relaxed and opened the door for Chase to enter.

Overwhelmed by how relieved she was to see him, Ashley rose. She needed some distance and rest. "I am exhausted. I promise I'll fill you all in on my past some other time."

Leslie stood and gestured toward the hall. "I'll show you where you're sleeping."

With a nod and smile to Chase, Ashley followed Leslie to a large bedroom. "Is this your room? I can't put you out of your own bed."

Leslie waved away her protest. "Nonsense. You need sleep. We'll camp in the living room." She gestured to a door. "Restroom's in there. Towels under the sink. We'll see you in the morning."

After Leslie left, Ashley showered and dressed in long flannel pants and a matching shirt that she'd purchased at Leslie's store for Christmas. Turning out the light, she prayed and then tried to sleep but her mind raced with nervous energy.

Finally, sometime after midnight, she couldn't take her sleeplessness anymore and padded out to the living room to find Leslie painting her toenails, Kaitlyn watching the news with the sound turned off and Chase sitting at the dining room table with a laptop open. His expression went from grim to commiserating when he lifted his gaze to her. "Can't sleep?"

Ashley shook her head. "I'm too nervous about tomorrow. Mind if I get a glass of water?"

"Help yourself," Leslie called out. "Glasses are in the cupboard next to the sink. There's filtered water in the refrigerator door."

"Thanks." Ashley went to the kitchen, found a short glass in the cupboard and rinsed it at the sink. Having grown up in the Mojave Desert, she'd formed the habit of always rinsing her utensils and drinking cups to wash away the dust. As she turned off the faucet, movement in the window above the sink caught her eye. Unlike the front window, there were no curtains or blinds for Kaitlyn to close. Ashley frowned, going on tiptoe to peer out.

A dark figure appeared in the window. Only the whites of the person's eyes were visible in the ambient light.

Startled, she screamed and she dropped the glass she held as she ducked to a crouch. The sound of glass shattering in the sink echoed through the house and assaulted her ears.

Chase and Kaitlyn ran into the kitchen. "What is it?"

Recovering from her fright, Ashley realized she'd dropped the glass into the metal sink and thankfully not on the floor. Cautiously, she rose and pointed at the window. "There was someone out there."

Kaitlyn grasped Ashley's bicep and pulled her into the living room. "Leslie, take Ashley into the bathroom and lock the door."

Leslie was already moving with her phone in her hand. "I'll call Daniel."

Chase had his weapon drawn. "Stay here," he said to Kaitlyn. "Don't let anyone in."

Kaitlyn nodded, her gun at the ready. "Be careful."

Ashley's heart tore as Chase disappeared out the back door in pursuit of the intruder. Then Leslie was tugging her into the bathroom.

Sinking to the floor, the heavy weight of distress spread through her body. She'd put these people in danger by staying here. She sent up a plea to God to keep them safe.

As Chase's eyes adjusted to the dark, he searched for the prowler. The dark shadows made his quest difficult. Bushes lined the sidewall, providing numerous places of concealment. His nerves stretched tight with readiness. Cautiously, he stalked forward, wishing he'd grabbed a flashlight. He wanted—no, needed—to find this intruder.

A wisp of noise on his left provided a split-second warning. He spun, bringing his gun up just as something metal crashed down on his right forearm. Pain exploded through his system and his hand went limp, his gun falling to the ground.

A person dressed all in black rushed at him.

Calling on his one year of high school football as a defensive guard, Chase dropped his shoulder and met the assailant's charge, taking him off his feet and propelling him backward onto the ground with an audible thud.

A siren rent the air, signaling that Daniel was arriving.

Before Chase could secure his attacker, the man rolled to his side, got his feet beneath him and bolted, running away from the cottage toward the pasture that stretched for acres in darkness.

Breathing hard, Chase picked up his weapon with his nondominant hand and contemplated firing after the suspect but he couldn't see the target. Awkwardly, he returned his weapon to its holster, then massaged his forearm where he'd sustained the blow. No doubt the tire iron lying on the ground had been the assailant's choice of weapon.

A moment later, a Sheriff's Department cruiser pulled to a stop and Daniel jumped out.

"What's going on?" he asked, as he raced to Chase's side. "Leslie said there was an intruder."

"One perpetrator. He got away," Chase said and recounted the incident.

"No way could we have anticipated an attacker coming at the house through the field in the dark," Daniel stated.

Logically, Chase agreed that he and the other deputies couldn't have secured all access points of the hundred-plus acre spread. But it made him so mad that the men hunting Ashley had even known she was here at the Quinn ranch. It was like Maksim Sokolov had eyes and ears everywhere. And everything Chase had read online about Maksim Sokolov had chilled Chase's bones.

The guy was a ruthless gangster with ties not only to Eastern Europe but to the Colombian cartel. His name was associated with gunrunning, drug smuggling, prostitution and murder.

And he always managed to evade the law.

Chase remembered Ashley saying that Gregor, the man who'd helped her disappear, had told her not to trust the police because Sokolov owned many of them. Anger burned in Chase's chest. That an officer of the law, who'd sworn an oath to protect and serve, would join forces with the likes of someone like Sokolov made Chase's blood run cold. Dirty cops were a blight on all law enforcement agencies.

He trusted his fellow deputies and the sheriff. He was confident none would reveal Ashley's location. Not intentionally.

But clearly Sokolov had spies in town. And Ashley wouldn't be safe until the man was locked away for good.

Daniel eyed him. "You okay?"

"My ego is more bruised than I am." Keeping his arm tight against his middle, Chase headed back inside, informing Kaitlyn of the escaped intruder.

"You chased him away," she said. "That's a win in my book."

He grunted his disagreement.

Kaitlyn went down the hall and returned a moment later with Leslie and Ashley following close behind.

Chase's gaze collided with Ashley's. Her eyes lit up, sending a ribbon of affection unfurling through his system. In three long strides, he met her halfway. Silently, she slipped her arms around his waist, resting her cheek against his chest.

"The intruder's gone," he told her. The relief that she

was unharmed heated his core, lessening the throbbing pain in his injured arm.

Ignoring the curious stares of the others in the room, Chase tucked Ashley's head beneath his chin and held her tight with his left arm. It felt good and right to hold her close. Part of his brain protested, claiming he was digging himself a hole he might not be able to get back out of. The other part of his brain, the one that acknowledged he cared for Ashley, had him placing both arms around her, despite the pain in his right forearm.

She drew back to stare into his face. Her eyes were red-rimmed and her expression troubled. "I was so scared for you."

Her concern touched him deeply. "I failed to capture him."

"He didn't succeed in his plans," she countered, gripping his right arm.

Her fingers dug into what promised to be a deep bruise and caused him to draw in a sharp breath.

Gasping, she quickly disengaged and stepped farther away from him. "You're hurt!"

He flexed his fingers and moved his wrist. "Only superficially."

Wrapping her arms around her middle, her voice dropped to a low whisper. "He's going to keep sending men to kill me."

"We'll deal with them," he assured her.

Pressing her lips together as if to prevent herself from saying something, she only nodded. But he could tell she wasn't convinced. Only time would prove his words true.

SEVEN

The next morning, after stopping by Chase's house for him to change into a fresh uniform, and rubbing some arnica cream that Lucinda had given him on the black-and-blue area of his forearm, Chase hustled Ashley into the conference room of the sheriff's station. A TV monitor had been hooked to a laptop and sat facing a lone chair.

Though her insides still quaked with worry, she'd recovered enough from the ordeal of the night before to find her composure. As long as she didn't let her mind dwell on the fact that Chase had been injured protecting her. Today she'd chosen to wear a pretty blue top borrowed from Leslie over her one good black pencil skirt and low heels. She'd tamed her hair a bit with a hair product she'd found in Leslie's bathroom that smelled of vanilla, a scent that gave her some comfort.

Daniel, wearing the same brown uniform that matched Chase's, was at the laptop. His head lifted as they entered. "Everything is all set on this end." He gestured for her to take a seat. "The sheriff will be in momentarily. He's on the phone with the district attorney in Los Angeles now. When they're ready, I'll conference in the DA. He'll appear on the screen to talk to you."

Daniel left the room as Ashley nodded and sank onto the chair in front of the monitor. She swallowed back the trepidation working its way up her throat. Nerves from the thought of giving her statement to the district attorney had her heart pumping with enough adrenaline to keep the fatigue from a sleepless night at bay.

Ashley, along with Chase, Kaitlyn and Leslie, had stayed up the rest of the night, finally resorting to playing board games to pass the time. He'd sat with an ice pack on his arm in hopes of reducing the swelling and bruising. And every time she'd looked at him, she wanted to cry but stifled the urge.

Now she couldn't wait to get this deposition over with, so she could figure out what to do about the rest of her life and how best to keep anyone else from getting hurt. Once her story became public knowledge, there would be reporters hounding her. Not to mention the ever-present threat that one of Maksim Sokolov's goons would manage to silence her before the trial.

She had no illusions that giving her statement would make her safe. Actually, she believed the opposite.

But she would keep her word to Chase and tell the authorities what she'd seen.

Chase stood at her side and placed a hand on her shoulder. His touch gentle and reassuring. "You're going to do just fine."

She hoped so.

A handsome stranger wearing a pinstripe suit with a red tie walked into the conference room. Of medium height with highlighted blond hair and piercing blue eyes, he surveyed them for a moment, pressing his lips together in apparent disapproval before striding toward Ashley.

Unnerved, she leaned closer to Chase.

"What are you doing here, Grayson?" Chase asked.

"The sheriff called to ask if I would represent Miss Willis," the man said. He shook Ashley's hand. "Donald Grayson."

Panic flooded Ashley's system. Was he here because she'd left the scene of the crime? Her gaze jerked to Chase as she extracted her hand. "Why do I need a lawyer?"

"You're not in trouble," Chase assured her. He turned his questioning gaze to the man named Grayson. "Isn't that correct?"

Mr. Grayson nodded as he set a briefcase down on the conference table. "Miss Willis, you're being deposed and this is a legal matter. The sheriff thought it would be good for you to have some preparation and, if the need arises, representation."

"That makes sense," Chase stated. He smiled at her encouragingly. "He's here to help."

Mr. Grayson sat down at the conference table and opened his briefcase. "I've read your statement. But there are a few things we need to go over in preparation for this deposition." He glanced up at Chase. "My client and I need a moment alone."

"I'd rather stay." Chase angled toward Ashley. "If that's okay with you?"

Uncertainty gripped Ashley as her gaze bounced between the two men. Finally, she decided she had nothing to hide from Chase. "I'd like Deputy Fredrick to stay, please. He's promised to be with me through this whole thing."

Mr. Grayson arched an eyebrow. "If you're sure."

"I am."

"Then let's get started." Mr. Grayson pulled out a notepad. "First off, tell the truth. I know that seems like a ridiculous thing to say but it needs to be said."

Wincing with guilt for having deceived everyone with her false identity, she nodded. "The truth and nothing but."

Mr. Grayson smiled but it didn't reach his eyes. Though they were blue like the handsome deputy's, Chase's were warm and inviting, whereas Mr. Grayson's were like a storm about to hit land.

"Also," Mr. Grayson continued, "I want you to refrain from volunteering information. If you are asked a question and you can answer yes or no definitively, do so. If you don't know the answer to the question, say I'm not sure or I don't know. You can ask to have the question repeated. Take a moment to think before you answer. And I want you to refrain from arguing. Answer only the questions that are directly asked of you."

A knot formed in her tummy as she absorbed his instructions. That was a lot to remember.

"I understand that Mr. Sokolov's attorney will also question you," Mr. Grayson said.

A stab of dread impaled Ashley. She thought she might be sick. "I didn't know that." Ashley turned her gaze to Chase. "Did you?"

"I wasn't sure," he said in a strained tone.

Anxiety spread through her chest. "You should've warned me."

"Actually," Mr. Grayson said. "You're not allowed to have any coaching from law enforcement. Only from your lawyer. Which is why I find it highly irregular to have Deputy Fredrick here."

"I'll be quiet," he said.

Grayson shook his head, clearly deciding that wouldn't do. "I think it's better for my client if you leave. We wouldn't want any suggestion of impropriety on the side of the defense."

Daniel poked his head through the doorway. "The video will be up and running in ten minutes."

"I need to prep my client," Mr. Grayson stated.

Chase took her hand and gave it a gentle squeeze. "He's right. I should go."

Disliking the sting of abandonment stealing over her, she clung to him for a moment. Dredging up strength from someplace deep inside, she released his hand. She needed to be brave for what was to come and to stand on her own two feet. "I understand."

There was no mistaking the reluctance on Chase's face as he left the room. Ashley stared at the table, willing herself not to tear up. Her throat worked and her insides quaked. Why did she feel so alone when Chase wasn't close by?

"Okay, then," Mr. Grayson said, drawing her focus back to the matter at hand. After walking her through the process of how to answer questions directed at her from the district attorney and the defense council, he slid a piece of paper in front of her with a long list of questions. Her stomach dropped, thinking she was going to have to answer each one.

"The district attorney will ask you some basic background questions," Mr. Grayson explained. "These are the most commonly asked questions. Take a moment to read through them and think about your answers. Be ready to respond if one is asked. I will let the sheriff know we are ready."

"Wait, that's it?" She didn't feel prepared at all. In fact, reading the long list of questions that might be asked, she grew flushed with anxiety. Some of the answers would be embarrassing. Like revealing her lack of education or her lack of family.

"Just tell the truth, Miss Willis." Mr. Grayson rose and walked toward the door. "I promise you everything will be okay."

She didn't take stock in promises anymore.

Staring at the paper in her hands, she decided the questions were pretty simple with simple answers. Her life until the night she witnessed Maksim Sokolov kill a man had been unremarkable in the grand scheme of things. Sure, she'd grown up on the wrong side of town, in a trailer near a refuse container, with a single mom whose desire to be a parent waxed and waned. Ashley had survived and had started to make a life for herself. One day, she hoped to again.

A few minutes later, the sheriff, Mr. Grayson, Chase and a pretty redheaded woman walked in. The woman went to the video monitor. Ashley remembered seeing her around town. But she didn't know her name.

Chase put his hand on her shoulder. "Ashley, this is Hannah Nelson. She is our crime tech specialist. She's going to run the camera and video feed. Daniel had to go out on a call."

Hannah waved at her. "Just call me the jack-of-all

trades." She smiled kindly. "Maya and Leslie and Kaitlyn all said to keep your chin up. They're rooting for you."

Hannah's words filled Ashley with warmth. It was good to know that these people had her back. She really wanted to trust them. There was a cold part of her that doubted any of them could promise her safety from Maksim Sokolov's reach.

"Okay," Hannah said. "We are live in one, two, three." She flipped a switch and a man appeared on the monitor. Clean-shaven, graying at the temples with steel-gray eyes, the man regarded Ashley grimly. "Hello, Ashley Willis, I am District Attorney Evan Nyburg."

Unsure if she should say a greeting back, she looked at Chase. He gave her a slight nod. She turned back to the monitor. "Hello. Can you hear me?"

"I can hear you just fine," Nyburg said. He introduced his assistant, Sarah Miller, and the defense attorney, Amos Henderson. "All right. Let's get this started."

For the next hour and a half, Ashley answered question after question. The district attorney and the defense attorney grilled her to the point that she wanted to scream. But she did as Mr. Grayson had instructed and kept to short, simple answers. She took her time, she thought about her responses and she stuck to only what she knew. She did not elaborate and she did not guess. Her palms grew sweaty and the muscles in her neck knotted with tension but she maintained her composure much better than she'd anticipated.

"I have everything I need," Nyburg stated with a satisfied nod. "We will be issuing a warrant for the arrest of Maksim Sokolov."

"And he will be out on bail within the hour," the defense attorney said. "Your witness is unreliable and will not hold up in court."

Ashley's fingers curled in her lap. Her heart rate tripled. What had she done wrong?

"We'll see about that," Nyburg bit out. "There isn't a judge in the state who will let Sokolov go free. I'll make sure of it." The monitor went blank.

Ashley slumped in her chair. "Is what the defense attorney said true? Am I an unreliable witness? Will Mr. Sokolov not go to jail?"

Chase came over and helped her to her feet. "He was posturing. You did really well. The district attorney will do everything in his power to take Sokolov off the street."

"Indeed, you did well, Miss Willis," Mr. Grayson said with an approving smile that enhanced his good looks. He handed her his card. "If you need anything, call me. I understand you're staying with Leslie Quinn?"

Taking the card, she said, "Thank you. And yes, I am."

But not for long. Now that this part was over. It was time for her to leave. Tonight. If Mr. Sokolov had wanted her dead before, he surely would double his efforts now.

Somehow she had to go into hiding again. It was for everyone's sake. With her gone, the danger that she'd brought to Bristle Township would also leave. Chase and the others would be safe. Her heart hurt at the thought of leaving, but she had to do what was right and best for them all.

He escorted her from the conference room with his hand at the small of her back. His touch was solid and warm and reassuring. She wanted to curl into him for strength.

"I don't think you should go back to Leslie's," he said, his voice dropping low.

Surprise washed over her. Though she agreed, she hadn't expected Chase to come to the same conclusion, that it was time for her to disappear again. But somehow she doubted that was what Chase had in mind. "Why not?"

He paused at his desk. "We can't take any chances that Lucca Chinn or anyone else won't leak your location."

A shiver of fear worked over her limbs. "Then I should disappear."

Would Chase help her? Hope spurted through her heart, stirring the affection she'd been trying hard to repress.

"Yes, in a way." He guided her into the sheriff's office.

The sheriff sat at his desk. His silver hair showed signs of him running his fingers through the thick strands, something he did when he was stressed. "Everything is all arranged."

"What's going on?" Ashley didn't like this out-of-control, vulnerable apprehension steeling over her. Decisions for her life were being made without her input. She breathed deep, trying to let go of the need to have some semblance of control.

"You'll stay at the sheriff's house tonight until we can come up with a long-term plan," Chase said.

Startled, Ashley stared at the sheriff. "Oh, sir, I couldn't intrude on you."

"No intrusion," Sheriff Ryder said. "My wife will enjoy female company. And Chase will be on-site for extra protection."

"That's right," Chase agreed. He captured her gaze and the intensity in his eyes held her enthralled. "I'm not letting you out of my sight."

His words and the situation landed like a rock in the pit of her stomach. There was no way she'd be able to slip away and disappear with both the sheriff and Chase watching her every move. Now what would she do? Panic crept in. Staying was dangerous for everyone. And leaving had just become more complicated, if not impossible.

Chase touched her arm. Concern darkened his blue eyes. "Don't worry. I'll protect you with my life."

Didn't he understand? That was exactly what she feared most.

It was bad enough to suspect that Gregor's death was because of her. The guilt was nearly paralyzing. If anything happened to Chase…she didn't think she could live with the blame.

Sunlight broke over the horizon, casting long shadows over the mountain. The creeping sensation of darkness that was at odds with the light of day worked over Chase as he sat at the sheriff's kitchen table drinking coffee, winding his nerves tight. He was thankful for fresh clothes, jeans and a chambray shirt that Lucinda had bought him a few Christmases ago. He had his holster on and his badge.

Sheriff Ryder and his wife had already had their breakfast and started their day. The sheriff had headed to town while Mrs. Ryder went to her Bible study, leaving Chase to wait for Ashley to awaken.

He was glad she was sleeping in. He could only imagine the stress she was experiencing. Living under the constant threat of danger and exposure had to wear on a person. Especially someone as sensitive and compassionate as Ashley. He admired her fortitude. She hadn't crumbled yet. In fact, she'd done so well during her deposition, if he hadn't known how nervous she was, he'd never have guessed. She'd been poised and forthright. He was proud of her.

Despite assuring her that the district attorney wouldn't have any trouble putting Sokolov behind bars, Chase understood Ashley would have to enter witness protection, commonly referred to as WITSEC. The sheriff had already reached out to the US Marshals Service and arrangements were being made.

But until they could put her in the program, it was up to Chase and the Bristle County Sheriff's Department to protect her. As they would, regardless. But she'd become important to them. She belonged to the community. And it pained him to know she would leave them all behind. He'd have no way to keep in touch. For both of their sakes.

The sound of his cell phone ringing broke the early morning silence. He grabbed his phone from his pocket, hoping the noise hadn't disturbed Ashley. The call was coming from the sheriff's station.

"Chase here," he said into the device.

"I have some bad news." Sheriff Ryder's voice was grim.

Chase's stomach plummeted. He braced himself. "What's happened?"

"The district attorney's office had a break in last night," Ryder said. "Ashley's deposition was destroyed."

"How could that happen?" Chase fought a wave of confusion. "Surely they had security procedures to safeguard against a situation like this."

"One would think," Sheriff Ryder said. "Unfortunately, Maksim Sokolov has been released."

The crime boss had been arrested late yesterday afternoon on the strength of Ashley's testimony. And now he was out!

"What!?" Chase ran a hand through his hair in aggravation and dread. "We have a copy of the deposition. Can't we send it to them?"

"That would be the logical solution, however, the defense has claimed there's no way to ensure that our video hasn't been tampered with."

Gritting his teeth, Chase forced himself to refrain from wishing bad things on the defense. The man had a job to do and despite his poor choice in clientele, the defense lawyer's job was to defend his client, not be logical.

"District Attorney Nyburg is coming to town to depose Ashley in person, but he can't make it today," Ryder said. "Until he arrives tomorrow, we have to be on high alert."

"I need to take Ashley somewhere off the grid."

Chase's mind whirled. Where could he take her to keep her safe?

"Agreed. My old hunting cabin would be perfect," the sheriff said.

"Isn't the cabin accessible only by horse or ATV?" He had neither one.

"Yes. Because we don't have ATVs readily available, Kaitlyn has agreed to escort you and Ashley. She'll provide you each with a horse from her family's stock. There's no cell service up there, but you'll have a satellite phone so I can let you know when Nyburg arrives and you can come back down the mountain."

Going to the sheriff's hunting cabin was a sound idea. Chase had been to the rustic dwelling a few times. The place wasn't a five-star hotel but the cots were decent enough. And it was so far off the beaten path there was no way anyone would be able to find them.

"As soon as Ashley wakes, we'll head over for the keys," Chase told him before hanging up.

"Where are we going?" Ashley stood a few feet away, wearing jeans and a lightweight sweater in a pale coral, the hue enhancing the color of her cheeks. Her short platinum hair curled becomingly around her sweet face.

Attraction and affection zoomed through his veins. He wanted to draw her close, tuck her into the shelter of his embrace and keep her safe from the world. This latest development would be a blow. And if he could spare her the distress, he would. But he had to be honest; she deserved to know what had happened, so he told her the disturbing news.

Her face lost its color, making her eyes seem too

large for her face. "Now do you see why I must disappear?"

"Yes. And we're working on it." He told her about the cabin and the district attorney coming to town.

"But what happens after that?" Her voice shook. "Mr. Sokolov isn't going to let me live long enough to testify at his trial. You know that, right?"

He didn't like hearing her say what he knew to be true. Sokolov would do his best to eliminate the threat to his freedom. The man may have a large network of guys willing to do the dirty deed, but Chase was determined to make sure none were successful in their quest.

"You'll enter the witness protection program as soon as possible," he said. His heart hurt to think she'd be taken to some undisclosed location and he'd never see her again. But to keep her safe, he had to let her go. She'd take a piece of his heart with her but that was a small price to pay for her protection. Until then he would do whatever was required to protect her.

Her delicate eyebrows lifted. "So we hide on the *mountain*?"

The way she said the word *mountain*, one would have thought he was saying they were headed to the moon. "Yes."

After waiting a beat for her to digest his answer, her lips pressed together and her eyes hardened as determination settled over her pretty face. "Okay. Let's go." She started to move toward the front door with quick purposeful steps.

He suppressed a smile. She really was a trooper. "Do you want to gather your belongings?"

She spun and gave him a wry glance. "Oops. Yes. I'll grab my bag."

As she headed back toward the guest bedroom where she'd slept, he said, "The place is only accessible by horseback."

She stopped and slowly turned to face him, her eyebrows rising nearly to her hairline. She held up her hands as if to ward off his statement. "I don't know how to ride a horse."

Moving to her side, he said, "I'm a novice as well, but we'll figure it out. Together." He held out his hand.

After a moment of hesitation, she slipped her hand into his, their palms melding against each other. The heat of her touch raced up his arm and wrapped around him. She was placing her trust in him. He prayed he didn't fail her.

EIGHT

Ashley bounced in the saddle as the quarter horse, Othello, hopped over a rut in the trail. She tried to keep her knees loose as Kaitlyn had instructed and not hold on to the saddle horn for dear life, but she was so far from the ground that it was hard not to cling to the horse.

Anxiety twisted in her chest and she kept her gaze straight ahead. Falling wasn't something she wanted to experience, and if she glanced down, she feared she'd find herself hitting the ground face first, and not even her puffy down jacket would soften the fall.

Adjusting her hold on the reins, she shook her head with disbelief at the situation. To evade any more of Sokolov's thugs, they were headed up Eagle Crest Mountain to some remote cabin the sheriff owned. In theory, the idea had merit but in practicality… How had she let herself be talked into riding a horse? This was a new and strange experience.

In front of her, Kaitlyn, wearing well-worn denim and a cinnamon-colored leather barn coat, rode a large black-and-white-spotted horse as if she were one with the animal and saddle. No bouncing, just a nice rolling movement. From what Kaitlyn had shared, the woman had been riding since before she could walk. Ashley tried to emulate her. But she was doing a poor job of it by the way her body was protesting every step the horse took.

Glancing over her shoulder at Chase nearly caused her to slip sideways as a grin fought to escape. He didn't seem to be faring that much better. But at least he'd been on a horse before. He gave her the thumbs-up sign with a cheesy smile as she righted herself. She couldn't help but return his smile with a small laugh.

Riding into the trees through the valley that separated Eagle Crest Mountain and a smaller hill where the Delaney Estate had been built at the top and could be seen in all its glory, she felt freer, albeit sorer, than she had in a very long time.

No one knew where she, Chase and Kaitlyn were or where they were headed, except the sheriff, Daniel and Alex. She had to trust they wouldn't reveal her location. She'd had to do a lot of trusting lately and she felt the stretch of it in her soul. There was no way for Sokolov to send anyone after her out here in the wilds of the forest.

Birds sang in the trees and animals she couldn't see scurried through the underbrush. The horses' hooves made a slight rhythmic thumping sound against the dry ground. She deeply breathed in the pine-scented air, letting the familiar aroma soothe her.

Kaitlyn held up her hand. Assuming she meant for Ashley and her horse to come to a halt, Ashley pulled back on the reins like Kaitlyn had taught her. The pale brown horse stopped so abruptly Ashley almost went headfirst over Othello's neck. Chase's horse bumped up against her horse's rear flank.

"Whoa," Chase said.

She glanced back to see his horse dance a little, turning him in a circle. Relieved her horse wasn't doing the same, she patted the stallion's neck. "Good boy, Othello."

Othello pawed the ground, no doubt anxious to keep moving.

Kaitlyn consulted the map the sheriff had given her with directions to the cabin. She pointed off to the right and led the way into the trees, leaving the hiking path behind.

Holing up in a remote cabin in the woods sounded like an ideal plan. Out of the way, not easy to access and devoid of any way to communicate with the outside world save the satellite phone Chase carried. She doubted her escorts would allow her to stay forever. She didn't want to go back to town. She didn't want to go meet with the DA. She wanted this nightmare to end without any more drama.

But she didn't think that was possible.

The world would keep turning, and she would do what was required of her and go into hiding from a monster with long tentacles. She prayed the US Marshals Service would be able to find her a place far enough and secure enough to be out of reach of Mr. Sokolov.

The sun was high in the sky by the time they reached a clearing where a small single-story building had been erected amid towering pine and evergreen trees. Ten feet away was a wooden corral with a gate. Kaitlyn brought her horse to a halt at the corral and hopped down. She hooked her horse's reins over the top railing, then turned to survey their surroundings.

Ashley's horse automatically came to a halt next to the big spotted horse.

"Give me your reins," Kaitlyn said.

Ashley handed the thin straps of leather over and Kaitlyn wound them around the rail.

Following Kaitlyn's instructions on how to dismount, Ashley attempted to climb off the beast, but her feet got tangled up in the stirrups and she lost her grip on the saddle horn. Panic stole her breath as she fell backward, but then strong hands wrapped around her waist, lifting her away from the saddle and setting her feet on the ground.

The heady scent of man and spicy aftershave filled her senses. It was all she could do not to lean back into Chase's strong chest, wanting his arms to slip around her and hold her fast so that he blocked out the world.

He was doing what he could to help her. That was all she could ask. Wanting anything more from him wasn't wise and would only lead to heartbreak. They both understood her time in Bristle Township was close to an end. Better to put some distance between them or she might give in to her longing for connection and let her heart fall for him.

She stepped away to face him and gave him a grateful smile. "Thank you." Her gaze included Kaitlyn. "For everything."

Above all else, she was thankful because these two people were willing to give up their own lives for her sake. She'd never had anyone do that and it left her strangely unsettled. She sent up a quick prayer, asking God once again to watch over them. So far he'd answered her prayers.

She didn't want to believe it was just coincidence that had allowed her to survive too many scary situations. Trusting the Lord didn't come easily. Trusting anyone didn't come easily to her.

She'd learned at her mother's hand not to trust in promises or in seeming kindness. However, Chase appeared so sincere. She searched her heart and found that she did trust him with her life. And was aware he would do anything to protect her. Trust him with her heart, she wasn't so sure. But she was learning. Learning not only how to let go of any illusion of control but to appreciate being cared for by others. A hard lesson that pushed and prodded, molding her into a more complete person.

"I'll take the saddles off and give these guys a rub down," Kaitlyn said. "You two take the supplies and get the house situated."

Attached to both of their saddles were packs filled with food, their personal belongings and other necessary items that they would need for their short stay at the cabin.

Chase reached past Ashley and undid the knot holding the packs tied to her horse's saddles. The packs slipped away, and he handed her two lighter weight ones. "I've got the key. I'll be right behind you," he said.

She nodded and made her way slowly across the uneven ground to the weathered front door of the cabin. The place was in need of some tender loving care. Kind of like her. Didn't matter that she was only twenty-eight, she felt ancient. The stress of the last year and a half had taken a toll.

Chase stepped up to unlock and open the door. They stepped into a one-room space. Cots were stacked against one wall. A wood-burning fireplace with a stove stood in the corner. A table with four rickety chairs sat by the window. She bit her lip. "No running water?"

"Nope. Though the facilities are out back." He shrugged and she nearly groaned, picturing herself fumbling around in the dark behind the cabin.

"But there's a stream about fifty yards east. We'll gather some water to boil so that we can use it for washing and cleaning. And we brought bottled water for drinking."

"This is very rustic." Though he'd warned her, she hadn't expected it to be quite this sparse. "You've stayed here before, right?"

He nodded. "Yes. Quite a different experience from what I was used to." He unpacked food supplies. "It's a bit like stepping back in time to a simpler life. Relaxing in a way."

She figured she could adapt easy enough. "I don't mind roughing it. Beats what is waiting for me in town."

His steady gaze led her to believe that he comprehended what she wanted. His words confirmed it. "We can't stay here, Ashley. Eventually someone would figure it out. We have one night here and then you meet with the district attorney. By then the US Marshals Service should have everything in place."

Why wasn't she as eager as she should be to enter WITSEC? "And then I'll disappear again."

He looked away and busied himself unpacking a second bag. "Yes, you will."

From the tone of his voice, she had the impression he didn't like the idea of her leaving for good any more than she did. Oh, she wanted to disappear, never to be found by Maksim Sokolov, but she didn't want to leave Chase. Despite her best efforts, he'd invaded her heart.

She cared for him in ways that made her uncomfortable and giddy at the same time. But she had to put a pin in her emotions and deflate her growing attachment to the handsome, kind, compassionate and honorable man. Nothing good would come from the fallout of leaving her heart behind when she finally did relocate with a new name and blank slate. "If I'm going to be on my own, away from you, who's going to protect me?"

With a twist of his lips, he heaved a sigh of frustration. "I'm not going to lie to you. You'll be under the care of the US Marshals Service, but they won't be able to provide you round-the-clock protection."

Her heart sank. Once again she'd be alone and vulnerable to attack. There had to be something she could do to protect herself. "Life is so unfair sometimes."

Facing her, he held her gaze. "God never promised fairness, only that He would be with us through all of life's circumstances."

His words slipped inside of her, spreading hope within her like warm butter on toast. She clung to that hope, even though she hadn't been aware of God's presence very often in her life. She had to believe God had kept her alive so far for a reason. Having the confidence that God would continue to sustain her through this nightmare bolstered her courage.

Resolute determination squared her shoulders. "Then I need to learn how to protect myself. I want you to teach me how to physically defend myself against an attack. I need to know what to do if someone tries to grab me again like that fake police officer."

Chase contemplated her request, then nodded. "You know, that's not a bad idea. Between Kaitlyn and me, we could show you enough basic moves so that you could at least incapacitate an assailant long enough to run away. And really that's all you want. Run and hide." His intense gaze bore into her. "Don't think you can ever take on somebody bigger and stronger than you and hope to win."

She bristled. He thought she was weak. Okay, so she wasn't physically strong but it infuriated her to know that he thought it, too.

He made a face and held up a hand. "Before you get upset, I just want to say this has nothing to do with your being a woman. It's simple physics."

"So you would give the same advice to Kaitlyn?"

He thought for a moment. "Yes and no. If her life depended on it, I would say fight. But she's had years and years of training."

"Not to mention muscles," Ashley muttered.

A smile played at the corners of Chase's mouth. "This is true. And she is a deputy with a gun. But the smart thing for you would be to disable your attacker and then run like the wind. Get as far away as possible and hide or find a public place where you can get help."

That made sense and seemed more doable than single-handedly taking down a bad guy intent on harming her. The thought turned her knees to jelly.

"In fact, I would suggest you should always stay where there's other people," Chase continued. "Going into that dark alley by yourself that night—should never have happened."

"It was my turn to take out the garbage," she protested.

"I'm not saying you did anything wrong by doing your job." He gentled his tone. "The responsibility lies with the person in charge."

"Gregor."

"Yes. He put you in an unsafe situation."

"I get what you're saying." She blew out a breath in an attempt to release the guilt that had sprung up. Gregor may not have thought she was in danger by sending her out with the garbage, but he'd helped her afterward. And it most likely cost him his life. "I have no illusions that a few hours of some basic self-defense will turn me into a black belt or anything. But it would make me feel better if I at least knew how to get away."

The cabin door opened and Kaitlyn walked in. "I just heard the very end of that. What is it that you want to do?"

Chase explained Ashley's request.

Kaitlyn regarded Ashley with an assessing gleam in her blue eyes. "I think a little self-defense clinic is an excellent idea. We can teach you enough to know how to break a nose or crush a foot."

"Namely, hobble an attacker," Chase added.

Kaitlyn grinned. "Yes, and there is one particular move that's my favorite. A blow to the knee does the trick nicely. Let's unpack and then we'll have a lesson."

Giddy anticipation raced through Ashley's blood.

Finally, she was doing something proactive, something that would keep her as safe as she could be without her bodyguards watching over her.

They made quick work of unpacking their supplies and arranging the cots for later when they would sleep.

They headed outside and found a patch of cleared ground.

"Okay." Kaitlyn rubbed her hands together. "First off, let's talk about the parts of your body you can use to defend yourself with." She touched her elbows. "You have two very hard pointy objects with which to jab." She drew her bent elbow back. "Strike or ram."

Keeping her elbow bent, she made a sweeping motion that brought her elbow up and around, plowing into an imaginary foe. Then she lifted her other elbow and swung her arm in a downward motion, like a hammer.

Rubbing her own elbows, Ashley could envision the blows would hurt, both the attacker and her.

Kaitlyn then held up her hands and hit the heels of them together. "The heel of the hand is an effective tool for a head shot, too. You'll want to aim for the nose, the ears and under the chin." She motioned to Chase. "Come at me."

Ashley held her breath as Chase faced Kaitlyn and reached for her. Kaitlyn's cocked wrist thrust upward toward Chase's nose, stopping a hair's breadth before contact.

Chase didn't flinch. The man had nerves of steel.

Ashley blew out a breath. "Wow."

"You can also go for a knee or the groin. Grab your attacker by the shoulders, using his body for leverage as you ram your knee into the vulnerable spots." Kaitlyn demonstrated on Chase.

Ashley winced. Hurting someone went against every grain in her body. She'd have to get over it.

Kaitlyn turned around so that her back was to Chase. "If your assailant grabs you from behind, trapping your arms…"

Wordlessly, Chase put his arms around her torso, pinning her arms to her sides.

"Immediately, stagger your stance and bend your knees." She demonstrated. "This will draw your attacker off balance. At the same time twist and pivot from your feet until you can get at an angle." She moved as she spoke and then brought her heel up and touched it to the outside of Chase's knee. "At this point I'd ram my heel here. He'd buckle because knees aren't made to bend from the side."

"Or she could also stomp on her assailant's foot," Chase said, releasing Kaitlyn.

"True. The heel on the instep or a kick to the shin will also be effective."

"Now your turn." Kaitlyn stepped aside.

Ashley's mouth went dry. "I don't think I can do that."

"You can," Chase said. "The other thing you should know is how to break a hold if someone grabs you by the wrist." He reached out and took hold of her arm a few inches above her wrist. "What do you do?"

She tried to move away and jerk her arm free but he held on tight. "Okay, that's not working. What do I do?"

He released her. "You grab my wrist."

She grasped his left arm. He immediately pinned

her hand to his arm, stepped toward her and swung the arm she held around in a swift move that put him in control and twisted her arm backward at an awkward angle. Then he pushed her so that she had no choice but to sink to the ground.

"Whoa," she breathed out.

"From here, with your attacker down, you could kick or knee the guy to give you a few more moments to get away." He released her.

Excited by the simple yet effective move, Ashley jumped to her feet. "Teach me that move." She held out her arm for him to grab.

Over and over, she practiced the various self-defense tactics until it grew too dark outside to see. Kaitlyn had left them to work together while she went to the creek for water. Chase was patient as he repeated moves and instructions, making sure she understood the techniques.

She couldn't have asked for a better instructor. Despite her best effort, she was falling for him. She had to fight it with every fiber of her being, yet the question that kept playing through her mind was, how was she ever going to leave this man?

Chase stared at the darkened ceiling, his hands cradling his head while he lay stretched out on a cot near the door. The ladies were sleeping side by side in the far corner. Every once in a while one of them would move, their cot creaking, the blankets rustling. No doubt Ashley couldn't sleep. They'd spent several hours vigorously training.

His heart was still pumping fast, though he acknowledged it wasn't from the physical activity but from spending extended amounts of time with Ashley. She was so determined and eager to learn. It made his heart ache with dread, knowing she would be gone from his life soon. He wished there was a way she could stay in Bristle Township. But there wasn't.

The best thing for her was to go into the WITSEC program where she'd have a new identity in an undisclosed location.

He could go with her.

The thought pounded through his head.

No. He had a life in Bristle Township. Friends, Lucinda and a job he enjoyed. He couldn't give that up. His tender emotions for Ashley would fade with time. And if he said it enough to himself, he might one day believe it.

The shrill ring of the satellite phone exploded in the silent cabin. Chase jumped from his cot and hustled to grab the device from his pack.

A flashlight beam illuminated the room as Kaitlyn joined him.

"You got it?" Kaitlyn asked.

"Yep." He lifted the antenna and pressed the button to answer. After a few seconds of silence while the phone connected via satellite, Chase said, "Hello."

"Chase." Daniel's voice came through the line. "We have a problem."

Dread and anxiety crushed Chase's chest. "Tell me."

"I found a listening device attached to the leg of a desk. We believe when the fake Detective Peters was in the station, he planted it."

That was how Sokolov's men had known where

Chase and Ashley were when they'd left for Denver. The ramifications of this disturbing news hit Chase like a hoof to the gut. Sokolov no doubt knew where they were now.

"Uh, Chase," Ashley's voice trembled. She stood at the window. "There's someone outside."

NINE

Chase dropped the satellite phone and vaulted across the room, launching himself at Ashley, tackling her in a full contact embrace and taking her to the ground just as the world erupted in a barrage of gunfire.

Bullets pitted the wooden walls. Glass shattered, raining down on Chase's back. Heart pounding in his ears, he braced himself for the painful impact of a bullet. He would protect Ashley with his body, with his life. He prayed Kaitlyn had found cover.

After a moment that seemed to last forever, the gunfire ceased. The ensuing silence was deafening. Breathing a small sigh of relief to not have a gunshot wound, Chase lifted his head slightly. "Are you okay?" he whispered against Ashley's ear.

"Yes," she squeaked.

He turned his head toward the spot where Kaitlyn had last stood. Embers in the cast-iron wood stove glowed eerily. "Kaitlyn?"

"I'm here, behind the stove," came her whispered reply. "I let Daniel know we're in trouble."

Appreciating Kaitlyn's quick thinking in picking up

the phone he'd dropped and letting Daniel know what was happening, he eased away from Ashley, but he kept his hand on her shoulder to ensure she stayed down. "We're going to crawl as fast as we can to the wood stove. You're going to get behind it."

He didn't wait for her to answer, but prodded her forward. They scrambled across the hardwood floor now littered with glass. The sting from shards of the busted window bit into his skin. When they reached the wood burning stove, he maneuvered Ashley behind it.

"What are we going to do? There's only one way in and out of this cabin." Ashley's panicked question made Chase wince.

"And they know that," Kaitlyn said grimly. "It's only a matter of time before they come in and finish what they started."

"No, we're okay. There is another way out." Chase groped the floor, searching for the lever. "The cabin doesn't have a foundation because we're on government land. The sheriff keeps the firewood under the floor. There's a hatch here somewhere."

"I'll help you search." Ashley's scared whisper brushed against his neck.

"No. Stay put." He didn't want her exposed. "Kaitlyn, are you armed?"

"Yes."

"Keep them busy. If someone comes through that door, shoot him." He placed his hand on his own weapon and unlocked the holster so he'd have easier access.

"Roger that." Kaitlyn moved to the window.

"We only want Ashley Willis," a man's voice shouted

from outside the cabin. "Our business isn't with you two deputies. Save yourselves and hand her over."

"Not going to happen," Kaitlyn yelled back. "You better take off or I'll take you down."

Coarse laughter met her threat.

"Keep them talking," Chase said, as he continued searching for the latch to open the trap door in the floor. Sweat rolled down his back from the anticipation of their attackers breaching the cabin before they managed to escape.

"Who sent you?" Kaitlyn called out.

"Doesn't matter," the same man yelled back. "Send out the woman."

"You know we can't do that!" Kaitlyn replied.

Silence met her announcement.

"What are they doing out there?" Ashley asked.

"They're going to wait us out," he said. "Obviously, they're in no hurry. They don't know that we've called for backup." His hand closed over the latch and he eased the hatch open. He lay on the floorboards and reached into the hole to find a large stack of wood. As quickly and silently as possible, he removed the short logs, haphazardly pushing them aside. A slight breeze blew through the opening as he created enough space for them to drop into and crawl out from beneath the cabin.

"Okay, ladies, get ready to move. We'll have to crawl out from beneath the house."

Ashley moved to his side and put her hand on his arm. "We can't go out there. What if they see us?"

"We have to. My priority is getting you to safety. Staying here isn't safe."

"Getting *all* of us to safety," Ashley protested.

"Yes. All of us." He appreciated her concern. "I'll go first, then you and then Kaitlyn."

"And…then what do we do?" she questioned in a whisper.

Good question. "Not sure yet. I'm winging it here."

"If I can make it to the corral and get to the horses, we can escape," Kaitlyn said.

"Assuming they haven't let the horses go," he replied.

"Dancer, Othello and Buttercup won't go far if they have been released," Kaitlyn assured him.

He wished he had as much confidence in the horses' loyalty. But the horses were Kaitlyn's animals and he trusted her to know. "All right. Let's go."

He squeezed through the opening headfirst with his arms out for support. Once he touched the ground, he belly crawled to the edge of the cabin's frame, on the opposite side from where the bullets had come from. When he was assured there was no one around, he shimmied out and gave a slight rap on the wall to let Ashley know it was her turn to crawl out. Crouched down, making himself as small as possible, he heard the faint noise of Ashley's movements.

"Give me your hand," he whispered, reaching out for her.

In the dark, her hand touched his, then held on as she made her way out from beneath the cabin.

After giving the wall another faint rap, he pulled Ashley behind him so that she was wedged between the cabin and him as they waited for Kaitlyn to join them.

"You two stay put." Kaitlyn's voice, barely discernible, came at him in the dark. "Let me check out the horse situation. If I can set them loose, then you two meet me in the woods behind us."

"Copy," Chase said, the one word barely above a whisper. It was important now that they stay as silent as possible so as not to draw the attention of their attackers.

Kaitlyn moved past him toward the edge of the cabin and then she was gone.

The whinny of the horses alerted Chase that Kaitlyn had reached the corral. He sent up a prayer that the men out front didn't understand the noise was the horses greeting their owner.

"What's got those horses spooked?" one of the men said, his voice carrying on the breeze that had kicked up.

"Maybe a copperhead snake," another man said.

"Oh, man, I hate snakes."

"Pipe down," a third man demanded. "I'm going in."

The sound of boots on the porch shuddered through Chase.

There was a rustling sound and then the pounding of hooves as the horses bolted from the corral, disappearing into the forest.

"What's she doing?" Ashley whispered in his ear.

"Creating a diversion," he whispered back. Kudos to Kaitlyn. The longer she kept the men from breeching the cabin, the more chance they had to get away.

"Hey! Who let the horses out?" one of the men shouted.

Not waiting to find out what the men decided to do, Chase tugged Ashley away from the cabin. "This way," he whispered in her ear.

He tucked Ashley close and together they ran toward the shelter of the trees. They found Kaitlyn behind the trunk of a large Douglas fir.

"We need to reach the creek," Kaitlyn whispered.

"What about the horses?" Ashley asked, also keeping her voice low.

"They'll come running when we're ready for them," Kaitlyn answered.

Shouts of the men galvanized Chase into action. Their attackers had discovered the empty cabin.

"Lead the way," Chase urged Kaitlyn.

He put Ashley in front of him so he could protect their flank. The going was slow in the dark. He kept a hand on Ashley's shoulder to steady her when she stumbled.

The rush of the creek, swollen from the winter run-off, led the way forward. When they reached the edge of the canopy of trees, the moon shone bright on the rippling water of the creek a few feet away.

Kaitlyn let out a shrill whistle. "It will be a moment or two."

"We should stay near the trees." He didn't like the idea of being exposed out in the open.

They took cover at the base of a tree that had large bushes growing up around it.

"Will the horses be able to find their way in the dark?" Ashley's voice held concern.

"Yes. They have excellent night vision," Kaitlyn replied.

"That's a relief."

Chase smiled to himself at Ashley's innate concern for others, even horses. She was such a caring and generous woman. One of the many things he'd come to admire about her.

"What was Daniel saying to you on the SAT phone?" Kaitlyn asked.

Remembering the disturbing news, a fresh wave of anger coursed through Chase's veins. "He found a listening device in the station house."

Ashley gasped softly. "How did it get there?"

"Only way I can think of is when the fake Peters showed up, he must have planted it," Chase told her.

"That's how they found out we were here." Kaitlyn's tone held a sharp edge. "I figured it had to be something like that. These bozos wouldn't know how to track anybody on their own."

Ashley made an irritated growling noise in her throat. "Mr. Sokolov has known our every move. He's insidious."

Chase slipped his arm around her shoulders. "He won't be privy to any more information on you now."

She leaned into him. "I hope not."

The bobbing of flashlights moving through the trees sent Chase's heart slamming against his rib cage. "They're coming."

Kaitlyn pushed away from the tree she'd been leaning against. "We need to cross to the other side of the creek."

Deciding it was better than waiting to be found, Chase urged Ashley into the knee-high flowing water. Through his shoes and pant legs, cold zapped his flesh to the bone. He kept a firm grip on Ashley's biceps as she sucked in a sharp breath of distress at the icy temperature of the creek.

She slipped, letting out a muted yelp, and he pulled her firmly against him. "Steady now."

"I pray we get out of this alive," she whispered. "And with all our toes."

"We will," he told her and sent a prayer heavenward that he wouldn't be proven a liar. Moving slowly over slippery rocks and against the current's tug, they reached the other side of the creek and hustled to the cover of more trees.

Kaitlyn let out another soft whistle that sounded more like a bird's call. A few moments later, the three horses appeared, their hooves splashing in the water as they ran along the creek. The three horses stepped onto the bank and moved toward their owner with Dancer in the lead.

Kaitlyn held up her hands. "Whoa," she cooed gently.

The three animals slowed to a halt.

"I didn't have time to put their saddles on," Kaitlyn told them. "Only their bridles. Not ideal but we'll have to manage."

Chase kept an eye on the light bobbing through the forest. They were getting closer every second. Worry chipped away at his confidence. Urgency sharpened his tone. "We need to go."

"I don't know about this." Ashley's voice was low and uncertain.

"It's not much different than with a saddle," Kaitlyn said. "Grab some of Othello's mane near his withers."

"His what?"

Chase could tell Ashley was on the verge of panic. He didn't blame her. It was one thing to ride while secure in a saddle with stirrups for your feet to help you stay in place. And with no experience riding, he understood her confusion about the animal. He stepped closer. "I'll help you up. The withers are the ridge between the horse's shoulder blades."

"Oh." Ashley reached to grab a handful of Othello's black mane. "Now what?"

"I'll lift and you swing your leg over," Chase said. "Ready?"

She gave an audible gulp before she let out a strained, "Yes."

He put his hands at her waist and lifted her off the ground. She swung her leg over and settled on the horse's bare back.

Kaitlyn handed her the reins of the bridle that would control the horse's head. "These horses are used to being ridden bareback, but it is challenging. You'll need to sit upright, no slouching or hunching over. Keep your legs draped over the horse. Try not to grip or draw your knees up. The horse is going to feel every movement you make. This is going to challenge your balance."

"Wonderful," Ashley muttered.

Committing Kaitlyn's instructions to memory, Chase hurried to Buttercup.

Kaitlyn moved with him. "Drape your torso over his back and then swing your leg over."

He did as instructed and easily found himself sitting on the horse. It was a very different sensation than with a saddle, and he figured he and Ashley would be sore when this was over.

Kaitlyn easily mounted her horse. "I suggest we head to the Delaney Estate."

"Lead the way, Kaitlyn," Chase said, eager to be

gone before the men pursuing them discovered their whereabouts. "You still have the phone, right?" he asked, with hope coloring his voice.

"Of course." She patted the cargo pocket on the thigh of her pants.

"Good. Let Daniel know where we're headed and about the men hunting us."

"On it."

The second Dancer took a step, Othello and Buttercup followed. Kaitlyn led them through the dark forest. Chase barely heard her talking to Daniel on the phone. Chase kept half his attention behind him, praying they'd outsmarted their attackers. The journey toward the safety of the Delaney's rolling mansion at the top of the next rise was harrowing and physically uncomfortable but a small price to pay considering the alternative.

By the time they arrived at the Delaney Estate, Ashley's body hurt. Tension radiated through every fiber of her being. Not only from the anxiety of being pursued through the forest but from sitting on a horse with no saddle. Riding bareback was a strange experience, one she didn't want to repeat anytime soon, but she trusted the horse as Kaitlyn had told her to do and the animal hadn't dumped her off, which was a win. Her core muscles were taut with the constant need to keep her balance atop Othello.

Lights flooded the Delaney property as they halted the horses in front of the large ornate metal gate. Kaitlyn buzzed the intercom.

"State your business," a man's deep voice stated, coming out of the box.

"Tell the Delaneys it's Deputy Kaitlyn Lanz of the Sheriff's Department."

"One moment, please."

Slowly, the gate opened and they rode the horses up the paved drive, past an illuminated manicured lawn and hedges that were trimmed into animal shapes. Ashley had never been here before and had never thought she would have an occasion to visit the Delaneys in all their splendor. The structure reminded her of a castle from a fairytale. She'd heard the elder Delaney was eccentric, the treasure hunt last year being proof of that, but this mansion was so whimsical that she wondered what type of person would create a place like this in the middle of the Colorado forest.

The front door opened and Nick Delaney, the younger of the Delaney brothers, stepped out and hurried down the large staircase, heading straight for Kaitlyn as she drew her horse to a stop. He wore designer jeans and a form fitting long-sleeved T-shirt that accentuated lean muscles. "Well, aren't you a sight for sore eyes."

Ashley's horse came to a halt next to Kaitlyn's, with Chase moving in next to Ashley.

Kaitlyn hopped off Dancer. "Where's Ian?"

Nick shrugged. "Not here. What can *I* do for you?" He grinned and wagged his eyebrows.

"This was a mistake," Kaitlyn stated, half pivoting away as if she were going to remount her horse.

Nick's expression cleared and grew serious beneath the house's outside lights. "Really, what can the Delaneys do for you? We're happy to help."

With a huff that Ashley decided was a mix of exasperation and surprise, Kaitlyn handed him the reins of her horse. "Hold this." She turned away, but said over her shoulder, "Don't let her step on you."

Ashley pressed her lips together to keep from laughing at the way Nick's nose scrunched up as if he'd eaten a lemon.

"Step on me?" He backed away from the horse, stretching the reins out as far as they would go. "Why would the horse step on me?" He eyed the big bay as if afraid the animal might charge him. "Are you a mean horse?"

Chase slipped off his horse and came toward Ashley.

Kaitlin took hold of Othello's bridle. "Okay, Ashley," Kaitlyn said. "You're going to fall into Chase's arms."

Ashley raised her eyebrows at Kaitlyn. "Excuse me?"

Kaitlyn's smile was much too innocent. "I mean, you're going to slide off. Pretty much like before. Grab the reins and some of the mane, lean forward and then swing your right leg over the back of the horse and slide down."

Chase moved closer. "Come on, you can do it. I'll catch you if you fall."

Ashley blew out a breath. Unfortunately, she doubted she'd be graceful. "You better catch me, Chase."

"Don't worry," he said. "Trust me."

He was always saying that, and it hadn't always worked out. "Who are you trying to convince? Me or yourself?"

Moonlight displayed the face he made. "Both."

Tilting her head, she said, "I trust you to catch me if I fall."

"I know I've let you down before," he said. "I—"

"Stop." She cut his words off. "You're human and not infallible. Evil is evil, sometimes unstoppable. You can't control all circumstances, no matter how determined you are."

He touched her knee. "You're right. I pray every moment that I'll be enough."

She wanted to tell him he was, but she remained silent, knowing if she spoke, she'd reveal just how enough for her he was. That if she weren't careful, she'd give him her heart.

Holding on as instructed, she leaned forward, lifted her right leg and brought it over the horse. Othello chose that moment to move. She lost what little balance she had and plummeted straight into Chase's strong arms.

He set her gently on the ground. "See, I didn't let you fall."

On impulse, she reached up and kissed his cheek. "No, you didn't and for that I'm grateful."

His lopsided grin sent her heart thumping. His gaze dropped to her lips. Her pulse jumped. Yearning flooded her system. She wanted him to kiss her. Instinctively, she leaned toward him.

Kaitlyn cleared her throat, disrupting the moment. Ashley jerked back, her cheeks heating. She hoped her blush wasn't visible in the glow of the house lights.

"Let's get inside before those bumbling henchmen decide to find us and climb the fence," Kaitlyn said.

"Hey, wait a second," Nick said. "Henchmen?" He handed Kaitlyn back the reins to her horse. "There will be no henchmen climbing our fence. Follow me."

He led them into the large sprawling mansion. Ashley marveled at the marble floors, sweeping views from the large windows and a wide staircase with a wrought iron railing leading upward to a second floor. Impressive paintings that she'd only seen in books adorned the walls. There was a museum-like quality to the home. Not as whimsical inside as outside.

Nick shut the big oak door behind them with a solid thud. An older man, wearing a black suit with the buttons mismatched as if hastily put on, stepped out from a side door.

"This is Collins, my father's valet and the house butler," Nick said. "If you're hungry, he can fix you something to eat."

They all declined. Ashley couldn't fathom being wealthy enough to have a valet/butler. She wasn't even sure what a valet was, but he seemed like someone only the rich needed.

"Then would you see to their horses," Nick told the man.

"Sir?" Collins's expression was a mixture of confusion and concern.

"Seriously," Nick stated. "They came riding horses. Old West style."

"Very well." Collins headed for the front door. "I will handle them."

"Make yourself at home." Nick waved toward a room to their right. "That's the library. You'll find bottles of water in the mini fridge."

"Do you happen to have any pain reliever?" Ashley asked. Her body was bruised and sore, but thankfully not broken.

Sympathy flashed in Nick's eyes. "Of course. My

father keeps a stash in his desk. Top right drawer. Help yourselves. I hope you find some relief." He strode away.

Ashley and Chase moved toward the library and stopped when Kaitlyn didn't move. She stood rooted to her spot, watching the younger Delaney brother disappear down a corridor. "I wonder what he's up to?" Her gaze narrowed. "I'm going to find out." She stalked after Nick.

Ashley wasn't sure what was up between the deputy and their host. But they seemed to be at odds on everything.

Chase shrugged and led the way into the library. Another wall of windows greeted them. Ashley wanted to see the view in the daylight. A few lights twinkled in the distance. Were they facing town? The other three walls were filled with volumes of books.

A large massive desk sat in the middle of the room. Ashley found three different types of pain relievers. She took two from a bottle. "Chase?" She held up the container.

He nodded. "I'll take two."

Chase went to the mini fridge in the corner, grabbed two bottles of water and handed one to her.

Ashley enjoyed the cool liquid as it washed down the pills. She hadn't known how thirsty she was until she'd drunk nearly the whole bottle. "I never suspected riding horses was so hard."

"We survived," Chase said, finishing off his water and dropping the empty bottle into a garbage can by the built-in bar.

"Yes. But for how long?" The fear that she'd kept at

bay while concentrating on staying atop a horse now rushed back to overwhelm her. "What happens when they realize where we've gone and they come after me again?"

"We need to get through the night, then put you in front of the DA tomorrow. The US Marshals Service will take over after you're deposed."

She should have been happy at the news. This would be the beginning of a new phase. She'd be whisked away to some undisclosed location where Mr. Sokolov couldn't find her. But she wasn't happy. Not in the least. Hiding again—using another fake identity, living a lie—twisted her insides into knots.

She moved to sit in a wingback chair. Sinking into the cushions, she absorbed the softness after the bony hardness of the horse. "I don't know how much more of this I can take."

Chase sat on the little ottoman in front of her. "Listen to me." His intent gaze demanded her attention. "You are doing great. You will survive this. You are a survivor and don't let anyone or anything tell you differently."

She wished she felt like a survivor. But she accepted she was a fraud. And a liability. A nuisance. An albatross around Chase's neck. Leaving with the US Marshals Service would be the best thing for everyone. Only it would be agony on her heart. She sighed. "Thank you. You always seem to know exactly what to say."

He frowned. "If the expression on your face is any indication, I'm not sure if I did more harm than good."

He'd done it again, reading her so well. She rose and stepped away. "No, everything is working out the way it's supposed to. I just have to—" She swallowed hard, her mouth suddenly so dry. "I have to trust that God's in control."

She went to the bookshelves and pretended to read the spines, but her eyes were misty with tears. Strong arms wrapped around her. She hadn't heard Chase move, but for some reason she wasn't surprised that he would offer her comfort, reassurance and his strength. She leaned back into his chest. She'd take it for now.

Because soon they would be separated by confidentiality and distance. The thought of leaving had never hurt so bad.

TEN

The sound of Kaitlyn and Nick Delaney in the entry-way of the Delaney mansion heading for the library forced Chase to release Ashley. She hurried away to stand near the floor-to-ceiling window overlooking a dark landscape. His arms were empty and cold without her.

He had to admit, it was better to not give anyone the wrong impression, though. They weren't a couple. No matter how much he liked, respected and cared for Ashley, the paths of their lives were set on different trajectories. There was no intersection where they could travel together toward a mutual future. Part of him wanted to accept the fact and another part wanted to rail against fate. He would do neither.

Grabbing a book from the shelf and pretending interest, Chase looked up as Kaitlyn swaggered into the opulent room with Nick on her heels.

"He armed the fence. Anyone touches it, they'll sustain a nasty shock," Kaitlyn announced as she halted near the desk. "I'm sure it was Ian's doing."

The precautions seemed over the top, but Chase figured with the kind of wealth the Delaneys had, they must also acquire enemies. Last year when the hunt for the Delaney treasure was in full swing, there were many people willing to kill for the prize.

Nick snorted and rested a hip on the edge of the desk. "Why do you assume he's the brains behind our family?"

Kaitlyn's mouth lifted at one corner in a smirk. "I'd be highly surprised to find out otherwise."

He wagged his eyebrows. "Oh, I'm sure I could surprise you in many ways."

She dropped her chin and glared. "Not going to happen."

He cocked his head with a glint in his dark eyes. "I'm not sure what you are inferring, Deputy Lanz."

Kaitlyn's eyes widened, and her mouth opened but no words formed.

Chase almost laughed out loud and his gaze sought Ashley's. Her lips were pressed together as if she, too, were holding back her amusement at the interplay between the other two.

Kaitlyn finally narrowed her gaze. "When is Ian returning?"

The humor in Nick's eyes dimmed. "Not any time soon. And because my father is with Ian, you're stuck with me as your host. I'm really not that bad of a guy."

Kaitlyn made a face. "I'm going to check in with the sheriff. Then we need to leave." She stalked out of the library.

"I don't think she likes you much," Chase commented.

Nick chuckled and shrugged. "Probably not. But

she's much too serious. Just like my brother. But don't get me wrong, I respect anybody willing to put on a badge and do the hard job."

When Nick wasn't doing the adult equivalent of tugging on Kaitlyn's braid, Chase thought he was probably a decent guy.

Ashley moved to stand beside Chase. "We really appreciate you taking us in like this."

"Of course," Nick said. "I'll drive you all into town when you're ready."

"Thank you." Chase itched to clean up. His clothes smelled of horse and creek water. His socks were still sopping wet inside his shoes. He was sure both of the ladies were eager to get going, as well.

"You have an extensive collection of books," Ashley said.

"My father's passion," Nick said, going on to talk about the rare and first editions that Patrick Delaney had collected over the years. Ashley seemed very interested and for that Chase was glad. Anything to distract them from the danger looming outside the estate's fence. Nick was well spoken and much more conversational when Kaitlyn wasn't present.

Kaitlyn returned, her expression pensive. "I just got off the phone with the sheriff. He'd like us to stay here tonight and come into town in the morning."

"You're welcome to," Nick said. "We have plenty of en suite rooms and Collins can wash and dry your clothing for you."

Kaitlyn stared at him a moment. "Thank you. Your hospitality is appreciated."

Nick nodded but made no comment.

Chase didn't hesitate to take the man up on the offer. At least they would be safe for the night and have clean clothes in which to face the morning.

"This baby is armor-plated and has bulletproof windows," Nick Delaney proudly explained as he drove the big army green Humvee out the front gate of his estate the next morning.

Nick had insisted on driving them to the sheriff's station, much to Kaitlyn's dismay. Chase's coworker really had an issue with the younger Delaney. Chase wasn't sure what had her dander up. The fact that he was a wealthy man who seemingly didn't take life too seriously or was there something more?

After making arrangements to have the three horses transported back to her family ranch, Kaitlyn had slid into the back seat of the Humvee with Ashley while Chase sat in the front passenger seat. Chase had noticed the glance Nick had thrown Kaitlyn as if he'd been surprised she hadn't insisted on riding up front. To be honest, Chase had been surprised, too.

And though Nick played off his attention to Kaitlyn as bantering, there was no doubt the man was attracted to the female deputy. There was no mistaking the way Nick's gaze followed Kaitlyn when she wasn't watching. The two couldn't be more opposite, and sparks flew when they were together.

Chase, on the other hand, was grateful for the Delaneys' help and their safeguards. Anything to keep Ashley safe. And he refused to analyze why she'd become so important to him.

Today would be a big one for Ashley. Right now the

Los Angeles district attorney was waiting at the Bristle Township courthouse. And the sheriff had nudged the US Marshals Service to hasten their timeframe for when they would secure Ashley into the WITSEC program. It was all coming together. So why did Chase's heart sag heavily with something akin to sadness?

As they neared town, the chime of a cell phone rang loud inside the cab. Nick pushed a button on the steering wheel and connected via Bluetooth to the call. "Nick Delaney here."

"Mr. Delaney, this is Sheriff Ryder."

"Hello, Sheriff. I have you on speakerphone with Kaitlyn, Chase and Ashley. We're almost at the courthouse."

"I need you to step on it. I need them at the station right away."

Something in the sheriff's tone sent alarm bells ringing inside Chase's chest. "What's up, boss?"

"We have a situation. I need all of you here. Now." The call ended.

A fist of dread slammed into Chase's gut. What was going on? Was there a problem with the LA district attorney coming to town?

"Well, that was mysterious," Nick said as he maneuvered his way through town and to the end of the main street where the Sheriff's Department sat. The two-story brick building had been repaired and enlarged thanks to the Delaney family after last year's blaze. More specifically, Ian Delaney. The man had expressed his remorse that his father's treasure hunt had fueled the arsonist.

"Pull around back," Kaitlyn instructed.

"As you wish." Nick drove down the side alley into the back parking lot and halted next to one of the official sheriff department vehicles. They piled out and hurried inside.

Chase's throat closed up as his mind registered that the sheriff and Daniel were dressed in tactical gear. Daniel, a former marine recon sniper, held a Barrett M95 manual bolt-action sniper rifle at his side.

Tension bunched Chase's shoulder muscles, but he didn't say anything, waiting for an explanation. Whatever was happening had to be serious. They didn't normally bring out the specialized equipment unless something bad was going down. A band around his chest tightened with anxiety.

Sheriff Ryder pointed to the two chairs off to the side. "Miss Willis and Mr. Delaney, take a seat." There was no arguing with the command. Ashley and Nick settled on the chairs.

"What's going on?" Kaitlyn asked with a frown. She bounced on her toes, a habit that Chase had noticed when his fellow deputy grew anxious.

Before the sheriff could answer, Alex stepped out from another room, also decked out in full body armor complete with riot helmet and two sidearms strapped to each thigh. His grim nod strained Chase's nerves.

"Kaitlyn, we need you to stay here and guard our witness," the sheriff said.

"Against what?" Chase reflexively demanded. He couldn't take not knowing what sort of situation required full-scale assault equipment in their small town. But he had a dreadful foreboding in the pit of his stom-

ach that this had something to do with Maksim Sokolov and Ashley.

The sheriff shifted his attention to Alex and gave
a nod.

The empathy in Alex's eyes slammed into Chase.
"Lucinda has been taken hostage."

The bottom of Chase's world fell away.

"Oh, no." Ashley's heart sank. She jumped up from
the chair and rushed to Chase's side, gripping his arm.
"She's in danger because of me."

Alex nodded. "Unfortunately, yes. They are demanding we trade you for her."

Stomach knotting with horror, Ashley stared at
Chase. His jaw worked but no words came out. Lucinda was his family. Like a mother to him. The only
person he was close to. He had to be devastated. Ashley's chest ached.

"You have to do it," she said despite the terror flood-
ing her veins. "Trade me."

Chase's gaze whipped to meet hers. The dark blue of
his eyes turned stormy. "No! Never. Not going to happen. Lucinda wouldn't want that to happen."

"But Chase—" Didn't he understand? She'd do whatever was necessary to ensure Lucinda was released unharmed.

He gave a sharp shake of his head and abruptly
turned from her. The dismissal cut deep.

"Where is she?" Chase asked the sheriff.

"She called from her cell phone and Hannah traced
the call back to your place," Alex supplied.

For a second Chase was silent, then he nodded.

"Okay. We can work with that. Let me gear up." He sprinted out of the room without waiting for permission.

Ashley sank back onto the chair. Fear for Lucinda drained her of oxygen. Her lungs contracted painfully, and panic fluttered in her chest. Ashley remembered what it was like when the man posing as the detective had been about to throw her off the cliff. She hated to think Lucinda was experiencing the same terror. If those men hurt Lucinda, Ashley would never forgive herself.

When Chase returned, he was dressed in a similar fashion as the other deputies. A shudder of alarm worked over her limbs. They were expecting the situation to turn deadly. Why else would they be wearing such intimidating outfits? Nausea roiled through her stomach.

Chase headed for the door. "Let's roll."

"Wait!" Ashley scrambled from her chair. "Take me with you. If worse comes to worst, you trade me. We might as well get this over with. Gregor died for me. I can't let Lucinda pay the ultimate price, too."

Skidding to a halt, Chase whirled to face her. The anger on his handsome face should have scared her but it only made her want to weep with despair.

Chase's voice was hard and unyielding. "No one is going to die at the hands of these thugs. We will rescue Lucinda. You need to remain here."

Aggravated with a potent mix of terror and anguish, she shook her head. He couldn't make that kind of promise. "I can't let them hurt someone else."

She had to do the hard thing and sacrifice her life to save another life. She would not let Lucinda pay the price for her. She bolted for the door. Kaitlyn blocked her path, hands raised.

"Ashley, no."

"But you can use me to draw them out," Ashley argued.

"That won't be necessary," Chase said. A muscle ticked in his jaw. He shook his head and trained his focus on his boss. "There's a root cellar in the basement that has an opening about ten yards from the house. I doubt these LA henchmen of Sokolov's would even know to look for it."

"We can split up," the sheriff said. "Daniel and I will work from the front of the house while you and Alex go through the back access point."

"What about me?" Kaitlyn asked.

Before the sheriff could respond, Nick stood. "I can keep Ashley safe inside the Humvee."

Kaitlyn turned to him, her expression startled as if she'd forgotten he was there. "You're not a part of this."

He stepped past her to address the sheriff. "I am a part of this community. I can help." He turned to Kaitlyn. "Ian is not the only one with skills. Plus, Ashley will be safest in my vehicle. Being armored and all."

"That's not a bad idea," Alex interjected. "We may need all hands on deck here."

"Gear up, Kaitlyn," the sheriff said, apparently agreeing with Alex. "We'll get the car ready."

Ashley recognized the way Chase's jaw clenched. He wasn't happy with the decision, but the longer they debated, the more likelihood that Lucinda would end up hurt.

Heart pounding in her chest, Ashley hurried out to

the Humvee and slid in the back. Chase left with Alex in a separate vehicle. A few moments later, the sheriff drove away with Daniel and Kaitlyn. Nick pulled in behind them and followed them through town toward Chase's house.

Ashley sent a desperate plea heavenward. *Lord, please don't let anything happen to Lucinda. I couldn't take it if she died when I could've done something to save her.* Losing Gregor had been awful, but Lucinda would be worse because of what it would do to Chase.

Chase parked a few blocks away from his house. His heart hammering in his chest and a prayer on his lips for Lucinda's safety, he and Alex hoofed it through Chase's neighbors' backyard to the fence separating the properties. Through the earpiece jammed in his ear, he heard the sheriff trying to negotiate Lucinda's release. Thankfully his boss was keeping the men holding Chase's former nanny hostage busy. Chase and Alex had a better chance of gaining access to the house unseen.

In the shadow of a full maple tree, Chase slipped over the fence and dropped down next to the tree's trunk. Alex joined him a moment later.

Daniel's voice came through the earpiece. "We have two suspects. I have a clean shot."

"No," Chase quickly replied, knowing Daniel could only take out one at a time, which would give the remaining one an opportunity to hurt Lucinda. "We can't take the chance with her life on the line."

"Let us get inside and neutralize them both," Alex said softly into his own headset.

Chase gave his superior a grateful nod.

"Copy," Daniel said.

Lifting a scope to his eye, Chase surveyed the back of the house. He didn't see anyone at the windows or any movement within. What were these goons thinking? What was their plan? How did they intend to escape once they completed their goal of eliminating the threat to Sokolov?

A horrifying thought flittered through his brain and made sweat break out on his neck. Was this a suicide mission? Did they plan to take Ashley out along with themselves and anyone else who got in the way? Could anyone be that loyal to a crime boss? Then again, it probably wasn't loyalty that motivated them, but fear. They likely had families of their own they were protecting.

"We need to be alert for explosives," Chase murmured into his headset.

Alex tapped him on the shoulder once to indicate he heard.

The sheriff's voice came through the earpiece. "Take care. Godspeed."

Chase lifted another prayer for guidance, then motioned for Alex to follow him. In a low crouch, they moved along the fence line until they were close to the place where the root cellar doors were visible. With another hand gesture, Chase indicated the entrance. Alex tapped his shoulder again one time in acknowledgment.

In tandem, they quickly moved from the fence, across the yard to the metal door. There was a combination lock that Chase quickly undid. He lifted one half of the door and Alex slipped inside the dark root cellar with his weapon at the ready.

Chase quickly followed, easing the door back into

place as quietly as possible. The clank of the metal latch settling into place reverberated through him and ratcheted up his tension.

Sudden light from Alex's flashlight dispelled the total blackness and revealed the rows of canned goods, baskets of vegetables and the incline ramp Chase had built for Lucinda, which led into the basement via a wooden door.

Calming his breathing, Chase retook the lead and opened the basement door. He swept the large space, determining it was clear, before stepping inside with Alex on his six. Another homemade ramp would take them into the kitchen. He and Alex positioned themselves on either side of the door, preparing to breach the house, when Chase heard Ashley's voice in his head. Or rather his headset.

"Sheriff, tell them to send Lucinda out and I'll go in."

Ashley's raised voice sent fear sliding through Chase. "No," he ground out as softly as he could, but loud enough for the sheriff to hear.

"Miss Willis, you are to stay back." Frustration vibrated through the sheriff's voice. "I will put you in handcuffs if I have to."

Forcing himself to stay focused on the job at hand and not on Ashley's stubborn refusal to keep herself safe, Chase turned the knob and slowly opened the door. Alex moved past him, turning to the left while Chase entered to the right. The kitchen was clear.

From the other side of the wall separating the kitchen from the living room, Chase heard Lucinda's soothing tone.

"Are you sure you want to do this?" Lucinda asked.

"Why ruin your lives when you don't even know why you're here?"

Chase had to smile. Leave it to Lucinda to pull out the men's story.

"Listen, lady, the boss gave us a job to do and we have to do it or—" The man's voice shook with agitation and sounded familiar to Chase.

"Shut up!" a second man barked out the command.

This man's voice also rang a bell. These were the same thugs who had found them at the cabin.

Where was the third man? Probably watching the sheriff's station.

Alex and Chase stacked up at the edge of the wall. With a quick tap on the shoulder from Alex, Chase and Alex stormed into the living room, Chase going to the left and Alex to the right. Two men stood on either side of the front plate glass window. The one on the left held a semiautomatic pistol while the other had a Glock, similar to what Chase used, tucked into his waistband. Lucinda was in her wheelchair in the middle of the living room.

"Hands in the air," Chase yelled.

"Drop your weapons," Alex shouted.

Surprise marched across both men's faces. The man closest to Alex held his hands up. Alex rushed forward and disarmed the man and cuffed him.

Chase advanced on the other guy holding a weapon. "Set it on the ground."

Slowly, the man complied, putting the pistol on the rug at his feet.

Chase rushed forward and kicked the gun aside. "Turn around."

For a moment the guy hesitated, then finally turned. Chase holstered his weapon and took out his cuffs, slapping them around the guy's wrists. Once he had the man secured, Chase knelt beside Lucinda, visibly searching for signs of abuse. "Are you okay? Did they hurt you?"

"I'm not hurt," she replied.

Hanging his head with overwhelming relief, Chase sent up praise to God for the blessing.

"Suspects secure," Alex said into his headset.

"Chase." The urgency in Lucinda's tone brought Chase's gaze up.

"There's another one. In the—"

A loud crash reverberated through the house.

"What in the world?" Alex exclaimed.

A black SUV broke through the garage door and shot out onto the street, tires squealing.

Through the front window, Chase watched the sheriff jump out of the way as the SUV sped onto the street, barely missing the sheriff's vehicle. Then a streak of green roared past. Nick Delaney's Humvee rammed into the getaway vehicle, sending the Escalade sliding into a telephone pole. A flash of blond hair in the back seat sent Chase's stomach plummeting. Ashley was in the Humvee.

Both automobiles came to an abrupt halt.

Fear galvanized Chase into action. "You got these two?"

"Yes," Alex replied. "Go."

Running out the front door, Chase couldn't help the litany of words streaming from his mouth. "Please, Lord, don't let her be hurt." Chase couldn't bear the thought he'd let Ashley down…again.

ELEVEN

As Nick rammed his vehicle into the escaping black SUV, the inside of the Humvee rattled from the vibration of the impact and shuddered through Ashley. The echo of metal colliding, twisting and bending as the two vehicles locked in a forceful battle rang in her ears.

Thankfully, the seat belt strap pulled tight, locking her in place in the middle of the back seat. She would probably have a bruise from the wide piece of heavy fabric, but that was such a minor thing, considering all she'd been through in the past few days. Her muscles already protested after bracing herself for the crash and made any movement painful as she shifted on the seat, trying to see out the front window.

Now that the black SUV was pushed up against a telephone pole, metal falling off it and steam rising from the engine, the rush of adrenaline ebbed but did little to ease the flutters in her tummy or slow her heart rate.

From what Ashley could discern, the Humvee had sustained minimal damage.

In the front seat Nick fought with the air bag, pushing it out of the way. Then he unclipped his seat belt and turned around to face her. "Are you okay?"

"I'm good. What about you? Did the air bag hurt you?"

He grinned, his dark eyes dancing. "Nope. You were right to have me push the front seat back as far as it would go. The air bag barely touched me when it deployed. And the seat belt kept me from flying out the window." He touched his chest. "I'll be sore, but it was worth it."

"We got him!" Jubilantly, she held up her hand for a high five and winced with the movement. Her whole body contracted and protested. She needed more pain relievers and some ice packs.

Nick slapped his hand against hers. "It was quick thinking on your part."

She dismissed his praise with a smile. When she'd seen that SUV smash through Chase's garage door and zoom past the sheriff, clearly intending to escape, all she could think about was stopping the men inside. And the only way to do that was for Nick to hit the gas and ram into the other vehicle.

Just then the door to the back passenger seat opened with a jerk and Chase ducked his head inside, his wide-eyed gaze frightened. "Ashley! Are you hurt?"

She unbuckled the seat belt and slid carefully toward him along the bench seat. "I'm fine. We're fine. But we got them."

"Him," Chase corrected. "There was only one person in the vehicle."

Through the front windshield, Ashley watched Daniel checking on the occupant of the SUV. A distant siren heralded the approaching ambulance.

Chase turned his stormy gaze to Nick. "That was reckless and stupid. You both could've been killed. What were you thinking?"

Quickly, Ashley held up a hand, keeping Nick from talking. "This was my idea. I had to do something to help. I'm tired of sitting on the sidelines, watching everybody else do the work, while I cower in the corner. If I could've driven this Humvee by myself, I would've." She cast Nick a glance. "But he wouldn't let me take over the wheel."

Nick held up his hands. "Hey, she's a force to be reckoned with. You have your hands full, buddy."

Chase's jaw firmed. "Yes, I'm getting that idea."

Heat flushed through Ashley and she was sure her cheeks were bright red. "I'm right here." She gripped Chase's forearm. "Lucinda? Is she—" Ashley's breath laid trapped in her lungs as she waited to hear his answer.

"Unharmed," he said.

A swoosh of relief overwhelmed Ashley. She sank against the backrest and released her hold on Chase. "Thank you, Jesus."

Movement over Chase's shoulder drew her attention. Alex and the sheriff led two handcuffed men toward the sheriff's vehicle. Behind them, Lucinda wheeled herself out of the house, confirming Chase's words that the older woman was safe.

Focusing on Chase, Ashley placed her hand on his chest. His gear masked his heartbeat beneath her palm, but she could see the rapid pulse thumping at the base of his neck where his collar and the vest revealed his skin. He was still hyped from the situation. "I'm sorry that you were scared. But we're fine. Everything worked out."

"This time." He covered her hand with his. "You can't do stuff like that. You have to stop trying to control everything."

His words pierced through her to the core. She did have an issue with control. How did she change that aspect of her personality?

Then he drew her out of the vehicle and into his embrace, his strong arms holding her close. Her arms went around his waist and she rested her head against his shoulder. She didn't want to ever leave the warmth of his hug. She wanted to snuggle closer, only there was all this stuff between them. Not only his tactical gear, but the specter of Maksim Sokolov and her imminent departure with the US Marshals into the WITSEC program.

"Nick Delaney!" Kaitlyn's strong voice rang out as the deputy marched toward the Humvee. "That was the most reckless, juvenile, thoughtless, inconsiderate and inconceivable thing I have ever seen anyone do! You could have been seriously injured."

Guilt for putting Nick in Kaitlyn's crosshairs blossomed in Ashley. She disengaged from Chase and hustled around to the other side of the Humvee to take responsibility, but this time it was Nick who held up a hand, staying her words.

He stood at the open door of the vehicle with a wide grin as he faced the female deputy glaring at him. "Deputy Lanz, I didn't know you cared."

Chase's chuckle drew Ashley's attention. He'd followed her around the Humvee and now stood at her elbow. He leaned close to say, "I'm sure Lucinda would like to see you."

Knowing he was right and that neither Nick or Kaitlyn needed them gawking as they verbally sparred, Ashley tucked her arm through Chase's and hurried to Lucinda's side. The older woman spread her arms wide, inviting Ashley in for an embrace.

Ashley bent forward to hug the older woman. Clung to her, really. Tears of gratitude that she was safe and sound stung Ashley's eyes. She finally released her hold on Lucinda and stared into her dark eyes. "I'm so sorry this happened. You should never have been in danger. This is all my fault."

Lucinda shook her head and waved a hand. "Not your fault, Ashley. Those men didn't know who they were dealing with." She beamed at Chase, obviously proud of the man she'd help raise. "And they are as scared of Mr. Sokolov as you are."

"Did they tell you that?" Chase asked.

Lucinda shielded her eyes against the April sun to stare up at him. "They didn't have to. Anytime his name was brought up, the two men cringed. Whatever hold he has on them, it's strong."

Chase rubbed a hand over his jaw. "I kind of figured as much." He glanced around. "I don't want to take any chances that there are more of them lurking about." He grasped the handles of Lucinda's wheelchair. "Let's get you both inside."

A shiver of apprehension traipsed down Ashley's spine as she hurried to open the front door. Once they were inside the house, the adrenaline that had pumped through Ashley's veins ebbed and tremors worked over her flesh.

Chase locked the wheels on Lucinda's wheelchair and rushed to Ashley. Rubbing her arms, he said, "You've had a shock." He led her to the couch.

Appreciating his kindness, Ashley held his hand before taking a seat.

He gave her hand a squeeze before saying, "I need to talk to the sheriff to see if I can buy us some time before we have to go to the courthouse."

"That would be helpful," she said. "I'm all sweaty and hot and I would really like to change my clothes."

"Same here." He left through the front door.

"Can I get you some water?" Lucinda asked as she unlocked her wheels.

Distressed, Ashley jumped to her feet. "I should be the one asking you if you need water or anything at all. You're the one who was just held hostage."

Without waiting for a response, Ashley rushed into the kitchen. She stopped as tears sprung to her eyes. Gripping the sink, she hung her head as the stress of the past few days washed over her. She'd never experienced such heaviness of heart. She'd put good people in jeopardy. Today could have ended so differently. Lucinda could have been seriously hurt or worse. Chase could have lost so much. But it would be over soon. They would be free of her and the danger she'd brought to this town and its citizens.

"Glasses are in the cupboard to the left of the sink on the bottom," Lucinda said from the threshold to the kitchen.

Ashley jerked upright and nodded with a forced smile. She grabbed two short water glasses and filled them with water from the refrigerator filter system. She handed one to Lucinda. Her hands shook, and she sloshed water onto Lucinda's slacks.

Grimacing, Ashley set her glass down and grabbed a towel to wipe up the mess. "I'm so sorry."

Lucinda waved her away. "It's only water. It'll dry." She wheeled herself over the threshold of the kitchen and moved farther into the living room. "Come on, let's take our glasses and get you back to the couch. You're going to collapse if we don't."

The thought of collapsing actually sounded good to Ashley. Unsteady on her feet, she followed Lucinda back to the living room and sat down. Placing her glass on the coffee table, Lucinda wheeled closer and took Ashley's free hand. "Honey, what are you going to do about Chase?"

Ashley tucked in her chin, her eyes widening at the question. "Do about Chase?"

Belatedly, Ashley remembered the first time she'd been here and Chase had commented about Lucinda playing matchmaker. Ashley couldn't let this woman hope for something that could never happen. "There's nothing between Chase and me."

Lucinda patted her hand. "I don't believe that for a second and neither do you. I've known that boy his whole life. He was upset that I was in danger, but it was nothing compared to the anguish I saw on his face when he thought you might be hurt. My boy loves you. He may be too stubborn to realize it yet, though, so you're going to have to point it out to him."

Ashley's heart jumped into her throat. She set her glass down and retracted her hand from Lucinda. "No, no, no." Standing, Ashley paced back and forth in front of the couch, agitation running rampant through her body. "That can't be true."

"What do you feel for him, Ashley?"

Lucinda's softly asked question stopped Ashley in her tracks. If she was going to be honest with Lucinda, and with herself, she would admit that she had deep feelings for Chase. Feelings that she had no business having for him. Feelings that she had locked away and couldn't let out of the little cage she'd locked them in. Because if she admitted how much she cared for— maybe even loved—Chase, leaving him would only be that much more painful.

She faced Lucinda. "As soon as I give my deposition, I will be leaving with the US Marshals Service. I will never see Chase, or any of you, again."

Lucinda made a face and waved her hand, a gesture that was so innate to the older woman, Ashley fought a smile. "We can get around all that. What I want to know, Ashley, is are you willing to take the risk on Chase?"

Risk? The word reverberated through Ashley's brain. "I can't risk that something will happen to Chase, or you, again. My being here, in your lives, puts everyone at risk."

Lucinda's expression softened and her voice gentled. "Honey, there are no guarantees in life. God never said life would be fair, only that He would be with us in every circumstance."

Those words echoed inside of Ashley. Words she'd heard before and words she clung to now. "Though I agree with you that there are no guarantees, there are some things I can control. My leaving is one of those. I will not, in any way, shape or form, destroy Chase's life by staying here."

"He could go with you, you know." Lucinda's steady gaze pinned her to the floor. "That happens with witnesses. My husband was a police officer. I know how the witness protection program works. Family members can go with the witness."

Ashley's heart twisted in her chest. "Please, understand. He's not my family. He's yours."

All this talk of family and love was giving her palpitations. Her heart acted like the injured bird she'd once rescued and transported in a cardboard box to the bird sanctuary. Tap, tap, tap. Scratch, scratch, scratch. If her ribs weren't already sore from the seat belt, she'd guess they'd have been sore from the pain within her chest.

The door opened and Kaitlyn walked in. She leveled Ashley with a stern scowl. "Chase tells me it was your idea to ram the Humvee into the SUV."

"And what a good idea it was," Lucinda said.

Though Ashley was grateful to the older woman for her support, she faced Kaitlyn's displeasure head on. "Yes, it was my idea. I had to do something"

Kaitlyn harrumphed. "Well, he didn't have to go along with it. He was in the driver's seat."

Ashley grimaced. "To be fair, I told him if he didn't do it, I would push him out and drive the Humvee myself."

Kaitlyn's gaze narrowed. "And you would've too, right?"

Squaring her shoulders, Ashley said, "Yes. I've

learned a lot from you and Chase and Leslie. I'm not going to be some idle victim anymore. I want to take control of my life. The first thing I need to do is tell my story to the DA and then—" Ashley's voice faltered as her determination tripped over itself. Taking a deep breath, she continued, "Then I'm going into witness protection. I am going to blossom. Because if I don't, then Mr. Sokolov has won even if he hasn't eliminated me as he'd like to."

The respect and admiration in Kaitlyn's eyes warmed Ashley's heart. "Good for you. I still think it was foolhardy to risk your life, and Nick's life, but I understand."

Ashley was certain Kaitlyn did. Because Ashley was pretty sure Kaitlyn would've made the same choice.

Chase stepped inside, his gaze meeting Ashley's. "You're right, Ashley, you do need to blossom."

Apparently he'd overheard her speech. Embarrassment heated her cheeks, but she refrained from putting her hands to her face or dropping her gaze. She meant what she'd said.

"And I will do everything in my power to make sure you can," he continued.

Ashley frowned, not sure what he meant and too afraid to ask. Then she mentally scoffed. She'd just told everybody she was going to take control of her life and stop being a victim. And yet she was too afraid to ask a simple question for clarification from Chase.

But with everybody staring at her, them—Lucinda's gaze was hopeful while Kaitlyn's was intrigued—Ashley decided the better course of action was to remain silent.

There was something in Chase's gaze that she

couldn't decipher, something between respect and affection and fear. She wished they were alone so she could explore what was going on, what he was thinking. But then again, did she really want to open herself up to that kind of heartache?

"So, what's the plan now?" Ashley asked, needing to change the subject and direct the conversation toward actions rather than emotions.

"Kaitlyn's going to take you to Leslie's, while the sheriff and Alex process these guys. Daniel went with the injured man to the hospital and will make sure he doesn't escape."

"And you?" Ashley asked.

"I'm going to get Lucinda somewhere safe," he said. "Then I'll join you at Leslie's."

That was good news to Ashley. She didn't like leaving knowing Lucinda could still be in danger. Ashley went to Lucinda and kissed her cheek and whispered in her ear, "I'm sorry. I'm just not brave enough."

Ashley walked out, following Kaitlyn to her car. The second she settled on the passenger seat, she tilted her head back and closed her eyes. Silently she prayed, *Lord, give me strength.* Why did life have to be so hard?

Once the door closed behind Ashley and Kaitlyn, Chase stood there for a moment, his head bowed as he murmured a quick prayer, "Lord, please watch over Ashley."

He had to trust that Kaitlyn and Leslie would take care of Ashley until he could get there. But his next order of business was to ensure Lucinda's safety. He turned to his former nanny. "You need to pack a bag.

I'm taking you out to the Johnsons' house. They've agreed to have you stay with them until this whole mess is over."

"That's awfully nice," she said. "I like them." She started to wheel away and then spun back toward him. "So, Ashley?"

Confused by her question because he'd already explained that she was going to Leslie's and then to the courthouse, he said, "I'm going to make sure she gets to the courthouse safely so she can give her deposition. Then I will wait with her until the US Marshals take her into protective custody." And he was going to make sure the marshals understood that if anything happened to her under their watch, they would have to answer to him, and all of Bristle Township.

"That's not what I meant." The intensity in her eyes made him twitchy. "I meant, what are you going to do about how you much you care about her?"

The question tied his stomach up in knots. He undid the straps on his flak vest. He had no idea what he was going to do about the emotions crowding his chest, emotions that all centered on one platinum blonde with big beautiful eyes. "I don't know what you're talking about."

"Seriously, you're going with that answer?" Lucinda wheeled herself to his side and leveled her arthritic index finger at him. "Chase Fredrick, I have known you your whole life. You have strong feelings for that young lady. And she has strong feelings for you."

Her pronouncement stilled his hands. He glanced at Lucinda and, noting the determined expression in her eyes, his stomach slid toward his toes. "Don't go getting any hopeful ideas about me settling down. I've already explained this to you. I like my life the way it is."

That the future stretched out in a lonely abyss before him was something he didn't want to address. "Ashley's leaving, so whatever emotion she, or I, feel toward one another stems from the circumstances. There's nothing lasting between us. I need to stay rational and keep my feelings out of this situation."

"You can't tell me that work is going to be the one and only thing in your life."

How many times had he heard this lecture? She sounded like a broken record. Only for some reason, her words stung now, where in the past he could laugh them off. He shrugged off his flak vest and set it on the couch before taking a seat to undo the laces on his boots. "Please, go pack your bag."

She hesitated for a moment and he thought she would continue her interrogation. But instead she whirled away and rolled down the hall to her bedroom.

Letting out a beleaguered sigh, Chase ran a hand over his stubbled jaw. He did have deep emotions for Ashley. Some of which he was afraid to label, but they were so muddled with fear and responsibility and protection, he didn't know which end of his emotions was up and which was down. But he'd told Lucinda the truth. He liked his life and he didn't want to make any changes. Or at least, that's what he told himself. And he used to believe it, 100 percent. But now…he couldn't deny the ache filling him, making him long to find a way to make a future with Ashley.

You could go with her.

The unbidden thought marched into his consciousness. That idea grabbed hold of his imagination and wouldn't let go. What would it be like to start over, a fresh and new life with Ashley by his side?

But he couldn't leave Lucinda behind. And he couldn't ask her to go. Plus, he would miss the community of Bristle Township, his coworkers, his friends and his church. He'd made a life for himself here. One apart from his parents, where no one wanted to use him as a way to gain access to the vaunted Fredricks.

Was he willing to give up his carefully constructed life for Ashley?

The answer should have come easily, but he was so conflicted. A state of being he didn't usually find himself in.

Frustrated, he marched into the bathroom and quickly showered and shaved, then changed into a fresh uniform. When he returned to the living room, Lucinda was waiting.

"Okay, this is the last thing I'm going to say on the subject," she said over her shoulder as she wheeled toward the front door. At the portal, she faced him, her earnest expression tearing his conscience. "Your job is not enough. You're going to grow old alone. You need Ashley and she needs you. Do what you have to do to be with her." With that, she opened the door and wheeled out, leaving Chase staring after her.

Shaking his head in a mix of exasperation and admiration, he hurried out and helped her into his truck, which thankfully the town's tow truck operator had dropped off while Chase was in the shower.

He started up the engine, but before throwing the

gear into Reverse, he turned to Lucinda. "And this is going to be my last word on the subject. I love you and I need you to stay out of my business."

TWELVE

Ashley took a refreshing shower and then donned a change of clothes—black pants and a red cardigan over a white blouse. She'd stuffed all of her belongings into her duffel bag and took a moment to pray, thanking God for His provision and asking for His continued blessing and protection.

Once she'd done a second sweep of Leslie's bedroom to make sure she hadn't left anything behind, Ashley walked out to the living room to find Kaitlyn and Leslie deep in a hushed conversation. The two women stopped talking as soon as they noticed her.

For a moment, Ashley questioned if they'd been talking about her. She smoothed a hand over her hair, noting that it had grown and needed another trim. Or maybe she'd let it grow out. And she'd definitely change the color. She was so done with the platinum.

Shaking off the self-conscious doubt, she reminded herself she was leaving and after today these kind and thoughtful women would be out of her life.

Every cell in Ashley's body ached with sorrow and regret, knowing she was going to be walking out the door of Leslie's little cottage for the last time. She set her bags down and then impulsively hugged Leslie and Kaitlyn. They hugged her back. She struggled not to cry.

"I'm going to miss you both." Ashley's voice shook with suppressed tears. "I know we won't be able to stay in touch, but I will be praying for you both."

Leslie took Ashley's hand. "I wish there was something we could do. We are going to miss you, too"

Kaitlyn squared her shoulders and blinked rapidly. "You're going to do fine. You are strong and you're a survivor."

Though Kaitlyn had said those words before, Ashley still struggled to believe them. But she smiled at the female deputy, knowing Kaitlyn was determined not to show any weakness. "Thank you, Kaitlyn. You and Chase have taught me a lot about who I am and who I want to be."

"Chase is the one I'm going to be worried about when you leave," Leslie said. "He has it bad for you."

Frustration welled within Ashley. She didn't need to hear this again. Lucinda had said the same and more. But there was nothing Ashley could do about how Chase felt about her, or how she felt about him. The situation was what it was. She was leaving. She couldn't dwell on what would never be. She only could look forward, knowing that she had to be as strong as Kaitlyn believed her to be in order to survive.

Picking up her bag, Ashley briskly said, "It's time we leave for the courthouse. I'm sure that the Los Angeles district attorney is getting antsy. I just want to get this all over with."

Kaitlyn moved to the window and looked out. "We have a few more minutes to wait."

"What do you mean?" Ashley asked.

Kaitlyn turned from the window. There was a mix of mischief and sadness in her eyes. "Chase wants to take you to the courthouse. I'm going to follow to make sure you make it there safely."

Ashley's stomach knotted. Though she would be seeing Chase again at the courthouse, she hadn't expected to be in close quarters with him. How was she going to make the trek from Leslie's ranch to town with Chase and keep from saying something she might regret?

Something like, I love you and I can't live without you. The thought rocked her back a step. Did she love Chase? As in forever and ever. The answer danced at the edge of her mind and she quickly tamped down the tender emotion. Love had no place in her life. She had to do the right thing. Leave with no strings tied to Chase or anyone else.

Her throat grew tight. She forced out what she wanted to say. "Can't you just take me?"

Kaitlyn's smile was gentle. "You need this time with Chase. He needs this time with you. I'm not going to ruin it for him, or for you."

The sound of tires on the gravel drive announced Chase's arrival.

"Here he is," Kaitlyn said as she opened the door.

Ashley hesitated, bracing herself and shoring up her defenses. No matter what her emotions were, no matter how hard it would be to say goodbye to Chase, she had to. She had to keep her emotions in check.

Leslie put her hand on her shoulder. "Be of good

cheer. For the Lord is with you and He will guide you wherever you go."

Ashley pressed her lips together for a moment to keep a chuckle at bay. "I think you're blending a couple of Bible verses."

Leslie grinned. "I'm sure I am. Memorizing Scripture was never my strong suit. But it sounds good and I do believe it."

Ashley quickly hugged Leslie with her free arm. "Thank you again."

Lifting her chin and straightening her spine, Ashley walked out of the cottage. Chase climbed out from the cab of his truck. He looked so good in a fresh uniform, his sandy blond hair still slightly damp and his jaw clean-shaven. She swallowed the lump in her throat along with the urge to run into his arms. On stiff legs, she walked forward as he jogged to the passenger side and opened the door for her. He took her bag from her hands, their fingers brushing briefly. Little zips of sensation tingled up her arm and settled near her heart.

She climbed into the truck and buckled the seat belt with shaky hands. If only things were different…she slammed the door on any thoughts that would lead her down the road to heartache. Folding her hands in her lap, she stared straight ahead.

Chase conversed with Kaitlyn before he climbed back inside the truck and drove away from the Quinn ranch. Once they were on the road headed back toward town, she glanced in the side-view mirror to see that Kaitlyn was, indeed, following close behind them.

The silence was thick in the cab of the truck. Ashley searched for something to say, for some inane topic to discuss to relieve the choking sensation of the air being sucked out of her lungs. But she came up empty.

So she settled for embracing the tension. She should have been used to this by now. Her whole life had been about dealing with one crisis and the next. Living with her mother had taught her how to cope, and going on the run had driven the lesson home.

Now, she was going to be joining the ranks of the many unnamed witnesses who disappeared from their everyday lives, reborn with a new name.

As they neared the courthouse, Chase eased up on the gas. "This isn't a good sign."

On the courthouse steps, a group had gathered. A TV news van from Denver was parked at the curb. Ashley spotted Lucca Chin with his notepad and pen. Her stomach sank. The last thing she needed was her face plastered all over the media.

Chase took a sharp turn down an alley and pulled around to the back of the courthouse to park. She could always count on him to know what to do.

He popped open his door, but Ashley put a hand on his arm. "Chase."

"Ashley?" He pulled the door closed and turned to face her, his eyes troubled. The longing in his tone had her heart pounding in her chest.

She tried to fill her gaze with all the love and affection she harbored for this man, because she could never say the words.

With her right hand, she unbuckled her seat belt while she fisted her left hand in his shirt. This was their one and only opportunity before she disappeared again. She leaned forward, hoping, praying he would close the distance because she needed this kiss. Something she'd been longing for from the moment she'd first laid eyes on Chase Fredrick.

Just one kiss to keep in her memories for the rest of her lonely life.

Chase's breath caught in his throat. There was no mistaking the invitation Ashley was extending. His rational brain said, *No, don't do it.* Giving in to the yearning to press his lips to this woman's would end up hurting them both.

But at the moment he didn't want to be rational, he didn't want to do the right thing by denying her something they both apparently wanted.

He wanted to kiss this woman more than he wanted to draw his next breath.

Closing the distance between them, he sealed his mouth over hers. Her lips were soft and pliable. He cupped the back of her head and deepened the kiss. Her right hand gripped his biceps while her left hand relaxed and splayed open across his chest. The heat of her palm burned through to his heart. No doubt she could feel the thunder of his heartbeat. He was surprised she couldn't hear the roar of his pulse. He certainly did.

When the kiss gentled and slowly ended, they drew apart and he dropped his forehead to hers. They were both breathing hard, their breaths mingled, fogging the windows despite the warmth of the spring sun outside. He searched for something to say that wouldn't shatter the moment, that wouldn't destroy the connection binding him to her. He remained silent, just breathing in her scent of vanilla and lavender and woman. He never wanted to leave the truck. How was he going to say goodbye?

Finally, she drew back. Her eyes misted. "Thank you."

He chuckled, his ego puffing up. "For the kiss?"

She gave him a soft, sweet smile that wrapped around his heart like a big red bow. "For the kiss. For everything. I wouldn't be alive if it weren't for you. I just want you to know how very grateful I am and how very much I will miss you."

His heart ached at the bittersweet melancholy that filled him. He reached for her, hoping to ease the pain in his chest. "I'm going to miss you, too."

She scooted back, out of his reach, pressing against the door. Her hand groped for the door release. "We need to go."

He hated hearing the sound of choking despair in her voice. This was hard for her. This was hard for him.

But she was right; they had to leave the confines of the truck and face what waited inside the courthouse. He gathered his rational side and wrapped it around him like an invisible cloak of sanity. He gave a sharp nod and opened his door. "Sit tight."

He climbed out, jogged around to her side and opened the door, his gaze searching the area to make sure there was no one in the vicinity who posed a threat.

He grabbed her bag and placed his hand at the small of her back, then guided her through the back entrance of the courthouse, past the restrooms and the court records room. They hurried to the main lobby. He could hear the clamoring outside the main doors. The media wanted in. A security guard Chase didn't recognize manned the door, keeping the news reporters from entering the building.

Taking a breath, Chase gestured toward Donald Grayson, the lawyer who sat on a bench down the main hallway. "We should talk to your lawyer."

As Chase led Ashley forward, he couldn't ignore the niggling at the base of his neck.

Donald rose from the bench outside the courtroom and stalked toward them, looking very citylike in his double-breasted gray suit and red power tie.

"It's about time you got here," Grayson said. "The district attorney and his assistant are getting nervous."

"We're here now," Chase said.

Grayson's mouth firmed. "I can see that. I would like a moment with my client alone, if you don't mind, Deputy Fredrick."

Knowing he had no choice, Chase nodded and stepped a few feet away. Far enough to give them privacy, yet close enough that he could reach Ashley within seconds if needed. For as long as he could, he would protect her despite his heart bleeding and breaking with the knowledge that he was going to have to let her go.

"Hi, Deputy." Mrs. Hawkins, the town librarian, walked past. She was a stout woman with auburn hair wrapped into a twist on the top of her head.

"Ma'am," he said. "What brings you to the courthouse today?"

She handed him a flyer. "We're starting a book club and I dropped some flyers off in the records office."

He glanced at the paper in his hands and thought about Ashley's love of books. This was something she'd enjoy. Sadness thrummed in his veins.

"You might want to go out the back door," Chase told her. "There's a lot of people out the front door."

"I saw that." She peered at him with curiosity evident in her gaze through her red-framed glasses. "What's all the ruckus?"

Not about to explain Ashley's predicament, Chase said, "Do you know the new security guard?"

Mrs. Hawkins glanced to the front door. "He must be Jarvis's replacement. I know he was going to retire."

That made sense. Just because he didn't know the new hire didn't mean there was cause to panic.

Every month people moved to the small mountain haven of Bristle Township in search of a simpler life. A simpler life had been very alluring along with a job with the Sheriff's Department. He'd thought that he'd grow old here in Bristle Township, serving its citizens and keeping the town safe. But now he wasn't sure that staying was what he really wanted.

You could go with her.

But did she want him to?

Ashley could feel Chase's gaze on her. It took all her effort not to turn toward him and see his expression, to discern what he was thinking and feeling about her. About the kiss.

Her lips still tingled. She'd known that kissing him would leave an indelible mark on her, not a visible sign but an inner stamp that would forever remind her of him. But more than that was the knowledge that no matter where she went or what she did in this life, there would always be a part of her missing. A part of her staying here in Bristle Township with Chase.

"Miss Willis."

Ashley blinked, realizing that Mr. Grayson was talking to her and she hadn't heard a word. The grim set to the lawyer's mouth had her stomach knotting and her muscles bunching with tension. "Is something wrong?"

"I don't like this situation at all," he said. "I find it hard to believe that the district attorney's office of Los Angeles had a burglary. Sounds fishy to me."

She shrugged, knowing the truth did stink. "Maksim Sokolov has people everywhere."

"I do believe you're right," Mr. Grayson said. "From all accounts this man has managed to stay out of the law's reach for a long time. Hopefully, now his reign of terror and corruption will end soon. Mr. Nyburg seems determined to bring the man to justice."

She was glad to hear of his determination. It would take a strong and stalwart personality to go up against a man as powerful as Maksim Sokolov. She hoped the district attorney watched his back.

"Let's get to the business at hand. Remember the drill from the last time?"

As if she could forget. The last deposition had left her drained. She could only imagine how much worse it would be in person. "Yes, I do. Only answer the question that is asked of me with as little verbiage as possible."

"Correct." He drew her to the bench seat. He opened his briefcase on his lap and handed her a stack of papers. "This is the transcript from the last time. I want you to read it over so your answers match. You won't have that inside the court, but at least this will refresh your memory just in case."

She didn't think her memory needed to be refreshed. She could remember every last detail of the video deposition, but she did as Mr. Grayson asked and read through the transcript. "Is there a reason the transcript can't be used in place of an in-person deposition?"

Grayson made a face. "The defense attorney protested using the transcript or the sheriff's copy of your deposition, saying there was no way to verify that the documents hadn't been doctored."

Ashley swallowed back a nervous lump. "Is the defense attorney here?" She remembered the coldness in his eyes and the way he'd grilled her, making her feel small and unworthy.

Mr. Grayson splayed his hands across the top of his briefcase. "He is here. But you have nothing to worry about. Don't let him intimidate you. If he gets out of line, I will stop him."

She had no doubt that Mr. Grayson would have her back. Just like Chase. She glanced over to where he stood with his back against the wall and his gaze on her. She gave him a soft smile, which he returned. Her insides strained with regret and longing.

The doors to the courtroom opened and four people walked out and headed in their direction. Ashley recognized the district attorney and his assistant. The other two men were strangers. Mr. Grayson stood, urging Ashley to do the same by cupping her elbow.

"Miss Willis?" the bigger of the men asked.

Ashley nodded. Her tongue remained glued to the roof of her mouth beneath the man's scrutiny. She was aware that Chase had stepped to her side. She could only imagine that, from an observer's point of view, the three of them were facing off with the four strangers. For some reason the music from *West Side Story* played through her mind.

"US Marshal Dirk Grant," the big man spoke. He had wide shoulders beneath his navy blue suit. He flashed a badge, then gestured to the other man, similarly dressed. "This is my partner, US Marshal Keenan Hawks. We will be taking you into our custody now."

District Attorney Nyburg stepped forward. "Not before she's disposed." He looked at Ashley, his gaze concerned. "You are ready, correct?"

Taking a fortifying breath, Ashley nodded. "Yes, sir, I'm ready."

"Good. We need your testimony to convict Sokolov of murder and put him away for life. Let's get this show on the road." Mr. Nyburg turned and hurried back inside the courtroom. His assistant hesitated, and then quickly followed her boss, her heels clicking on the linoleum floor.

"This way." Marshal Grant indicated for Ashley to step between him and Marshal Hawks. "We will escort you into the courtroom."

Every cell in Ashley's being rebelled. She didn't want to go inside the courtroom. She didn't want to become their responsibility. She didn't want to leave Chase. But she had to. She handed Mr. Grayson back his papers. She glanced up at Chase, wanting to say something but afraid that only a squeak would come out because her throat was closing with despair and anguish. His jaw was tight, his eyes turbulent. She gave him a nod and stepped between the two marshals.

"Wait." Chase stopped them.

Ashley turned to him, her heart pounding in her ears. She wanted to run into his arms and ask him to whisk her away. She stayed in place.

"I need a moment with Miss Willis," Chase said, his voice strained.

Marshal Grant sighed. "Deputy, she's in our custody now."

"This is personal," Chase said. "I need to talk to Ashley."

Desperate to have one last moment alone with him, Ashley looked at Marshall Grant. "Please," she managed to say, her voice barely making it past the constriction in her throat.

The two marshals exchanged a glance. Marshal Grant nodded.

"Two minutes," Marshal Hawkes said.

Ashley hurried to Chase. He wrapped an arm around her shoulders and led her out of earshot of the men watching them. She stared at him, memorizing every line and angle of his face.

Keeping their backs to the men, he met her gaze. "I will go with you."

His words caused confusion to tear through her veins. She couldn't have heard him right. "With me?"

He had to mean he would go into the courtroom with her. Right?

"Yes." He nodded as if affirming his decision. "I will go with you into witness protection."

Her heart fluttered in her chest. The world tilted on its axis. What was he saying? "Why would you do that? Your life is here. Lucinda is here."

A muscle ticked in his jaw. "I can't stand the thought of you being alone and unprotected."

She wanted to weep. It wasn't a declaration of love but she understood that he wasn't making this offer lightly. Lucinda's words replayed in her head, telling her that he loved her. And as much as she wanted to grab hold with both hands and say, *Yes, come with me*, she would not let him sacrifice his life for her. As much as it wounded her, she accepted what she had to do. "Chase, you and I are never going to work. This is just a momentary blip in the grand scheme of things."

He frowned. "Ashley, I—"

"No." She cut him off, knowing that if he said the words, she would not have the strength to deny him. And deny him she must. "I'm sorry. I can't risk my heart to anyone. Life is too precarious and I'm not willing to be hurt or to hurt anyone else. And that includes you." Then she sealed her own coffin by uttering the words, "I can't love you."

An agonizing cry of grief built inside her chest. Tears burned the backs of her eyes. If she didn't walk away now, she was going to embarrass them both by breaking down into a sobbing, quivering mess. She turned and ran for the restroom she'd seen on the way in.

"Miss Willis!" Marshal Grant's shout followed her.

Once inside she slumped against the wall and let the tears flow.

THIRTEEN

Chase watched Ashley dip into the women's restroom at the far end of the corridor. The two marshals hurried after her, stopping outside the door, their expressions frustrated as they banged on the door.

I can't love you. The words echoed through Chase's brain, knocking against his skull until he thought they might break free. His feet were rooted to the floor. He wasn't sure what to think. He'd thought she'd be happy for him to go with her. But evidently, he'd misread her feelings for him.

"What did you say to her?" Donald Grayson asked.

Rubbing his jaw, which was as sore as if he'd been punched, Chase said, "Obviously something she didn't want to hear."

The courtroom doors banged open again. The district attorney's assistant walked out. She hitched her purse higher on her shoulder as she came over to them. "Excuse me? Where is our witness?"

Chase gestured down the corridor. "Restroom. She'll be out soon."

The woman's gaze narrowed, then she walked past

them. She spoke briefly to the marshals. The two men didn't look happy, but they walked back to where Chase stood.

"Deputy, it would be better if you left the witness to our care," Marshal Grant stated.

Chase nodded but didn't move. He couldn't leave, not like this. He had to make sure Ashley was okay. He hadn't meant to upset her. He only wanted to make her happy and keep her safe.

Ashley had ignored the banging on the restroom door and Marshal Grant's demand that she come out at once and was glad when the noise finally ceased. She wasn't ready to face them. She wasn't ready to face anyone yet. She needed this moment to grieve, to let go of the foolish notion that she could somehow live a normal life, fall in love—who was she kidding, she did love Chase— and become part of the Bristle Township community.

There were voices outside the door, one of them definitely female. A moment later, the door to the restroom opened and the Los Angeles district attorney's assistant, Sarah Miller, walked in, looking cool in her gray pencil skirt, white blouse and high heels. The brunette's green eyes assessed Ashley.

Self-consciously, Ashley pushed herself away from the wall and pulled herself together as best she could. She splashed water on her face, washing away the tears. However, nothing could wash away the anguish burrowing into her heart.

Sarah leaned against the counter, holding onto her purse strap. "I know this can be hard. You don't have to do this if you don't want to. You can back out."

Ashley doubted Mr. Nyburg would appreciate his assistant saying Ashley had a choice in testifying. "I want to tell my story. It's my duty. I have to do the right thing."

Sarah grimaced. She reached in her purse and pulled out her cell phone, quickly sending off a text. "I was afraid you were going to say that."

"What is that supposed to mean?" Ashley asked. She dried her hands with a paper towel and tossed it into the trash bin.

"We all have to do what we have to do," Sarah said. "Sometimes to protect ourselves, sometimes to protect those we love."

Ashley didn't understand the woman's cryptic remark. And she didn't have time for riddles. Straightening her shoulders, she headed for the door. "I'm ready to get my deposition over with."

Sarah pushed away from the counter and blocked her path. "Not just yet."

Ashley frowned, not liking the anxiety roaring to life within her gut. "What do you mean, not just yet?"

The shrill sound of the fire alarm going off jolted through Ashley. And then the ding of an incoming text punctuated the noise.

Sarah looked at the text message and then shoved her phone back in her purse. When she withdrew her hand, she held a small black gun and aimed the barrel at Ashley.

Stunned, Ashley stepped back, aware there was nowhere to run. "What are you doing?"

The woman's hard expression didn't bode well. "I'm sorry, Miss Willis. But you're going to come with me."

Was the woman working for Sokolov? Fear slid over Ashley's skin like sandpaper. "The marshals are right outside the door." As was Chase and the courthouse security guard. What did this woman think she was going to do?

"Don't worry about them," Sarah said.

She gestured with the gun for Ashley to precede her to the door. As soon as she was behind Ashley, Sarah crammed the business end of her weapon into Ashley's ribs. Fear exploded inside Ashley. Her mind scrambled through the self-defense tactics that Chase had taught her. Kicks and jabs came to mind, but would she be quick enough or would Sarah pull the trigger before Ashley could get away?

Sarah said, "Open the door slowly."

Deciding to comply for now, Ashley was met with a face full of billowing smoke. Her eyes instantly watered and her nose stung as she coughed in a lungful of acrid smoke. Where were the marshals? She could hear voices shouting but couldn't see anything in the thick gray smoke.

Sarah coughed behind her but managed to say, "Make noise and I pull the trigger. Turn to your left."

Left was in the direction of the door out of the building. But Ashley needed to go right to find Chase. The gun pressed harder into her rib cage.

"Do it. No screaming," Sarah demanded. "I'll shoot you where you stand if you so much as make a peep."

Ashley clamped her lips together and closed her eyes. She sent up a silent plea to God for help.

Letting Sarah get closer, Ashley spun while at the same time jabbing her elbow into Sarah, knocking the hand holding the gun away. Free, Ashley turned to escape but tripped over a body lying on the ground in front of the door. She went down hard on her hands and knees.

Hands grabbed her, lifting her off the floor and securing her in a strong grip. For a moment hope flared that Chase had found her in the smoke, but an arm slid around her throat, putting pressure on her trachea and disabusing her of the notion that her helper was friendly. She kicked and clawed at her captor.

She let out a scream that was cut off as something touched her side and sent an electric shock through her system. Her whole body stiffened as pain ricocheted through her muscles. The shock was only an instant but enough to make her body go limp with relief when it ended.

Her feet no longer touched the ground as the man holding her lifted her and tightened his arm around her neck, cutting off her air supply. She scratched at the arm, trying desperately to turn her head and wedge her chin into the crook of his elbow the way Kaitlyn had instructed but she was so weak from the electrical shock.

"Cooperate or I'll zap you again," a deep male voice said into her ear.

She stilled, her mind rebelling at suffering another jolt of electricity.

He released the pressure on her neck.

Her attacker set her feet on the floor and pushed her forward. "Move it."

Using the hem of her shirt as a filter against the thick gray smoke, Ashley couldn't see anything so she put her free hand out in front of her. She bumped up against the wall.

"Find the door," Sarah gasped from behind her between coughs.

Holding her breath, Ashley groped around. She found the hinge of the door. She finally had to breathe in. Her lungs hurt and she doubled forward to cough.

Her attacker shoved her hard into the door and the bar released upon impact. Ashley stumbled out into the fresh air with the man, who wore a face mask and was dressed as the courthouse security guard, and Sarah following her. The door slammed shut behind them.

Ashley breathed in deep, trying to clear the smoke from her lungs. She wiped at her watery eyes. They were at the back of the building. The fire alarm continued its cry and mingled with the sound of the fire engines arriving at the scene.

A big black car rolled up in front of them and the door opened. "Get in!" shouted a gruff voice.

A voice Ashley knew from her nightmares. She shrank back, looking for a way to escape.

"Go." The security guard shoved Ashley forward so that she had no choice but to climb into the back of the limousine. She settled on the seat and stared at the man who wanted to kill her. Sarah climbed in behind her, while the security guard joined the driver in the front seat.

Maksim Sokolov looked at her like she was gum stuck on the bottom of his shoe. "So you're what all this fuss is about."

He knocked on the window separating the back compartment from the driver, apparently giving the signal to go. The Lincoln Town Car drove away from the courthouse, dodging pedestrians and emergency equipment. Ashley twisted in her seat in time to see Chase and the marshals burst through the back entrance door. Chase ran after them but the speeding limo was too fast. Within moments, they were leaving downtown Bristle Township.

"I love you," Ashley whispered, convinced she would never see Chase again.

The moment the fire alarms sounded, Chase had known something was wrong. The billowing smoke was thick and hard to navigate. People poured out of the courtrooms and the court's records room. He'd raced to the restroom, urging people to move out of the way, only to find it empty and the marshals unconscious on the ground.

After making sure they were both alive, Chase ran for the back exit in time to see a black town car speeding away with Ashley in the back seat. Frantic, with fear freezing in his veins, he ran after the car but was no match for the moving vehicle.

Still running, he doubled back and jumped into his truck. As he started the engine, Marshal Grant jumped into the passenger seat. "I'm coming with you." He had a nasty knot forming on his head that no doubt hurt. "Hawks will follow in our vehicle."

"Shouldn't you be checked out by a paramedic?" Chase asked the question as he threw the gear into Drive. Before the man could buckle up, Chase stepped on the gas and drove in the direction the town car had taken.

"I'm fine," Grant said, bracing himself on the dash-board.

"Call for backup," Chase told the marshal. "Ashley's been taken. We have to stop them before they kill her."

The terrorizing thought robbed him of breath. He fought to maintain his cool and not give in to the rising panic.

At the intersection where he had the choice to turn right toward Denver or left toward the backside of Eagle Crest Mountain, Chase faltered and prayed for inspiration.

He thought about the private airstrip at the top of the mountain attached to the Eagle Crest Resort and the car service the resort provided for its guests. Chase was sure he recognized that limo as one used by the resort. He had to take a chance. He turned left, heading toward the mountain pass.

Beside him, Grant was talking to the sheriff.

"Put that on speaker, would you?" Chase said.

Grant complied. "Sheriff, I have you on speaker now with Deputy Fredrick."

"Sir," Chase said, "we're going up the mountain to the airstrip at the top."

"Playing a hunch?"

"Yes, sir." Chase tightened his grip on the steering wheel as he took the corners on the winding mountain road at top speed. "A man like Sokolov wouldn't go commercial."

"Agreed."

Stomach churning with anxiety, Chase said, "But in case I'm wrong, alert the state patrol to watch for a black limousine with the license number 359 XTL."

"Roger that." The sheriff's deep timbre filled the cab of the truck. "Marshal Hawks and Daniel are headed your way."

Marshall Grant clicked off and frowned at Chase. "I hope you're right about this. If we lose Miss Willis, it's your fault."

Chase didn't need that reminder. Guilt threaded through his system like the laces of his boots. He should've waited until after the deposition to talk to Ashley about joining her in WITSEC. Or better yet, he shouldn't have said anything at all.

Now that he grasped she didn't share the same emotions about him, he regretted letting down his defenses and opening himself up for rejection. Though he couldn't find it within himself to harbor any ill will for the woman who had captured his heart. His love was unconditional. And he would do everything in his power to ensure that the woman he loved lived to see that Maksim Sokolov rotted in prison.

Ashley noticed the terrain outside the speeding car's window. They were driving the same road that the fake Detective Peters had taken the day he'd forced her into his SUV. They were headed up the backside of the mountain. What was Mr. Sokolov's intention? To throw her off the cliff?

Her insides clenched with dread. She would fight to the end. She would not be easily disposed of. She hadn't come through this nightmare only to have it end like this.

But they passed the turnout spot where Chase had shot the fake detective and he'd been the one to go over the cliff. Was there another turnout they were heading for?

The car kept a steady pace, rounding the curves that hugged the mountain with a squeal of tires. The seat belt bit into Ashley's chest, poking at her already tender spots. Maksim Sokolov sat on the bench seat facing Ashley, his gaze never wavering.

He was older than she remembered, his skin weathered and wrinkled. Up close like this, Ashley could tell the man had scars on his hands and one running down the length of his neck that disappeared beneath the collar of his black suit. She shivered with fear as she met his dark reptilian gaze.

Shifting her attention to the woman sitting beside her, Ashley asked, "Why are you a part of this ugliness?"

Sarah stared at her for a moment as if startled by the question. Her green eyes were anxious as the gun in her hand quivered. Her mouth moved but no words came out.

Maksim Sokolov sat forward to snatch the gun from Sarah's hand. "We don't want this to accidentally go off. That would be a mess to clean up."

He set the gun on the seat beside him.

Ashley focused on the weapon, her mind working out how to get her hands on it. Though she'd never fired a gun before, she figured simply pointing the weapon and squeezing the trigger would get the job done.

Maksim shook his finger at her. "Don't even think about it, young lady. I may be old, but I'm faster than you."

Ashley jerked her gaze back to his. "You should have

just left me alone. I wasn't going to say anything to anyone until your assassin showed up."

He shrugged. "I couldn't take the chance that one day you'd grow a conscience."

A stab of guilt pricked her. She'd always had a conscience. She'd just been more afraid of him. And with good reason. But maybe if she'd come forward sooner on her own, Gregor would still be alive.

"Did you kill Gregor?" Her heart twisted with grief at the loss of her friend.

Maksim's lips thinned. "An unexpected casualty. But he'd outlived his usefulness, anyway."

Her fist clenched at his callous words. Gregor had been twice the man Sokolov was. "Did you set fire to the restaurant?"

He waved the question away as if swatting at a fly. "I no longer wanted the business," he said. "The insurance payout will allow me to open a new venture."

By burning down The Matador, he'd put people out of work and killed a man. Which she doubted bothered him at all. Talk about not having a conscience. "You're a horrible man," she said. Deciding she had nothing to lose, she asked, "Why did you kill Detective Peters?"

Maksim sneered, his face twisting in a way that had Ashley's skin crawling. She pressed her back against the seat, wishing to put more distance between them.

"He betrayed me." Maksim nearly spit the words. "No one betrays me and lives."

"How did he betray you?" Ashley pressed. "He was a police officer doing his job."

"He may have been on the job but he was taking my

payoffs until he decided to become greedy and wanted more," Maksim stated.

"So he was dirty," she murmured, disappointed that the officer had sold out his honor and integrity to Sokolov. What could have enticed Peters to turn against his oath to protect and serve? She guessed they'd never know.

"Everyone has dirt on their hands," Maksim said.

Once again Ashley turned her gaze to Sarah, who stared out the window with tears rolling down her cheeks. Reaching across the seat, Ashley gripped the other woman's hand.

Sarah startled, her head swiveling as her watery gaze met Ashley's.

"Tell me why you're doing this. Is it for money?"

Sarah shook off Ashley's hand. Her terrified gaze darted to Maksim before bouncing back to the side window. Sarah curled away from Ashley, keeping her hands out of Ashley's reach. Whatever hold Sokolov had on Sarah was strong. Ashley wasn't sure how to help her.

They finally reached the plateau at the top of the mountain. In the distance she could see Eagle Crest Resort. Ashley had never ventured to the resort but from what she could see of the large four-story structure with its peaked roofline, she understood the draw.

The hotel sat strategically on the tip of Eagle Crest Mountain and provided a panoramic view of the surrounding mountains. Though there was scant snow on the ground this late in April, there were people riding the lifts up and down the ski runs on the north side of the mountain. The other sides of the mountain were crisscrossed with hiking trails, which was a big draw for Bristle Township in the sunny months.

Why were they taking her to the resort?

The vehicle veered in an arc away from the main road leading to the resort and headed toward a private airstrip a football field length away from the main building. A small white jet with three round windows along its side stood on the tarmac. The jet's door was open and a set of stairs extended to the ground.

"Where are you taking me?" she asked.

Maksim's lips stretched in a smile that reminded Ashley of an evil clown. "Somewhere no one will ever find your remains."

Ashley's mouth dried at the blatant threat. She had to find a way to escape, but there was nowhere for her to go even if she managed to run off. She doubted she'd make it to the resort for help before they shot her. And taking off into the woods, well, the mountain had its own set of dangers.

The town car came to a halt. The driver jumped out and opened the back door, reaching inside to clamp a hard hand around her biceps. He yanked her out of the car. Maksim and Sarah followed.

Ashley had to do something to delay them. That is if Chase managed to figure out where she'd been taken. But she had no idea how he would know. She could only pray that God would give him the right knowledge.

Digging in her heels, she forced the driver to drag her. She wasn't going to make this easy for them. She kicked and punched at the behemoth man but her attempts to hurt him bounced off his hard muscles. She screamed at the top of her lungs, hoping somebody at the resort might hear.

Maksim smacked her across the face. Pain exploded in her head and she tasted blood in her mouth. She lunged at him with her fists raised.

He darted out of the way. "This one's a wildcat," he said. "When we get on the plane, restrain her."

Sarah stopped walking. "What about me? We're square now, right? You'll let my son go?"

Ashley's heart sank. No wonder Sarah was helping him. Her child's life was in danger. Ashley asked the woman, "You destroyed the video deposition, didn't you?"

Sarah ignored her. "Please, Maksim, you promised me."

"Indeed, I did." Sokolov held the gun that Sarah had used to force Ashley from the courthouse and aimed it at Sarah. "I'm done with you. You're nothing but a loose end."

There was no doubt about his intent. He was going to shoot Sarah. "You can't kill her," Ashley yelled. "She has a child. Don't you have any sense of decency in you?"

Maksim laughed. "No. Any sense of decency I had was beat out of me in prison years ago."

"There's no reason for you to harm her," Ashley pleaded. "Please, don't hurt her, too."

"You bleeding heart types," Maksim muttered and lowered the gun. "Get on the plane, both of you."

Maksim made a whirling gesture with his finger in the air. Ashley followed his gaze to where a man wearing a navy blue pilot's uniform appeared in the open doorway of the jet. The pilot disappeared and a few moments later the engine roared to life.

The man holding on to Ashley tugged her toward the jet. At the bottom of the staircase leading to the plane's door, Ashley grabbed the railing with her free hand and wrapped her legs around the bars. They were going to have to pry her loose and carry her up the stairs.

The squeal of tires on pavement rent the air. Chase's truck followed by a Sheriff's Department vehicle screeched to a stop a few feet away. Ashley nearly collapsed in gratitude. God had come through and sent Chase to the rescue.

Moving quicker than she deemed possible, Maksim rushed forward, pushing his man aside to grab Ashley. "Let go or I kill her." He aimed the weapon at Sarah.

Ashley released the stair railing. Maksim strong-armed her in front of him like a shield.

Then he shot Sarah. Ashley screamed as the other woman crumpled to the ground. The driver and the pilot both disappeared inside the plane, leaving Maksim to fend for himself.

Maksim put the gun to Ashley's temple. "Climb the stairs. Those cops are going to have to go through you to get me."

Ashley could only pray that somebody would take the shot, regardless. Maksim Sokolov needed to be stopped.

Chase jumped out of the truck with his breath trapped in his lungs and his sidearm at the ready. Fear and anguish squeezed his insides at the gut-wrenching sight of Maksim Sokolov hiding behind Ashley. Her eyes were terrified and her face had lost all its color.

Holstering his weapon, Chase put his hands up and moved forward. "Mr. Sokolov, let's be reasonable here. There's no way you're getting off this mountain. If you harm her, you're going home in a body bag. I don't think you want that. You can run your operation from inside prison."

"I've been in prison," Maksim yelled back. "I'm not going back."

Marshal Hawks parked his vehicle in front of the plane, blocking the aircraft from leaving. Behind him Chase could hear Daniel saying he didn't have a clean shot.

Chase made a wide circle so that he wouldn't be in the pathway of the bullet when the opportunity for a shot presented itself.

Seeing that Maksim's finger wasn't on the trigger, Chase's gaze locked on to Ashley's. He couldn't let Maksim take her onto that plane. She would be as good as dead. He prayed that Ashley wasn't too freaked out. He needed her to keep her head and be focused.

"Now!" Chase shouted.

Without hesitation, she reacted. In one swift move, she cupped her fisted left hand with her right while jamming her elbow into Maksim's rib cage. At the same time she stomped on his instep.

The man let out a yowl of pain. She jerked out of his grasp but he grabbed her by the wrist before she could get away. She used the lessons in self-defense to lean into Maksim, swiftly yanking him off balance as she reversed her hold on his wrist and twisted his arm behind him.

Chase's breath caught and pride swelled.

But Maksim didn't go down as planned. He braced his legs apart, clearly understanding the move.

With a sickening laugh, Maksim cackled, "You think you're so smart." He brought the gun around and aimed the barrel at Ashley's face.

"Let her go," Chase yelled, even as he was running toward her.

Ashley released her hold on Makism. He tried to grab her again, but she dove to the side.

Three shots rang out as the two marshals and Daniel fired on Maksim, hitting him center mass. Blood blossomed in a widening crimson stain across his white shirt. Shock twisted his features as he went to his knees and then fell face first onto the tarmac.

Marshal Hawks and Daniel ran forward and entered the plane to apprehend the pilot and the driver.

Chase caught Ashley as she barreled into him. She clung to him and buried her face into his neck. Her body trembled within his embrace. "Shh. You're safe now. It's over."

She was finally free. She could resume her life, wherever she wanted it to be.

Chase longed to tell her that his love for her was real, that he would follow her to the ends of the earth. She only had to say the word. But he held back. He wanted her to have the choice. She no longer had to live a life looking over her shoulder.

Daniel had Sokolov's two henchmen cuffed and sitting on the ground.

The two marshals stepped forward, taking Ashley from Chase. "We'll take our witness with us," Marshal Grant said.

"Chase?" The confusion in her eyes scored him.

"It's okay. You go with the marshals for now," he said. "Daniel and I will take care of this. You still need to give your deposition."

"But he's dead," she said. "He can't hurt me anymore."

Marshall Grant cleared his throat. "Maksim Sokolov may be gone, but until we take down his network, you need to stay in our custody."

Chase's stomach dropped. He should've thought of that. Would Maksim's men seek revenge against Ashley?

"But I don't know anything about the rest of his organization," Ashley said.

"We have another witness," Marshal Hawks stated. "You can give us the information we need in regard to Detective Peters's murder. Our other witness will provide the rest."

Chase frowned, wondering who this other person could be. But he wasn't given an opportunity to ask as sirens heralded the arrival of the ambulance and the squeal of more tires as Alex, Kaitlyn, the sheriff and the district attorney also arrived.

The sheriff stopped to talk to the marshals. Kaitlyn listened for a moment, then stalked toward Chase. Alex went to help Daniel with the two men. The district attorney rushed to Sarah's side and helped her to a seated position. One paramedic hustled to stop the bleeding in her shoulder, while the other checked Sokolov's body, then placed a white plastic sheet over his still form.

Ashley stood apart from everyone with her arms wrapped around her middle. She kept glancing toward Chase.

"Dude, really?" Kaitlyn walked up to him and punched him in the arm. "Are you going to let them take her away? You better fight for her! She loves you and you love her."

"Ouch!" Chase said, mostly to buy time as he processed her words. "She said she couldn't love me."

Kaitlyn slapped a hand to her forehead. "She didn't mean it. She doesn't want to make you choose her over your life here."

Chase's mind whirled. Did Ashley love him? Had she said she couldn't love him because she hadn't wanted to take him from his life in Bristle Township? He did love this town and the community, but he wanted to be with Ashley. And that was what he was going to do, if she'd have him.

He hurried to Ashley's side. Relief shone bright in her eyes as she gripped his hands.

Marshal Grant frowned. "What is it now, Deputy?"

"I need to tell Ashley something," Chase said.

"Again?" The marshal shook his head. "Last time didn't turn out so well."

Ignoring everyone else, Chase focused on Ashley. He squeezed her hands. "I know you said you can't love me. But I love you, Ashley Willis." He swallowed the lump of dread and apprehension forming in his throat. "And I want to spend my life cherishing you, protecting you and loving you."

Her eyes widened and a mix of doubt and joy filled her gaze. "Are you really willing to give everything up to be with me?"

"Yes," he said. "Whatever it takes."

Her eyes softened and she beamed at him. Joy spread over her lovely face. "When I told you I couldn't love you, that was a lie. My last one, I promise."

"So what is the truth?" he asked, his heart pounding with anticipation.

She cupped his face and looked deep into his eyes. "The truth is, Deputy Chase Fredrick, I love you. And I want to be with you, no matter what, no matter where."

Elated, he captured her mouth in a toe-curling kiss. He accepted and acknowledged that whatever the Lord had in store for them, for their future, they would face it together, forever.

EPILOGUE

Three months later

Overhead, lights danced in the night sky in a brilliant burst of colors. Ashley sat next to Chase on the park lawn in downtown Bristle Township. Lucinda sat in her wheelchair next to them with a blanket over her legs.

An unfamiliar warmth spread through Ashley as she contemplated the fact that Lucinda's matchmaking had come to fruition. However, Ashley believed God had brought her and Chase together. No other man could have breached the barricades of her heart. His innate kindness, loyalty and honor had drawn her to him, but his love had captured her heart. Soon they would marry and start a new life together. With children and love. Lucinda would one day get her wish of grandbabies to spoil.

All around them sat families and friends on blankets or in chairs, as they watched the Eagle Crest Mountain Resort's Fourth of July lights show. "This is actually better than fireworks."

Chase tucked a chin-length strand of hair behind

her ear. She'd gone back to her natural color of walnut brown and was letting it grow out.

"Every year is different," Chase said. "I enjoy the cartoon characters."

Ashley laughed. "I'm enjoying the flower display." A large rose blossoming held her interest.

"You're more beautiful than any flower," Chase murmured in her ear as he tightened his arm around her.

"Ashley?" a deep male voice asked.

Her heart skipped a beat. She recognized that voice. She'd never dreamed she'd hear it again. Ashley's gaze sought the man standing at the edge of their blanket. His hair was whiter than she remembered and his shoulders a bit more stooped. But it was him.

She gave a little gasp and jumped to her feet. "Gregor!"

After everything that had happened on the mountain, the marshals had finally revealed that they had faked Gregor Kominski's death to keep Maksim Sokolov from killing him. In return, Gregor had given them everything they needed to take down what remained of Sokolov's operation. Even though the mastermind behind the organization was dead, there'd been people who were loyal to him and who had expressed the need for revenge. The police had arrested them all.

The marshals had released both Ashley and Gregor from protective custody. They were given permission to go back to their lives with their own names. She, of course, returned to Chase and Bristle Township. Though she knew Gregor lived, she hadn't been able to see him and had no idea where Gregor had disappeared. But now he was here in Bristle Township. Her heart swelled with happiness.

His face and hands bore scars from the fire, but his eyes were still so kind. She hugged him tight. "I didn't think I'd ever see you again."

"I wasn't sure if you would want to see me," Gregor said, hugging her back.

"Of course I would," she exclaimed, choking back tears of gratitude. "You are a part of my life. An important part."

He leaned back to search her face. "I am glad. I never meant for you to be hurt."

She shook her head. "I wasn't, thanks to you."

Chase stood and shook the man's hand. "Thank you for coming. And for all you did for Ashley."

Ashley turned to her fiancé. "You invited him here?"

Beaming, Chase slipped his arm around her waist. "I knew you would want to see him."

Love filled her to overflowing. Chase was the man she would marry and spend the rest of her days loving. And she couldn't be happier. "You are the best man in the whole wide world."

Chase laughed and introduced Gregor to Lucinda.

"Pull up a chair, young man," she said to Gregor. There was no mistaking the curiosity in Lucinda's eyes.

He smiled and seemed to stand taller. "Oh, I think I'm going to like you."

Chase somehow found a folding chair and put it next to Lucinda's wheelchair. Gregor sat and the two became fast friends.

Resuming their seats on the blanket, Ashley leaned

back against Chase's chest and stared up at the beautiful display of lights in the sky.

She couldn't have asked for a better ending to her story.

But it wasn't an ending. It was the beginning. She looked at the diamond engagement ring sparkling on her finger, almost as bright as the lights overhead. The beginning of a new life with a new name—Mrs. Ashley Fredrick.

She liked the sound of that.

* * * * *

SPECIAL EXCERPT FROM

LOVE INSPIRED SUSPENSE

INSPIRATIONAL ROMANCE

*A K-9 trooper must work with her ex to bring
down a poaching ring in Alaska.*

Read on for a sneak preview of
Wilderness Defender *by Maggie K. Black,
the next book in the Alaska K-9 Unit series,
available May 2021 from Love Inspired Suspense.*

Lex Fielding drove, cutting down the narrow dirt path between the towering trees. Branches slapped the side of his park-ranger truck, and rocks spun beneath his wheels. All the while, words cascaded through his mind, clattering and colliding in a mass of disjointed ideas that didn't even begin to come close to what he wanted to say to Poppy. Years ago, he'd had no clue how to explain to the most incredible woman he'd ever known that he didn't think he was ready to get married and have a family. He might not have even had the guts to tell her all his doubts, if she hadn't called him out on it after he'd left a really unfortunate and accidental pocket-dial message on Poppy's voice mail admitting he wasn't ready to get married.

Something about being around Poppy had always made him feel like a better man than he had any right being. Even standing beside her made him feel an inch taller.

He just hadn't thought he'd been cut out to be anyone's husband. Something he'd then proved a couple of years later by marrying the wrong woman and surviving a couple of unhappy years together before she'd tragically died in a car crash.

He heard the chaos ahead before he could even see it through the thick forest. A dog was barking furiously, voices were shouting, and above it all was a loud and relentless banging sound, like something was trying to break down one of the cabins from the inside.

He whispered a prayer and asked God for wisdom. Hadn't been big on prayer outside of church on Sundays back when he'd been planning on marrying Poppy. But ever since Danny had been born, he'd been relying on it more and more to get through the day.

Then the trees parted, just in time for him to see the two figures directly in front of him dragging something across the road. His heart stopped.

Not something. *Someone.*

They had Poppy.

Don't miss
Wilderness Defender *by Maggie K. Black,*
available May 2021 wherever Love Inspired Suspense
books and ebooks are sold.

LoveInspired.com